Susan Sallis is now firmly established as one of the most successful writers of engaging family sagas. Her novels include the Rising family sequence, *Summer Visitors*, *By Sun and Candlelight*, *An Ordinary Woman*, *Daughters of the Moon*, *Sweeter Than Wine*, *Water Under the Bridge*, *Touched by Angels*, *Choices*, *Come Rain or Shine* and *The Keys to the Garden*. She lives in Clevedon, Somerset.

THE APPLE BARREL

Susan Sallis

CORGI BOOKS

THE APPLE BARREL
A CORGI BOOK : 0 552 14747 8

Originally published in Great Britain by Bantam Press,
a division of Transworld Publishers

PRINTING HISTORY
Bantam Press edition published 2000
Corgi edition published 2000

1 3 5 7 9 10 8 6 4 2

Set in 11/12pt New Baskerville by
Kestrel Data, Exeter, Devon.

Corgi Books are published by Transworld Publishers,
61–63 Uxbridge Road, London W5 5SA,
a division of The Random House Group Ltd,
in Australia by Random House Australia (Pty) Ltd,
20 Alfred Street, Milsons Point, Sydney, NSW 2061, Australia,
in New Zealand by Random House New Zealand Ltd,
18 Poland Road, Glenfield, Auckland 10, New Zealand
and in South Africa by Random House (Pty) Ltd,
Endulini, 5a Jubilee Road, Parktown 2193, South Africa.

Printed and bound in Great Britain by
Mackays of Chatham PLC, Chatham, Kent.

To my family

One

The house was in a hollow, sunk between fortresses of cliff-rock and cushions of thrift, as if it might be sinking into one of the old tin-mining shafts which burrowed through this country like rabbit warrens. It was long and narrow with windows both sides but in spite of the constant sound of waves, no sea views; the front windows might well frame banks of flowers running downhill to the stand of trees, but on the other side the only possible aspect would be of ragged granite tops with sky above. One half of the building was derelict; the slate roof had collapsed in the middle and brambles grew from the broken windows. The other half had been re-roofed with corrugated iron; the windows were catching the evening sun and gleamed cheerfully and the front door was painted canary yellow.

Jack made a moaning sound in his throat.

'Oh God, Ho . . . I am sorry. I suppose it had to be like this, so damned cheap. I should have guessed. I'm sorry . . . what can I say?'

But Hope, naturally optimistic like her name, was seriously enchanted.

'Darling Jack. It's beautiful. Tucked away like this – to protect it from the wind, d'you think? Look at that door. Imagine that welcoming you when it's raining – isn't it marvellous? Darling – I love it. I think you're a genius to have found it!'

Jack refused comfort. 'I didn't find it, Ho. I told you. A chap in a pub knew someone who knew the Penhaileses at that farm where we left your car—'

'I know, I know!' She kissed him briefly. 'Never mind all the talk – let's have some action!'

'Well . . . are we going to stay here? Actually stay here?' He looked at her helplessly. 'We've got enough cash for a couple of nights in Penzance.'

She was impatient. 'Of course we're staying! This is our honeymoon cottage! We've driven over two hundred miles to get here. We are definitely staying!' She looked at him expectantly.

He said, 'I suppose so. All right then. I'll go back to the car and get our stuff.'

She detained him. 'Not yet. There's something you have to do first.' She grinned at him. 'That front door is open. I want you to carry me over the threshold!'

He looked at her. Her eyes, made up darkly to look like Elizabeth Taylor's, were alight with laughter. Her hair, straight at the sides, a riot of curls on her forehead – also à la Taylor – was still lacquered into the shape that had accommodated her small pearl wedding cap. But the fashionable pale lipstick had long gone, the enormous stud earrings had been tugged off some time during the drive down here and the daring pleated mini-skirt of her going-away outfit was crumpled and lopsided. She looked like the girl he had fallen for only a year ago when she was just twenty and still at Miss Marchant's secretarial school.

He said, 'I can't believe what's happening. Are we really married?'

She nodded, suddenly unable to speak. Then she moved close to him, put her hands on his shoulders and her forehead against his throat. He stroked the crisply set hair and told her throatily how much he loved her. She nodded with difficulty.

'Look at me, Ho. Kiss me.'

She shook her head with even more difficulty. But then she said, 'I know I've always had my way. I know you think I'm spoiled. But those promises we made . . . you know, sickness, health, all that stuff. I meant them. I really meant them, Jack.'

'I know. I know, my darling.' He had told her once she should have been named 'Hopeless' because she couldn't darn a sock or make a decent cup of tea. A week later she had been waiting for him outside the Inland Waterways office by the docks, with a Co-op carrier bag. From it she took three socks. 'They're Daddy's. I darned them. Mummy made me unpick the first darn five times until it was neat. What do you think?'

He had examined them, pop-eyed with amazement because she had taken him seriously. Then he had said the wrong thing. 'Don't you

9

know that it doesn't matter that you're hopeless? With your face and figure you'll get anything you want. Always.'

He had not meant to be insulting but she stared at him, violet eyes filling, as if he had slapped her across the face. And then she went to the edge of the harbour and threw the socks into the murky water, turned and started to run back up towards Bearland.

He shouted, 'Hope! What the hell – those are your father's socks!'

She knew Gloucester like the back of her hand and had disappeared down one of the alleys that led into Westgate. He went back to the office, saw that the socks were floating just below the wall and shouted to one of the bargees to use his pole to fish them out. That night he washed them in the china basin at his digs, dried them in front of the popping gas fire and wrapped them in tissue paper. It had been his turn to present her with three socks. He had done so outside Miss Marchant's the next afternoon.

She had taken them and said in a small voice, 'I bought them for him. So that I could cut the holes in them.'

'You're mad,' he said.

'No, I'm not. And I can make proper tea now. I'm not hopeless. Not really hopeless.' Like a child she was instantly ebullient. 'Let's go on a picnic on Sunday. Then I can show you. We've got a paraffin stove. I'll bring the sandwiches.'

He looked at her steadily. 'Who will make them?'

She stared back, then said, 'Me. Of course.'

'Where shall we go?'

She was delighted at his tacit acceptance. 'Let's go to the Forest. Cannock pool.'

'How do we get there?'

'I've got a car. Daddy bought it for me when I matriculated!' She stopped speaking for an instant, then resumed. 'Or we could go on the train to Speech House. Or a bus.'

But, of course, in the end they had used her car. Just as they had used it to drive down to St Buryan today.

He said now, 'I meant them, too. The promises. Vows. I'm going to look after you, Ho. Properly. This . . .' He gestured towards the cottage. 'This will seem funny later.'

'No.' She moved her head against his neck again. 'Not funny. We shall smile probably. But not at it. It's waiting for us – welcoming us. We'll never think it's funny.' She looked up into his face. 'Dear Jack. This is the most wonderful surprise I've ever had. Thank you.'

'You don't have to say that—'

'I'd like a kiss now.' She closed her eyes and waited. Then she said, 'Thank you. And now will you carry me over the threshold?'

'The key—'

She wound her arms more tightly around his neck. 'You weren't listening. I said the front door is ajar. That's what I meant about the welcome.'

So he scooped her up, staggered down the bank and shouldered the door wide. And then, of necessity, stood very still because almost immediately inside the small square room stood a table, covered with a snowy cloth and laid with cups, saucers and plates, a jug covered with beaded net, a teapot standing next to a fat tea cosy in a cat shape, a butter dish and a breadboard bearing an enormous cottage loaf.

Hope breathed, 'Oh . . . goodness gracious!'

Jack let her slither to the floor and added, 'My God! This is a proper welcome!'

'You see?' She turned to him exultantly. 'Now will you just . . . be happy!'

And at last Jack grinned and then began to laugh. She laughed too. It had been a long day; they could not stop laughing. They reeled around the table to the range which held a kettle but no fire; that set them off again and they went on through a door at the side of the range into a scullery which was so dark it might have been carved out of the cliff itself. Here they discovered a shallow stone sink served by a small hand-pump and an orange box covered in American cloth and holding a primus stove.

Before he could think of, let alone mention, her mother's kitchen at Horsley, she said, 'It reminds me of the kitchen at home, Jack! Not the pump, of course, but the flagstones and the red check covering. Isn't it pretty?'

There was a second's hesitation while he registered that by 'home' she meant the Sandhurst cottage he'd managed to rent from the old harbour master.

He said, 'I'm not sure about pretty. But it's dark and it's got an old-fashioned sink and is furnished with orange boxes. So I suppose—'

She pushed him quite roughly. 'Stop it! It's a form of self-pity, you know! Poor old Jack Langley. Got married today – some harridan he met in Gloucester park. Had to find a house for them to live in. Did that. Had to fix up a honeymoon. Did that. It's a shame, isn't it?'

She went on shoving him towards another door and he let himself go, flapping protesting hands, pretending to be cowed and then, suddenly, when she opened the door to disclose steep wooden stairs, roaring at her, scooping her up over his shoulder and charging at the stairs like a bull. She screamed and beat at his back as he crouched to go through a low doorway and then she was flying backwards, crashing on to a bed and he was kneeling above her grinning and the bed was protesting loudly but holding up.

'You – you – devil!' she panted, laughing.

'Fine. If I'm a devil, you're most certainly a she-devil!'

It was all so foolish and so sweet. The 'sixties had so far passed Gloucestershire by, and this was their first time. They treated it as a joke at first, something naughty they were doing in the equivalent of the bicycle sheds behind the docks. They imitated the scufflings and squeaks they had heard. And then, quite suddenly, it was serious and they held each other, clinging for dear life, supporting, helping and holding, he apologizing, she whispering fiercely, 'Oh my darling . . . oh I love you – it's all right. It's all right.' And, amazingly, in spite of their ignorance, it was all right and they lay exhausted but in perfect accord and let the old bed settle around them comfortably.

When she turned and looked at him, he smiled somehow. His mouth worked uncontrollably. She said again, 'Oh Jack. It's all right.'

And he nodded and whispered shakily, 'With

my body I thee worship. Makes sense, Ho. It makes such bloody good sense.'

And then she wept and so did he and they clung again and comforted each other. Years later, decades later, when she felt an old woman though she was in her forties, Hope remembered that time and thought how young they had been. Young and so innocent. Back then, it had not occurred to them to repeat that first successful lovemaking. That might happen again in the evening, or tomorrow, but for now they had to get up and go and fetch their stuff from the car and find out how the paraffin stove worked and eat together and walk together. Sex, that newly discovered delight, was only a small part of what was going to happen. Living together meant exactly that: laying tables, cooking and washing up in the tiny cottage, finding out how they could wash and brush their teeth. And more than that, too: learning to read the other's expression, the way they sat in a chair, moved around a room, breathed, sneezed . . . everything. Sex was amazing, but it had its place and it was not everything. Then.

Mrs Penhailes announced she was 'tickled to death' by them. She opened a five-barred gate so they could drive through and bring the car and luggage much closer to the cottage.

'Widdershins it's called. That means it's okkard.'

'Okkard?' queried Hope.

'Okkard in every way. 'Gainst the sun, 'gainst the wind. The gaffer was going to let it all go back to the moor. You can see the moor nearly 'ad it . . . brambles growed inside as well as out!

14

But then this young artist chap took it on for a season and we put a roof on the half of it.' She grinned. 'Mind, he couldn't stand it for long. Too lonely, 'e said. But you two got each other, 'aven't you? Reckon you won't notice much else.' She was a dark, stringy woman, sallow-complexioned with a sardonic expression.

Hope said enthusiastically, 'We think it's lovely! And the way you laid the table – oh, it's just lovely.'

'Plenty more where that came from. I got rabbit pie for your dinners tomorrow. And there's plenty of fish in the sea.'

Jack looked hopeful. 'Any chance of some fishing?'

'The gaffer'll take you out any time. I'll send 'im down tomorrow. Not too early!' She laughed uproariously, slapped the boot of the car as if it were a horse and began to close the gate. 'You two!' she called back. 'Tickle me to death, you do!'

It was such fun settling in. Hope had to keep running outside to look at Widdershins from different angles. 'You're not a bit okkard!' she sang to it when the moonlight bathed its granite slabs to the smokiest blue. Then she gave a small scream and dashed back in. 'Jack! It's on fire! That paraffin stove—' She stopped mid-sentence. Jack was crouched in front of the range coaxing a small flame around paper and wood. He looked up, grinning.

'I know we don't need it, but it's one of those things. D'you remember? Our picnic in the Forest? The Foresters could claim ground on which they built a house overnight.'

Her face felt soft and wobbly. 'Between sunset and sunrise,' she said. 'And there had to be a fire in the hearth.'

'So the crafty devils built the fireplace and chimney first!'

He put his face close to the bars and blew gently and the flame licked through the kindling and started on the logs and small coals. They sat quietly watching the fire grow and establish itself and then they ate supper. They had not eaten since the wedding breakfast and that had been a buffet affair of unfamiliar food. Now Jack hacked wedges from the loaf and topped them with cheese and Hope wiped the tomatoes given to them by the tickled Mrs Penhailes and they munched them like apples and washed everything down with the contents of the milk jug and then they watched the fire again until it died down and they went to bed.

Hope woke early and lay very still in the big brass bed, watching the patterns of shifting sunlight on the faded wallpaper. There must be a tree just outside their bedroom window because the sun and shadows danced across the ceiling and down the walls with surprising vigour. She worked out that the cottage faced the east so it was getting the morning sun, but she could not remember any trees until the little copse at the end of the cleft. She was consumed with curiosity and turned her head to look at her watch which she had hung from its strap on the bedpost. It wasn't six thirty yet. There were small sounds to accompany the shifting light; she wondered whether a family of mice lived in the tumbledown half next door. She moved her head cautiously the other way. Jack was turned from her, his right ear just above the sheet, bright red, tender, folded miraculously against his head, surrounded by his brown hair and some darker stubble . . . She forgot the dancing shadows and the mice and stared at his head as if she had not seen it before. It was incredible to her. Perhaps because it was next to hers; actually on her pillow as well as his own. She reached behind her cheek cautiously; yes, she was supported by a flock-filled bolster. That made her feel less guilty about the possibility of waking him and she propped herself on one elbow to extend her view. Now she could see the jut of his forehead and brow over his closed eyes, his short straight nose; snub really. And his mouth was curly and good-tempered. She knew he got depressed, especially about what he called his 'lack of prospects,' but she had never seen him lose his temper. He always looked happily boyish. As if he ought to dress perpetually in cricket flannels and an open-necked shirt.

She smiled to herself at the ridiculous thought and then wanted him to smile back at her so she leaned down and nibbled his earlobe. It was unexpectedly fleshy and apparently dead because however hard she nibbled he did not move. She lifted her head slightly and blew right into the ear and he gave an almighty jump, turned on his back and opened his eyes wide.

'What?' he asked loudly.

'Nothing. I was looking at you and I wanted you to look at me.'

'The farmer hasn't turned up? Penhailes? Wossa time?'

'Six thirty.'

'Six what? Six thirty? He's not coming early. Don't you remember, she said—'

'I know. I know. Sorry – sorry, darling man boy husband. I'm a selfish, horrible, possessive . . . wife! Yes. Wife!' She leaned down and kissed him. 'I just wanted you to be awake with me.'

He smiled slowly and then took her by the shoulders and rolled her on to her back, kissing her as he did so. She was going to protest and ask him to lie and watch the sun dappling so crazily and now a bird – a blackbird? – singing fit to burst somewhere near at hand. But then she knew she mustn't. She wondered, even as she let herself become aroused, how it was that she was suddenly so wise. Perhaps it was also because she knew that she was spoiled and self-ish and probably hopeless. It might be guilt. It might be a form of over-compensation. She didn't care. She wound her fingers into his short crisp hair and hung on for dear life.

Farmer Penhailes appeared at ten thirty with another pitcher of milk, a fresh-baked loaf and the promised rabbit pie.

'There's a rill goes down through that thicket. 'E's always cold. Stick the milk jug in 'im – wedge it with some stones, mind, and keep 'en covered – and the missis says there's turnip and potato, onion and carrot in the pie so you don't need more. An' I'm a-going out tomorrow at six. Be in the cove then if you want to come.' He was talking to Jack and though it had not occurred to Hope to go fishing with Jack, she might have been slightly piqued at her exclusion had she not been so delighted with everything else. She had never heard the word 'rill' actually spoken before and was enchanted with that. The rabbit pie was still hot from the oven and its heavenly smell almost, but not quite, masked the wonderful aroma of new bread.

Jack, more practical, asked about the paraffin stove and they all went inside where Hope had been trying to wash up the supper and breakfast things in cold water. They watched as the little Cornishman – half the size of his wife – lit the wick and adjusted it carefully.

'See you lit the range last night,' he commented. 'Chimney all right, was it?'

They looked at each other guiltily then nodded.

'Well then. There's your 'ot water supply.' He pointed to a witch's cauldron at the back of the range. 'Fill 'en up and keep 'en just over the grate like. Still be warm in the morning. You won't want no baths with the sea just over the cliff. I got some sea soap if you need 'en.'

'Sea soap?'

'It do lather in the salt water.'

'Oh how marvellous.' Hope smiled ecstatically. 'Thank you so much, Mr Penhailes. Everything is just . . . marvellous.'

The dour old man smiled right at her. He was short on teeth but uninhibited about the smile. 'Don't be calling me Mr Penhailes like that, my maid. Peter. That's me. Peter Penhailes. You en't going to forget that, are you? Peter Penhailes.' He chuckled as he scraped past the table. 'They used to call me Peppy at school but then the missis said it sounded as if I was some foreigner and she did always call me the gaffer. But everyone else had to call me Peter. And when she says a thing, then it's so.' He glinted at Hope. 'Don't forget. She said, no other vegetables with the rabbit pie. Woe betide if she finds you in St Buryan buying cabbage or spuds!'

He laughed and departed and once again Hope skipped around the room, into the kitchen and back again as if unable to believe that the cottage was real. She was delighted with everything and Peter Penhailes was top of the list.

'He's lovely!' she carolled. 'A rill! Did you hear that? A rill in which to cool the milk! Okkard . . . okkard my foot! This is Arcadia!'

Jack, on his knees again, lighting a fire in the range, smiled into last night's ashes and remembered when he had seen her first, one among a gaggle of ex-schoolgirls coming out of what the elderly Miss Marchant insisted on calling the Gloucester Commercial College. It was as if that one girl had been surrounded by an aura of light, shining like a lamp, making the tatty old spa buildings look like something from ancient Greece. He registered she was dark with violet eyes and then tried to dismiss her. All the girls at Miss Marchant's were barely out of school, at least six years younger than he was. And he wasn't staying here in Gloucester anyway; nothing to keep him; dead-end job, National Service over, brother in Australia . . . He had held out against her . . . what a fool he had been . . . he could have lost her and his life would have stayed grey and anxious always. He said, 'He fell for you, Ho. I watched it quite objectively. He was holding out against you until you told him how marvellous everything was. Then, plonk, he went.'

She laughed. 'What rubbish. But I was right, wasn't I? Everything is marvellous?'

'You were right,' he said soberly.

But the flames were a long time dealing with the whitened embers and Hope, impatient to be off, flitted around him like a butterfly.

'I want to see the rill! Come on – we can do that later!'

He had arranged a trellis-work of wood and coal. He stood up. 'Let's fill the hot water system and then go and find this blessed rill!' he said with mock disgust.

They found the rill and named nearly all the trees in the thicket. Henry was the tallest; an elm housing a shabby rookery. The blackbirds apparently lived in a stand of alder – christened Marble Arch – around the rill. There were birds everywhere, mostly seabirds swooping and screaming above them and disappearing over the cliff; a heron standing solemn and unafraid, one leg held delicately clear of the water.

They went back for towels and set out to discover the cove. The rill tipped over the cliff edge at an impossible height, but there were paths either side of it and by taking the one that seemed to be dropping, they discovered a rough flight of steps hacked out of the granite and leading down to a small cove, sandy, rock-strewn and pierced in rather a sinister way by the entrance to a cave.

'Look, the tide comes right up to the cliff.' Jack was in his element, like a Boy Scout. 'See the wrack caught in the mouth of the cave? It's dry sand beyond – oh and there's the Penhaileses' boat, I suppose.'

Hope came up to the cave and looked in rather apprehensively. A large scow-like boat took up most of the space. It looked robust enough but she had expected a jetty and life-belts.

'It's all a bit . . . amateurish,' she said doubtfully.

'Must be a devil to launch. Tide's going out so I suppose it's high at six tomorrow. Look at the tyres. They're fenders of course. Must take some beating against the side of the cliff.' He lifted one of the tyres to reveal 'PZ' (for Penzance) and the name of the boat: the *Mirabelle*.

'You don't suppose . . . ?' she said.

'No. Bessie or Nancy. But not Mirabelle.'

She giggled. 'Gladys.'

'Helga.' Jack grinned. 'I just hope Mirabelle was his mother. Don't fancy incurring the wrath of Mrs Penhailes!'

He let the tyre fall back and some flakes of paint drifted to the sand. Hope was apprehensive.

'Is it safe? I wouldn't want to come. Not that I was asked . . .'

'You didn't mind? I thought you would rather lie on the beach. Or something.'

'I didn't mind at all. I can't see what the attraction is.'

'I want to bring home a catch!' He flung his arms about and pretended to be Tarzan. 'I want to provide for my woman! From the land – from the sea – from the air!'

'The *air*?'

'Birds. Probably Peter P has got a gun. An ancient fowling piece—'

'We can't eat *birds*! Rabbits, OK. Although I hope Mrs P will deal with them. Fish . . . I think I might cope with fish. But birds, definitely not. And ancient fowling pieces even more definitely not.'

They laughed for no reason, hugged each other, decided on a swim. In spite of his catcalls she undressed behind a rock and, emerging in her new swimming costume, noticed that he was behind another. They ran hand in hand into the small summer waves.

There was no time to watch the sun and shadow dance the next morning. She cut sandwiches for him while he got the range going, then she pulled on a shirt and cotton skirt to go with him to the cove. The tide was indeed lapping at the foot of the cliff and she stayed on the steps and watched as Peter Penhailes instructed Jack on how to manoeuvre the 'old girl', as he called the boat, through the tangle of weed to where it could wallow helplessly in half a fathom of water.

'Hold her steady, m'boy! Dun't want her slamming against that cliff, fenders or no!' They were both waist deep, obviously straining every muscle.

Hope muttered aloud, 'How does he manage when he hasn't got Jack, then?' She watched with some trepidation while Peter scrambled aboard, leaving Jack to hang on to the stern and push it away from the cliff. 'He could be crushed! What do they think they're doing?' she asked in anguish.

But then the engine roared into life, making Jack splutter helplessly, and the boat moved away and suddenly Jack was swimming and Peter was leaning over the side and hauling him aboard. The sandwiches, wrapped in grease-proof paper, bobbed into the cave.

'Damn!' Hope said loudly.

'See you tonight, darling!' Jack yelled, obviously thrilled to bits.

'You're wet through! Come back!' Hope yelled.

Peter and Jack laughed uproariously, then Peter unlashed the wheel and they headed straight out to sea.

Hope stood and watched them helplessly. 'Well, I'll be . . . blowed,' she said.

She was cold so she went back to bed until the fire got under way. She felt rather peculiar without Jack; she'd had him by her side for forty-eight hours and they had grown together already. She wasn't exactly lonely; she was strangely at a loose end. The light patterns weren't the same and when there was a rustling next door she was certain it was mice and leaped out of bed hastily and conversed with herself quite loudly.

'I'll find out what tree is sending these patterns on to the wall. Then it will be low tide so I can look for firewood. I wonder if the dry seaweed burns? I bet it does. I'll collect that as well. Then I'll go for the milk. And I might take the car into Buryan and get some fruit. I'd like an orange. Or a banana. And some pop. I'd love some pop.'

There were no trees around the cottage and she came to the conclusion that the patterns were made by the fronds of fern which edged the hollow like the crochet around the milk-jug cover. She made up the fire and filled the cauldron with water and then wandered rather aimlessly to the beach. It was almost mid-morning and the tide was ebbing fast and had left half a dozen charred spars on the sand. She gathered them up and went into the cave to pick up dried seaweed. It was eerie in the semi-darkness and she left there quickly and clambered laboriously back to the cottage armed with her firing. Then she cleaned the tiny scullery from ceiling to floor and opened the windows on to the rock face to dry it out. She had never done any real house cleaning before and she surveyed her work from the middle door with much pleasure. She wanted to go upstairs and make the bed and wash the windows in there, but that would mean walking on her pristine floor so she left that and retreated to the range where she took some of the 'hot water supply' and made tea. Unfortunately neither she nor Jack had remembered to replace the milk in the rill last night and it smelled slightly tart. She poured some more tea and drank it black, screwing up her face, determined to enjoy it.

The sun was hot outside the front door. She poured more tea and took a chair on to the front path. She said aloud, 'It's like those cottage teapots and this is the spout leading down to the rill.' She tipped the chair against the bank and laid her head on a cushion of sea pinks. Some time later, when the sun had dipped behind the house and the lip of garden was in shadow, she roused. It was four thirty by her tiny square watch. She jumped up and went indoors. The fire was out and though the scullery floor was dry she thought there probably wasn't time to clean the bedroom. She would do it tomorrow. She needed some food for the evening meal; certainly milk. She found her handbag and looked at her face in the mirror of her compact and did some quick repairs. How could she have wasted the whole afternoon? She dashed out of the door and began climbing to the top of the cliff. It was tempting to take the car but that seemed too hopeless for words, so she tramped along to the Penhaileses' farm, walking now straight into the eye of the setting sun.

Mrs Penhailes was in the yard crouched over a barrel of apples, transferring them individually and with great care into shallow boxes. 'Shouldn't be doing this now,' she said, straightening her back with some difficulty. 'Could smell 'em. There's a rotten one here somewhere.' She looked down grimly. 'Always one in every barrel and if you don't rout 'n out, the whole barrel's done for.'

Hope said eagerly, 'Let me.' She knelt on the old flagstones. The smell was heavy and sweet and very slightly rank.

Mrs Penhailes said that it was Monday so it was no wonder her back ached and she was a fool to start on the apples but then everyone knew she was a fool. She had started on the washing as soon as that Peter left this morning; the washhouse warmed up quickly with a good fire going under the copper. Plenty of sun, plenty of wind so everything was dried before she could heat the irons. All afternoon it had taken her because she did the overalls for the colly-cutters too, but she'd be finished and everything put away before the gaffer got in. That was the way to deal with a Monday.

Hope nodded but did not really understand. Her mother had had a washing machine very soon after the end of the war. She had recently installed a dryer as well. Any day of the week could be washing day and there was a girl in the village who came in to do the ironing.

'Oh dear.' She looked up. 'Think I've found it. Mushy.'

'Good girl. Into the pig pail with it and let's have the others all nicely spread out.'

They sorted the apples between them and then Mrs Penhailes led her proudly into the dairy which – she boasted – was scrubbed out every day. Along the marble slabs were metal bowls, one of which contained butter the colour of sunshine. They both washed their hands at the shallow stone sink and Mrs Penhailes showed Hope how she patted out the butter between two wooden boards and then gently impressed their acorn mark on each pound. 'I don't often have to weigh it,' she boasted. 'I knows 'zackly how much to pat out each time.' She demonstrated. 'Look at that,' she said, setting her load on to greaseproof paper and then transferring it to the hanging scales. 'Couldn't be nearer if you tried, could it?'

'It's perfect,' said Hope. Then, 'What time will they get back, d'you think?' she asked, wondering what she could get for supper and how quickly she could light the fire in the range.

'On the tide. About six thirty, I'd say.' Mrs Penhailes was laconic. She wrapped the butter and put it alongside a cloth-wrapped loaf in a basket. 'Use some of this when you do cook your mackerel,' she said, indicating the butter. 'There's a dish in the cupboard by the range. Lay them nose to tail, bit o' salt, bit o' pepper. Parsley will have grown out – you can take a bunch with you—'

'Mackerel?' Hope queried.

'That's what they'll bring back most likely. But whatever it is, you can cook it the same. When you gut the fish, press 'en down like this . . .' She demonstrated on the marble slab in front of her. 'That way you'll loosen the backbone and draw it out before cooking.'

Hope blinked. She had heard Jack saying he wanted to supply them with food but somehow it hadn't occurred to her that they were waiting on his success. The thought of a real fish with eyes and tail and . . . 'guts' . . . was not reassuring.

'Keep a good fire in, then the oven will be hot and they'll take no more than half an hour.'

That was something she *could* do. She walked back briskly carrying the basket, trying not to stumble as she descended the tussocky path which rimmed Widdershins. She loved going through the front door and edging around the table; everything was beginning to be so familiar and dear. Jack would be home within the hour: she longed for him to see the spotless scullery. She began to lay the table. It looked wonderful. 'The hunter home from the hill,' she murmured,

seeing it through his eyes. Plates, knives, forks –
no such things as fish-knives but who cared. The
salt was in an open cellar with its own little
spoon. She knocked some on to the cloth and
pinched it up to throw over her left shoulder –
not that she was in the slightest bit superstitious
but when you were living in a cottage called
Widdershins it might be as well to propitiate the
god Pan.

Then came the fire. She riddled out the dead
ash and laid paper and kindling with great care.
On top of that she placed some of the dried
seaweed and then some smallish logs. She lit
it and grinned delightedly as flames crackled
around the weed, popping the little bladders
and licking the wood in a most heartening way.
Once the small stuff had burnt through, it died a
little. She went back and forth to the scullery
with a jug filling the cauldron, then threw on
some more seaweed and watched as the flames
leaped around it. More logs. More weed. It was
going really well now. She glanced at her watch
and decided to go down to the cove to meet the
boat. From the front door the cottage looked so
satisfying she almost chortled aloud. The table
was so inviting, the fire more so, the cauldron
beginning to sing. She almost ran down to the
rill and then the cliff and then the path and
then the amazing zigzag through the rocks to
the cove. And there, coming up to meet her,
looking like someone from the Old Testament,
was Jack.

She almost knocked him flat with her
welcome.

'Oh darling, you definitely pong! It's lovely –

fish and more fish!' He was laughing at her, kissing her saltily, trying to save his line of mackerel from falling off his shoulder. 'Where's the boat? Where's Mr Penhailes? Peter?'

'Steady. If this lot goes back in the sea you'll have your first sight of a strong man in tears!' He adjusted the fish. 'Peter says we can smoke the ones we don't want. Smoked mackerel, Ho! Our very own smoked mackerel!'

'Lovely. Wonderful. Where *is* Peter? And the boat?'

'It's a lugger, darling. A Cornish lugger. We got her into the cave and up on the dry stuff and he's hosing her down. Told me to get on. You'd be anxious.'

'I haven't been. I've been so busy, Jack! Like a proper housewife. I thought at first it was going to be a long day but it hasn't been half long enough! I've done the scullery and I wanted to do the bedroom but there wasn't time. What about you, darling? Has it been hard?'

'I missed you.' They were at the top of the cliff now and he held her against the mackerel and kissed her. 'It was a long day for me. It's exciting when you get a catch but there are lots of hours when you don't!' He kissed her again. 'You must come next time, Ho.' He laughed suddenly. 'I see what you mean about the pong. I couldn't smell it on myself but I can smell it on you!'

'You rotter!' She dashed off and he chased her and kissed her again and she knew that for two pins he would have made love to her there and then. It made her feel all-powerful, as if she could do anything in the world. But as she was wondering what to do about it, there came a shout from across the rill. They looked at each other wildly and then tore through the coppice and into the little lip of garden. A man was standing outside the front door; a stranger. He was choking. From every window and crevice of Widdershins, smoke and soot poured like black liquid. He recovered gaspingly just as they arrived.

'Christamighty,' he panted. 'Are you trying to kill me? I wasn't doing any harm! Just sleeping over for a coupla nights. Putting seaweed on that fire when that chimney haven't been used for God knows how long – that's asking for it!'

He pushed open the door. The little living room that had looked so welcoming less than an hour ago was blackened with soot. Everything on the table was the same. As Hope gave a moan of despair, so another fall filled the grate and rose in clouds around the cauldron.

Jack said, 'Oh my God!'

The man took pity on them both. ''S all right. The soot fall has put out the fire. It's just smoke and soot. But it came through my half and near choked me, I'm telling you!'

Hope was too stupefied to comment. She rushed in and picked up the milk jug. The net had held back most of the soot but underneath it a film of what looked like black oil floated on top of the milk. The butter was unrecognizable. She gathered it and the loaf in her arms and went into the scullery. The soot was in there too. She wept then, dusting the loaf into the sink helplessly.

She heard Jack say, 'What the devil d'you mean? Your half?'

'I came back coupla nights ago. Heard you in residence and guessed the Penhaileses had let the place to someone else. So I went in with the brambles!'

It was the last straw. She remembered the old bed and its unquiet accompaniment as they made love. This man had heard them. Heard them making love. Something that had been sacred and wonderful was suddenly tarnished and cheap.

She put the bread into the soot-filled sink, lowered her head and cried enormous tears. And when Jack held her and told her it didn't matter at all and they would soon clear it up, she refused to be comforted and would have gone to bed except that the tiny grate in the bedroom had also belched a layer of soot over the counterpane.

So the three of them laboured through the twilight and the stranger – the invader, who turned out to be the artist and was called Jem Trewint – cleaned the fish in the rill and made a fire in the garden and by the time they had scraped the butter, swilled the bread under the pump and skimmed the milk, the fish was ready to eat.

Jack, who was getting on well with Jem by this time, said, 'You'll have to join us, old man. The place might have burned down if you hadn't been here.'

Jem grinned, shaking his head. 'I told you. The soot put the fire out. And the chimney's clean now.' He squatted on the grass looking as comfortable as a cat. 'You can light the fire in the morning. Hang the rest of the fish in the chimney and smoke 'em. You all right now, little lady?'

'Hope.' She was eating the fish with her fingers. It was delicious. She was beginning to feel better. 'I'm sorry about . . . that. It's just that I'd cleaned up so nicely and laid the table . . .' She felt tears choking her throat again and stopped.

He nodded. 'I heard you. I'd have come and given a hand but I might have given you a heart attack instead!'

She remembered her bad habit of talking aloud and blushed deeply.

He said, 'You're very beautiful. I expect you know that. Would you sit for me?'

'Well. We're rather busy, you see.'

'We're on our honeymoon,' Jack said, suddenly direct and not quite so friendly.

Jem Trewint rolled back on to the grass laughing helplessly. 'I might have guessed it!' he crowed. 'And you wouldn't want your wife taking her clothes off for me. So the answer is no. And you'd rather I wasn't next door.'

Jack said, 'Much.'

Hope was enormously hot. She chewed busily and looked at her bare legs ending in sandalled feet. She pulled her skirt down to her ankles.

'Ah.' Jem Trewint still grinned but he began to stand up. 'I'll just get my paints and stuff. Bella will let me sleep in the barn tonight.' He held out a fishy hand to Hope. 'Goodbye. Perhaps we'll meet again and you won't feel quite so embarrassed by my presence!'

Hope put her own greasy hand into his. 'I'm so sorry, she stammered. 'Will you be all right?'

She asked the same question of Jack after the artist had disappeared at the top of the cliff.

Jack was brusque. 'Of course he'll be all right. He's one of those hippies.'

'How do you know?'

'Didn't you notice his hair? He looked like Jesus.'

'Oh Jack. He was here first. And we've turned him out.'

'Did you want him to stay next door listening to everything we said and did?'

'Of course not. But . . . he was so helpful. Clearing up and cooking and everything. And you liked him at first.'

'That was before he asked you to take off your clothes!'

She looked up at him. 'He didn't actually say . . . oh, you're teasing! Oh Jack. I'm so sorry. I've spoiled everything, haven't I?'

He told her she had done no such thing; he kissed her fishy mouth and told her she smelled wonderful and suddenly they were laughing again. She spluttered, 'Mrs Penhailes *must* be called Mirabelle! He – the painter man – called her Bella, did you hear?'

'I heard.'

They were still laughing as they cleared away the remains of the meal and went upstairs to the sooty bedroom. And it was all right. Everything was all right. But it wasn't the same. Before, they had not known they could be overheard. Before, it had just been the two of them.

Jack Langley had no parents, they had been killed when he was three and his brother, Giles,

34

was ten. The two boys had been brought up very strictly by grandparents and Jack's childhood memories were coloured largely by furious rows between Giles and his grandfather, after which an icy silence would include Jack himself. Giles had done his National Service during the Korean War and had confessed to Jack that it had been 'a piece of cake' compared with life with Grandfather. When the armistice had been signed he had come home and got a job in the Shire Hall at Gloucester but he hadn't stuck it for long. Apologizing profusely to Jack, he had emigrated to Australia in 1956. 'I can't take it here, old chap,' he had said. 'I had a few Aussie mates in Korea and from what they told me it's the place of the future. They call the immigrants "ten pound Poms". That's what I'm going to be.' He had grinned. 'You've only got a couple of years before you do your National Service and then you can join me. How does that sound?'

It had sounded all right. But, strangely enough, life without Giles in the small terraced house in Brook Street had not been as bad as Jack feared. Grandfather frowned a great deal but he took Jack to football matches and had him measured for a suit when he got the job at the docks. When both grandparents died during Jack's peace-keeping stint in Korea, he had genuinely grieved. But, like Giles, the travel had burst his horizons wide open, and until he met Hope he had fretted at the narrowness of his job and had constantly toyed with the possibility of joining Giles in Australia.

He still toyed with the idea. He was imbued with his grandparents' notions of prideful independence and the fact that Hope was giving up so many of her material comforts to marry him was irksome to put it mildly. In his grandfather's day, the men had been the providers and he was determined that was how it was going to be in his own marriage. That was why he so loved bringing home his catch from the sea; why he had gone shooting with Peter Penhailes for rabbits; even accompanied him to the abattoir when the Penhaileses' lambs had been slaughtered – 'Painlessly, Ho. I promise you that.' The honeymoon venue, which had seemed so unpromising at first, was turning out to be ideal. He could play at being a pioneer and he did it quite successfully.

There had been an odd sort of pleasure in finding that Hope had almost wrecked the cottage in his absence. He had enjoyed comforting her, taking over, putting everything right. After the first shock of discovering that Jem Trewint had been camping out almost within arm's length of them, he found the whole situation quite comic; something to tell the lads about at work. Even the bit about him wanting to paint Hope. Jack was proud of himself for being so forthright in his refusal. He had been defending his wife. That was what he wanted to do now: he wanted to look after Hope and, if need be, defend her.

They went to bed that night laughing at the pervading smell of soot. He held her close, quite certain that nothing would ever destroy this happiness. They were all right and they would always be all right.

* * *

Hope was only too happy to be 'looked after'. Somehow, during the caring she had received all her life, she had come to the conclusion that she was not one of life's copers and Jack's protectiveness was exactly what she needed. She was a typical child of older parents, perfectly content, happier with adults than with other children. When Jack had first looked at her across the heads of the other girls at Miss Marchant's, she had not dared to hope he was attracted to her. He was an older man, which meant he must have done his National Service, probably in the Far East. It set his age group apart, made them special. When he was waiting for her in the park the next day, she was overjoyed. She knew immediately she loved him and she would never love anyone else. She had never been certain of anything much before; but she knew she loved Jack.

Her parents, Edward and Milly Marsh, had moved to Horsley when a new branch of the Three Counties Friendly Society had opened in Ledbury. Edward had been in the City all through the war and the old-fashioned Three Counties snapped him up to launch their new branch. It was 1945, the war was over, and at fifty-five Edward was thinking of retirement. Horsley House was to be their retirement home. It was as if the house and village had been waiting for them and they had settled into their ways within a month of moving. Milly joined the Women's Institute and they both took up bowls. On Saturdays they drove into Gloucester and shopped. On Sundays they attended morning service at the grey church with its squat Saxon tower. Milly took up petit point and Edward began collecting old maps.

Then like a bolt from the blue, Milly, twelve years younger than Edward but looking forward to retirement just as avidly, became pregnant. They could not believe it. Milly was under the impression she had started 'the change' and did not see her doctor until her stomach began to swell and she thought she had a growth.

The doctor was young and jolly. 'Well, you've certainly got that, Mrs Marsh! But no need for any operations. I would say you will be losing it in about three months.' He was amused by her complete bewilderment. 'You are expecting a baby, Mrs Marsh.'

'But I can't be!' Milly wished she could see her old doctor in London. 'I'm too old!'

Dr Booth studied her card. 'Forty-three? That's not too old. My goodness, you're still in the prime of life!' He could not imagine being forty-three; anyway, the threat of a National Health Service would doubtless be the death of him.

'My husband will be retiring in five years!'

'This will be quite a sho – quite a surprise . . . for him, then?'

'Absolutely.'

'No other children, I see.' He kept his eyes on her card. He wanted to laugh but gathered it was not a laughing matter.

'We tried. We would have loved children but we accepted it was not to be. And then of course, during the war, it would have been wrong to bring a baby into the world.' She swallowed. 'I really *am* too old, Doctor.'

'You are perfectly healthy, Mrs Marsh. There is no reason on earth why anything should be wrong.' He reached for a prescription pad. 'Listen. I'm going to prescribe some vitamins. And if you would like to see an obstetrician . . .'

'A what?'

'A specialist.'

'Well. No. I don't think so. After all, you are qualified.' She sounded doubtful and he looked up and grinned, nodding. 'I'll see what my husband has to say. Oh dear.'

'He'll be as pleased as Punch, you'll see.' Dr Booth had an account at the Three Counties and knew that the manager was generous with overdrafts.

Edward was not only pleased, he was delighted. And frightened too. They did not choose a name or buy a thing, crossing their fingers and making sure they never walked under any ladders. When a perfect girl baby was born without any trouble at all, it was he who said, 'She is our hope for the future, Milly.'

Milly said, frowning slightly, 'Hope? It's rather an old-fashioned name, Edward.'

'I meant hope with a little h. But . . . sweetheart, it's a beautiful name. Shall we?'

And Hope had fulfilled all their hopes, as beautiful as a dream, not clever but not stupid either. And when she fell in love with Jack Langley, they were pleased. He was older than her, determined to look after her. They admired his stubborn, independent streak; he was not a money-grabber. Edward Langley had met a lot of money-grabbers in his line of business, so this quality was important to him.

Hope was not spoiled. But she was cherished. She was never pushed; she was always told that her best was good enough. When she met Jack Langley and he told her she was hopeless, it brought her up with a jolt. But then, gradually, she saw that he liked that quality in her. Perhaps so much approval made her too trusting.

Two

When they got back to the Sandhurst cottage which was as unpicturesque and as inconvenient as Widdershins had been, they were still like children playing at house. Hope's parents had driven from Horsley village to arrange the bits of furniture, clean the sink and the awful old gas cooker and make up the bed. Wedding presents gleamed unexpectedly from walls and shelves; a brand-new toaster sat oddly on the soggy wooden draining board and the tablecloth still retained its creases.

Hope viewed it all ecstatically then ran outside while Jack carried the cases upstairs, returning with a bunch of dandelions and buttercups. She arranged them in a cut-glass vase donated by the Women's Institute back in Horsley, and placed the vase in the middle of the table.

Jack nodded appreciatively but still asked, 'Is there any food?'

'I expect Mummy got us a loaf and some milk. Somewhere.' She opened cupboard doors vaguely and found plenty of supplies. 'There's everything! What would you like for supper, darling? I'll cook whatever you like! There's a fondue set somewhere and plenty of cheese here. Or pancakes? With cheese filling?'

'I'd love a stew,' Jack said. 'With carrots and plenty of dumplings.'

She stared at him, aghast, and he burst out laughing and held her against his shoulder and told her that cheese anything would be wonderful.

'You're a devil,' she said contentedly, sniffing the salt which still clung to his neck. 'It doesn't have to be cheese. There are tins.' She looked up at him. 'Hey – there might be some stewed steak somewhere!'

'No. I'd prefer cheese.' He frowned slightly. 'Your mother must have spent a month's housekeeping on stocking us up.'

'Oh – please don't go all independent on me now. Let's make a pot of tea and sit by our lovely flowers and just . . . be married!'

Those first few summer weeks were idyllic. The river running almost past their door was chocolate brown, turgid; a workaday river full of boats and barges. They were less than a mile from the docks. Traffic and goods for Tewkesbury and Worcester still used the waterways occasionally. Up beyond Wainlodes a grand house was being restored and barges of Bath stone went past daily during their first month. Milly and Edward bought one of the new colour television sets and tried to persuade Jack to accept their old black-and-white one. It was Hope who told them thank you very much but they did not want a television set because there was so much to do and see in Sandhurst. And then, at the end of September, when they went to Horsley specially to watch the new *QE II* being launched, Hope began to be sick every morning.

Everyone was apprehensive at first. It was so soon and really they had relied on Hope's salary for the nest egg that would eventually become a deposit on a house. But, as Milly said, 'When it happens like this, God must have had a hand in it – after all, think how surprised we were when you came along, my darling.'

Jack said, 'Well. We really have pushed the boat out, haven't we?' He was delighted, his face wreathed in smiles.

Milly said, 'Oh Jack, you are witty. I take it that's a sort of pun based on the launch of the new liner?'

They all stared at her. Edward Marsh said gently, 'I don't think so, my love. It's a current phrase, actually.' And then they burst out laughing which made the unintended joke really funny.

The sickness came and went. Hope made herself a couple of rather elegant smocks and a wrap-around skirt for later but she did not tell many people about the baby. She kept her worries about money to herself. Jack seemed to take it all in his stride.

'You must give up work immediately, Ho. We mustn't risk anything.'

'Darling, I don't want you to make a fuss, I want this to be a perfectly natural thing. No one will know at the office for at least four months. And the extra money will be so useful.'

He shook his head violently. 'We'll be getting

the family allowance. And if you stay at home we shall actually save money. You'll be able to get the cheaper cuts of meat and make nourishing stews – you know it's my favourite meal. And I can walk to work – need not take the car out at all. In fact we might as well sell it.'

She felt a small pang about that but nodded anyway. 'Yes, I suppose that's sensible. We must do some sums, darling. Mummy and Daddy will want to get us a pram—' She saw his face and added hastily, 'Grandparents always do that. And you mustn't be too prickly about them, Jack. They will want to share this so much—'

'Not to the extent of paying for every damned thing!' he protested immediately. 'All right, the pram. But that's it. I'm perfectly capable of providing for my wife and baby!'

'Oh darling.' She went to him and sat on his lap. 'I'm going to love it when you get all patriarchal.' She lifted his silky brown forelock and kissed the forehead beneath it. 'You'll be such a lovely father, Jack. I never thought of it before, but now . . .'

'Just say you'll give in your notice on Monday,' he whispered. 'Please, Ho. I do so want to come home and find my dinner waiting!'

She started to giggle and bite his ear quite hard and he screeched and stood up, lifting her easily. Later he told her how happy she made him. All the time.

In November the Petersens came on the scene. Mandy and Henrik Petersen were from Norway and had submitted plans for a Severn barrage to supply giant generators. Norway knew all about

44

hydro-electric power and already public opinion was cautious about the new nuclear power stations, so in a small way the Petersens were VIPs. Everyone in Sandhurst knew about them. They'd bought Salmon Cottage further along the bank and 'spent a fortune' having it done up. The landlord of the pub reckoned they'd have a big house-warming party and invite all the village, but when they didn't, the rumour went round that they weren't married at all; he had a wife and sixteen children back in Bergen. Oh, they had parties all right, more like orgies on the lines of the fast London set. Drugs and sex and all. That's how they were going to get their plans passed by the notoriously slow Inland Waterways, not to mention the City Council and the Docks Authority. But they were hoeing up the wrong furrow there; they'd have to have more than a few crazy parties to get past that lot.

Jack would come home and report all this in his best rustic accent. Hope would laugh, inordinately grateful to the Petersens for providing light relief. Now that she was pregnant her mother frequently spent the day with her. Jack wasn't keen on that. Jack wasn't exactly possessive. It was simply that having no family of his own he did not understand Hope's need for hers.

And then one Sunday at the end of that dreary month, when she and Jack could have spent the day at Horsley but he had said they should be together properly – Hope had come close to asking him snappily what on earth he meant by that – there was a knock at the door and there were the Petersens. Hope knew who they were because they drove past the cottage in their Volvo car at least twice every day. She smiled widely and said, 'You're our new neighbours. Welcome. Will you come in?'

Jack leaped up from his chair and held the back of it for Mandy to sit down. She was exquisitely beautiful. Blond and blue-eyed and very Nordic. Possibly almost thirty. She made Hope feel like a gawky schoolgirl.

'How sweet of you!' In spite of her Scandinavian looks, her slight accent marked her out as a Londoner. 'We thought it was about time we made contact with someone. I'm Mandy and this is Henrik and we live in Salmon Cottage – as you know – and we're walking down to the pub for lunch. We thought you might join us.'

Jack and Hope were amazed. They never ate Sunday lunch 'out', nobody they knew did.

'Do they do lunches?' Jack prevaricated.

'Oh yes. We eat there most days. It's easier than looking for a proper restaurant and anyway Gloucester doesn't seem to have many.' She turned her dazzling smile on to her husband. 'Henrik, my lambkin. Tell them. Insist.'

Henrik was older than his wife, probably by about ten years. He was rail-thin and distinguished looking and very definitely from Norway.

'Certainly I will try to persuade them.' He turned courteously to Hope. 'We would be so pleased if you would accept our invitation. Because afterwards I would like to show your husband my plans. I understand he works for the Inland Waterways and he might be able to share his local knowledge. Which would be most helpful to me.'

Nobody had asked Jack's advice before. He stammered, 'Most pleased . . . you are very kind.' He glanced at Hope. 'We would be delighted . . . I think . . . yes, Hope?'

It was a gift from heaven; suddenly the dreary Sunday afternoon blossomed. 'Oh yes,' she said, beaming at Mandy. 'But lunch . . . I'm not sure . . .' She had not wanted cooked food for some time.

Mandy leaped from the chair, clasped Hope to her sweet-smelling shoulder and kissed her cheek. She seemed to know about the pregnancy although Hope had been careful not to tell anyone in the village.

'My dear girl. How rotten. We'll settle that. I've got some special coffee at home. Henrik will go back, fetch it and bring the car.' She held up a hand as Hope and Jack began to protest. 'I won't hear a word against it! My coffee will settle you instantly. You drink it black. It is bitter but it works! Afterwards, we will drive you to the inn, you will eat a large lunch which will be delicious because you have not had to cook it beforehand, then we will go back to Salmon Cottage and while the men are looking at their dull papers, we will drink tea and gossip!'

It sounded delightful. Henrik was already walking smartly back along the towpath.

'I don't want to be a trouble,' she murmured, glancing at Jack. But he was smiling, not minding a bit that Mandy had appropriated her completely.

Mandy said, 'Now listen. Pop upstairs and

throw up. Wash your face and come back down a new person!'

Hope was to learn that Mandy never used terms like sickness or nausea. She referred to vomiting and throwing up. Often. She made Hope feel part of the brave new world of the 'sixties and after a few months it was hard to remember that she and Henrik had not always been around. The really good thing about the Petersens was that Jack did not resent them. If he arrived home and found Mandy there, he was positively pleased about it. 'Nice of you to keep Ho company,' he would say. And Mandy would come back with something pert. 'Henrik threw me out,' or 'I came for a cup of sugar . . .'

Hope was pleased by his reaction. 'After all, when you get home from work you're tired and entitled to have your home to yourself.'

'I don't mind Mandy. She doesn't share a past with you.' He realized that was an implied criticism of Milly and went on quickly, 'Besides which, Ho, Henrik's plans are absolutely marvellous. And I think he'd like me to take more than just a passing interest in them.'

'Sounds exciting.'

'It is.' He grinned. 'I feel full of hope in more ways than one!'

The old jokes on her name often failed to amuse, and her smile was more by way of encouragement. The trouble with expecting a baby was that you gave up something . . . was it identity? Or control? Mandy was a help with that too. She insisted that Hope should 'go into pants'. She took her into a small maternity shop

48

in St John's Lane and showed her how they worked.

'You see, honeybun, they're called kangaroo pants because the flap allows your tummy to ooze out of the line of cut. Stand sideways. Put your smock – and by the way I have to admit it is gorgeous – over the flap. Now do you see? The line of the pants is not interrupted.'

Hope had to agree. 'It's a bit like that king in the fairy story who had a golden patch put on his slippers to make room for his bunion. Or corn. Or whatever it was.'

'Quite, sweetie.' Mandy signalled imperiously to the sales assistant. 'We'll take two of those. And—' she indicated Hope's smock which was in corded velvet with a mandarin collar and wide sleeves, '—that is an original Hope Langley. Would you care for something similar for the window display?'

The assistant looked flustered. 'I'd have to ask the manageress. She is on holiday at the moment.'

'Very well. I do feel that a so-called boutique should stock some designer clothes. A maternity boutique more so than most.'

'I'm sure you're right.' The assistant surrendered to Mandy's obvious superiority and was won over by Hope's wide smile. 'I will certainly mention it to Mrs Bagnold when she comes in.' She slid the maternity trousers into a bag and picked up a pen. 'What was the name again?'

Hope wanted to giggle; she busied herself with her horrible wraparound skirt while Mandy continued with her act. Not that it was much of an act. Mandy Petersen swept through life like a combine harvester. Everything was dealt with and packaged in one fell swoop. She was in the process of packaging Hope.

They left the maternity shop and went for coffee in the Tudor Tearooms. 'I'd like to take that place over,' Mandy said, fitting a Russian cigarette into her holder. 'It's in a decent position. People coming out of Marks and Spencer's can't miss it. But what a name! The Maternity Shop, I ask you.'

Hope adjusted her lump surreptitiously and recalled that Mandy had liked her smock. 'But that's what it is, Mandy. How would anyone know if it was called . . . I don't know . . . Mandy's Smocks?'

Mandy made one of her perfectly hideous faces and Hope giggled at last.

'Well, I wouldn't think anyone would be cretinous enough not to know that Mandy's Smocks referred to pre-natal wear!' She inhaled luxuriously, narrowed her eyes and let the smoke trickle from her nostrils. 'What about – Expectancies? Just the one word. Full of excitement and anticipation.'

'Gosh. Yes.' Hope gazed admiringly at her friend. 'You could do it too. Not that there's a call for two maternity shops in Gloucester. The big stores have got maternity departments.'

'Will you stop using that word over and over! It sounds so puddingy, I can't bear it. Maternity is at one end of the scale and ladies in waiting at the other. One stodgy, one so pretentiously twee it makes you want to throw up!'

Hope laughed in outraged delight. She remembered when Mandy had first made contact last November. When Jack had eventually thanked her for calling, she had said to both of them, 'My dears, I don't call on people, I make contact with them. I have wanted to make contact with the two of you ever since Henrik and I arrived.' Even though Hope had been feeling so dreadful in the first weeks of her pregnancy, she had noticed that Henrik and Mandy Petersen had not moved in: they had arrived.

Now Mandy accepted her black espresso with a curling lip. 'One of the many things that make me want to throw up is espresso coffee,' she said. 'Unless you have that frothy milk effort like yours, espresso is a dead loss.'

'Well then . . .' Hope said blowing her froth aside and inhaling with closed eyes.

'Well then. I have to watch my figure like a hawk. Something you know nothing about!'

'I know I'm a fat lump but—'

'You also know I was not referring to Lump. You are naturally slim. I am not. It's sad but true.' She leaned forward. 'Darling, seriously now, when you told me you were running up your own smocks, I had no idea. If that girl talks her Mrs Peabody into displaying it, you'll have a business on your hands!'

'Mrs Peabody?'

'Whatever her name was.'

'I think it was Bagnold.'

'What a suitable name for the manager of a boutique! Mrs Bagnold! What is the world coming to? Well, obviously it will always be the Maternity Shop. Someone with a name like Mrs Bagnold couldn't reach for anything higher.'

'Anyway, Mandy, she's not likely to agree to

displaying anything I make, is she? That ancient hand-sewing machine on the kitchen table . . . all the seams are raw and just look at my buttonholing!' She poked a finger through one of them, caught her nail in a thread which puckered the whole of the front edge. 'Now look what I've done!' Hope grinned. 'That's all your fault!'

Mandy sipped her coffee and narrowed her eyes again as she studied her friend. Then she said, 'You're still doing it, aren't you? When I said I'd take you in hand, you promised me that you wouldn't even think the word "hopeless". Well, I heard it then. A sort of sepulchral echo, even as you laid blame at my innocent feet. Just stop that schoolgirl giggling. I wish I had a tape recorder sometimes so that you could hear yourself. No, not the giggling. As a matter of fact that can be enchanting at times – infuriating at others. But it's OK. The other thing.'

Hope shook her head. 'It's just a joke now. A sort of . . . defence thing. You know, self-deprecating. Whatever. I broke a cup yesterday – one of our wedding present cups. And I said it then.'

'What did Jack say?'

'He wasn't there. I wish you wouldn't assume that it's Jack who thinks I'm hopeless. It's me.' Hope waved her hands. 'And actually – like I just said – I use it to – to – make something awful into something bearable.' She looked defiant. 'It's better than swearing!'

'It's not better than swearing. Swearing is perfect. Will you promise me that next time you break a cup you'll say very loudly, fu—'

'Mandy!' Hope put out a hand. 'For God's sake! We're in the Tudor Tearooms.'

'And it's 1968.' But Mandy smiled. 'You said for God's sake. That's better than you used to say. Gosh and golly and goodness gracious . . . I couldn't believe you when we met.'

Hope said, 'I can't believe how I was either. I was sheltered and spoiled to a degree, wasn't I?' She quite enjoyed these conversations when they analysed her character. Jack was so full of the situation at the docks, he had no time for what he would term frivolities.

'I don't know.' Mandy inhaled, narrowed her eyes, exhaled. 'You were a hothouse plant perhaps. I watched you coming and going. When you went out to the road to buy bread or vegetables or fish . . . it was the way you put yourself in the hands of those traders. They could have sold you any rubbish. They never did.'

'They wouldn't. They're good people.'

'No. They're not good people. And they would have sold me rubbish if I'd given them half a chance.' She leaned forward suddenly 'Listen, honey. I promise you that that ridiculous little shop whose name shall not be mentioned will display your smock, and the next one you make. And the one after that.'

'Oh, Mandy! I do love you. But you're hopelessly biased—'

'That bloody word again! And you said you loved me. See what I mean? You are already vulnerable and you deliberately make yourself more vulnerable. My God.' She leaned back. 'You need me.'

'Of course I do. But not to sell my smocks. Just to be my friend.'

Mandy flung herself further back. 'I think I'm going to cry.' Then she grinned. 'No, I'm not. I'm going to buy that shop, change the name to Expectancies and sell exclusive clothes designed by Hope Langley!'

They both laughed inordinately and then ordered more coffee and did the *Telegraph* crossword between them.

Hope knew she had never been so happy. She had rarely been unhappy and the time at Widdershins, being in bed with Jack, and her childhood in Horsley House had all been idyllic. But the arrival of Mandy and Henrik Petersen had emphasized the rest of her good fortune and – somehow – completed her life. Henrik came and went, always smiling, always happy to do whatever Mandy demanded, encouraging Jack to offer his opinions on the barrage project; to discuss the merits and demerits of fossil fuel power, of nuclear power. He was a wonderful host at small dinner parties in Salmon Cottage, would drive Hope and Jack anywhere they wanted to go. 'He works like stink . . . plans, calculations . . . he's done it three times before. In the end nothing comes of it.' Mandy laughed. 'So he puts up his fees each time!'

'It will happen this time.' Jack was terribly enthusiastic. He had been up to the converted loft in the Petersen cottage and gone over the designs with Henrik. He wanted desperately to be in on it; to get away from the boredom of clerking for the transport company in the docks.

'The government had such a majority in sixty-six they can do anything. They're nationalizing the Inland Waterways . . . building motorways.' Henrik beamed at him and Jack spoiled it by adding, 'And we won the World Cup!'

'Ha!' Henrik said, 'Football! It conquers all!'

But Jack's imagination was fired. He took on some of Henrik's calculations: mathematics had been his best subject at school and he had used it to work on statistics in Korea. Henrik offered some instruction and suggested he should attend evening classes in the brand new field of computing. Jack had a feeling about it all. This was his chance: he knew instinctively that Henrik would help him. He knew too that there would be a price to pay; he had been in the world long enough to know there was always a price to pay. He thought the price was Mandy's patronage of Hope.

Mandy had announced quite baldly at the beginning of that year that she intended to take Hope in hand and she was a woman of many interests. She involved Hope in many of them. They went to auctions where she bought 'pieces' for Salmon Cottage. She took her to expensive shops and fashion shows, to art exhibitions and the ballet. He didn't mind; it seemed to him sometimes that Mandy was grooming Hope for a different life, but he was always included in it.

Lately Jack had heard a lot about fabrics. He came home from a day of checking bills of lading to find Hope up to her eyes in billowing masses of cloth.

'Isn't this the most gorgeous fabric?' she

asked, whipping up her own enthusiasm in an effort to fire his.

'Fabric?' he queried, looking at the brocade which his grandmother had favoured for front room curtains. 'D'you mean material? Cloth?'

'Of course.'

Mandy had told Hope to go 'beyond limits' when she chose fabrics for her smocks. 'Think drama. Think body – stiffness – no one wants a smock that clings to every curve. Let's go to Cheltenham. I've got an account at Cavendish House. We'll use Henrik's car, it's bigger. More comfortable for the Lump.'

So they had taken the Swedish Volvo and driven it to Cheltenham and Cavendish House where Mandy watched, narrow-eyed, while Hope went through the bolts of cloth, shaking her head at each one. It was Mandy who had said, 'Come on, honeybun. Let's go into furnishings.' And almost immediately, Hope had said, 'The brocade. It's got body. It's got drama. It would be marvellous in the evenings.'

Mandy had asked about yardage and gone to the counter. A male assistant had carried the enormous bulk of the brocade to the car. Hope knew it had cost the earth and was apprehensive.

'Supposing I muck it up?'

'*You* will not muck it up. There's bound to be wastage. We buy some more.'

'But the cost—'

'We stick it on the retail price.' Mandy had given her wonderful smile. She had the stark bone structure of a Marlene Dietrich but when she smiled it was as if she revealed her soul.

Hope, full of heroine worship, had said fervently, 'You know, you are as beautiful inside as you are outside!'

Mandy had replied dryly, 'Well, that about sums it up. Takes me nearly an hour to get my face right each morning. Probably took me years to do the same with the soul!'

'Oh shut up!' Hope said fondly. And, for once, Mandy did.

Hope had been all day struggling with the heavy brocade, cutting it out on the floor to make a sample smock. Twice she had had to unpick her machine stitching and for a moment she thought Jack's question about fabric was his way of getting at her. So her 'of course' was terse.

He responded immediately to her tone. 'Are you overtired? What are you doing exactly? That stuff is heavy. If it's for curtains we can get them made—'

'It's not for curtains!' She got up and went into the kitchen. 'I'll leave it out if you don't mind. Have another go after our meal.'

'You will not. You're exhausted, I can tell.' He was angry. He picked Hope up bodily, carried her into the tiny front room and laid her on the single bed she had covered with cushions. 'Just lie down and think of nothing. I'll cook the tea. What's today? Monday. Is it cold meat and bubble and squeak?'

She admitted to herself she was tired. 'Oh Jack. Sorry. Yes, that's what it is – doesn't it sound boring?'

'It's my second favourite, actually. Stew and dumplings being the first.'

'Mandy and Henrik wouldn't be seen dead eating cold lamb and bubble and squeak.'

'No. But then they haven't got what we've got.' He knelt and stroked her short dark hair. 'You mustn't let Mandy tire you out, darling. If it weren't for this—' he gestured towards the machine, '—you would have been lying down.' He kissed her. 'Are you all right, Ho? Really, really all right?'

'Yes, of course. I should have given up earlier. I'm just so hopeless, Jack. If it weren't for you . . .' She knew he was right and she clung to him and let him make a fuss of her. She had to think of the baby more. She must not make a mess of having the baby. After they had eaten and everything was all right again, she remembered something he had said.

'Sweetheart.' She was delightfully sleepy. 'What did you mean about us having something Mandy and Henrik haven't?'

She wanted to talk about the Petersens objectively; she and Jack together, talking about the Petersens. Even being a little critical perhaps.

'I meant . . . I don't know. They're in love, that's obvious. But not like us, Ho. We've got something so special.'

She snuggled into the crook of his elbow. 'I wonder why they haven't got children? Henrik must be in his forties.'

'His work takes up too much time?'

'Well, you work hard, Jack. I don't really think that's got much to do with it!' She giggled, expecting him to take her up on that one.

'It's different for Henrik. He's making a great deal of money. He asked me to help with his accounts and my God . . . but it's more than money. It's creative. All civil engineering is. He – he sort of generates things.'

'But according to Mandy they rarely grow – flower – whatever.'

'He's got the imagination to see them in his mind's eye. That's probably enough for him.'

She thought about it. 'Maybe that's why they don't need children? We – you and me – we like to see the result of our work.' She was starting to giggle again. 'My smocks. Your fishing.'

'The baby.' He was kissing her through her spluttering laughter. She had been tired, so tired. Jack could always rejuvenate her.

But then when he insisted on doing the washing up and had arranged her legs carefully and put a pillow in her back, he almost spoiled it all.

'I'll never forget the result of your first attempt at housekeeping! I can still get the taste of soot sometimes.'

He was teasing, of course. She hadn't minded before; not ever. But now . . . since Mandy, she did mind. And for the first time, she honestly felt inadequate.

Mandy took Hope into Cheltenham again that June and this time insisted she should buy chenille tablecloths.

Hope was very doubtful. 'Mandy, brocade is used for curtains but it has that sort of regal dignity . . . Chenille says – quite simply – old-fashioned table cover.'

'Sweetie, let your mind stretch. Look at the borders on the things. Look at the fringes. Now

59

. . . think.' She closed her eyes momentarily above the pile of cloths. 'Think . . . ponchos.'

Hope paused, pursing her mouth, frowning slightly. Then she picked up one of the table covers, folded it twice into a square, took the centre point between thumb and forefinger and let the cloth hang loosely.

'Hmmm. I see what you mean. So we have enormous, shawl-like sleeves, fringed, and a round neck. Easy to slip over the head of course.'

'Try one, sweetie. Wear it yourself.'

Still Hope demurred. 'Mandy, you have invested quite a bit of money in materials—'

'You've invested time and labour,' Mandy put in.

'And so far the maternity shop has not accepted a display piece.'

'They will,' Mandy said confidently. 'These smocks are all winter and party wear. Wait until the autumn. Then I'll strike! And meanwhile, this is light-weight stuff. Easier for you to work with. You'll probably finish one tomorrow and come waltzing down the lane showing it off.' She signalled to the shop assistant and got out her chequebook. 'You know, darling, if you have another baby – and I see you as a sort of glamorous earth-mother type – you should think about modelling your own stuff.'

Hope adjusted her lump into the kangaroo pants and sighed. 'Let's get this one born first. It's not much fun at the moment.'

Mandy was instantly sympathetic. 'Poor Hope! Come on, we'll go up to the restaurant and have lunch and then I'll take you home and put you to bed. Don't worry about supper. Henrik and I will take the two of you to the Boat House and Jack will be as happy as Larry because Henrik wants him to do some stuff on tide times. Charts. Graphs. You know.'

It was so wonderful to be with Mandy and have everything arranged. Hope knew in her heart of hearts that it was a continuation of her parents' care but Mandy wasn't that much older than she was herself, so it didn't count. And she was repaying as best she could with the smocks . . . She said gratefully, 'It's sweet of you. But I've done a casserole for tonight. And Jack gets awfully tired towards the end of the week.'

In the end she managed – almost a point of principle – to get out of being put to bed for the afternoon. She went into the Petersen cottage for a cup of tea and then walked back along the towpath to their own tinier, much shabbier cottage, clutching the parcel containing the table cover and planning to begin on it as soon as she got in. It was too hot for her to lie outside as Mandy planned to do and the flies were a nuisance at this time of year. She would cut out a neck shape in facing and stitch it on to the middle of the 'poncho' before she actually made a cut in the chenille; it might fray or pull sideways, she'd never worked with it before. It was fascinating to plan what shape it would be. A V-neck? A scoop line perhaps – that seemed to be all the fashion at the moment.

She stopped as the baby inside her kicked imperiously. Jack loved to feel the movements; she must tell him about this one. It was like someone knocking on a door. Urgently. She looked across the river, unseeing, wondering what the actual birth would be like. Her mother was most reassuring. 'You were born at home, darling. Didn't have time to get to hospital and – really – afterwards it seemed it would have been a waste of a bed someone else could have.'

Hope smiled. Mummy was so sweet, so gentle, so completely wrapped up in Daddy. Just as he was in her. Maybe that's how it was as you got older. Maybe Jack would be content then . . . and Mandy and Henrik would be there, but so much further into the background.

Hope sighed. She was divinely happy. Of course. But she thought quite suddenly of Widdershins and the rill running through the thicket of alder and the enormous cliffs falling down to the tiny cove. The isolation that was never lonely. She thought of Jem Trewint who had doubtless returned to the cottage as soon as they left. He had told her she was beautiful and had wanted to paint her. She had hated the thought of Jem being next door and hearing . . . whatever he had heard. But then he had tramped off towards Penhailes Farm and she and Jack had stripped off their filthy clothes and gone to the rill to wash and then walked back to bed like Adam and Eve in Eden. The whole incident – the whole day of separation and then closeness – had been some kind of rebirth. As if they had played at courtship and getting married, and then after that day they had been . . . married!

She smiled and moved slowly on down the towpath, trying to see in the closeness of water and land an echo of Widdershins. She had been delighted when Jack told her about the end-of-terrace cottage by the river. And though he had not been able to spare any money for new furniture and carpets, she had made the tiny house into a cosy home for them and seen in it something of the sparseness of Widdershins. Unfortunately the Petersens' alterations to their detached place further downstream had somehow lessened that illusion, but as her mother so often said, 'comparisons are odious'.

Hope was tired. She was about two hundred yards from the cottage but it had never seemed so far. The sun shot diamonds of light up at her so that she could no longer look at the water, but she was conscious of the sheer power of the river right next to her, pushing down to the sea, as inexorable as the child inside her. It was almost frightening in a way. Birth, death . . . there was no stopping time, no stopping anything really. She shivered, not smiling any more.

It was good to reach the tiny strip of garden full of ferns and house leeks. She had planted the back with lettuce and radishes and gladioli and lupins, but the front was how they had found it. River plants, Jack called them. They smelled of the river, and when she opened the front door the little hall smelled the same. She went quickly into the kitchen where the casserole she had prepared that morning gave out a lovely aroma of onion. She smiled again. Was there ever a more homely smell than that of onions?

She made more tea and let the last twenty minutes subside. They said pregnancy brought strange emotions: though her mother had shaken her head at that. 'I just got on with doing things,' she said. 'If ever I feel a bit down, I just get on with things.'

So Hope fetched some interfacing material from her sewing box and fashioned it into a wide ellipse. She found the centre of the tablecloth, stitched the oval around it and cut out the middle. Then she threw the tent over her head and went laboriously upstairs to look in the wardrobe mirror. She knew instantly that Mandy had been right; the effect of stripes, fringes and soft chenille combined into a stunning cover-up. If she could cut the sleeves in exactly the right place so that the drape remained as it was, they had a winner. She turned sideways, then right around and viewed the back over one shoulder. She struck poses; she was grinning, giggling aloud in the dusty heat of the bedroom. Her mother was right as always; in working on the smock all her ghosts had been laid. And it was a success. Her mother was right and Mandy was right. And so was she!

And then, without warning, a pain started from her diaphragm and seemed to slice her abdomen in two. She gave a gasping scream and held on to the bed knob, doubling over convulsively. It ripped down her legs and was gone.

She stayed still, crouched, hardly breathing, not terrified, but scared and very aware. It didn't happen like that. She had been to talks at the local welfare clinic. There were all sorts of warnings: backache, exhaustion. But also a need, a longing to work. She'd had that.

She straightened inch by inch and glanced into the mirror. Her face was white and stretched but in the flowing poncho she did not look pregnant any more. That was frightening too. She held the chenille close to her and looked at the shape of her abdomen. As she watched, it moved, she actually saw the movement. It was immediately followed by another ripping, tearing, agonizing pain.

'Oh God. Oh God.' She was on her knees by the bed, clawing at the counterpane. It slid off the bed towards her and she clutched it and wrapped it around herself. 'Oh God. What's happening?'

There was just enough time for her to get downstairs. She knew she had to get outside so that someone would see her. At the end of the terrace lived one of the teachers from the school. She would be home soon and she had a telephone.

'It's too soon . . .' She spoke aloud because, as usual when things weren't quite right, it was somehow a comfort to hear her own voice. 'It's not due yet. It's too soon . . .'

The pain was upon her before she got to the door. She fell to her knees and pressed her forehead to the scuffed lino of the parlour. Behind her on the table her sewing machine loomed hugely, closer and closer. She was certain that it would fall on her. When the pain abated she saw that it stood there, perfectly still and inanimate. 'Oh dear God. Hallucinations . . . oh dear God.'

She got outside the door and fell into the ferns. They were a comfort, damp and cool. She was so hot in the poncho, but she could not get it off however much she tugged. The pain would not go away now, it was sending jabs all over her body. She heard screams and with part of her mind she knew they were her own.

And then she heard a car. It was strange that through all the turmoil and confusion she recognized the sibilant engine note of Henrik's Volvo, even stranger that he – so quiet, almost reticent – took immediate action. She might have expected him to drive on and fetch Mandy and use the telephone. He did not. He crouched by her and dug her out of the ferns and into his arms, poncho and all, and put her in the car so tenderly yet so swiftly she was hardly conscious of movement. He spoke to her in his native Norwegian so she had no idea what he said, though she felt comforted. He parked the car right outside the maternity wing of the hospital and carried her inside. She was rigid with the pain, holding on to him with frantic fingers, moaning into the collar of his beautiful tweed jacket. And then expert hands took over and a mask came across her face and she was breathing as deeply as she could, sucking in unconsciousness, never quite reaching it . . .

It was a long labour and Faith was not born for another twelve hours. Hope forgot that she was having a baby: it was just her and the pain and she tried, often, to give in to the pain and let it win, let it take her wherever it was going. And then Jack's voice, urgent in her ear, would say, 'One more push, my darling. Just one more.' And then another and another and then there was no more strength and pain engulfed her and pressed her into the bed. Jack would not let go, would not release her hands. She whispered, 'Jack . . . it's hopeless . . . hopeless.'

And he shouted like a madman, 'You are not hopeless! You are my hope. My salvation. Do you hear me?'

They were getting her ready for an emergency Caesarean when he said that and she reared up, holding his hands, and gave him 'one more . . . just one more'. And Faith came. Puckered, wizened, underweight, but perfect.

Hope, exhausted, without an emotion left, watched as they dealt with it all and as Jack knelt before her, weeping helplessly, and telling her how marvellous she was.

'I was so frightened . . . this must never happen again, my darling. No more babies. No more.'

She nodded thankfully. She never wanted to go through it again. She had done it once, and once was enough.

Three

Faith was the ideal first baby for a young couple who were without money or prospects. She loved everyone, needed no more entertainment than to watch the aspen leaves moving above her pram and went from breast-feeding to sieved foods without a burp or any other protest. When she woke in the night she would cry as if her heart was breaking but immediately Hope's face appeared above the cot, her mourning changed to rejoicing and she tensed her arms, rolled her tiny fingers into fists and reshaped her pitiful expression into one of apparent excitement. Edward and Milly Marsh took her in their stride.

'She's just like you,' Milly said to Hope. 'So pleased to be alive.'

In case Jack felt left out Edward added quickly, 'I bet you were a pretty cool customer as a baby, weren't you, Jack?'

'Giles reckoned I was a little perisher,' Jack said. 'Kept him awake when he was sitting his scholarship.'

'Look at her now!' Milly enthused. 'She's trying to pull herself up on my thumbs! How old is she? Barely four months. I can remember you trying to stand up on my lap at that age, Hope!'

'Mother!'

Hope left them to it and went to make some tea. The horror of childbirth had receded and, like Faith, she was happy again and with a new intensity. She felt her life had accelerated amazingly: she had no need of her old car any more. Mandy brought shopping in daily and because she 'knew where to go' the bills were much less than when Hope had done it herself. The ecstatic grandparents came every week with gifts of fruit cakes and fresh vegetables, Henrik appeared most days on his way home from Weston and the neighbours in the little terrace by the river were always dropping in to see the new baby. It was as if the riverside cottage had become the hub of the universe.

Edward and Milly always timed their visits for the weekend, imagining that Jack would feel left out if they came while he was at work. They came at four o'clock and left at seven and it was a pleasant ritual. They had what Hope called 'a Sunday-school tea' around the table in the dining room where she still occasionally ran up one of her smocks, though Mandy's far-fetched plans had not yet materialized. Her father said, 'I love sardine sandwiches. When did we last have sardine sandwiches, Milly?'

'We don't eat tea, darling.' Her mother cast an eye towards the door where Faith lay in her carrycot playing with her toes. 'D'you think she's warm enough, Hope? There's no heating in the hall. And it's Christmas in two weeks.'

'It's not cold, is it?' Hope licked her finger

and held it aloft. 'The wind is in the west!'

Everyone laughed but Jack got up and fetched the baby and kept her on his knee while they went on with tea. Faith gurgled delightedly.

'Her feet are clammy, actually, Ho.'

'She won't keep anything on them and she's not worried by cold feet and hands. Her body is always warm.'

Milly leaned across the table and felt the minuscule toes and fingers. 'Perhaps you should have some of those electric radiators around, darling,' she said. 'Would you like something really practical like that for Christmas?'

Hope did not even look at Jack. 'I was hoping for a new cardigan. Or a skirt – do you still make those sort of tapestry skirts, Mummy?'

'Yes. And of course you shall have something personal. I was thinking of Faith. She's too young to appreciate toys – anyway Mandy and Henrik will go mad in that direction!' She smiled though she did not entirely approve of this new and close friendship. 'The radiators would be for Faith, not you and Jack!'

Again everyone laughed, Jack less than the others.

Hope got up and went into the kitchen, reappearing with toasted buns. Edward clasped his hands theatrically. 'Teacakes! My favourite. Why don't we have sardine sandwiches and teacakes, Milly?'

Milly was about to protest again that they did not eat tea and then caught his eye. 'You shall have sardine sandwiches and teacakes, Edward dear. Tomorrow. And Tuesday. Wednesday and Thursday too if you so desire!'

Edward made a face at Jack. 'This is what I have to put up with, old man. Please note. It is quite possible to kill with kindness!'

Milly caught herself thinking of Mandy and Henrik Petersen; were they trying to kill off the young Langleys with kindness . . . ? She almost laughed at herself.

She said thoughtfully, 'D'you know, I am wondering about those radiators. Faith is doing so well. And anyway you put her out every day in the pram whatever the weather. I think we'd better let things stay as they are, don't you?'

Jack smiled and looked down into his daughter's face. She was almost asleep in the comfort of his arms. He felt a surge of love.

'What do you think, little Faith?' he murmured. 'Are you happy with life as it is?'

The baby tightened her grip on one of his fingers and her lips curved in a smile. They all cooed with delight.

The Petersens did in fact shower Faith with soft toys that Christmas; Jack received a watch and Hope a pair of diamond earrings.

'Oh how lovely!' She held them up to the grey light at the window. They were spending Christmas at the cottage; Jack insisted that Faith's first Christmas should be spent in her own home. The grandparents were unable to join them because Milly's much older sister had come for two weeks and did not want to venture out.

The diamonds sparkled with a blue fire. They were genuine.

'Henrik chose them,' Mandy said. 'I told him

you didn't have pierced ears, but he said you would have them done for the sake of the earrings!'

'Henrik, they really are gorgeous. You shouldn't have done it! But perhaps – one day – I will get my ears pierced. When Faith gets married!'

'And I chose your watch,' Mandy said to Jack. 'Let me put it on for you. It's a Rolex. If you don't like it, they'll change it.'

Jack was red with embarrassment. 'My God. Mandy – Henrik. You're too good – we just can't keep up with this!'

'Silly boy!' Mandy slapped his wrist and turned to Hope. 'You have given us friendship. We value that more than any other present we have had.'

'I made you some cushions.' Hope gathered them from under the tree; they were wrapped in thin, holly-sprigged paper. 'It's a kind of quilting thing I read about. And you're always on about unusual materials, so see what you think of these!'

They were in unbleached calico, with an occasional dark thread running through the natural fibres. For some obscure reason Hope said, 'Actually, Jack chose it.'

Mandy was delighted. 'Darlings, you couldn't possibly have got us anything we could like better! And this is another of your trendsetters, Hope! Oh, my dear girl, I can see a dark green carpet with these cushions scattered over it . . .' She looked at Henrik. 'Shall I tell her now?'

'You'll have to, won't you? She'll die of curiosity if you leave it at that!'

'Hope. Jack. I've sold all of your smocks. All twelve. That ghastly woman, can't remember her name, made out the cheque to me so I've paid it in and written one for you.'

She delved in her handbag and came up with a cheque. Hope, already jumping around the room like an excited child, stopped beneath the mistletoe and took it. It was made out for £960. She was aghast.

'Mandy! Whatever did you ask for each one?'

'Eighty pounds, my dear. If you don't put a good price on them people will think they're home-made rubbish—'

'But they are!'

'They most certainly are not!'

Hope passed the cheque to Jack who stared at it with equal disbelief.

Henrik said, 'Change the subject! Stay exactly where you are, Hope!' He approached, pointed upwards to the mistletoe and took her in his arms.

Mandy looked swiftly at Jack and said, 'Never mind the mistletoe, Jack. What's sauce for the gander . . .' She put her arms around his neck. When Henrik drew away and left Hope laughing, Jack and Mandy were still clasped closely. Henrik guffawed and Mandy lifted one leg until the heel of her shoe touched her buttocks. And then she drew away pretending to swoon.

Jack was grinning foolishly. He made a big thing of folding the cheque into a postage-stamp square and pocketing it. He took Hope's hand and they stood there, obviously unable to find words of thanks.

Mandy clapped her hands. 'Let's go for a walk with Faith. I simply must be seen on Christmas Day pushing a pram! I might be childless but it's the thought that counts!' Which piece of nonsense was welcomed by everyone with relieved laughter.

Mandy took Hope to the January sales. 'For materials. Especially calico. I want you to start on the cushions – they're not so bulky, are they? Jack had a word with me after Faith was born. He thought the brocade was too heavy for you to handle.'

'Actually I was looking at the chenille when Faith started. It wasn't heavy,' Hope said. 'And where on earth do you think you're going to sell cushions? They won't take them at a shop full of maternity wear!'

'I don't see why not. Lying on the floor seems to be all the rage for pregnant mothers. A few cushions dotted around the carpet, as I was saying to you at Christmas—'

'We said and did a lot of things at Christmas that were . . .' Hope had not tried to put her feelings into words, not even to herself. And Mandy and Henrik were so kind and generous she wished she hadn't started now. 'Well . . . over the top.'

Mandy crowed with delight. 'You were jealous when I kissed Jack, weren't you?'

'No. Not a bit.' Hope started to laugh.

Mandy said, 'Quite. It's funny. I'm old enough to be his mamma, damn it all!'

'You certainly are not!' Hope turned around to look at Faith in her carrycot on the back seat.

'I meant . . . oh, you know, the presents. They must have cost—'

'Don't mention money!' Mandy turned into Hare Lane and then into Archdeacon Street. She manoeuvred the car into the last parking space and sat back. 'Gloucester is getting dreadful for parking. There are just too many cars around.'

'We haven't got one,' Hope reminded her.

'No. And that's why you're special people. The things you haven't got become . . . positive.' Mandy turned and looked at her friend quite seriously for once. 'Listen, Hope. All Henrik and I have got is money. He cut himself off from his family when we moved in together. You realize we're not married? Henrik has a wife at home who was getting edgy because there were no children. I don't want children. We met when I was working as a hostess at a hotel in Bergen – I've always done hotel work, started in a boarding house in Sussex Gardens – and we knew immediately that we were meant for each other. So we live away – we feel sometimes as if we're on the run. Ridiculous in this day and age, isn't it? That's the sort of influence families have. Not good. We don't need them. But we do need friends and you give us something more precious than we could ever give you. Believe me.'

Hope stared into the sea-blue eyes and swallowed wordlessly. She had always known there was a lot behind Mandy's stunning looks and flippant manner. But this . . . living in sin in old-fashioned Gloucester; it was unheard of. It was all very well not wanting children but you couldn't always plan these things. What if Mandy had a baby? Her heart went out to her; no wonder she needed a friend.

She said, 'Sorry. Sorry, Mandy. You know how wonderful your friendship is for us too. It's – it's transformed our lives. I mean that.'

'I know you do. It's not true of course. Your lives might well have been better without us. But . . . we do our best. And that was why . . . you know. The earrings et cetera.' She grinned. 'If Henrik wants you to get your ears pierced, give it consideration, my lamb. It would mean a lot to him.'

Hope laughed, again slightly uncomfortable. She spread her hands in a gesture of surrender and Mandy leaned forward immediately and pecked her cheek.

'Come on. Let's get Faith on to her wheels and go look at fabrics.'

They bought calico remnants for a song, and some mattress ticking. Mandy was doubtful about it but Hope, with a new-found confidence, went ahead anyway.

'I'm ploughing your cheque back into the business!' she joked. 'Petersen and Langley have got to experiment now and then. Mattress ticking will be so very avant-garde!'

'All right. But Langley and Petersen. Sounds better.'

'Mandy Hope sounds better still.'

'Oh God, I hate my shortened name. Amanda Hope. Please.'

They carried on like that while they packed their parcels in the tray beneath the push-chair and then they went for coffee and Faith began to weep for her bottle which was in the car.

Mandy handed over the keys. 'I'll come with you to the lift. Then I need to look at little black frocks! Can you manage? We're going to a do. Chamber of Commerce or something. Henrik has asked me to knock 'em out. The estimates are higher than his tender.'

'Of course. Take your time. Faith will!'

Hope joggled the pushchair along Northgate Street, talking to Faith encouragingly. Immediately, the baby was happy again, making her usual clenched-fist salute to the sky. Hope made to turn into Hare Lane and then paused and went on into St John's Lane and through to College Court. The Maternity Shop was as hideous as ever, smocks and trousers displayed on hangers and a doll's pram in one corner of the window. There was no sign of an Amanda Hope smock. Hope gnawed her underlip then manoeuvred the pushchair into the shop. Thank goodness the assistant was not familiar to her; perhaps it was the mysterious Mrs Bagnold.

'Have you got any designer smocks?' Hope asked with a bright false smile. 'I'm looking for something completely unique and I understand you do stock some specials. At a higher price,' she added quickly.

'We have no call for expensive stuff, I'm afraid.' Mrs Bagnold had a nice enough smile. 'You might be lucky in Cheltenham. Let's face it, Gloucester is still a working city.'

Hope thanked her and left feeling hot and extremely bothered. She went back to the car and unscrewed Faith's carrycot from its wheels.

By the time she'd put them in the boot and got out the terry-wrapped bottle, Faith was heart-broken again. There wasn't time to think about anything until she was feeding her. And then she hardly knew what to think. No wonder Mandy had had the smocks for a long time; she had been turned down in Gloucester and probably toted them all around Cheltenham. Had she eventually sold them? Hope gnawed again at her bottom lip; obviously she hadn't. She would have given a name to the shop instead of letting Hope believe they had gone to Mrs Bagnold.

But what on earth was to be done? This was definitely charity. For the first time Hope fully appreciated how Jack felt when her parents tried to help them. She couldn't bear the thought that Mandy and Henrik were plotting how to subsidize their 'friendship'. If only she had discovered this before Mandy's little speech earlier this morning, she could have come into the open and said it could not happen. But Mandy had been somehow . . . not like Mandy. Not exactly pathetic, but . . . yearning. She'd have to talk it over with Jack. Yes, that was what she would do. This evening she and Jack would sort out the whole thing.

Mandy appeared on the driver's side and slipped into her seat as quickly as possible.

'My God, it's cold. I think we might have snow this month.' She peered over Hope's shoulder at Faith. 'Oh, isn't she just adorable. Oh Hope, it's been good today. Hasn't it?'

What else could she say except, 'It has.'

*   *   *

Jack was strangely withdrawn from the whole situation.

'I can't see it as a problem – well, not yet anyway. Obviously she's sold the wretched garments. Why she told you they'd gone to that particular shop, I don't know . . . did she in fact say as much?'

'I can't remember now. Perhaps I ought to come out with it. Ask her. Point blank.'

'Ho, you can't do that. It's looking a gift horse in the mouth. She's got the money somehow, from somewhere. To question that would be awful.'

He was right; she could not question it. But not because of ingratitude. To question or criticize anything Mandy did now would be a kind of condemnation.

She said, 'What if she's got it from her own bank account?'

'She wouldn't. As a matter of fact, they're quite businesslike. Henrik's found a computing course. In Bristol. He suggested I went on it then it might be possible for me to do some work – professionally – for him. I told him we couldn't afford it and he just smiled and suggested I hock the watch.'

'Jack! My God. D'you suppose they gave us those ridiculous presents as – as a kind of payment in kind?'

'Payment for what?'

'Well, I don't know. What they hope to get from you in the future? Mandy is always saying how helpful you are to Henrik. If he's now talking of employing you – well, you couldn't refuse if he's paid for this thingummy course, could you?'

'He's talking of me setting up my own consultancy!'

She was stunned. It was all happening too fast for her. She drew a deep breath and said, 'Darling. Are you sure you don't want to reassure me about the smocks because you need to keep in with Henrik?'

'Ho-ho!' He made his usual pun without humour. 'Darling girl. I truly believe that Mandy has sold those smocks. But if you're unhappy about it, why don't you open a bank account, put that money into it and leave it. You can always pay her back later.'

She swallowed, not wanting to admit she had already used some of it for today's fabrics. She said in a small voice, 'What are you going to do about this course thing?'

Jack laughed. He was excited. 'Take a month's special leave from work. Hock the watch just as Henrik said.'

'Mandy chose it.'

'She'll understand. And this is our chance, Ho. I've got a feeling about it. This computer business is going to take off and the people who are in on the ground floor are going to go with it.' He gathered her up and whirled her around the table. When he put her down he was suddenly serious. 'You don't know how much I want to give you everything, Ho. Everything. You had so much before we married. Your parents have never criticized me but I feel . . . I've wondered about emigrating, all kinds of things. But now . . . this is it. Henrik says if we get in on the ground floor we can undercut everyone else. He says he'll use me exclusively for quantity surveying and tendering. Other engineers will follow suit. I can name my own price. We can get out of this damp hole and into something higher up with a proper bathroom and kitchen units and – and—' he raised his hands above his head, 'a – a dishwasher!'

She laughed, knowing he meant so much more than a dishwasher. She hugged him and kissed him and did not remind him that they had a baby to look after. She would have to believe that Mandy had sold the smocks now.

She had not intended telling him about Mandy's confidence, but much later she said sleepily, 'Darling, Mandy told me today . . . she and Henrik are not married.'

Jack snuffled a little laugh into her hair. 'Of course they're not.'

She was relieved he knew already. And then curious as to how he knew. But she never asked him that.

The course was a month-long stint, seven days a week. It was scheduled for June and was run by an American company. The list of rules sounded formidable.

'My suit won't do, Ho. I'll have to get a new one!' Jack groaned. 'White shirt, tie, well-polished shoes. Sounds completely irrelevant. What is it – a course for male models?'

Hope was impressed. 'They mean business, Jack. They don't want the place cluttered up with hippie types.' She turned her mouth down. 'It's the hours that worry me. Eight hours a day, plus private study – that's homework, I suppose. Seven days a week. That works out at . . .'

'Two hundred and twenty-four hours,' Jack supplied. 'Sounds like brainwashing.'

'No weekends at home. I shall miss you.'

'Will you be all right? Would you like to go to Horsley?'

She knew he wouldn't really want that. 'No. Of course not. This is home and I shall be quite all right.'

'I'd say Mandy and Henrik will look after you but I know that's what you don't want.'

'I think I've got the whole friendship thing on a much better level.' Hope nodded sagely. 'I haven't done anything with the calico and ticking Mandy and I bought in the sales. She's asked me about cushion covers several times and I've said I've been too busy to sew.'

'Good idea.' Jack fiddled with the papers detailing the course programme. 'You haven't . . . well, choked her off or anything, have you, Ho? I mean, if you were right about the smocks . . . well, she meant it kindly.'

'Of course I haven't choked her off!' Hope covered his hand with hers. 'Listen. I know how much this course means to you – and Henrik's support too. I'm not going to jeopardize that.'

'I wasn't thinking of the course!'

'You were!' She laughed, ducking away from an imaginary blow.

He held her, tickling her unmercifully, then kissed her and drew away and said seriously, 'Darling Ho. They need us. I don't quite know why, but they do. Don't you feel it?'

'Yes.' She put her finger on his forehead and ran it down his short nose to his mouth. 'I've thought about it a lot actually. They're not entirely happy. They love each other but happiness isn't quite there. I suppose because they are living in sin.' He laughed and she shook her head. 'I just mean . . . they need us because we're properly happy.'

He took her hand to his mouth, kissed it and held it against his heart. 'It's your doing, Ho. Your mother says Faith is like you, pleased to be alive. And she's right.'

'Only half right. You are the other half. It's together we make happiness.' She looked at him steadily, her darkly fringed blue eyes solemn. 'Be careful when you're away, Jack. Won't you?'

'I will. And you too.'

It was amazing that immediately Jack left she felt so ill. She told herself it was psychological, but it made no difference. Every night as she lay down in bed the summer darkness would whirl around her like a dervish so that she had to clutch at the pillows to stop herself from being flung around the room. The 'turn' as she called it usually ended with vomiting and then, weak as a rabbit, she would sleep until Faith woke her at dawn and the whole thing began again. She declined Mandy's offers of help with untypical brusqueness and told her that, until things were better, she would prefer Henrik not to drop in to see Faith. Mandy nodded reluctantly and begged that if she needed help she would send up a smoke signal. 'I mean it, Hope. Light the fire in the parlour. I can see the smoke from my kitchen window and I'll be over in two seconds.' Hope nodded back and then stopped abruptly as the kitchen slid around her. But it was a relief to know that she had the house to herself and could sit around, watching Faith doing her strange sideways crawl around the playpen, nursing her occasionally and doing nothing until the next feed. She wondered whether this summer cold or whatever it was would turn out to be a blessing in disguise. It was certainly breaking the pattern the Petersens had set up.

Her mother drove over from Horsley and saw immediately that something was really wrong.

'Come home with me, darling. Please. I can get Dr Booth in to look at you and I can nurse you and Daddy can take Faith for walks around the village – it will be a little holiday for you.'

It sounded like heaven. 'Let me sweat it out, whatever it is.' Hope sat in a hard chair hunched over the table, frightened to lean back more comfortably in case the room began to move. 'Besides, I couldn't go to Doc Booth – it would be unethical. Dr O'Brien would be cut to the quick. He saw me through that awful labour . . . oh Mummy, you don't suppose I'm pregnant again, do you?'

Milly said delicately, 'Well, you should know, darling.'

Hope threw delicacy to the winds. 'I use my cap always! I couldn't bear to go through that again!'

'Well then . . .'

'They say there's no such thing as complete birth control!'

Milly tried to be sensible. 'Listen, Hope dear. Did you have this dizziness when you were expecting Faith?' She answered herself. 'No. It's a most unlikely pregnancy symptom, in fact I've

84

never heard of it before. Much more likely to be a virus, aggravated by being on your own here. Please come home with me.'

Hope was sorely tempted but felt she must do something to prove herself.

'Let me stick it out a bit longer, Mummy. I'm so . . . reliant . . . on people. I'd like to feel I can cope on my own. I'll ring you. Promise.'

But after her mother had driven into the kind of sunset that provoked Hope to tears, she had the worst night of all. She promised herself that she would phone Horsley at nine o'clock and beg her father to come and fetch her. But by the time she had heated Faith's bathwater and made her some of the porridge stuff she had for breakfast, she felt slightly better. She put Faith into the bath and managed a watery smile as the little girl thumped the water with her fist. Then nearly jumped out of her skin as Henrik's face appeared at the kitchen window.

She opened the back door.

'I'm all *right*, Henrik! If Mandy has asked you to check up on me, just tell her, I'm all right. Really.' She stood in the doorway and he looked past her at Faith in her bath. The child crowed her delight.

'I'm missing Faith.'

He sounded bereft. She sighed and stood back.

'Come and say hello. Sorry. It's just that when I feel rotten I'm so much better on my own.'

'You won't let Mandy mind Faith? She would love it, you know.'

'There's no need.' But he stood there so helplessly, looking down at the bath on its little stand. 'Sit down, Henrik. I'll dry Faith then I'll make coffee. Can you spare the time?'

'Of course.' He sat down with alacrity and leaned over Faith, making little waves over her stomach. 'Try hitting with open hand. Like so.' He slapped the water gently and she shouted with pleasure and scissored her legs. 'Careful! You will have a flood!' He looked up. 'Hope, may I dry her?' She began to shake her head and stopped abruptly as his face blurred into the cooker. He said sadly, 'How have we offended you, child? Don't deny it. Somehow we have hurt you – we both know it – we don't know how.'

Hope held the edge of the shallow stone sink until things steadied, and then, because she could no longer prevaricate tactfully, she blurted, 'Mandy didn't sell those smocks. I went into the shop and they told me. She's still got them at home, hasn't she?'

He stared at her. Faith slapped the water with her open hand and sprayed his smart summer suit with droplets.

He said, 'Yes. But not for long. You don't understand, Hope.'

Hope said wearily, 'She told me that both of you needed friendship. Don't you realize that when you try to buy it, you kill it off? Completely?'

'Is that how you see us? Wanting to buy you? Because of the smocks?'

'You gave Jack a watch and then told him to sell it.'

'Of course! I wanted him to know it was his to do with as he wished.'

'Me too? You bought me earrings when you knew my ears weren't pierced—'

'I hoped that one day . . . listen, Hope. Listen. Please. Mandy did not tell you at Christmas because she was still negotiating. But she is buying that little shop. She wants to turn it into a boutique. In another few weeks you will be able to go again into the city and see your smocks in that shop window. She did not see why you had to wait for your money. Was that wrong of her? Was it wrong of me to buy you something I hoped one day you would wear? Diamonds are my favourite stones. Mandy does not like them, she says with her fair skin she needs rubies or emeralds. And you are dark.'

There was a long pause. Faith continued to slap her bathwater on to the floor. Hope stared into the sink and thought about Henrik and Mandy and their predilection for generosity. At last she reached for the towel and passed it across the bath.

'Just wrap her up and take her into the front room. It's sunnier in there. I'll bring in the coffee.'

She lit the gas and spooned coffee into a jug. Henrik wisely said no more to her; his conversation was entirely with Faith. Hope loaded the tea trolley which the girls at the commercial college had given her and clung to it as she followed him into the old-fashioned parlour. He looked ridiculous sitting in her low nursing armchair next to the baby basket, his jacket front powdered with talcum, two nappy pins in his mouth. She made no comment and did not interfere. Somehow she felt it was the least she could do.

At last he struggled up, put Faith into her playpen and picked up the coffee which Hope had poured for him.

He said, 'Aren't you having one?'

'No, thanks. And congratulations. You managed that nappy better than Jack could.'

'Nephews. Nieces.' He sipped. 'Hope, does Jack feel the same way as you do?'

'Not really. He is so excited at what you have offered him.'

'I have offered so little, my dear. Already he has done work for me. I have not paid him for that work. In the future I shall feel bound to do so. Will it drive him away too?'

'Of course not. He will be selling something.'

'As you did to Mandy.'

'Please, Henrik. If Mandy had explained . . .'

'I told her to be frank and open about it. But already she felt you . . . withdrawing.' He leaned forward. 'She has not had enough to do, Hope. That has been her trouble. But now . . . she is very enthusiastic about this shop. She would like you to go into it with her, but obviously you would not want that. However, it would seem you have a natural aptitude for design. I think – if you look at it as Jack is looking at his computer course – you could contribute a great deal.'

She shook her head. 'I can't think about it now, Henrik.'

'If you can imagine us as belonging to Jack's side – grandparents perhaps, or godparents – it might not be so difficult.'

Perhaps it was Henrik's subtle foreignness that made the idea almost acceptable. And if that was how he saw himself . . . she stared down at Faith who was pulling herself upright on the bars of the playpen. She made a mental note to tell Jack about it when she went to the phone box that evening. And then she blurted, 'I think I'm pregnant again. And I'm scared stiff.'

She heard Henrik's indrawn breath, saw from the corner of her eye that he put down his coffee cup and jack-knifed himself upright. She glanced at his face and before the room turned over, she saw the blaze of sheer joy on it. She closed her eyes and waited for everything to settle down.

Henrik said, 'Hope, this is wonderful! I thought you and Jack would not have more family. I am so happy for you!'

She waited, clutching the edge of her chair in case she fell off it. Then she said, 'You didn't hear me. I am scared stiff.'

'My dear child.' He folded his skinny height into a kneeling position before her. His long arms encircled the chair, holding her in her place. 'Listen. My brothers and sisters. They all have children. No one baby is like another – who would expect such a thing? Therefore, it is not logical to deduce that no two pregnancies are alike? Also no two birthings!'

She kept her eyes closed but she felt better. Henrik's off-beat phrasing made this conversation possible; even easy. His thin, linen-clad arms were not touching her but they were a framework around the chair. She was safe. She made a sound in her throat.

He went on, 'When I found you last summer, collapsed in the garden, I knew it would be bad.

This time, I know it will be good. The discomfort is now. After this it will be easy. You will have a little holiday and when you come back you will be well and you will stay well.'

The sunlight made patterns behind her closed lids. 'Don't be silly, Henrik. We can't afford a holiday. And no, you can't treat us. And I am not going to sell my earrings!' She felt her mouth curve into a smile and was conscious that he sat back on his heels.

He said, his voice lighter, 'All right, all right. I am glad. But sorry too. What about going to your parents' house?'

'Can't do that either.' She opened her eyes and looked straight into his. 'I'm not sure. You realize that? I've said nothing to Jack. You won't . . . ?'

'Of course not. He asked me to telephone if anything was wrong.' He held her gaze. 'It's not, is it?'

'No.' She felt an enormous sense of relief. 'No, it's not. Thank you, Henrik.'

'For talking to you like a Norwegian uncle?'

'Yes.' She took a breath. 'I'm all right now. You can stand up.'

He did so. She put up her hands for him to draw her up as well and as she stood facing him, looking at the granules of talc clinging to his shirt front, she really did feel all right. She experimented, turning her head to the right to look down at Faith in her playpen, then up into Henrik's face.

'I might go for a walk. Could you put Faith in the pushchair, Henrik? I'll go and see Mandy. Will that be all right with her?'

'Naturally. I will walk with you.'

'No. I'd prefer to go by myself. I want to apologize.'

He hesitated, then nodded and went into the hall to get the pushchair. She waved him good-bye and set off along the towpath. It took her no longer than five minutes. If she hadn't been frightened of the dizziness returning she could have run. She had missed Mandy more than she realized.

Mandy saw her coming, opened the kitchen door and came to the gate.

'I didn't see any smoke! Are you all right? My God, you look awful!'

Hope started to laugh. 'Do I? I don't think I've done my hair – oh Mandy, I'm so sorry. Not for looking a wreck – for misunderstanding. Henrik's told me that you're buying the shop! I thought you were just giving me a handout! When we went to the sales . . . you remember? I went into the maternity shop and the woman didn't know anything about any smocks! So I thought . . .'

'Darling!' Mandy put her arms around Hope's shoulders. 'Oh, I'm so pleased to see you! I don't know what you're blabbering on about, but come inside – it's too hot – Faith, my dearest baby lovely girl! Look at your curls! How come you're blond when Mummy is so dark?'

Hope was laughing inordinately, mainly because it was wonderful that she felt well again. She went into Mandy's modern stainless-steel kitchen and let Mandy tug the pushchair over the step.

The telephone rang and nearly startled her into another attack of vertigo.

Mandy grabbed the receiver and stroked Faith's head at the same time. 'Silly phone . . . oh it's you, Henrik! No, I was talking to Faith. Hope has just arrived with her . . . yes. Yes. Oh. Of course, yes, I understand. She was saying something about it when she arrived but I was so pleased to see her I didn't take it in. Obviously, sweetheart. Don't worry.' She moved away from the pushchair and into the hall as far as the cable would let her. Hope sat at the kitchen table and took Faith on to her lap and bounced her gently. It was still all right. There was a curious sensation of fuzziness behind her eyes, but everything in the kitchen stayed where it was. She hugged Faith's curly head beneath her chin and looked around her. A washing machine hummed in the corner, the electric kettle and toaster were shades of duck-egg blue to match the cushions on the kitchen chairs and the curtains at the two windows.

Behind her, Mandy said quietly, 'Henrik says you might be pregnant again.'

'I'm not sure.' She turned to look behind her and the cushions and curtains merged into one. She blinked hard. 'The symptoms aren't right. I was just so scared . . . you know.'

'You both said no more children.'

Hope felt her brows lift in surprise. 'Well, yes. We can't afford another baby. And . . . it was so awful, Mandy.'

'But you must have known what you were doing – the risk you were taking.'

Hope moved her chair around with some difficulty. 'You're worried!' she said. 'You're just as worried as I am.' Somehow that was even more reassuring than Henrik's positive reaction. 'Mandy, it's all right. Really. If that's what it is, then – so be it. Better than something awful inside my head!'

There was a pause; Mandy seemed to be reassembling her feelings in some way. She suddenly emitted an enormous sigh and collapsed with it on to her knees, just as Henrik had done.

'Darling Hope. I'm so sorry. Oh God, what a mess. Henrik's just told me properly about you going into Mrs Dreadful's about the smocks. Darling, I'm sorry about that too. You do see – surely – that I wanted to spring the shop on you like a bombshell?'

'I suppose so.' Hope smiled into the beautiful, carefully made-up face so close to her own. 'And I don't know what difference it makes really – but it does. So long as they sell! If they hang about for ages—'

'They'll go like hot cakes. Plus anything else you can think of. I want you to come in with me and help me run it—'

'No. Definitely not, Mandy. I couldn't give you enough time and anyway . . . no.' She was glad Mandy did not press any further. It was only when they were drinking coffee that she asked about Henrik's phone call. 'He could only have got as far as the post office!'

'Yes, he called from there. He'd left some plans on the studio table and he didn't want Mrs Malkin to dust them away.'

'I thought Mrs Malkin wasn't allowed in the studio?'

'Well, sometimes.' Mandy was joggling Faith expertly. 'Also, Henrik had another of his bright

93

ideas. He suggested that you and I take a holiday while Jack is doing this course. Just a few days.'

'I told Henrik already—'

'Not expensive. In fact Henrik was wondering whether we could take your honeymoon cottage. That was going for a song, wasn't it?'

Hope thought again of Widdershins and her heart swelled slightly but definitely.

She said, 'I couldn't do that to Jack.'

Mandy said quickly, 'Of course not. Silly of me. Forget it.'

'And there isn't really time. He'll be home in ten days.'

'Yes. Quite.' She kissed Faith and held her aloft. 'Oh she's beautiful, Hope. Stay and have some lunch and she can nap in the garden while we sunbathe.'

Hope looked at the two of them, Faith already half asleep, her blond curls mingling with Mandy's. She must keep thinking of the Petersens as belonging to Jack. In-laws. Wonderful in-laws. Because then they had a right to be generous. There was no question of them wanting anything in return.

'That would be lovely,' she said.

Four

The dizziness came and went but it was no longer the nightmarish experience it had been during the first two weeks of Jack's course. She was able to call him from the Petersens' telephone too, which obviously delighted him. She had not realized how worried he had been by what they all now called 'the rift'.

'Darling Ho. I'm so glad you've healed that rift. It was so stupid after all. They're just so generous.'

She could have reminded him that it was her parents' generosity that made him so touchy, but of course she did not.

'Only another three days, Jack. Has it been worth it?'

'Well, I don't know yet, do I? But my God, it's interesting, Ho. I reckon in a few years' time the world will be run by these things.'

'Computers? You sound like a science fiction film.'

'Leave out the fiction. If we can think of the right way to put questions, they can answer anything.'

She smiled into the receiver. 'Darling, you've

forgotten how hopeless I am at maths. When you were talking about a binary base, I gave up then and there!'

'OK, try this. D'you remember that peculiar plant we came across? Just outside Widdershins?'

Again that slight swelling of her heart. 'Yes,' she replied, prepared to melt.

'Do you also remember how we looked it up? In the *British Flora*, in Penzance Public Library?'

'Yes.' She frowned, knowing the melting moment was not appropriate. 'It was a case of either yes or no. And if it was yes turn to page thingamijig. And if it was no, turn to page . . .'

'D'you see what I'm getting at? You had to keep asking questions. The book could either say yes or no. But when you got to the end of that, there was the answer . . . and that's how it is with computers!'

She smiled again, this time at his boyish enthusiasm and the fact that he wanted her to share it. 'You're wonderful, Jack,' she said.

He made a sound, half pleased, half frustrated. 'You can't fob me off with compliments. I want you to see – to understand – the enormous possibilities.'

'I do. I do.'

His voice softened to the consistency of porridge. 'I do too,' he said.

'Oh Jack.'

'There's a queue for the phone. Until to-morrow.'

Mandy, jiggling Faith within hearing distance, said, 'Didn't he want to hear his daughter? What did he say – not the last bit, I almost threw up at that!'

Hope grinned. 'He tried to explain about computers.'

'And you switched yours off.'

Hope laughed. Her mother had taken her to see Dr O'Brien that morning and he had confirmed that she was almost three months pregnant and the dizziness was anaemia which could be dealt with easily. She realized, in retrospect, that she had been terrified of a brain tumour; the normality of her symptoms was such a relief that she no longer feared the actual birth. Besides, as Henrik said, no two births were the same. It had been awful with Faith; this one would be easy – like her mother's in fact.

Milly had reassured her, 'I had you in about two hours, darling. And that's how it will be for you this time. I promise.'

Jack arrived home late on Friday night, still incredibly smart in his new suit, brimming with a new-found confidence. He talked almost non-stop until Faith woke at two o'clock in the morning and came into their bed. She was over-joyed to see him and wanted to play and he was too wound up to sleep so the two of them went downstairs and Hope fell asleep, exhausted.

The next morning she found him beside her, curled round like a cat, snoring slightly into his pillow. Faith was similarly sleeping in her cot. Hope let them both lie and laid breakfast in the tiny back garden. As the smell of toast wafted through the house, Jack woke up and stumbled downstairs. She let him come to while she bathed Faith and put her in her playpen. Then she told him about the baby. She was a little apprehensive; he had been as adamant as her

97

about not having any more children. But she knew before he said a word that he was pleased. He waited, tensely, trying to discover her real feelings and when she smiled tremulously, he swept her into his arms.

'Ho. Dear . . . dearest Ho. Are you sure? How are you? How long have you known? Why didn't you say something before . . . ?'

Between them, they arrived at the present. He was near tears. 'All this has happened and I wasn't here! If only you'd told me – your mother could have phoned – I would have come home.'

'Idiot! That was exactly what we did not want you to do! Be honest. You said you wouldn't have missed this month for *almost* anything – and if me being pregnant had been the *almost*, where would that leave us? You need that training more than ever now – oh Jack, four mouths to feed!'

'I can do it. I feel like a giant. I can do it!'

'Oh darling. I know. And you can see – everything is all right now. It was all in the mind. Henrik came round and explained about those wretched, *wretched* smocks, and I felt better immediately. And it was great when dear Dr O'Brien told me the news.' She paused. 'Are you sure you're pleased?'

'I am – I am!'

She had known. But it was sweet to hear him say so.

They settled down again. Milly and Edward came on Sundays as before and often in the middle of the week as well. Edward declared that computers could never take over from a good bank clerk but he was interested in spite of himself. When Faith had her first birthday party, he accompanied Henrik and Jack to Henrik's studio and spent the evening poring over Henrik's sketches and checking Jack's figures.

'What will happen to the sand?' he asked, frowning at one point.

'How do you mean? You refer to the sea bed?' Henrik leaned over the plan. 'The flow of water will be intense, naturally. That is what we require. The tides here are the highest in the country and by restricting them judiciously . . .'

Edward's frown deepened. 'Eventually that artificial bore will make a deeper channel. The sides will silt up. What about the sand? The beaches at Burnham and Weston? Will they be scoured away or made into enormous dunes? And how will that affect the buildings on either bank?'

Jack nodded. 'I thought of that. It is very difficult to project. But . . . it is possible that if it were fed the correct information, a computer could do just that. The only other alternative is to make some kind of model and wait for . . . twenty years?'

'Not viable,' Henrik said.

Edward had a sense of déjà vu. Hopeful loan applicants had approached him in the past with similar limitations. Henrik Petersen needed time and time often had to be bought and paid for. 'A test situation could be created for the duration of, say, one year and then projections made from the results.'

Henrik glanced at him. 'I need to know soon.

I am hoping that Jack will be able to help me. If there is no immediate risk of over-silting, I think I can persuade Somerset that this is their chance to be in the forefront of technology. And then I can go all out to sell the whole package to the electricity board.'

Jack glanced at his father-in-law. 'I can work in the evenings, Dad. Compile a program – that's a kind of dossier which you feed into the computer to get out what you need. Then there's a place in Bristol where I can buy some time on their computer to feed in my programs. Henrik will pay for that and take me down.'

Edward nodded. 'What if the answer comes up the wrong way?'

Henrik grinned. 'Then I must use more persuasive means. I think Mandy will help me there!'

He turned and started back downstairs. Jack did not meet Edward's eyes.

Edward cleared his throat. 'How soon do you need your information?'

'Soon. The wolf is at the door. Before Christmas.'

'I see.'

Edward wondered how dependent Jack was on this foreign engineer. Perhaps it would be as well if the project was turned down by Christmas. Before Jack actually gave up his job at the docks.

They walked back to the others and then, as the tide was out, they carried Faith down the bank to the river's edge to launch the flotilla of boats they had bought for her. Edward sat on his shooting stick and watched them. Hope showed no sign of her new pregnancy. She wore a tight-bodiced dress of blue-flowered cotton which belled into an enormous skirt; her hair was glossy and sprang from her head in a riot of curls and her dark blue eyes were intent on Faith, who was staggering about on the pebbles clutching Jack's hand. Mandy stood close to her, also watching. Henrik took Faith's other hand and the two men swung her over the water so that she screamed with delight. Hope laughed. Mandy did not; Edward had the feeling she was near to tears and felt a pang of sympathy for her.

He said, 'For goodness' sake, you two! You'll dislocate the child's arms!'

Quite suddenly he knew he would have to help: he recognized an ambition in Jack which he had not seen before. And this was Jack's chance. And Hope's happiness depended on Jack. He began to plan a way of financing the Petersens' project with very definite provisions to include his son-in-law.

That autumn, Mandy opened her shop in Gloucester with a cheese and wine evening. Hope modelled her own smocks and managed to find the time to make six ponchos and a dozen calico cushions. If it hadn't been for this second pregnancy, she knew she could have taken a much bigger part. As it was, Mandy went brazenly into a furnishing shop in Eastgate Street, asked who did their curtains and loose covers and discovered Mrs Martin who lived in a tiny terraced house in Tredworth. Hope visited her and showed her some of her designs. Mrs

Martin was quite used to taking measurements and making patterns for covers and curtains but she had never gone in for dressmaking. She had a way of sucking in her lips until they disappeared, and when she shook her head as well Hope gave up on her. Mandy did not. She made her an offer she could not refuse. She never told Hope what it was but Mrs Martin moved into the flat over the shop the following week. She was shop assistant by day and seamstress by night.

Mandy took on the role of buyer and would have taken Hope with her to look at new lines except that Hope suddenly and inexplicably lost interest. Mandy was certain that things would change once the new baby was 'up and running', as she put it. She called her shop, Expectancies and juggled her new life with apparent ease. The only difference was that she had very little time to spend with Hope. But Henrik continued to drop in to play with Faith and to tell Hope how excellent was Jack's work for the 'project'. He could not come up with the necessary information before Christmas after all, but the chairman of the planning committee had agreed to give them more time. If only Jack would give up that ridiculous job at the canal . . . 'We have to live on his money, Henrik!' Hope said with a sharpness that might have been excessive. Certainly Henrik did not broach the subject again.

Chatty was born the week before Christmas. Just as her mother had said, Hope had no problems at all. Dr O'Brien, making a routine call, found her clutching the edge of the playpen, unable to pick Faith up. He lit the fire in the parlour and within three minutes Mandy was at the back door. It was unusual for her to be at home during the day and Hope had expected Henrik to pick up the smoke signal; she was thankful it was Mandy though she did not know why.

'She's in bed,' the doctor explained brusquely. 'No time for hospital. Can you telephone this number, then get back here to help until Mrs Green arrives.' Mrs Green was the midwife. Mandy turned and ran back down the towpath. By the time she had also telephoned Jack and Henrik, Mrs Green's Morris Minor was outside the cottage. Mandy whipped in through the back door and scooped up Faith who was crying lustily for her mother. With the child on her hip she managed to find a biscuit for her. As one cry died, so another started. She looked at Faith.

'Well . . . another member of the family. At least Henrik can't pretend this one belongs to him. This one's mine! And by golly, I've earned it!' She laughed and Faith laughed with her.

Jack would have liked a boy and Hope felt a sense of guilt as he arrived at the bedroom door. He made a wry face at her.

'Trouble is,' he said, 'poor little devil has to be called Charity. What a name to carry throughout her life!'

Hope laughed. 'We can shorten it to Carrie,' she said, looking down at the shaggy dark hair. 'Or choose a second name and use that.'

'We'll see.' He came to her. 'You were too quick for me this time, Ho. Sorry I wasn't around.' He too stared at the new baby. Not even her proud parents could describe her as beautiful.

Hope said, 'She was a bit too quick for herself, I think. Dr O'Brien says her head will be a better shape in a few days. She won't look so . . . scrunched up.'

Charity might not be a pretty baby but she was very vocal; it seemed apt to shorten her name to Chatty. Faith had already christened herself Fay and could just about manage a version of Chatty. So Fay and Chatty the girls became. Meanwhile, Jack called the new baby Screamer and Henrik insisted on Number Two, not realizing the English connotations.

In February Jack left the Inland Waterways and went to work all day – and half the night – in Henrik's studio. It was a huge step to take; Hope was terrified but could say nothing in the face of his ebullience. She saw less of him than ever and the responsibility of two babies exhausted her. By Easter, when they were going to have a double christening, she wondered how much longer she could go on. And then something unexpected and quite marvellous happened. Edward and Milly brought the news that their small parish was to be united with two other local villages to become a large benefice. This meant that the vicarage at Horsley would not be required and it was expected that the church would sell it. However, the local Parish Church Council had put forward a suggestion that it could be let to the churchwarden. As Edward was the churchwarden, he and Milly planned to move in quite quickly and suggested that Hope and Jack might like to rent Horsley House.

Milly drove herself over a few days before the christening: she was bubbling with the news.

'Darling, I know dear Jack will go all proud and pretty about this, but can't you talk him round? Just think – you'd be fifteen minutes' walk away! And I'd just love to think of Fay and Chatty growing up where you did – the swing is still on the apple tree, as you know. And with four bedrooms Jack could have an office at home and you could join the Women's Institute . . . oh Hope, it would be lovely!'

But Hope was appalled. 'You're doing this – moving into that barn of a place – just for Jack and me! Aren't you? Mummy, Daddy is seventy-nine! Nearly eighty! He shouldn't be having to move house at his age.' She wanted to add that Milly herself was sixty-eight but her mother was reticent about her age.

'Darling girl, it's not that much of a barn. The basement is the Sunday school and youth club. The upstairs flat is entirely self-contained and the two floors we shall occupy have been refurbished recently. Just think of it – no more responsibility for repairs and maintenance! Someone on the premises if anything goes wrong. Daddy can't wait to move in.' She saw doubt still on her daughter's face and said seriously, 'Hope, we shall move whether you take Horsley House or not. But as the house will be yours one day, it seems only sensible for you to live in it now while we can enjoy your company.'

Hope was icing a batch of cakes. She frowned

over the wire tray. The prospect, which had sounded completely cock-eyed at first, was becoming solid and real. She thought of living in her old home, away from the damp river which could well be the reason that Chatty woke night after night with a blocked nose. She thought of Fay playing in the orchard. She thought of her mother's little sewing room where she might be able to start working again.

By the time Milly left, she wanted to live in Horsley House very badly indeed. And she was certain Jack would turn it down.

She thought about it for the rest of the day and half that night. When Jack crept into bed at midnight she rolled into his arms and kissed him. He was surprised.

'I thought you'd be fast asleep as usual,' he whispered, propping himself on an elbow and looking down at her in the darkness. 'Aren't you tired?'

She shook her head, kissing him again. After a while they made love very quietly because of Chatty but she woke anyway and Hope sat up in bed, feeding her and thinking of all those bedrooms in Horsley House. She looked down at Jack who was already curling himself up as he always did.

'I wanted to ask you something,' she murmured because Fay's room was only a partition away.

Jack snorted a little laugh. 'You sound like Mandy,' he said.

'What on earth d'you mean?' She was startled.

He smiled sleepily. 'Well . . . you know.'

'I don't. Has Mandy been asking you something? About the shop?'

'Idiot. How do you think Henrik got extra time for my research? Don't you remember he needed results by Christmas? It's Easter now.'

'I haven't had time to think of anything since Chatty was born!' She was inexplicably annoyed. 'And I still don't get it. What's Mandy got to do with Henrik's reprieve?' Jack continued to smile a cat-like smile, eyes closed. 'You don't mean . . . she – she's been – making up to the planning people?'

He laughed again. 'I like that. Making up. Surely she's told you – she's so horribly frank most of the time! She's been more than making up!'

She continued to stare at his face. 'You don't mean . . . She hasn't actually . . . ?'

'Oh Ho. Use your loaf.'

She sat there, thinking, feeling utterly naive. 'I don't believe it!' she said at last. 'Henrik would guess. He would *know*!'

'He knows. Obviously.' Jack rolled over. 'Do shut up, darling. You can ask me whatever it is in the morning.'

But she knew she would not, not now. After all, if she made love to Jack and then asked him if he would be willing to move house, it might occur to him that she was following in Mandy's footsteps. She continued to think about Mandy while she finished feeding Chatty. She did not know whether to feel sorry for her. Or for Henrik. She did not feel sorry for Jack, however. He thought it was funny. He probably admired Mandy. She laid Chatty in her cot and stroked the rough black hair until the child snuffled herself to sleep. No, she would not ask Jack for any favours. But, oddly, she wanted to live in Horsley House more than ever.

As if he could read her mind, Henrik arrived in the middle of the morning with an enormous bunch of freesias.

'They will last until Sunday. For the christening,' he said, standing them in a bucket of water beneath the sink. Hope had just finished the washing and eyed his appropriation of the nappy bucket with scarcely veiled annoyance. 'Ah. Number two daughter is ready. And Fay?'

'She is resting.'

'I have come to take you to town. Do you not remember? Mandy and Mrs Martin are planning the Easter parade.'

She had forgotten. Mandy had been full of it: Easter bonnets for babies. A milliner's in Somerset had closed down and Mandy had bought the stock.

'I know, I know,' she had said in response to Hope's amazement. 'Hats are out. Even for funerals. In 1970 we go bare-headed. Finito.' She grinned. 'But bonnets . . . for Easter . . . that's something else.'

Hope sighed and looked at Henrik. 'I can't, Henrik. Sorry.'

'But the children, they will love it. I will look after Fay and you can cope with Number Two. Mandy will be devastated.' He looked at her; she was conscious that her face was very hot. He said slowly, 'Mandy is doing this for you, Hope. Just as she is always doing things for me. She cannot help herself.' He lifted his shoulders slightly. 'We have to learn to . . . accept.'

She tried to meet his dark eyes. 'Accept? How much? Everything? Anything?'

He was silent for a moment then said, 'Jack has told you things. How Mandy persuaded Mr Charles Clements to give us extra time? Once again, you are . . . alienated from us.'

'No, I don't think so. You are both so different from us.' She shrugged. 'What you do is . . . your business.' She willed herself to be unembarrassed. 'It's just that I am so busy. The christening on Sunday . . . and I don't get much sleep.'

He nodded. 'I wish we could help. Jack is working so hard. I feel guilty, Hope, but it is his chance to get established. You do understand?'

'Of course. Of course I do.' She swept her hand around the tiny rooms. 'We're so cramped here. If Chatty could have her own room she would settle into a night-time routine, I'm sure of it.'

He was so damned astute. He said, 'You have heard of somewhere else?'

She found herself telling him about Horsley House: the sewing room, the four bedrooms which would mean Jack could have an office. She did not need to tell him about Jack's stubborn independence.

He said slowly, 'It sounds ideal for you. Mandy will miss you terribly. As I will also. But . . . it sounds ideal.'

She said flatly, 'It won't happen. I will tell him of course. But . . . it won't happen.'

'I think it will, Hope. I think it will. If you like – if you do not think it is interfering – I will talk to Jack.'

She was tidying toys into a cardboard box. She paused and looked up at him. If it had been anything else, anything else at all, she would have turned him down out of hand. Because it *was* interference. But this was different.

She said, 'Do you think he will listen to you?'

Henrik said without hesitation, 'Oh yes. It is, after all, good business.'

She drew a deep breath. 'Even if he accepts the . . . first proposition – the actual move . . . he will know that we cannot live there without being . . . what do they call it? Subsidized?'

'No. It is not a subsidy, dear Hope. It is an investment.' He sat on her low nursing chair which brought their faces close. 'I believe in Jack. I will invest in him. That is not a subsidy. Do you understand?'

She wanted to believe him, that was the trouble. Jack had wanted to believe him for some time now: Jack had actually sniggered at the thought of Mandy 'persuading' the necessary councillors to give Henrik more time. And now she wanted to believe Henrik.

She said slowly, 'I do understand. He will listen to you, Henrik. So . . . thank you.'

He shrugged and said nothing for the space of several seconds. She moved back from him and shoved the cardboard box into a corner. Then he stood up briskly.

'Right. Now go and get ready, wake up Fay and I will load the pushchair into the car.'

He went into the hall and she could hear him talking to Chatty. She straightened her aching back; she did not want to go into Gloucester and smile at prospective customers and allow Mandy to put bonnets on Fay. But she knew this was her side of the bargain.

In the event it was not at all bad. The shop, swathed with Mrs Martin's drapes, had a new opulence; the renovated pre-war bonnets were so pretty they sold out before midday. Mrs Martin, flushed with success, took over while the others went over the road to the tearooms for sandwiches. Henrik nursed Fay and Hope gave Chatty her bottle and smiled as Mandy outlined plans for the future.

'As soon as you're into a proper routine again, Hope darling, we'll really go to town! I want to get another shop in Cheltenham or Tewkesbury and do evening wear.'

'In a maternity shop?' Hope queried.

'Absolutely. Maternity evening wear. Lots of floating voile. Terribly décolleté. I've noticed how gorgeous your breasts are since the children. Why not show them off?'

Hope coloured but also laughed, and Chatty tried to do likewise and dribbled milk all over the place. 'Damn, I shall smell all sour again!' But Hope suddenly did not mind. It was so good to be with frank and outrageous Mandy again. And if they moved house then they wouldn't be on each other's doorsteps. And meanwhile she was going to go into business . . . Life was full of possibilities. She wanted to match her friends' generosity with some of her own. She looked at Henrik and said, 'What are you doing this afternoon?'

He made a face. 'Back to the drawing board, I guess. Literally.'

'Can you spare me another . . . I don't know
. . . half an hour?'

'Naturally. You need shopping?'

'No.' She smiled at them both. She thought
how lucky she was to have friends like Mandy
and Henrik. 'I want to get my ears pierced!'

They both clapped their hands; it was as if
she had given them a gift. And it proved so easy
and completely painless. When they reached
home again and Henrik unloaded the pram and
carried Fay back to her playpen, Hope felt as if
they had all been to a party. The girls were
exhausted but content and she felt quite different. No longer tired and dreary. Full of . . . yes,
hope!

She smiled at Henrik. 'I would go and put in
my diamond earrings except that they said I had
to keep these gold rings in for a bit. But thank
you, Henrik. I'm so glad you called for me . . .
it's been a marvellous day.'

'Thank you, my dear Hope. It has indeed
been a very excellent day.'

She laughed again at his un-Englishness and
then leaned up and pecked his cheek. 'I am
lucky to have in-laws like you!' she said teasingly.
'Don't go back to Norway just yet, will you?'

'Don't worry.' He put a hand to his cheek
momentarily. 'We will not go until the investment is secure.'

Her laugh became uncertain; sometimes his
foreignness sounded distinctly odd.

He kissed Fay and Chatty and went down the
garden to the road. She stood at the door,
waving with one hand and with the other
moving one of her earrings around in her ear as

they had told her to do. She had no idea why her elation was such a personal thing: after all, the investment, as Henrik so diplomatically put it, was in Jack, not her. And yet . . . and yet . . . she knew that she and Fay and Chatty were also part of the investment even if she did not know how or why.

After Jack had come home and eaten a scratch meal and gone straight back to Henrik's studio, she put the children to bed, pulled the bedspread from the double bed and took it downstairs. She ignored the dishes and the muddles and flung the bedspread over the table. It was a wedding present: leaf green satin embroidered with a writhing Chinese dragon. She picked it up by two corners and held it around her; then fastened it with a clothes peg on one shoulder and adjusted the fullness so that it fell in folds over her abdomen.

She heard Mandy coming down the garden path and flung open the back door.

'What d'you think?'

Mandy was ecstatic. 'Darling! It's wonderful! You look like the sexiest member of the Roman Senate! Sweetheart, how many can you make in – say – three months?'

Hope was breathless. 'I don't know. Too many other things really.'

'I know, I know.' Mandy looked at the sink of crockery and made a face. 'Henrik has told me of the plans to move. I hated the whole idea at first, but it could be the answer, couldn't it? Your mother can have the children and you can work.'

Hope made a face too. 'I'm not sure about

that. Daddy might well object. And anyway, Jack
. . . he might object too.'

'You leave Jack to Henrik! I used to think the
best carrot to dangle in front of donkeys . . .
sorry, men! . . . was sex. But after flirting
with every man-jack on that bloody committee, I
know it is money!'

Hope swallowed. She did not like the impli-
cation that Jack could be bought. But Mandy's
words also made her exploits almost innocent.

'Is that what you've been up to?' she said.

'You must have guessed! I'm quite good
at it although I shouldn't say so.' She made a
ridiculous moue and they both laughed. 'Oh
Hope! I don't see enough of you these days and
I shall see less when you move. We must have an
arrangement – weekly lunches or something.
After all, the men have business lunches, why
shouldn't we? And you'll have to bring some
drawings for Mrs Martin. She's worth her weight
in gold. Doesn't have ideas like you but she
knows how to copy.'

Somehow it all sounded settled. The move,
the designing and the sewing. The weekly
lunches. It was, as Henrik would say, absolutely
excellent.

Five

Four years seemed to disappear without trace. They moved to Horsley House and Hope joined the Women's Institute but rarely went to meetings because of the children. The same thing happened with her sewing and designing plans. She would run up the occasional smock, or design maternity pants with flares and embroidered turn-ups, but her heart wasn't in it. There were two miscarriages which drained her and she found it difficult enough to keep the rambling old house going and cook meals.

Jack took over the biggest bedroom as an office and seemed to be doing well although he rarely discussed his work with Hope any more. The days of playing at house were over.

It was Chatty's first day at school. Jack, who had promised to be there, had left early to accompany Henrik to another interminable meeting. She had not reproached him but he had glanced at her face and said tightly, 'I've told you before, Ho. This is real life. OK?'

Mandy had also promised to be at the gate and was conspicuous by her absence. But after all it was a ten-mile drive from Sandhurst to

Horsley and Mandy had her hands full with her two maternity shops. So Fay, whose sunny nature had won her friends without effort, took her little sister by the hand and led her away from the gate and across the playground. 'You're going to be very happy,' she said firmly, noticing with dismay that Chatty's bottom lip already protruded on a level with her pointed chin. 'You're not going to cry and you're not going to chatter. You're going to listen!'

Chatty looked over her shoulder. Her mother was still at the gate wearing an encouraging smile and Chatty knew that parents were not allowed in the playground. She also knew that her aunt Mandy was a law unto herself.

'Where's Andy?' she asked loudly. 'She's supposed to *be* here!'

Chatty had always telescoped 'Aunty Mandy' into 'Andy'.

Hope's smile shrank somewhat. Chatty and Mandy had a special bond. Just as Fay and Henrik had.

'I expect she's busy at the shop. Shall I telephone and ask her to come to tea?'

Chatty's small, gloomy face lightened. 'Yes. She'll bring chocolate biscuits.'

'I expect so,' Hope said. 'Now off you go with Fay.'

The two girls got as far as the door of the cloakroom and then Chatty jerked backwards, bringing both of them to the ground. She started to scream. As usual where Chatty was concerned, bedlam broke out. Mrs Mayhew, the reception teacher, emerged from the cloakroom and picked the children up, only to receive a

116

sharp kick from Chatty. Fay began to cry quietly, not because she was hurt but because she was so ashamed. Hope started across the asphalt and was waved away by Mrs Mayhew even as she rubbed at the sore place on her shin.

And then there was a second commotion, at the gate this time, and the knot of mothers parted like the Red Sea to make way for Mandy who tore across the playground and swept Chatty into her arms.

'Darling girl! I'm so sorry! Wretched traffic hold-up! Some awful man wouldn't let me get across the road. Shall we go in?' She smiled widely at Mrs Mayhew and made for the cloak-room doors.

Hope heard Chatty asking with enormous interest, 'What did you say to the awful man, Andy?'

'I told him to retake the course at the charm school, darling.'

Mrs Mayhew looked across at Hope and grinned reassuringly. She had been to tea several times at Horsley House and had met Mandy before. Hope sighed and settled against the gatepost to wait for Mandy. It would be fun to hear the latest about the shops and Mrs Martin and the old neighbours at Sandhurst. Oddly enough Hope was lonely at times. She saw her parents almost every day, but other people respected the fact that Jack worked from home and the two children were always there. She missed her life at Sandhurst more than she had dreamed possible. The cottage might have been inconvenient and much too small but it had always seemed full of people. However, as Jack had pointed out only that morning, she was the one who had been so keen to move.

'Come on, Ho. You have a marvellous time here. Coffee with your mother every morning. Christmas fairs, summer fêtes. No more scrapping around with Mandy making ghastly smocks!'

'I didn't mind . . . and anyway it was Chatty who stopped that, not the move.'

'Good for Chatty,' Jack had come back. 'Cheer up, old girl. Don't let Henrik see you with a long face. I never told you, but it was Henrik who talked me into coming here.'

Hope could have wept. She watched the two men drive away and wondered what on earth was the matter with her these days.

Back at Horsley House, Mandy was her usual ebullient self. She stacked the breakfast things from the kitchen table and fetched clean mugs while Hope made the coffee.

'I feel it's midday instead of nine o'clock,' she complained. 'How on earth d'you get cracking so early every morning?'

'Chatty sees to us getting cracking at all sorts of times.' Sometimes Hope wished Chatty was not always quite so happy in Mandy's presence; it gave an entirely false impression. 'Thanks for salvaging everything this morning. Poor Fay. She wanted to drop through the ground.'

'Poor Fay indeed. It was poor Chatty. Everything strange – why on earth didn't you go with her into the cloakroom?'

'You know very well it's a rule that parents stay by the gate. And Chatty knows that too – we take and fetch Fay every day after all.'

'Don't worry, she was as right as rain when I left her. So was everyone else. They all wanted to show me the pictures above their pegs . . . where they sat . . . told me their names . . .'

'My God, you must have been popular with Mrs Mayhew!' But Hope was laughing as she poured coffee. 'You haven't changed in all the years I've known you. Seven this November. Seven years. Can you believe it!'

'Actually it is hard to believe. Normally we would have moved on to the next job. This one is proving . . . well, impossible.'

Hope looked up sharply from her mug. 'What do you mean? Surely you're not giving up? Not now?'

'No. That's the trouble. We've invested so much time and effort, we can't afford to give up.' Mandy made a hideous face. 'Too many bosses, Ho. The local council, the environment people, the electricity board, the engineering firm who tendered for the job. I can't keep up with them all!' She laughed.

Hope did not return the laugh. For one thing she had never been sure how much Mandy was involved in what Jack called 'diplomatic persuasion'. And for another, if Henrik and Mandy left England now, Jack would be in a very difficult position. What with the three-day week and the miners' strike and poor Mr Heath having to call an election and Mr Wilson about to call another, everyone was in a difficult position.

Mandy glanced swiftly across the table and sobered, then said, 'If it weren't for my shops, we'd have had to cut our losses and go. And you were the one who got me started in the

119

rag trade, Ho. I'll never forget that.'

Hope shrugged. 'They've done well considering the recession.'

'People will keep having babies!' Mandy said and laughed again.

There was a little silence then Hope shrugged again. 'I'm not likely to forget that if it weren't for you, we wouldn't be living here—'

'That is surely down to your parents!' Mandy protested.

'You know what I mean.' Unconsciously, Hope touched her stud earrings as if reminding Mandy of Henrik's part in talking Jack into the move. 'And not only persuading Jack it was the right thing to do, but setting him up in the consultancy like you did. It gives him a feeling of independence, and that is so vital for Jack.'

'Yes.' Mandy looked past Hope at the sink full of washing up. 'Dear Jack.' She focused again and laughed. 'Dear all of you. The Lovely Langleys.' She lifted her coffee cup in a salute. Hope smiled but did not follow suit.

Mandy said quickly with her usual perception, 'What's wrong? You seem in a different world this morning.'

Hope shrugged once more. 'Probably missing Chatty. Which reminds me, can you come to tea? And bring some chocolate biscuits? She's relying on it.'

'Of course. Henrik will come too. He misses Fay terribly, you know. You realize that the girls are our children once removed, don't you?'

'I think I've picked up on that!' Hope tried hard for a laugh.

'And you don't mind?'

'How could I mind? Jack's got no one and I'm an only child – it's wonderful for them to have you two as honorary aunt and uncle.'

'Thank goodness!' Mandy puffed an exaggerated sigh of relief. 'I thought you might be getting all huffy in your old age. If you'd shrugged once more I might have had to hit you!'

Hope gave a genuine laugh and asked why.

'Because it's a physical display of that awful word.'

'Hopeless?'

'Don't say it!'

'All right then . . . what about . . . neededness? D'you know, Mandy, that's what's the matter with me today! I've lost my neededness! Fay and Chatty have both started independent lives, Jack is completely absorbed in this blessed programing business and though I adore living in the village alongside Mummy and Daddy, I'm not actually . . . needed!'

'Listen, idiot child. This is what we've been waiting for! You must now go back to the drawing board. Mrs Martin simply replicates your old stuff over and over again. We need new designs! Jack won't be able to tell you it's too tiring any more. You've got all day to yourself. Don't get caught up in village life – get caught up in your own life!'

Hope felt a tiny shoot of interest begin somewhere around her diaphragm. She grinned and Mandy grinned back.

'See, it's not going to be that difficult, is it? You'll have the place to yourself for six hours every day. Henrik will pop in when Jack's not here – he loves being domestic so you can leave a duster lying about not too obviously . . .' She laughed. 'Come on, Ho. Cheer up. We haven't seen much of each other for the past four years. But we will.' She heaved a sigh. 'My God, you need me!'

And Hope laughed as she always did when Mandy was in this mood, and said dramatically, 'I do, I do!'

Mandy did not even smile. She leaned forward and put her manicured fingers over Hope's red hand. 'And we need you too, darling. Together we make a perfect whole. Don't you feel that?'

Hope was surprised but nodded. 'Yes.'

'You mean that?'

'Of course.'

'Thanks, darling. You are so understanding. Generous.' She sat back, still serious. 'You are our surrogate family. You know that.' She looked around. 'Now, let's get everything ready for Chatty's tea party. And for Jack. Flowers, candles, the best wine glasses. And something special for you to wear.'

'You sound like the advice column in a magazine!' Hope protested. And when Mandy did not reply, she went on slowly, 'You think I need it too, don't you? Do you think Jack and I . . . are losing something?'

'Of course not. You're simply . . . growing up.' Mandy stood up decisively. 'I'll do in here while you tackle the dining room. Then I shall leave because I want you to start thinking georgette.'

'Georgette?'

'Everyone is asking for georgette. I thought a dark plum colour. Not so décolleté as usual.

Maybe even a loose bow at the neck – a floppy one, like an artist.'

Hope grinned. 'You are a she-devil,' she said.

Hope had intended to go to her mother's for half an hour before collecting Chatty and Fay, but after Mandy left she found herself sitting at the kitchen table sketching an evening outfit. She did not like the thought of plum-coloured georgette; she thought black silk. A top cut in a voluminous bell shape which clipped gently in at the hips and was worn over a narrow black skirt. Time ceased to have meaning and when the telephone rang she was amazed to hear Mandy say, 'I've got the chocolate biscuits plus Henrik and we will be outside the school in plenty of time, so keep working!' Hope glanced incredulously at the clock; it was just gone three. She laughed and Mandy said, 'You see? I know you better than you know yourself.'

It was true. In the weeks that followed Mandy kept in touch on the telephone, pre-empting practically everything Hope did, structuring her day so that life had a purpose and direction again. When Milly mentioned – very uncomplainingly – that she saw less of Hope than she did before Chatty went to school, Mandy was delighted. 'This is what she has been waiting for! A chance to get back to designing again.'

It was as if Hope had fresh inspiration. Chatty seemed to have settled in at school and the house was tidier for her absence. Out of the blue, Henrik would appear at odd hours of the morning and afternoon with messages for Jack. He would disappear upstairs for an hour then come down and stand at the sink peeling potatoes, in spite of Hope's protestations.

'I can do that when the girls are home – leave it, Henrik. Please.'

But he would smile gently and put a sandwich in front of her, kiss the top of her head and vanish as unobtrusively as he arrived. She knew she was being organized again by the two of them and this time she did not mind. What was distinctly odd was – neither did Jack. He pretended to grumble but it didn't mean a thing.

'They've taken me over and they act like the girls are their own,' he said one day when Henrik had collected Fay and Chatty in his car and brought them home. 'Now they've got you on the payroll again!' He grinned without rancour. 'I don't know what we'd do without them though.'

'We're their family,' Hope said. 'Poor Henrik has been practically disowned by his people and Mandy seems to be absolutely alone in the world.' She glanced at him curiously. 'Do you really feel Henrik has taken you over?'

'Well . . . I suppose . . . not exactly. It's just that the bulk of my work comes from him still. He's putting tenders in all over the world and I do all the calculations of course. But nothing comes of it. I simply wondered if they were going to transfer their interest to the rag trade.'

'Do you work at the shops too? For Mandy?'

'Yes. I'm doing the accounting at the moment. But that's all it is, simple accounting. The stuff Henrik deals with entails projections on a grand scale.' His eyes lit up and she hugged him.

'The thing is, Jack, they give us this – this –

enthusiasm. A sort of excitement comes off them. Don't you feel that? Can't we just go along with it and see what happens?'

He made a face. 'I don't think I've got much choice, Ho. It's different for you. If you really have got this flair, you could get some training – work on your own . . .'

She shook her head. 'I couldn't do it without Mandy.'

He said slowly, 'Neither could I.'

The following year Edward Marsh had what he called 'a turn' during evensong. Dr Booth had retired the previous year but Edward went to see him anyway, ostensibly to talk about over-wintering the fuchsias.

The doctor, no longer young but even more cynical, listened to his erstwhile patient and good friend, nodded wisely and said, 'I think you've had a warning. A heart attack. Small but definite. What did Milly say?'

Edward pretended astonishment. 'What are you talking about? One minute we're on potting compost and the next . . .' He grinned sideways. At eighty-five he cut a magisterial figure; his hair was thick and snow-white, and beneath his warm green sweater his white shirt and tie were immaculate. 'Yes. All right. I'm not going to beat about the bush any more. It could have been a little heart spasm. And Milly doesn't know.'

'She should. Yes, I know it will worry her but . . . she should know.'

Edward shook his head. 'I think I could tell Hope,' he offered.

'Good. Tell her. And then watch yourself.'

'No tests? No questions?'

'They're for your doctor to arrange. I'm talking as a friend.'

Edward said comfortably, 'That's what I wanted.'

He made elaborate arrangements to ensure that his subsequent chat with Hope seemed casual. He dropped in one afternoon with some special candles for the cake he knew she was making for Chatty's sixth birthday.

'They blow out then they relight themselves.' He busied himself giving a demonstration. 'It will mean she can have several goes and then pass them on to someone else.'

'She'll probably go crazy with frustration.' Hope grinned as she worked marzipan into various unidentifiable flower shapes. 'Sit down, Dad, and I'll make some tea. Henrik is meeting the girls and taking them to see the Christmas lights in Gloucester.'

'Yes. So your mother said.'

Hope looked round sharply and then said, 'Ah.'

He told her about his turn and Doc Booth's advice. Hope sat down, her face drained of colour. He said rallyingly, 'I am an old man, Ho. Did you think I would go on for ever?'

'No. But I – we – can't spare you. You know that.' She swallowed painfully. 'What about Mummy?'

'Quite. She'll have you. Won't she?'

'Of course. But I'm not you.'

'In many ways you will be.' He covered her hand. 'It was a tiny little spasm, Ho. Nothing to worry about. I simply want you to know . . . some things.'

She forced a smile and nodded dumbly.

'Your mother will have to give up the old rectory. Can she come here?'

'It's her home. Of course.' Hope clasped her hands in front of her. 'The children. Will she be able to stand the children?'

Edward said steadily, 'Yes.'

'And will she want to come?'

'I think so. But she will have money, Ho. If she wants to go somewhere else, she will be financially independent. I want her to stay that way, my dear.'

Hope stared. 'What do you mean?'

Edward spoke levelly. 'I don't want it to go into the bottomless pit that the Petersens have dug.'

Her eyes opened very wide. 'My God. I know you don't feel entirely happy with Henrik and Mandy, Dad. But are you saying . . . ?'

'I am saying that I have invested heavily in Petersen's. I do not wish to invest any more and I do not wish your mother to do so in the future.' He covered her hands with one of his. 'Stop twisting your fingers like a Victorian heroine, Ho.' He grinned. 'I have not lost more than I could afford. But I want what is left to benefit your mother and then you and my granddaughters. That's fair enough, surely?'

She was devastated. Her father had lost money . . . because of Jack. She swallowed and whispered, 'Does Jack know?'

'About my investment? Naturally.'

'But he must find it so hard to accept.'

'It's business, Hope. Not charity. And I think that when the Petersens pull out – as they will do – Jack's reputation will be strong enough for him to keep going independently. That's what I had in mind.'

She continued to stare at him and now, because his hand was stopping her from twisting her fingers, she bit her lip.

'Pull out? Do you mean leave the project? The country?'

He turned down his mouth. 'I don't know, Hope. They are shifting their interests. Maybe they intend to stick it out. Mandy has the two shops, others could follow. She intends to exploit your talents, Ho. That is why your mother will be able to help. With the children.'

'But . . . Jack. I'm not sure he could . . . stand alone. He seems almost to be under Henrik's thumb. That's silly, of course. He is no more under their thumb than I am. Than the children are.'

'You are the centre of his universe, Ho. Same with Fay and Chatty. Always will be. Mandy and Henrik represent glamour. That's all.'

She said nothing and after a while, squeezing her hands slightly, he said, 'Is Jack still the centre of your universe?'

She nodded automatically. Then smiled. 'Dad, this is all a bit much. I think I should be saying something really encouraging. And I don't know what it is. I wish you would talk to Mummy.'

'You know I can't do that. Not about the money and where she will live.' He patted her hand and stood up. 'You're so strong, Ho. Just forget this conversation for now. If – when –

anything happens, remember it then. Petersen has always made his money by taking on new projects. He will cut his losses and do it again eventually. You and Jack will go with him. Perhaps that is when Milly will come into her own. Looking after the children.'

It was as if he was thinking aloud. Hope was terrified. How could she leave her mother, leave the children?

'Oh Daddy.' Belatedly, there were tears. They hugged each other. They both felt completely inadequate.

But Chatty's birthday came and went; Christmas came and went and it was 1976. Hope watched her father like a hawk and could see no change in him. Very gradually she began to relax. Everything appeared to be going well; Henrik was working hand in hand with a consortium who had dedicated themselves to ecology and he was encouraging Jack to design a windmill to generate electricity. The shops were still showing a profit – as Mandy said, people kept on having babies however grim the outlook. Perhaps Mr Callaghan with his twinkly smile made things look better than poor Mr Wilson had.

When Edward Marsh died early in 1977, it was as if a light had gone out. Even the Petersens were affected and some of their ebullience was dimmed. Not one of them had realized how much he contributed to their lives. The children were bewildered. Whenever they saw Milly they wept uncontrollably and she wept too, unable to help herself. Jack looked . . . frightened. Hope tried to remember that her father had said she was strong. She knew she wasn't but she did not weep, and when Milly held the girls and broke down with them, she put her arms around all three and held them close.

'Come on now. He wouldn't want this. We must be proud we knew him – proud for him. Lift your heads. We belong to Edward Marsh – that's something to be proud about!'

Her mother managed a watery smile. 'You sound as if you're going to break into "Onward, Christian soldiers"! But you're right, Ho. We certainly can be proud.'

They got through the funeral and then the long business of clearing out the old rectory, saving the pieces that Milly wanted, selling the rest. By that summer, Hope felt as if she had looked at a million old photographs and letters. Jack and Henrik were often away inspecting possible sites for their prototype windmill. Milly arranged for a builder to come into Horsley House and add another bathroom and kitchen. She said conversationally over a sandwich lunch, 'I do wish Daddy hadn't tied the money up so tightly. The builder is going to have to wait three months before I can pay for this work. Luckily it's Murchison's – they know I'm a safe bet. But it could be awkward.'

Hope was surprised. 'Hang on, Mummy. There was over ten thousand in the joint account you and Daddy had. It won't cost more than that, surely?'

'Darling, there was the money for the engineers. Don't you remember?'

'Engineers?'

'Who made the windmill for Jack. It cost more than ten thousand. Poor Jack didn't know which way to turn.'

'So you let Petersen's have all your ready cash? You cleaned out the account?'

'Not Petersen's, Ho. This project is Jack's own, darling. You realize that, surely?'

Hope said carefully, 'I don't think I did fully realize.'

She tackled Jack that weekend. He was apologetic. 'I was going to tell you. I felt terrible, Ho. You can imagine. Henrik said if I could raise the cash I could take on this project – in other words he'd work for me instead of me working for him. It was too good a chance. It won't be a long-term thing, obviously. These ecology power people will put money up front as soon as they can see our windmill in situ and working.'

'So it's Henrik's project as well?'

'He contacted the consortium. Used his influence. Backed it with his expertise. Of course. But . . .'

'It was you who asked Mummy for the loan. I can't believe this, Jack. You have never accepted a brass farthing from either of them and now you go cap in hand—'

'Ho! You know it's not like that! I could have got the money from the bank but I didn't see why Milly shouldn't have the interest!' Jack was red-faced and no longer apologetic.

'OK. Sorry. It's just that if we're talking about Henrik's design, I can't quite see why Henrik couldn't have applied for a loan himself.'

'I just told you! It's my project. Weren't you

listening? Henrik is working for me on this one. He was generous enough to say that as we put in equal effort, it was about time I had a turn at the wheel.'

Hope did not understand it. She said again, 'Sorry.' She shrugged. 'I couldn't help being amazed. But I'm glad the money is for you, Jack—'

'My God, it's not for me! It's for all of us, Milly included. Can't you get that into your head?'

She swallowed. 'All I meant was . . . I should have explained before. Daddy was worried about Mandy and Henrik. He thought they might persuade Mummy into investing a lot of money . . . well, let's just say, I'm glad it was you and not Henrik who needed the loan.'

Jack made no response and she knew she had hurt him. She got up and went to put her arms around his neck. He caught one of her hands and put it to his face. 'Sorry. Sorry, Ho. Didn't mean to snap. Rather a lot on my mind lately.' He retained her hand, making it impossible for her to hug him. 'Actually, Ho, you have no idea of money, not really. Ten thousand is a drop in the ocean compared with what Petersen's have to take on.'

She laughed. 'Is that meant to reassure me?'

'No. I just want you to know that I wouldn't ask Milly to lend me anything she couldn't afford.'

Part of her almost held her breath for the next few months while the wind project got under way. And then, in February 1978, quite suddenly

Jack was a different man, laughing and dancing her around the furniture just as he'd done when they were first married. It was his happiness that made her realize how introverted he had become over the past three or four years. Even on family outings she always knew that at least half of his mind was not with them.

'They want us to put up twenty of the things, Ho! Twenty! They're calling it the Windpower Project – I've got a name, Ho! I've actually got a name!'

'You always had a name, darling,' she said but she laughed with him and grabbed Fay's hand as they did a sort of sideways conga through the hall and into the dining room. Milly came out to see what all the fuss was about and got caught up with Chatty.

When they calmed down, Jack said, 'Now listen, Milly. You can have your money back, plus interest. Or you can buy into the Windpower Project!'

Hope said, 'Hang on! Let Mummy think about it.'

Jack looked at her almost sharply and there was the tiniest pause in their celebration. Then he said, 'Of course – take all the time you want, Milly.' He kissed Hope's nose. 'It's your birthday next month. And I've just had the most wonderful idea.'

'I don't want shares in the Windpower Project!' she laughed.

'You'll regret that decision, my girl!' But he was exuberant again and would say no more.

In June that year, when Edward Marsh had been dead for eighteen months, Jack gave her

her birthday present. It came in an enormous buff envelope.

'I've had the devil's own job with the solicitors,' he explained almost nervously. 'There were no deeds or anything. I mean, it was just a sort of shepherd's place . . . fisherman's hovel . . . Peter Penhailes built it with his own hands. So a deed had to be drawn up – land bought – there were affidavits and things.'

She swallowed and opened the envelope and stared at the legal documents that slid out on to the kitchen table.

'What is it, Mummy?' Chatty bounced around like a rubber ball.

Fay said, 'Is it a windmill? Has Daddy bought you a windmill, Mummy?'

She gazed in disbelief.

'He's bought me a house.' She picked up the thickest document and stared at it. 'Oh Jack. It's Widdershins. You've bought Widdershins!'

'It's in your name.' He pulled the papers towards him and began pointing to the words. 'See? It's yours, Ho. You loved it so much. And I always wanted to get you something that no one else would even dream of!'

She felt tears in her throat. She whispered, 'Jack, it's the most wonderful present. I certainly could *never* have dreamed of something like this.'

He was triumphant. 'That's what I thought. No one will be able to match it, will they?'

She looked at him. She had wanted to weep with joy. Suddenly the tears dried up. It was as if he was paying her off.

She shook her head. 'No one,' she said.

Six

It was incredible that nothing had changed. It was eleven years since Hope had seen this little lost corner of the country, and then she had not been driving. Now, once off the A30 she knew her way almost by instinct.

'See that enormous tower right against the sunset? That's St Buryan church. Widdershins is about four miles from there.'

The girls, who at the last minute had not wanted to leave Horsley and Daddy and Andy, rallied somewhat.

'It looks haunted,' Fay said, intrigued by the enormous broken-tooth silhouette.

'How many more minutes, Mummy?' queried Chatty. 'Grandma, how much longer? I need another wee something terrible.'

'You *are* something terrible, Charity Langley,' Milly told her, almost at the end of her tether after eight hours of close proximity with her granddaughters. 'Just sit still and stop thinking about the time. So long as we get there before dark, we'll be all right.'

Fay's big blue eyes swivelled towards her

grandmother apprehensively. 'And if we don't. What will happen?'

Milly was tempted to say that the Cornish piskies would come and cannibalize them, but she forced a smile and spoke soothingly. 'It's just that it will be awkward unpacking in the dark, that's all.'

Fay said, 'Oh dear. I wish Daddy and Uncle Henrik had come.'

Hope grinned into the mirror so that Fay could see her. 'What's the matter with you? What can two men do that four women can't? We're the Female Four! How does that sound?'

The girls, Chatty eight and Fay just ten, snuffled giggles. Chatty boasted, 'I'm as strong as all the boys in my class. We done arm-wrestling at playtime and I beat Mark Jinty and he's bigger than all the other boys.'

Milly said automatically, 'We *did* arm-wrestling, Chatty, not we *done* it.'

Fay said scornfully, 'He let you win. He wants to marry you, that's why.'

Chatty was furious. 'He don't – he don't!'

Fay was maddeningly calm. 'He doesn't, not he don't. That's how he talks. You talk like that because you like him.'

Chatty gibbered with rage. 'I can't marry him anyway. Not with that silly name. Chatty Jinty. It's horrible!'

Milly and Hope in the front seats exploded with laughter and by the time everyone had calmed down, they were past Buryan and the gates of the Penhaileses' farm were in front of them. Hope pulled up.

'I don't know whether to knock on their door,'

she said. 'Last time we just drove on as far as we could. But it seems rather unfriendly . . .'

She got no further. Mrs Penhailes emerged from the door of the dairy and almost ran down the track to the gate. She was as bony as Hope remembered; was her name really Mirabelle? A more unlikely name for her was hard to imagine. Behind her trundled Peter, an enormous grin cutting his face in two.

'We bin watching out,' Mrs Penhailes announced, crouching by Hope's open window. 'Dear God. You 'aven't changed one little bit. Eleven years. And two bonny girls to show for 'em.'

Hope got out and embraced them somehow. They were embarrassed but bore it stoically. She then introduced the others.

'My mother, Milly. And Fay and Chatty.'

'We were christened Faith and Charity,' Fay said solemnly, shaking Peter's enormous hand. 'But we couldn't say our names properly, so we're Fay and Chatty.'

'And you've come to see your house,' Peter said. 'No one's bin there since your ma and pa. Only Jem Trewint in the winter. But Bella and me, we bin down with a paintbrush so it's all fresh and nice.'

'I've made up the beds,' said Mrs Penhailes. 'And the gaffer, he's dug a fresh pit.'

Hope had forgotten the toilet arrangements. Eleven years had made a difference to their expectations and after the bathrooms at Horsley House they were all spoilt.

Peter grinned. 'And we've swep' the chimney!' He reached into the car and gathered Chatty into his arms. 'Did your mam ever tell you about the chimney fire, my 'an'some?'

Chatty gave a sort of gasp. 'I need—'

Hope said swiftly, 'I wonder if we could use your privy?'

But it was too late. Chatty gave a wail. 'I done it! In my knickers! I done it!' she keened.

Peter's face was a picture. Consternation, embarrassment and finally a kind of triumph creased his leathery face a dozen ways.

'Well! You takes after your mam, I must say! Hopeless! The pair of you! Hopeless!'

Strange that he made the description into something so special. Even Chatty eventually laughed through her tears.

Hope had thought it wouldn't be the same without Jack and of course it wasn't, but in a different way it was just as magical. Anyway, the Jack who had rented Widdershins eleven years ago from a man in a pub had changed immeasurably and Hope wondered whether he would enjoy the simple life any more. She found it difficult to imagine him here now. The Female Four, as they called themselves, slept in the same room, Hope and Milly in the double bed, the girls on the floor. They went to bed when it was dark and got up when it was light. They washed in the rill where it ran through the grove of alder – which a younger Hope had called Marble Arch – and thought it great fun. No one was quite so happy with the toilet arrangements, so they went into Penzance where they bought a chemical toilet in a camping shop which they set up with great ceremony in the ruined half of the cottage. They continued to name things and the 'throne room' was duly opened with red ribbon and a pair of garden shears. Henry, the elm tree, had succumbed to Dutch elm disease, so they bought a willow from a garden shop and planted it in his place. Chatty insisted on calling it Andy.

'I don't think Mandy will be pleased,' Milly commented to Hope. 'It's distinctly stubby. Not a willowy willow at all.'

Hope, half lying in a deckchair, watching the girls make a bridge across the rill with stepping stones, replied, 'To be honest, I don't think Mandy would like Widdershins. Not unless I let her modernize it completely. And I don't want to do that.'

'No.' Milly turned in her chair with some difficulty. 'It's not charming. Not in the picture-postcard sense. And of course having that tumbledown bit hanging on to it for dear life doesn't help.' She turned back and relaxed, closing her eyes. 'There's something about it, though. I haven't felt quite so . . . peaceful . . . since Daddy died.'

'Oh Mummy. You put up such a good show. Organizing the alterations and sorting out your furniture. You fooled me into thinking you had accepted it.'

'Well, I have. I mean there's so much going on . . . the girls and you and Henrik popping in. Doing things. You know – much the best situation for me to be in. What I meant was, I've been so busy, I haven't had time to think until I go to bed and then I cry. Here, there's all the time in the world and I haven't cried.'

Hope made a little sound in her throat. Then she cleared it and said, 'Funny you should say that. I haven't cried at home. But here . . . I look out to sea and my eyes fill. Not just for Daddy but for times gone. A loss of . . . time.'

She gave a little sob and Milly leaned over and put a hand on her arm. 'Death does that. Brings you up short. But I've got this theory . . . I think that somewhere, somehow, all time is rolled up into one. It's not lost – it doesn't rely on memory – it's there. Waiting for us.'

'Rolled up?'

'Like a carpet. A magic carpet. We can go where we like.'

'Oh Mummy, that's – that's wonderful!' Hope leaned across the space between the two deck-chairs and flung an arm across Milly's chest. 'Oh Mummy, you've always been like that. Making things sound . . . well, wonderful. And you were over forty when you had me!' She looked down into her mother's face, still pretty at seventy-six. 'Maybe I should have waited before having the girls. I was too young.'

Milly struggled beneath the pinning arm. 'Darling, of course you're not too young. You're young, yes. Not too young. You and the girls – you're on the same wavelength. It's much better your way than mine.'

Hope released her mother and smiled wryly. 'Come on. You know that without you and Daddy and Mandy and Henrik I would have got nowhere.'

'What utter rubbish!' Milly was angry. 'We all rely on each other. That's part of the human condition.' She sat up and surveyed her daughter through narrowed eyes. 'Were you always like this, Ho? Was your natural optimism mistaken for confidence? You're still optimistic, I suppose. Fairly, anyway. But, considering you're married to a man you adore and who adores you back, and you've got those two beautiful daughters – and now a house of your own – you lack a sense of . . . I'm not sure what it is . . . self-worth.'

Hope made a face. 'Don't worry about it. I know myself, that's all. My – my capability threshold—' she laughed at herself, '—is low. Just like some people have a low pain threshold. What is absolutely marvellous for me, Mummy, is that I have always been surrounded by people who *think* I am all right. Special even.' She picked up her mother's hand and held it loosely between both of hers. 'You and Daddy. Dear Jack. Mandy and Henrik.'

Milly was silent for some time. Then she said quietly, 'Most of us are like you, darling. And then we're tested. And we're quite surprised at ourselves.'

Hope squeezed her mother's fingers then released them.

'We're getting heavy. I'll go and make a picnic if you'll keep an eye on the girls.'

As she walked up the tiny valley to the house she could hear Milly saying, 'We're going to have a picnic. Then we'll walk down to the beach and swim. Then we'll come back and light the fire and we'll each take a turn at telling a story. So start thinking!' She felt her eyes fill. Her mother made everything sound so . . . secure.

*   *   *

Halfway through the school holidays, Jack came down for a few days, driving himself in Mandy's car. The children were ecstatic, Jack slightly less so. He too had forgotten the domestic inconveniences and it did not help to have to sleep on the floor in the tiny living room and shave in the cave-like scullery behind. He had to drive into Buryan twice in order to use a public phone. 'Why?' asked Hope. 'It's just for a weekend, Jack! Surely Henrik can cope with everything for three days?' He replied with a shrug. She wondered whether he had picked up her shrugging habit; it was easy to see why Mandy objected to it.

On the Saturday, when he should have been starting back, Peter Penhailes called in. ''Tis high tide in an hour. We could take the ladies for a cruise if they fancied it.' Peter grinned at Jack. 'I remember you was good at getting the old tub out of the cave. Still up to it?'

Jack was going to turn down the offer but the girls were jumping around him crazily and Hope's gaze was on him as it so often was these days, as if she expected something of him.

He said, 'All right then. Ho – will you come?'

Hope shook her head. 'Mummy and I will stay put. Try and set the chimney alight!'

Everyone laughed obediently and Jack said, 'Well then, will you go into Buryan and ring Henrik? Tell him I'll be home bright and early tomorrow.'

Hope nodded. 'Of course. You'll enjoy it, Jack. It will do you good.'

Peter rowed them into the cave in a dinghy, the girls clutching each other as they felt the sheer strength of the sea beneath them. They scrambled aboard the *Mirabelle* and sat down obediently, their sunhats brilliant white patches against the dark rock. As before, Jack untied the boat as she nudged quietly against the cliff, then waited for the wave that would lift her into the sea. As before, he got soaked and had to swim out and be hauled aboard. Hope felt the same thrill of terror as she watched the whole operation. She could tell it wasn't as easy for him as it had been eleven years before. When Peter eventually pulled him on board he was obviously at the end of his tether and sat soggily by the girls, head down until they were free of the cove. Then he waved back at her and stuck up his thumb. She found herself saying quietly, 'Let them all have a good time. It can't be the same. Nothing can ever be the same, but let them have a good time.' She had a sense of trying to pull Jack back in time. It was strange: 'weird', as Mandy would say.

She and her mother plodded up to the car and drove into the village and did some shopping, then Milly sat on a bench outside the church while Hope made her phone call. It was a perfect day, no wind, the sun brilliant yet the air still fresh off the sea. It was difficult to imagine Henrik's studio at Sandhurst; the big tables covered in plans, the sun beaming through the skylight and holding the dust motes, making the room stuffy. She had opened one of the smaller lights one day and Jack had leaped to close it because the plans would scatter so easily.

'Henrik? It's me, Hope. How are you?'

'Lost without all of you. I find myself taking the Newent road by mistake some mornings.'

'Fay misses you too. But she loves it down here. We all do. Jack has taken them out in the boat today. That's why I'm ringing. He won't be back today. He says he'll start early tomorrow morning. I told him you wouldn't mind two hoots!'

'It will be all right. Yes.' Henrik's precise voice made him sound as if he were granting permission. 'Tell him that. Tell him it will be all right.'

'Of course. Yes.' Hope watched herself in the tiny mirror above the phone. Her mouth was turned down. Was Henrik always so . . . pedantic? No, worse than pedantic – possessive. 'I've already told him, actually. No one is indispensable.'

'Only to themselves. Yes. Certainly.'

'Henrik – are you all right? Is Mandy all right?'

'Both. Yes. You are happy with your present? The gift of the little cottage?'

'It's a dream come true.'

'I am glad. Tell Jack I will see him tomorrow. And I will see you on the first day in September.'

'Yes.' She hesitated, then said, 'Goodbye, Henrik.'

'Goodbye, Hope.'

She pushed at the heavy door of the kiosk and sat by Milly. Across the road, the post office was doing a brisk trade in cauliflowers; a knot of holidaymakers were examining the stand of postcards. Milly said something about cauliflower cheese for supper and Hope nodded. And all the time something worried at the back of her head.

That night she waited until Milly was asleep then she stepped carefully over the girls and crept downstairs. Jack was propped up on his airbed reading the paper she had bought in Buryan. He grinned a welcome and cast it aside.

'Darling! Come and snuggle. It's quite cosy down here especially when we've lit the fire.' He gathered her against his shoulder and kissed the top of her head. 'It was a great afternoon, Ho. The girls loved it. I'm glad you persuaded me into going.'

She leaned back, surprised. 'I didn't say a word!'

'You didn't need to. You gave me one of your looks!'

'Jack!'

'It's true.' He kissed her hair again then leaned forward to find her mouth. 'Shall we?' he murmured.

She didn't want to. She felt a wave of guilt; after all she had come down to him, joined him in bed, the message must have been obvious. But their lovemaking had lost its spontaneity and she was terribly conscious of her mother and the girls upstairs.

'It's just that there's no proper ceiling. Only planking,' she apologized.

'I'll make you forget about the planking!'

He couldn't and again she felt guilty, remembering that first time when he had carried her upstairs and thrown her on to the bed. They had laughed so much and then stopped laughing. There was no laughter any more. It didn't matter of course because the intensity could still be there. But the laughter had been so . . . joyous. Now, unexpectedly she found she was weeping. And what was even worse, so was he.

'Ho. Darling. Did I hurt you? I'm sorry, Ho. I'm sorry.'

'Of course you didn't.' She sniffed and smiled. 'You know what an idiot I am.'

'You're pleased with the cottage?'

'That's what Henrik asked me.' And that was why she had come downstairs; she had wanted to talk about Henrik, about the cottage. Now she wasn't sure that she wanted to talk about anything. 'Of course I am. I love it. You know that. But you don't seem . . . quite . . . connected.'

He knew what she meant and made no protestations. 'It's just . . . I didn't remember it as being so primitive.'

'My God, the fuss you made when you saw it first! Have you forgotten that?'

'Only because it appeared to be derelict.' He gave an upside-down grin. 'When I arrived on Tuesday, I wondered what sort of present it was. A heap of stones.'

'Don't be silly.'

'I was talking to Peter Penhailes. Jem Trewint still comes down every year. He would stay here over the winter if we liked. Renovate the place.'

'I like it as it is, Jack. You sound like Mandy. Widdershins isn't meant to be smart.'

He said sharply, 'What's Mandy been saying?'

'It's what she would say if she came down. New kitchen, modern bathroom, extra bedroom . . . you know.'

'Oh. Yes.' He sat up, delved in his discarded

pyjama top for a handkerchief and blew his nose. Then he said, 'Couldn't afford that. But Jem would clear out the ruined bit. Tidy it up.'

'We'll see.' She slid off the airbed and stood up. She wondered what else Mandy might have been saying. 'Sleep well, Jack. I'll see you in the morning.'

Only much later, when she was at last dropping off to sleep, did it occur to her that neither of them had suggested she should sleep downstairs.

There was no sense of anti-climax. Milly, who had anticipated the girls being downhearted, had devised a treasure hunt and then a paper-chase for them. They looked towards Buryan church where Jack must be just skirting the War Memorial.

'It's such a nice day, Grandma,' said Fay. 'Let's save that for when it's dull and go down to the beach. Shall we?'

Chatty nodded vigorously, so Milly took them down armed with swimming costumes and towels while Hope cut sandwiches and tidied up the tiny cottage. She tried, consciously, to think of Jack on the first leg of the long journey home but though she inserted a sense of loss into her mind, underneath the forced imaginings, the equally forced feeling, she knew that there was also relief.

She said aloud, 'It's just that he brought some of the tensions with him. And that wasn't his fault. He wasn't here long enough to relax and forget all about business.' She looked around the cramped living room. 'Perhaps I could ask Jem

Trewint to do something. Just so that Jack would feel more comfortable. I could use the sewing money.' She felt a sudden thrill of achievement. 'I've got that money – it's mine! I could . . . invest it.' She laughed. 'I could invest it in Widdershins!'

She picked up the picnic basket and set off for the beach. She thought of the long day ahead of them in the sunshine; this evening she would watch the sunset and probably weep for her father; she would sleep next to her mother and listen to the girls breathing gently, almost in time with the sea; and there were two more weeks before they went home. She did not want to go home, but now all her work would be for Widdershins. It would have real meaning. So she was happy. Yes, at that precise moment she was happy; she could almost take her happiness out and contemplate its many facets. As she reached the top of the cliff and looked down at the children already in the crystal-clear sea, she realized with a little shock that she had missed Jack out of the scenario. Very quickly she went back to imagining him driving home. He would be through Penzance now, heading for Truro.

Her mother looked up and waved and Fay screamed, 'She keeps splashing me, Mummy! Tell her . . .' Hope abandoned all coherent thought and laughed as she ran the last few yards to the beach. She was happy. And she hung on to that.

The school holidays in Widdershins became the highlight of the next few years. The following summer of 1979 was probably even better than that first one. The Female Four were firmly established; they knew their own limitations as well as the limitations of the others. Even Chatty knew when to stop talking and Fay, slightly apprehensive about travelling into Gloucester next year to the 'big school', made a real effort to be helpful. Morning tea in bed turned the blanket-strewn bedroom into a boarding-school dormitory. Fay would arrive at the door, balancing the tray precariously in one hand as she stepped over Chatty's sleeping form to put the cups carefully on the mantelpiece.

'Darling, it would be much easier to come downstairs for this,' Hope said, reaching out desperately to stop the milk and sugar from cascading down the tray.

But Fay was insistent. 'Anyone can have their tea downstairs,' she said reproachfully. 'But we're the Female Four, remember!'

That year Bella Penhailes told Hope that Jem Trewint was in the area and Hope was able to leave a message asking him to call at Widdershins. He turned up one afternoon when she had returned early from the beach with a headache. She was sitting in the shade of the fern-fringed cliff, eyes closed, waiting for aspirin to work and nearly leaped from her chair when a voice said, 'Reckon thunder's around.'

'Dear Lord!' She gripped the chairframe. 'I didn't know . . . it's Mr Trewint? You make a habit of being invisible, don't you?'

He laughed. She remembered him as a typical hippie, so very long-haired and bearded it had been impossible to see whether he was plain or downright ugly. Now, shaven but stubbly, his probably bald head protected by an embroidered African hat, he was definitely ugly. Recognizable only by his beaded neck and wrists and a writhing snake tattoo on his arm, he looked a stereotypical convict. She stood up and held on to the back of the chair, wishing very much she hadn't asked him to call.

His laugh burbled away and he said, 'My God, you haven't changed. You're still stunning. And so formal! The name is Jem. Your bloke called me Jem.' He stopped grinning and said ruefully, 'But you didn't like me.'

She shook her head. 'Nonsense. I was a bit put out that you'd been living next door and we had no idea you were there.'

He had changed; aged. She tried to work out how old he might be. Over forty probably. And still no proper life.

He too shook his head. 'You didn't like me. Be honest. You didn't like me then and you don't like me now.'

She began to feel alarmed. His words were definitely aggressive. Yet he was smiling again, challenging her to be frank.

'Well, I left a message with the Penhaileses. I wanted to see you.'

His grin widened. 'Well fielded.' He spread his hands then suddenly folded himself down and squatted on the grass. 'Sorry. Please sit down and relax again. Then you can tell me why you wanted to see me.'

She felt stupid as she fumbled her way ungracefully into the deckchair. Why on earth hadn't she contacted a local builder instead of laying herself open to this kind of exchange?

Nevertheless there was no getting out of it now.

'I was hoping you would take up residence again this winter and . . . perhaps . . . try to repair some of the . . . stonework. And things.'

He was silent, staring at her. Then at last he said, 'Do you mean it?'

'Of course.'

'You don't like me. You can't call me by my name. Yet you trust me to live in your house – Bella Penhailes told me it's now your house – and work on it?'

'Well, I gathered that you are still painting. And I don't think a builder would tackle it. And I just wondered . . . hoped, really . . . and of course I don't not like you.' Her words sounded like something Fay or Chatty might say. She concluded defiantly, 'Jem.'

He snorted a small laugh but said nothing. His stare was unnerving. She said, 'Well?'

'Sorry. I can't believe that you are still so . . . vivid.' He shrugged then nodded. 'Of course I'll do it. Whatever. It will be wonderful to have a roof this winter – be independent. If you tell me what you want done . . .'

'I don't know. Not really. You might not be able to do anything. Just take it away – the ruined part, I mean. But if you could . . . sort of . . .' She shrugged. 'It sounds hopeless, doesn't it?'

'It can't sound hopeless coming from you. Can it?'

'How do you mean?'

'Well, you are Hope. I've never forgotten. Can't remember much about that summer. The chimney fire of course and cooking mackerel.

151

But I was pretty well stoned most of the time. Your name. Hope. Like a beacon.'

She was shocked. 'Do you still take drugs?'

'I smoked. And no. Bella says you have daughters. I'm quite safe, I promise.' But he was grinning, mocking her naivety.

She said, 'Look, I'll have to ask my husband about this. But – in general – you'd give it a try?'

'There will be a charge.'

She was taken aback again. 'Of course. I've saved some money. That's another thing: you'd have to give me some kind of estimate.' This wasn't going to work, it was all too un-businesslike.

'Not money. I would like to paint you.'

She recalled something of this before. 'No. I'm sorry. I couldn't.'

'It's all right. Fully clothed. I wouldn't ask you to sit. Might take some photographs. But . . . your permission.'

'Well . . . all right.'

'Thank you.' He smiled and was transformed. The grin had given him a cynical, gargoyle look; the smile was sweet-tempered. She found herself smiling back and thought that perhaps she hadn't made a terrible mistake after all.

'Would you like to have a look round?'

'No thanks. I remember it well. And I don't want to disturb you any more. Close your eyes.' He stood up, unfolding himself without effort. 'Here.' He went over to the cliff and pulled at a root of sorrel. 'Chew the leaves. They taste good and if you happen to have a headache, they help.'

She hesitated, about to deny any likelihood of

a headache; then took the plant and smiled, relaxing. 'We used to call them vinegar leaves when we were children.'

'Try them again.' He gave her another smile. 'I'll get a key from Penhailes some time this autumn, shall I?'

'Yes. Do that.' It was so informal. She didn't know what he would do and neither did he. Jack would never agree to this.

He was gone as swiftly and silently as he had arrived. She sat there, eyes closed, chewing on the sorrel like a cow on cud. When the first thunder rumbled menacingly up the little valley and the children arrived hotfoot and excited, her head was clear and she gathered them into the house and held the door open for Milly as the first heavy drops fell.

They did not see Jem Trewint after that, but each year something else had been done. She never asked Jack's advice, simply told him that Jem would spend each winter making good the ruined half of the cottage. She received two notes from him. Early in 1982 he wrote and told her there was a firm in Falmouth who would dig and install a cesspit and clear it every year. He wrote down the cost of the work and the cost of what he called 'bathroom furniture'. She wrote back and sent a cheque. When they went down that summer, the joy of having a bathroom almost eclipsed the fun of bathing in the rill. But not quite.

By 1987 Widdershins boasted another downstairs room with a bedroom above it. That year Fay did not come with them. She was nineteen and had just finished her first year at Sheffield

University. There was a boy from the Orkneys in her year, a geology student, who was a member of a group planning a field trip to Iceland. Fay was an English student specializing in myths and legends. When he suggested that she should join the group and look at the Heimskringla in Reykjavik it made sense, though both Hope and Jack had no illusions about her real motivation. 'Icelandic sagas, my foot!' Jack commented, much to her annoyance. However, she allowed them to spend a weekend in Sheffield, during which she introduced them to Martin Craigie. He shook their hands at the same time, Jack's with his right hand, Hope's with his left. 'I believe I'm meant to produce some credentials.' He had eyes as blue as Fay's and full of laughter. 'My ma knits and looks after my sister's children while my sister flies around with her husband who is a pilot. And my pa farms and fishes. And . . . that's it.'

Jack said, 'Sounds all right to me. What about you – what are you planning to do when you've finished here?'

'I don't want to teach,' Martin said firmly. 'I'd like to get a job with one of the oil companies. Prospecting.'

'Daddy's into alternative power sources,' Fay said with a transparent eagerness.

'Really?' Martin released Hope and continued to pump Jack's hand. 'I'd be really interested . . . some time . . . perhaps . . . that is, if you didn't mind. And had time to spare. This Chernobyl thing in Russia last year has made everybody worry about nuclear power.'

Jack nodded. It was true. Even Henrik's

languishing project for a Severn barrage had taken on a new lease since last April. 'Of course. You must come and stay and I'll show you the windpower field. They're calling them farms now. Man's use of land and weather.'

Fay said, 'Martin would be more interested in the barrage actually, Dad. He might be able to help with that silt-shift problem you still have.'

Hope felt a wave of small shocks. She hadn't realized that the awfulness of Chernobyl might help Jack and Henrik. That Fay knew more than she did about Jack's projects. And that Fay was in love.

Unfortunately Chatty was not keen to go to Widdershins without Fay.

'It's not that I wouldn't love it with you and Grandma,' she tried to explain, spreading her hands helplessly. 'It's just that . . . well, we wouldn't be the Female Four, would we? And Fay and me do lots of things together . . . I don't know. Shall we go for a week this time?'

Milly said, 'Listen, I'll drop out this year – no, seriously, let me finish. I'll look after the house and field Jack's phone calls. Let Jack go. Just the three of you. It'll be great – different but even better. You haven't had a holiday as a family . . . ever.'

Hope was thankful that it was Chatty who said, 'Oh come off it, Gran! Daddy comes down every blessed summer and is bored to tears!'

It was Henrik who came up with the perfect solution. He called in, ostensibly to pick up Jack but really to ask if there was news of Fay.

'Jack's in Bristol. At the computer centre. He should have told you.' Hope sounded short; she

155

was on the point of suggesting that she go down to Widdershins on her own and have a real holiday for once.

Henrik made apologetic sounds and picked up the postcard from Iceland. Around him, the argument continued. It now appeared that Mark Jinty was going on a French exchange, otherwise he could have come with them. Hope commented sarcastically, 'That would have been fun,' and Chatty suddenly rounded on her and accused her of not understanding anything at all.

Henrik said tentatively, 'Why don't you ask Mandy to go with you, Ho? She and Chatty get on so well and I rather think she could do with a break.'

There was a pause then Chatty erupted ecstatically. Hope and Milly exchanged glances. There was nothing they could say. Hope, thankful for the bathroom and separate bedroom, smiled and agreed. Chatty crowed, 'Yippee! We'll still be the Female Four!'

But somehow it wasn't like that. Chatty and Mandy went out with Peter in the old *Mirabelle* and persuaded him to moor in one of the Fal inlets where they could get a meal and a drink at a pseudo smugglers' inn; they drove into Penzance and shopped crazily, returning to the cottage with arty wall hangings and wind chimes; they got in with some of the art colony in St Ives and joined in with what Chatty called a weekend binge. Even if Hope had wanted to do those things, she could not have left her mother. But she did not want to do them. Widdershins was no longer basic and cut off from the world as it had been in the 'sixties; its isolation had to be protected now from walkers or people looking for the open-air theatre. To go outside and visit the frenetic tourist spots seemed to court an invasion of their precious privacy.

So she and Milly did what they had always done: when the weather was good they made picnics and lugged them down to the beach; when it was poor they took slow walks along the cliff, lit the fire in the evenings, read and chatted amiably.

Unexpectedly, halfway through the month, Jem Trewint turned up. It was mid-afternoon and Mandy and Chatty, claiming to have hang-overs, were sitting in deckchairs near the rill with slices of cucumber over their closed eyes. Their ears must have been alert, however, because when a man's voice was added to those of Milly and Hope, they stood up with one accord and made for the cottage.

'Jem!' Hope was genuinely pleased to see him and after their eight-year correspondence found no difficulty in using his name. 'How nice to see you! We're so pleased with all your work – we wanted to thank you . . .'

'You've done that. Often.' He actually looked embarrassed. This time his hair had grown and sprouted little curls above his ears; the stubble around his chin had gone. 'Thought I'd slip by and thank you for the last eight years' lodging!' He gave his cadaverous grin. 'When those gales came last winter, I was more than thankful to have a roof over my head.' He turned the grin into a smile and looked at Milly. 'I'm not very young now.'

She was fascinated by him. 'What did you do . . . before? I mean, where did you sleep?'

'Barns. The Penhaileses' dairy. They've always been good to me.'

'Oh dear. How uncomfortable.'

'Lots of people doing it then. Not now.'

Hope said awkwardly, 'You know you can use this place any time. And that's not charity. You've earned a place here, Jem.'

'I've got a room. In Falmouth. I call it a studio but it's just a room.' He looked round at Chatty's arrival. 'My God, you've grown. Where's your sister?'

Mandy appeared from behind Chatty. 'Well, I'm not her.' She laughed. Hope knew she must be nearly fifty but she hadn't changed. Even after her latest foray into the artistic social life, she looked delicately beautiful. Since the old days in Sandhurst, Hope had seen Mandy several times 'in operation', as Jack put it. She watched her now without amusement.

Chatty said, 'Fay's in Iceland. With her boyfriend.'

For some reason Hope said, 'A friend. Who happens to be a boy.'

Mandy laughed again and Milly said quickly, 'Why don't we have a cup of tea? Come and sit down . . . Jem. I want to thank you personally for the bathroom. I couldn't manage without it.'

He actually reddened. 'Well . . . I talked to the firm who did the pit. And one of them came and helped me with the pipework. It's all right then?'

'It's grand.'

They were lavish in their praise. Only Mandy, who after all had not seen the cottage in its original state, said nothing. She watched Jem, smiling slightly. He knew she was watching him and his colour did not fade.

He gulped tea and said, 'I came to see – well – what's next.'

Chatty said, 'What about knocking the dividing wall down, then we could have a big farmhouse kitchen. Bit like Bella's.'

Hope said, 'Hang on. Having that little sitting room also gives us an extra bedroom. If Daddy comes down it would be useful.'

'Daddy won't come down,' Chatty said confidently. 'And anyway, we can always double up.'

'What about the kitchen?' Jem asked. 'You might be able to get a cable laid for electricity, then you could have a cooker.'

'And a washing machine,' Milly said.

'And one of those sandwich toasters,' Chatty added.

Hope held up her hand, laughing. 'Stop!' She shook her head, gently. 'I'm sorry, everyone. I don't want anything else changed.' She waited for Chatty to stop groaning. 'I love the two new rooms and the bathroom is wonderful. But I also love lighting the lamps at night, taking a candle up to bed, that horrible old oil cooker, the pump in the sink . . . I want Widdershins to stay Widdershins.'

Jem nodded and looked pleased and Milly said, 'Hear, hear.'

Mandy said, 'Oh God. The tea will continue to taste like paraffin then.' Jem laughed and then caught her eye and stopped laughing. She went on in her amused voice, 'Perhaps we could invite

Jem to stay in the little sitting room so that we can show him how grateful we are.'

Chatty looked deliberately bored and Milly said how nice that would be if he could spare the time. Hope hesitated then said belatedly, 'If you would like to. Of course.'

Jem looked at them all then back to Hope. 'It would be a good chance to do the portrait,' he said tentatively.

'Portrait?' Mandy was suddenly sparkling. 'Your portrait, Ho? You never told us about this. How absolutely marvellous – an original portrait! We could hang it in one of the shops – it must be romantic, Jem! She must wear something she has designed herself.'

Hope was annoyed with her. 'It's so long ago. I thought you'd forgotten all about that.'

'I couldn't bring it up again until everything was finished. It was the final payment, after all. But if you're certain you don't want anything else done . . .'

So he stayed that night and for the rest of the holiday. Mandy hovered around like a fascinated gnat, but there were no formal sittings. He sketched unobtrusively, appearing quite suddenly with his pad when Hope was shelling peas or washing clothes in the rill. Mandy said delightedly, 'He's in love with you! My God, it's so romantic! All these years you've been sort of connected! And now this painting is going to be a culmination of eight years of complete adoration—'

'For goodness' sake, Mandy!'

'It's true. He knows I know. He's uncomfortable when I'm around. I like that. I'm going to be around a lot to save you from yourself.'

'Mandy if you don't shut up I'll make sure there is paraffin in your morning tea.'

Then Mandy said, casually as if it didn't matter, 'I think you're an idiot. I'd sleep with him this minute if he wanted me. He's lovely. Like that chap in *Lady Chatterley*. Earthy and real.'

Suddenly Hope had had enough. She said, 'Are you joking? I hope you are, Mandy! When I think how Henrik adores you – how can you talk in that silly way?'

Mandy stared back, surprised. 'Darling. What I say means nothing at all, you know that. I adore Henrik too. But . . . honey, I thought you knew and perhaps I had better tell you now.' She smiled. 'Sweetie, Henrik is impotent. That's why his family let me have him. He can never father a baby. Why do you think he loves Fay and I love Chatty? They are the children we could never have.' Her smile gurgled into a laugh. 'Don't look like that, Ho. You didn't really understand what I was saying until I mentioned the babies, did you? It's all right, darling. We manage very well. And we have a perfect understanding. Honestly.'

Jem appeared in the doorway and Mandy swept up to him and took his arm. 'Jem. Be a darling and walk with me. Not too much to ask? Hope needs a little time to herself.'

Hope stood where she was and watched the two of them walk down the little valley towards the copse of trees. She thought of Henrik; that kiss underneath the mistletoe so many years ago, his care of her when she had Fay. He was possessive, demanding, generous. And now it made sense.

She must have stood there for a long time because Milly, who had gone to the farm for mik and exchanged gossip with Bella, arrived some time later and found her still in the same spot.

'Anything wrong, darling?' she asked.

'No. Yes. Mummy, I'm glad there's only another few days to go.'

'Oh.' Milly swallowed. 'You haven't enjoyed it?'

'Very much. It's been special for us, hasn't it? You and me.' Hope smiled and took the milk from her mother. 'Let's have a coffee and sit for a bit. It's just that . . . I need to see Jack.'

Milly sat down thankfully. 'I'd love coffee. Bella does go on and on and she never sits down.' She smiled. 'I've felt this has been a special time for you and me too. Thank you, darling.' She sighed sharply. 'Anyway . . . why do you need to see Jack? Something wrong with Chatty?'

'No. Nothing wrong at all. Everything very right, actually. But I thought, quite suddenly, that Jack and me . . . we've grown apart in many ways, Mummy. And he's my husband and the father of my children.'

Milly laughed and reached for her daughter's hand. 'Something all wives need to remember now and then, Ho,' she agreed.

Chatty came bursting in, hair wet and straight, eyes red-rimmed with salt.

'Guess what?' She was giggling helplessly, holding the table. 'Andy and Jem. They're kissing.

I was dressing inside Marble Arch and they didn't know I was there! They're kissing and cuddling and sort of stroking each other . . .'

Milly said, 'Honestly! Mandy is the giddy limit, Ho! That poor man – I knew he didn't stand a chance!'

Hope tried to echo Chatty's giggle. 'Your aunt Mandy is a case, Chatty! But you'd better not mention it.'

Milly said, 'Did she get up to these sort of shenanigans when you went to that awful party? Because if so, I'll have to speak to her—'

'No such thing, Mummy!' Hope turned her head away from Chatty and made a face at her mother. 'You know it's only Mandy having a bit of a fling.'

Chatty made for the stairs. 'If you're going to make a fuss about a kiss – it's not Andy's fault, Gran! Takes two to tango, you know!'

Milly waited fumingly for Chatty to clatter up the stairs then turned to Hope again. 'It was because he showed an interest in you, Ho! That's what maddens me. Whatever you and Jack have got, she wants.'

'Mummy, stop it. She's so generous—'

'Don't you see . . . it's only to get something. It's like a payment.' Milly shuddered.

'Come on now. Don't let's spoil anything.'

They laid the table in silence. Hope glanced through the window to where, at the end of the miniature valley, the copse hid the rill. It was half an hour before Mandy put in an appearance. She was flushed and very happy.

Seven

Fay seemed to shine with happiness. 'I'm effulgent!' she said, spinning around the kitchen like a top. 'That's my latest word! I . . . am . . . effulgent!'

Hope and Milly took it in turns to hug her. Milly said, 'This is exactly how your mother was when she met your father!'

Jack said, 'I hope Martin is just as effulgent!'

Chatty said unhappily, 'Everything is going to be different now. I don't want it to change.'

'It will just be better!' Fay carolled. 'Better and better and better!'

Henrik and Mandy came for a proper Sunday tea before Fay went back to Sheffield. The leaves were banana yellow and orange and scarlet. Beyond the slope of the garden, the squat Saxon tower of the church was framed in silver birch.

Mandy's reaction to Fay's excitement was to hug Chatty to her. 'Don't you go giving your heart away just yet!' she commanded.

Henrik said austerely, 'It's first love, Fay. It might not be the last. Be careful.'

'Oh I know.' Fay was assured, believing herself

to be totally realistic. 'I've done all that. But we care about the same things. He – he under*stands* things. People. He even tries to explain how Sinn Fein *feel*! I mean, he knows they've got a point of view—'

'We all know that, Fay.' Henrik was looking like a character from an Ibsen play. 'We also know they are wrong.' He drew his mouth down. 'And where is he now? Why hasn't he come home with you? Made sure you arrived safely?'

'Henrik, stop it! He lives in the Orkneys, for goodness' sake! And nothing's been *said*. It's just me – I am seeing everything so differently. I can't explain!'

Jack said, 'You have said.' He grinned. 'You are effulgent.'

Hope suddenly went over and sat on the arm of his chair. She thought gratefully: neither of us has forgotten . . . it's not the same any more, but at least we haven't forgotten.

And Mandy, watching the two of them and then glancing at Henrik who stood to one side, subtly excluded, tightened her hold on Chatty. 'We saw plenty of effulgence in St Ives, didn't we, darling? Didn't cut much ice with us!'

Chatty relaxed and grinned sideways. 'Andy – you're a realist! We're both realists!'

It came as no surprise to anyone when Fay rang towards the end of the term and asked whether Martin Craigie could spend Christmas at Horsley House.

'He wants to be home for the New Year,' she explained breathlessly, 'so we thought, Christmas with my family and New Year with his. Will that be all right?'

It was Jack who said it would be fine. Hope was not at home: in November, Milly had found a lump beneath her arm and was undergoing tests in Gloucester Royal. Hope felt as if everything had suddenly turned upside-down. She stopped her sketching and sewing abruptly. When Chatty asked whether she could go away with Mandy to Paris for her eighteenth birthday, she nodded absently, thinking it would be as well if both girls could be away during this time. Jack protested.

'Ho! It's her eighteenth. The official coming-of-age now! Shouldn't we do something together?'

'I can't think about parties, Jack!' she said passionately. 'My God, d'you realize what this could mean?'

'Of course. But your mother wouldn't want you to push Chatty aside like this. After all, Milly is eighty-five, Ho. Almost as old as your father was. She couldn't have gone down to Widdershins again.'

'Oh God!' Hope had not thought of that. Now, looking back, it seemed as if her mother had known it would be their last holiday. The Female Four. Never again.

'Look . . .' Jack was talking to her with great reasonableness. 'Let's suggest that Chatty and Mandy go off for their Paris weekend before the actual birthday—'

'Don't you see, Jack? I don't want to celebrate . . . anything! Not Chatty's birthday, not Christmas, not New Year—'

He stopped being reasonable and said tightly, 'Shut up, Ho! Stop being so bloody selfish! You have to let your mother go – my God, you've managed it with both your daughters, not to mention me!'

She was shocked, astounded. 'I don't know what you mean,' she said.

He stared at her for a long time and she expected him to hold out his arms in comfort. He did not. 'You really don't know, do you?' He spoke slowly as if to himself. 'You haven't been interested in what I've been doing for the past twelve years. You let Henrik make your lunch and when Fay started school in Gloucester, he usually drove her in—'

'Only when she missed the bus!' she protested.

'Chatty is always with Mandy—'

'That is not true, Jack!'

'It's not far from the truth. Basically you're still the spoiled only child, Ho. And your attitude now confirms that.'

'You're not being fair! How can I be interested in what you are doing when you never tell me! You're hardly ever here so when Henrik pops in – to see *you*, remember – I have to take him on!' She heard herself sob against the sheer injustice of his attack, and at such a time too. 'He simply happened to be around when I went into labour with Fay – he's always felt he had a share in her because of that. And it was the same sort of thing when Chatty was born, only with Mandy. You know all this! My God, it's you who relies on him – for work, for money, for . . . everything!'

He ignored her words and went on in the same measured voice. 'I know he's in love with you, Ho. Are you in love with him?'

She almost screamed then and put a hand to

her mouth. When she could speak she said flatly, 'He is impotent, Jack.'

He frowned impatiently. 'I know that. Mandy fell in love with him knowing that. Have you?'

The shrill note of the telephone cut short her scornful reply. She snatched up the receiver and an impersonal voice said, 'This is Sister Morris, Mrs Langley. Your mother's results are ready now and Doctor would like to talk to her. It would be best if you could be here too.'

She knew then that the results were the worst. If they had been clear there would be no need for any support. She closed her eyes momentarily, then said clearly, 'I'm on my way.'

She looked at Jack and wanted to hurt him, so she said unforgivably, 'I don't think you'll have to pay back that money after all. Ten years, it's been. No interest. Rather a good deal.'

He flinched physically and she would have given a great deal to retract what she had said. But there was no going back.

Chatty did not go to Paris that year because Milly died just before her eighteenth birthday and the funeral was just after it. Fay brought Martin home as planned but very tactfully he caught the sleeper back to Aberdeen when he realized the situation. Hope should have been infinitely comforted by the presence of her two daughters; as Chatty said, 'We'll always be the Female Four, nothing can spoil that.' But somehow, her row with Jack, cold and controlled and unresolved, poisoned everything. Even her grief for her mother seemed tainted and wrong in some way. It was Jack who broke down after

168

the funeral, turning away from the others and walking back to the line of cars entirely alone.

Fay said sadly, 'Gran was the mother he never had. They were so close. But he still hasn't got our blood links, has he?'

Hope looked at her, surprised, shocked. 'Blood links! What do they matter? I am glad you think Dad was close to her.'

'Yes. He was. But sharing the same genes and things does matter. It gives you rights.' She linked arms with her mother and sister. 'It's the Icelandic sagas. They're about families. They're so consoling.' She smiled. 'You go and have a word with the vicar, he's waiting for you. We'll join Dad. Come on, Chatty. We're Dad's links with Gran. He needs us.'

Hope watched the two girls in their dark duffel coats as they homed in on Jack. The vicar came over and shook her hand and then made for Mandy. And that left Henrik. She looked up into his patrician face as he put his arms around her. Was he really in love with her?

He said in a low voice, 'It will be all right, Ho. In time.'

'Yes.' Her voice was muffled by his enormous overcoat. She moved her head and saw Mandy leave the vicar and move over to Jack. 'But it will never ever be the same. That's the trouble.'

Fay stayed at home until the second day of the new year, and then she left for her promised visit to Lerwick. Jack was all for it and even Chatty agreed that she ought to go. Only Hope was silent. When Mandy brought up the Parisian visit again and Jack was for that as well, Hope could hardly believe her ears. She said nothing. Her feeling of being bereft intensified into self-pity. She could actually see Chatty and Fay putting their grief aside and coming back to life. She wanted to claw her way back into the past; the future seemed completely empty.

Jack said, 'Why don't you start work again, Ho? You'll have the place to yourself after Monday. Henrik and I are going to talk to the consortium about opening another field.' He held out his hand. 'I'm sorry about . . . well, you know. Those things I said.'

She made an enormous effort and took the hand. 'It was me. My fault. I can't think what happened now. Our nerves were stretched, I suppose. It was terrible – what I said. I was in such a state. Still am. I don't think I can bear to get the machine out. Sorry, I know it's ridiculous.'

He was silent and then he said, 'Your mother had faith in me, Ho. She backed me to the hilt. Now she's gone . . . I miss her.'

She held on to his hand, remembering Fay's talk of bloodlines. She had to remind herself that Jack and her mother had got on well; once Milly had accepted the streak of stubborn independence in him, there had never been any friction. She squeezed his fingers gratefully. It was the nearest they had come to comforting each other. She hoped it was a new start for them.

So it was a terrible shock when she received the letter from her mother's solicitor. She telephoned him immediately.

'Mr Rawlings?' His secretary had not sounded

surprised and put her through immediately. 'Mr Rawlings, I got your letter this morning. I don't understand. I thought my father tied up his money so that my mother could not invest any more in Petersen's. Yet according to this there were large payments made to Windpower on several occasions.'

'Windpower is your husband's firm Mrs Langley. Obviously if she had been putting more money into Petersen's I would have advised her against it. She talked it over with me and she saw it as simply transferring her capital to the people who would benefit from it anyway in the end. Which, surely, is the case?'

Hope was staggered. 'They are such huge sums of money!'

'As you see, your mother has left substantial bequests to your daughters.' He hesitated. 'She always said she would prefer to see her money being used while she was alive. That was why she gifted the house to you after your father's death.' He paused and when Hope said nothing, added, 'Your husband dealt with all of that, Mrs Langley. Your mother knew you would argue about it and she thought it best to act quickly. The seven-year clause, you know.'

'Seven-year clause?'

'Any gifts such as property have to be made seven years before the donor's death if they are not to be included in the estate for tax purposes.'

'But – but my father specifically asked me to make sure my mother's capital was protected, Mr Rawlings! You knew that!'

'Protected from investment in the Petersen

projects. Not from her own family.' His voice changed and became soothing. 'Mrs Langley, I understand your husband's windpower ideas are taking off in a big way. I don't think your father would have objected to helping with them, do you?'

But of course only she knew how intricately involved Jack and Henrik were.

Hope put down the receiver, frowning at the kitchen as if she had not seen it before. She told herself that everything was all right, but she could not believe that Jack had borrowed so extensively and not told her about it. And her mother had said nothing. As if they were in some kind of conspiracy against her. She shivered, recognizing her own paranoia. But surely her mother realized that money loaned to Jack was also money loaned to Henrik?

She could not rest. There was a need to do something and she did not know what. She went upstairs to Jack's office and sat in front of the computer screen with some idea of making it give up its secrets. But it had always been a mystery to her; Jack had told her she was not interested in what he did, but it was simply that she did not understand it. She sat there, still frowning, moving the revolving chair back and forth. Everyone was away. She would not see Jack until late tonight and he would be in no mood for her questions. Henrik was away too and Mandy was in Paris with Chatty. But she had a key to the Sandhurst cottage and in it would be Henrik's notes, made in the precise script she could always understand.

She drove with exaggerated care, almost

frightened that she was not in total control of herself. The feeling of being suddenly alone in the world was overwhelming. She desperately wanted her mother, but her mother had not told her everything. And Fay . . . not only were Fay's interests otherwise engaged, she had seemed to understand more about her father's business than Hope did. And Chatty . . . one thing that last holiday at Widdershins had revealed was that Chatty's first loyalty had somehow shifted to Mandy.

Once in Gloucester she drove around the docks, telling herself it was to see some of the new development, but in reality to recall those first days of knowing Jack. What she was doing now was, in fact, proving that after twenty years she no longer trusted him. She should get back into Westgate Street and head home . . . There was a moment when she almost did. Then she turned right on to the new ring road and headed for Sandhurst Lane.

Nothing had changed. The general ambience was one of gaunt trees etched against the January sky, of mud seeping on to the road, of the turgid river on her left. Yet in its way it was familiar and reassuring. Jack had driven them all to the Petersen cottage for Christmas lunch because she had been completely uninterested in making a Christmas at Horsley, but she had barely looked out of the car window. Perhaps it had been raining. In any case, with the funeral just five days before, she had been living inside her head, hardly registering anything outside.

She passed the terrace of houses, built for bargees and lightermen in the nineteenth century, and noted that the front garden at the end house, where she had collapsed in labour so long ago, had been gravelled over and sported some clipped bay trees in elegant pots. She remembered with a pang how Henrik had arrived and scooped her up into his big car. Taken her over, in fact. It had been from then on that the Petersens had subtly changed from being friends to being family. Fay had said that sharing genes gave you rights. Somehow the Petersens had overridden the genes.

She drew up at the edge of the road before she reached their cottage. She could justify what she was doing from here to next week, but she knew it was wrong. To use her key and go inside their home, to riffle through Henrik's papers for some indication that he had appropriated her mother's money, was awful. Probably illegal too. She switched off the engine and wound down the window and let the damp air fill the car, and after a while she said quietly, 'I'm not going to do it. If I do it, it will mean I don't trust Henrik and I don't trust my husband. So . . . I'm not going to do it.'

It was as if a weight was lifted from the top of her head. She stretched her neck and smiled ruefully. What on earth was the matter with her – seeing conspiracy where there had simply been an informal arrangement between her mother and her husband. She should be pleased about it. Delighted in fact.

She breathed deeply and decided that she would go home and get out the drawings she had started back in the autumn; before Milly had discovered the lump. She would go back to using stiffer materials just as she'd done when she started; make something that was absolutely straight at the back but had an expansion panel in the front, a mandarin collar. Gold piping? She started the engine and drove past the cottage in order to turn. And there, almost out of sight, but not quite, was Henrik's car. The car in which he and Jack had driven off this morning.

She braked and pulled over again. If something had gone ordinarily wrong, Jack would have phoned. Therefore something had gone really wrong. Her heart hammered a warning and she pulled on the handbrake, switched off and was out of the car, running across the gravelled sweep in two seconds flat. She passed the kitchen window: no one was in sight. Nor was anyone in the enormous living room that took up the whole ground floor of the house. They were upstairs in the studio, of course. She used her key and took the stairs two at a time and swung around the newel post to go on up to the converted attic, and then stopped. The bedroom door was wide open. Jack was lying on his back on the bed. Mandy was above him. They were both naked.

Hope had a very limited recollection of going back down the stairs, running across the gravel again and into the car. There were shouts from Mandy and from Jack. Despairing shouts. She could not pay attention to them. Her priorities had to be elsewhere: to jump the last four steps into the hall, remember that Mandy's front door opened outwards and needed slamming hard to shut it – she knew she had to shut it, to shut away what she had just seen. Luckily she had not locked the door of the car but to switch on, use the clutch and get the gear into reverse seemed to take all her energy and a great deal of time. She backed into the lane without checking her mirror and registered fleetingly how lucky she was that nothing was coming from the farm below the cottage. And then she was roaring back down the lane towards the pub, not re-alizing until she reached the ring road that she was in third.

After that she recalled nothing of the journey until she pulled into her own drive and for some reason got out, opened the garage doors, parked the car carefully and closed them again. If she imagined that Jack might think she had gone elsewhere – although where would she go? – she was mistaken. Ten minutes later, when she was still in her outdoor things, her gloves on the kitchen table and her stiff hands held over the stove, he burst in through the back door, fully clothed but, as if she needed a reminder of how she had last seen him, definitely unkempt. She felt sick.

He said, agonized, 'Ho – it means nothing! Mutual comfort – call it what you like! It has nothing whatsoever to do with you and me! Forgive me, Ho. Please.' He stopped a yard away from her as if frightened to touch her. She was grateful for this; even so she could not look at him.

He waited. She wanted to ask him how long it had been going on; wasn't that what wronged wives always asked? But if she spoke she would be physically ill; she needed all her strength to stay where she was, hands outstretched.

He made a noise halfway between a groan and a sob. 'Ho. Aren't you going to talk to me?' A long pause and then, although he did not move, he seemed to fall back into himself with a kind of despairing surrender. He said, 'You have to listen to me, Ho. I don't know how you found out about today but obviously you must have suspected something. Probably for some time now. Mandy said you were distant even on the holiday at Widdershins. And when we had that . . . row . . . just before Milly died, I thought then that you knew.'

She did not want to hear this; she blocked her mind and physically tightened the muscles of her throat. If she went to the bathroom she would have to pass him; maybe touch him. She must not be sick. She must stay exactly where she was standing now and she must not be sick.

His voice becamse hoarse. 'You see . . . Mandy still loves Henrik. And I still love you. Henrik has known all along and doesn't mind. So I thought . . . perhaps . . . as you don't want me any more . . .' She must have made some kind of sound because he stopped speaking for a moment. When he went on his tone changed. He began to justify what he had done. She knew he was using Mandy's arguments.

'You can't deny it, Ho. I can't really remember when I realized it. Was it that first visit to Widdershins? I came down for a weekend and you joined me on the floor in that ridiculous little living room . . . You couldn't wait to get back upstairs, could you? And there have been

177

other times too. You must admit it, Ho. Sex doesn't mean much to you. It does to most people. Please – please – admit that.'

She wanted to ask how you separated the act of sex from love. But she dared not speak. She must have put the kettle on a low heat because it was steaming. Should she make tea? Would that solve anything? The thought of tea made her retch slightly. She clenched her teeth and closed her eyes.

He said almost belligerently, 'Well?'

She lowered her head still further, eyes shut.

'You can't say the words, but you know it's true.' He turned suddenly and went to the window. She opened her eyes and for the first time saw Henrik's car outside. Her heart leaped into her throat. Was Mandy sitting in it?

He put his hands on the window ledge and lowered his head too. 'Ho . . . if you can see that – face up to it – then there is just a chance you can forgive me. That we can start again. Make something positive out of this fiasco.'

Her mind hung on to those words. She had lost her husband and her best – and possibly only – friend. How could anything positive come of that? She mumbled something and he looked round quickly.

'What?' He held out a hand. 'What did you say, Ho? Can we start again?'

She forced her teeth apart and whispered, 'Two negatives. You. Mandy. Will they make a positive?'

'There is no me and Mandy. We are finished, Ho. That is one thing you have to believe. I have known – all the time I have known – that what I was doing was wrong. Just because it was all right for Mandy did not make it all right for me. Today . . . well, that fact was brought home to me.'

She forced her lips to go on moving. 'You're not in love with her?'

'God, no! I have tried to tell you that! There is no love – none at all. Either way.'

She could not make it to the bathroom but she got to the sink. He tried to hold her heaving shoulders; to give her some kind of comfort as he had done when she was sick at the beginning of all the pregnancies. She flailed him away with her arms. He fetched a kitchen chair and as her convulsing body gradually stilled, she collapsed on to it and put her forehead against the chill stainless steel. She felt as weak as a kitten and she was shaking and cold.

He made tea and put the rest of the water into a hot-water bottle. She clutched it to her abdomen but she could not stop shivering. He poured the tea and then sat at the table and tried to sip his.

At last he spoke. 'Ho. Please. I promise if you'll just sit up and try to drink some tea I'll go. You need not throw up again on my account. But I can't leave you like this. I can't.'

She understood that. Very slowly she managed to right herself. She remembered feeling nausea like this before. Before Fay? Or Chatty? Henrik had been with her then.

'Will you let me hold your cup – just try – please, Ho . . .'

He was too close. His clothes smelled familiar but they had still been flung somewhere in

Mandy's bedroom. She sipped and then turned her head away and he sat down again. She closed her eyes with relief.

He said, anguished, 'Oh God. How am I going to leave you like this?'

She whispered, 'Where is Chatty? Did Mandy bring her home?'

'No. Mandy had an invitation to a show. She let Chatty go.'

She lifted her head wildly. 'Chatty is on her own? In Paris?'

'She's eighteen. But Henrik is with her by now. He flew. This morning.' She was looking right at him and he dropped his eyes. 'I know. More deceit. But at least you know that Chatty is not alone.'

'He's a pervert! She's with a pervert!' Her voice rose a register.

'Henrik? What are you talking about?'

'He arranges . . . sexual partners for Mandy! What does that make him?'

'Darling . . . he allows certain things to happen. Turns a blind eye, I suppose. That has nothing to do with—'

'When is she coming home? Chatty? When is she—'

'Tomorrow. He's bringing her back tomorrow. She planned to stay at Sandhurst and sketch some of the clothes she's seen for Mandy . . . she wants to do what you do, Ho. But in a much bigger way.' He looked at her face and said urgently, 'Don't look like that, Ho. How could she talk to you about all this? With Milly just dead and Fay not here—'

She dropped her head, assailed again by the

terrible nausea. Her feeling of isolation was appalling. She had never felt like this in her life.

'Where . . . where will you go?' she gasped when she could risk speech.

'I don't know.'

'Mandy's.' She answered herself. 'Of course you will go to Mandy's.'

'No.' He sounded weary. 'I thought you accepted that at least, Ho. I am not going to see Mandy again. And I shall try to disconnect myself from anything to do with either of them, except business.'

'Except business?'

'You know how involved I am with Henrik. I couldn't go it alone.'

'In spite of all my mother's money?' Suddenly anger stiffened her spine. She said, 'Did you think I wouldn't hear about that? The solicitor rang this morning. Everything, Jack. Gifted either to you or the girls. Thousands of pounds. Didn't that make you independent of the Petersens? Or isn't that what you want? Do you want to be in a position where you can't disconnect . . . was that the word you used? Disconnect?'

'Ho, it wasn't like that. It was for us. Not me. Your mother wanted my business to be strong – and, yes, disconnected from Petersen's. She wanted to see it happen in her lifetime . . .'

'Did she know about you and Mandy?'

'Christ, no! Of course not!'

'Does Chatty know? Fay?'

'No one else knows, Ho. Henrik and you.'

She stared at him for a long moment, then down to the table again. Her anger receded with the nausea and left her drained.

She said dully, 'The house is big enough. I need not see you. Stay if you want to.'

'Thank you. Thank you, Ho. Perhaps we can go on talking? Later? I'll cook something light—'

'Do what you like, Jack.' She clutched the table and pulled herself upright. 'I'm going to bed now. I'll get up and make myself some food later. But I don't want to see you.'

From the edge of her vision she saw him flinch but he said nothing. And after a pause she steadied herself and made for the hall and the stairs.

Eight

Chatty arrived home so full of news that for two days she did not notice anything was wrong. Andy had given her the most marvellous time she had ever known. Had they heard of Jean Lascelles? He was the designer for Jules Ferrier no less! Andy had met him years ago, before Henrik in fact, and they must have had a bit of a thing because he still obviously adored her. He had taken Chatty around his studio; she had talked to the models; she had handled the materials which were going to be used in next spring's collection; she had shown him some sketches—

'I didn't know you had done any sketches,' Hope said dully.

Chatty laughed. 'It's hardly been the time to show you my stuff, has it? You know I'm doing Art A level next summer.'

Hope had almost forgotten that too. She had forgotten that Chatty would be going away. 'I suppose it's this term you will be making some applications for a college place?' she said.

There was a small pause in Chatty's flow then she swept on regardless. 'Jean thought my stuff had promise. He meant it. I'll have to get lots of experience of course. Start from the bottom.'

'Make the tea?' Jack suggested in an effort to sound normal.

But Chatty nodded eagerly. 'Yes. If that's what it means.'

Hope said slowly, 'Are you suggesting that you go to Paris next September? Instead of university?'

'Not next September, Mummy! For goodness' sake – the job is to help with the spring collection!' She registered her mother's expression for the first time and went on quickly, 'Don't be all stuffy about this. You didn't go to university and neither did Daddy. And you're both doing very nicely, thank you.' Chatty reached across the table. 'Mummy, don't look as if the world is falling apart! This is the most fantastic thing that could have happened for me!' She hung on to her mother's hand and looked from one parent to the other. 'Most girls would kill for this opportunity. Seriously. Andy has got it for me – given it to me on a plate—'

'Could be something to do with your talent!' Hope said sharply.

'That's what she said.' Chatty laughed because no outright disapproval was forthcoming. 'Mum – Dad – you *can* see, can't you? It's a chance I just must not miss! To work with the chief designer for Jules Ferrier!'

There was a long silence. Jack said, 'We don't know enough about it, Chat. It's all very well . . . You'd have to get somewhere to live. And how much money will they pay you? You still have to eat, after all!'

Chatty said, 'Listen, talk it over with Mandy-Andy. She's sure to come up to see me tomorrow – she'll want to know . . . well, everything! She'll convince you!'

The impossibility of talking anything over with Mandy was immediately obvious to Hope and to Jack and there was another silence. Then Jack said, 'How about if you continue with your A level subjects, get a place at university – hopefully – and then keep it up your sleeve for a year? Until you know definitely that designing is what you want to do.'

Hope nodded. 'That would give you something to fall back on.'

Chatty withdrew her hand, lifted her head to the ceiling and howled like a dog. 'You haven't listened, have you? This is definitely a now-or-never opportunity! If I take it, I take it next month. Just two weeks to find somewhere to live and settle myself in.' She looked at their closed faces. 'What's the matter with you two? At least talk to Andy about it! I'm not exaggerating about this.'

Hope said, 'I'm sorry, Chatty, but—'

Chatty interrupted, turning to Jack desperately. 'You understand, Dad! You've had to take chances with Henrik. Mandy's had to take chances with the maternity shops. Mum doesn't know what it's like out in the real world – please say yes! Andy will set me up – I promise. Or you two can come over for a week and help me find somewhere to live . . . please, Dad!'

Jack frowned and Hope realized suddenly that he was holding back tears.

'We must talk about it, Chat. You've sprung

all this . . . everything is happening too quickly.'

'There's no *time*!' Chatty said, clenching her fists.

'There's tonight at least. How have you left it over there?'

She let her breath go and was silent for a moment, then spoke quietly. 'I had to say yes. I couldn't be . . . ungracious enough to hedge my bets. Could I? Think about it. It was a gift and you don't um-and-ah about a gift.'

Jack went to the sink and stared out of the window. It was raining and the old swing squeaked a protest as the wind twisted it. He said, 'I suppose, if we say no, you will be reminding us that you are eighteen and do not need our permission to do this.'

Chatty swallowed. 'I love you,' she said simply.

Hope gave a small sob and went to her. Chatty held her and then gave an embarrassed laugh. 'Hey – Mum, you're hanging on a bit tight there!' She drew away and looked into Hope's drawn face. 'And you've gone all skinny!' She glanced sideways at her father's rigid back. 'Are you all right? Is . . . everything . . . all right?'

'Everything is fine.' Hope forced a laugh, straightened and went back to her chair. She suddenly knew that it was up to her. And she could not inflict any of this on her children. Jack would take his line from her, she was sure of that. She cleared her throat and managed to produce a new vigorous voice. 'It's just that . . . we worry about you. Can't help it.' She thought, if I don't let her go now, I'll lose her. She patted the table top. 'Sit down and let's talk it over properly. Jack, how about a cup of tea?'

The sudden and spurious normality should have warned Chatty but she wanted this so much that she allowed herself to be fooled. She accepted without question her mother's assurance that Andy had spent enough time away from her businesses – and Henrik – and that Hope would come with her to Paris to find a suitable room somewhere.

'Couldn't you come too, Dad?' she asked, only too aware that Hope had never travelled outside Britain.

Jack looked at Hope for a moment, then said, 'I've had a lot of time off, love. Perhaps I could pop over for a weekend in two or three weeks?'

Chatty nodded and then realized that the question had been directed at her mother. Hope said in her new voice, 'Why not? We can take it in turns to come and see you if you're the littlest bit homesick.'

'Oh yes!' Chatty beamed. She had not expected this kind of cooperation. 'But honestly, you must *not* worry about me! I'm not going to have time to be homesick. They work through the night and – and everything . . . it's so exciting – Mum, you will just love it. They hold fabric up like you do, and watch the way it falls! And the sketches – sometimes just four or five lines on the paper . . . but you can *see* it. You can actually see it!'

Hope smiled in spite of herself. Perhaps after all this wasn't another terrible mistake. Perhaps Mandy had not intended to deliver a final blow to the people she professed to love as her own family. Perhaps this might turn out to be something good. It would certainly be something

Hope herself could do for the next two weeks. It was going to give her some time to think.

But two days later when Chatty had repacked her bags and Hope had got a visitor's passport for herself and Jack had gone into Gloucester to see the solicitors, Chatty picked up the telephone in the kitchen and rang Mandy's Sandhurst number. Hope, standing at the sink peeling potatoes for the evening meal, did not realize what was happening until Chatty said, 'Andy? Where have you been? Mum said you'd be busy after taking time off for Paris but I thought you'd ring to find out what was happening.'

Hope forced herself not to look up. She had fended off all enquiries about Henrik and Mandy but this had to come. She cut a large potato in half and stared down at it as a spot of blood stained its whiteness pale pink. She had nicked her thumb.

Chatty said, 'She's fine. No, honestly. Of course she misses Gran – we all miss Gran. That's why this is so wonderful. It's helping us to – you know – think about something else. And it's all down to you. We'll never be able to thank you enough.'

Hope squeezed her eyes shut in a physical effort to hold back thoughts. She knew that as far as Chatty was concerned, the normal thing to do would be to look up and mouth a message for Mandy; send love, ask how they were. She began to peel the stained potato.

Chatty said, 'Actually, you sound funny, Andy. Aren't you pleased about . . . a cold? Listen, we'll come over. Bring some stuff . . . Well, I've got to

say goodbye! After all, you got me the job!'
There was a long pause. Hope started on another potato; she was going to cream them and
have some cold meat with the tomato chutney
she had made last summer. Creamed potatoes
would make the scratch meal into a celebration.

Chatty's voice was suddenly rough. 'You can't
just . . . go! Why haven't you said something
before? You must have known when we were in
Paris!' She put a hand over the receiver and
hissed something across the kitchen at her
mother. Hope did not look up. 'Of *course* I know
you have to go where Henrik's work takes him!
Yes, I remember ages ago Dad saying something
about South Africa . . . but now? It's in a terrible
state, you can't go there now! It's dangerous!
Have you talked to Mum about this?' She did
not bother to cover the receiver but called across
the kitchen, 'Mum, come and have a word with
Andy! You obviously don't know what's going
on—' She stopped talking and listened and
Hope did not move. For a long time she stood
holding a potato in one hand, the knife in the
other. Chatty made sounds, little sobs of protest.
Then at last she said, 'But listen, Andy, I understand. I do – I'm not as silly as everyone thinks,
you know! If they're angry – if they see this as a
desertion – well . . . yes, I do see that. But you
and me . . . I have to say goodbye, Andy! I have
to say goodbye!' It was almost a wail of despair
and Hope knew a moment of pure jealousy.

And then Mandy made one of her splendidly
generous gestures. Chatty seemed to change;
first of all to flinch as if Mandy had hit her
physically, then to straighten, to harden. She

said falteringly at first, 'I didn't realize . . . of course I know that you are used to travelling the world, seeing places. Yes, I agree, Sandhurst is a bit of a backwater – although I've always loved it and I thought you did too.' From the sink Hope could hear Mandy's tinkling laugh. Chatty listened again, her jaw gradually thrusting forward in the aggressive, stubborn way Hope knew so well.

She said, 'Yes, I do intend to stand on my own two feet, Andy. Of course – that's exactly what I want!' She half turned to the wall. 'Actually, I wish I did take after them! They haven't done so badly. You've no right to say . . . yes, perhaps we will again, in the future. But if we don't, I still say, thank you for your help. And goodbye.' She replaced the receiver quickly and turned to her mother.

'I wish you'd told me! I walked right into that, and you let me!'

Hope closed her eyes again and took a deep breath. 'Told you what?'

'Oh come on! About them leaving. About the row because they're leaving. About her getting the job for me as a sort of farewell gesture!' She sat down abruptly at the kitchen table. 'I feel . . . horrible. Sort of like it's some kind of bribe or something. I don't know. In a way I should tell her to stuff her job—!'

'Chatty!' Hope protested automatically. She put down potato and knife and went to her daughter. 'Listen, I hoped you wouldn't have to know about the row. But I assure you that Andy got you this opportunity in good faith—'

'You don't know what she said. About me

190

having to pull my weight in the world – stand on my own two feet for once—'

'I can imagine. You have to be careful not to take after your mother!' Hope managed a little laugh. 'Don't worry about that, darling. She's angry with me, not you. Go ahead and prove to everyone that you can do it. Our little quarrel is nothing to do with you and you mustn't let it spoil anything. Really.'

Hope held the dark curly head to her old tweed skirt. She wanted to cry and run up to her room and shut herself away again. But she could not.

Chatty put her long arms around her mother's hips and held herself hard to the tweed. 'Really?' she repeated.

Hope laughed. 'Really.'

'And we'll go over on the ferry like we planned? Dad says he might not be able to come. Will that be all right? Just you and me?'

Hope said, 'Remember the Female Four?'

'But Gran was there then.'

Hope felt a moment of panic. Then, very calmly, she said, 'I think she'll be around this time too.'

Chatty was still for a moment; she hated what she called 'that kind of talk'. Then she relaxed again. 'You mean like Fay was saying? Blood links and all that? Well, yes. She's in you and me, so she will be around. Yes.'

It was amazing how well things went after that. Hope told herself that Milly was guiding the whole expedition. Jack offered again to take them over and leave immediately he'd ensconced them in a hotel but Hope was quite definite that they could manage.

'If the Petersens really are leaving, you will need to be around the office.' She gave him one of the swift glances which were still all she could manage. 'Did you know they were going to South Africa?'

'No. But I have already cut all my links. That was why I went to see the solicitor.' He hesitated. 'It's not going to be easy, Ho.'

She hated the intimacy of her shortened name. She shrugged.

He said, 'I know you're not interested. But we're talking about Fay at university. And now Chatty in France.'

She said, 'Lots of people much poorer than we are keep their children at university. Anyway, as far as I can make out, Chatty is going to be independent.'

'Not very likely, is it?' He too shrugged. 'Time will tell, of course. But meanwhile . . . yes, it might be as well if I stayed close to the phone.'

It was an enormous relief to get away from the house. The house now meant Jack and although he was scrupulous about keeping out of her way, she knew he was there. She shivered at the thought of the future; both the girls gone, her mother dead, her husband estranged, her best friend . . . no longer her best friend. What would happen about the shops? Once Mandy and Henrik really had gone – if they did go – she might call and see Mrs Martin. Perhaps between them they could come to some arrangement. She shivered again. She knew that somehow she had to become independent of Jack. And her mind wasn't working properly.

Chatty was understandably nervous but she had done the trip so recently she was able to guide her mother through the intricacies of the underground, the boat train, the boarding and the trip to the Gare du Nord from Calais. But then she seemed to go to pieces and it was Hope who got the taxi and managed with her half-remembered schoolgirl French to direct it to the tiny hotel in Rue Ste Jeanne d'Arc. Here, the phlegmatic concierge was won over by Hope's smile and her undoubted likeness to Elizabeth Taylor. She arranged for English tea and French pastries to be served while they unpacked. Hope sipped the tea cautiously and then nodded.

'Chatty, my darling, things are looking up. But the sooner you learn French the better, so pop downstairs again and see if that nice little woman can let you have a map of the Métro!'

Chatty looked at her mother with surprise and then said sadly, 'D'you know, you sounded just like Andy then.'

Hope refused to be daunted. She made a ghastly face and groaned, 'Oh God . . .' and was not comforted when Chatty paused in the door to nod.

'See?'

The plan was for Hope to accompany Chatty to the small studio where M. Lascelles worked and then begin looking for accommodation within a walking radius of it. They got the Métro to the Tuileries then walked back down the Champs-Elysées, passing the brass plate that announced Jules Ferrier's 'House'. The design studio was behind that, in an alley that had not yet been cleared of last night's rubbish. Someone had eaten a lot of oranges and the gently rotting smell of peel and pith was not unpleasant. Chatty stood in front of what was obviously a fire door and looked beseechingly at her mother.

'I don't know what to do!' she said. 'No one will hear if I knock. And if they do they won't speak English.'

But their good fortune had not deserted them. Hope took off her glove and hammered on the door which opened immediately as someone emerged. It was a girl not much older than Chatty. She wore a plaid pleated skirt several inches above her knees, a very conventional twinset which looked very unconventional on her, thick black stockings and ankle boots. She was shrugging into an army greatcoat.

'Oh hello.' She stopped and grinned at Hope and Chatty. 'I'm the other English apprentice. They said you'd be arriving. They don't know what to do with us now we're here! Lascelles is sleeping apparently, and no one speaks much English so they've sent me off to find a room. I slept in the station waiting room last night!'

Hope was delighted to see her. It was one thing to leave Chatty entirely on her own in Paris, quite another to leave her with this girl who seemed so capable. They all shook hands and Chatty said, 'You could have come with us. We're in a funny little hotel off Concorde.'

Hope said, 'We didn't know there would be another student. We can look for a flat together.'

Both girls nodded enthusiastically and Chatty

looked much less nervous. 'My . . . aunt . . . said there might be someone else. What a bit of luck. Shall I go in? Or come with you?'

'Let's all go in. Someone might take a bit of notice of us then. My name is Fiona Tabb by the way. Call me Fi. I know you're Charity . . . because Lascelles told me when I had the interview. I've been working in London and then Madrid which I hated so I wrote to Ferrier and said I was a Jean Muir type and I wanted some French experience and they must have liked my cheek because I got this interview. Do I call you Charity or do you shorten it?'

Chatty pretended to look stunned. 'I'm called Chatty because I talk so much.' And they all laughed.

In the end, Hope found herself searching for a room for the two girls. She felt greatly reassured by Fiona Tabb who could so obviously talk her way out of anything. Once Chatty gained some confidence they would be a similar pair – she even grinned wryly at the thought of them talking against each other. For an instant, she considered battling with a telephone and ringing Jack to reassure him as well, then realized she could not do that. In any case she would be going home earlier than expected, probably. As she trudged up uncarpeted stairs in the artists' quarter on the Left Bank she felt another wave of utter desolation and had to pause, hanging on to the rail and bending her head as if caught in a storm. And then, quite suddenly, in that unpromising place, she knew what she could do. She could go to Widdershins. It was hers;

nothing to do with Jack. She could take her mother's treadle sewing machine and set it up in the kitchen, close to the range, opposite the window which looked down the tiny valley to the stand of trees and the little alder grove called Marble Arch. She could make some smocks and take them into Penzance and try to sell them. Bella Penhailes would sell her milk – maybe bread too – and Peter would bring her some fish now and then. She could plant cabbages and beans and lettuce and potatoes. She could . . . she could survive!

She straightened and took a deep breath. She had a premonition that this room on the second landing was going to be the one for Fi and Chatty. That they would be friends. That this would be a wonderful experience for them both. She climbed the last flight of stairs and knocked on a door. An elderly man opened it. He was American and told her that when he retired he had tried to realize his dream of becoming an artist in France. Now he was awake and going home. She smiled and said the studio looked exactly what she had in mind for her student daughter . . . he smiled back.

It was strangely easy to leave Horsley House. For one thing it gave her something to think about other than ghastly images of Jack and Mandy. She telephoned a removal company in Gloucester and they sent a representative who went with her around her mother's little flat, making notes of what was to go.

'Is that all, Madam? We won't be needing more than a transit van. It's clothes, bedding, that coffee table, photographs, the sewing machine? Nothing else? What about one of the televisions?'

'No electricity,' Hope explained briefly. 'You understand that the van will have to wait at the top of the valley? There will be a walk . . . about ten minutes actually.'

The man nodded. Jack stood in the doorway, watching miserably.

He had been appalled by Hope's decision. 'I thought . . . perhaps . . . in time. I know – I know. However much time passes, it was still unforgivable. But . . . Widdershins. Let's get you a car. At least let me drive you down.' She kept shaking her head, still unable to look him in the eye.

'They've gone, you know. The Petersens. They've actually gone.'

She said evenly, 'It makes no difference really. I'm sorry. I can't help it. I have to start another life.'

'Ho – listen. Mrs Martin has got some sort of lease arrangement on the shops. I went to see her and she can still use your designs.'

'I told you—'

'I know. But you could work from Widdershins. Post them.' He flapped his hands. 'I thought you would like that.'

'Perhaps. I don't know yet.'

He was holding the inevitable mug of tea. It seemed to be shaking in his hand. He said, 'How will you manage through the winter? It's only January now!'

'I shall manage because I have to manage,' Hope said wearily. 'I have to manage here. It will be easier there.'

'You must have some money. You've got that savings account. Let me—'

'I don't want anything from you! Please understand that. Nothing!'

Jack flinched but said no more.

She wrote almost identical letters to Fay and Chatty. They were so-called explanations of her sudden desire for a winter holiday in the wilder part of Cornwall, but when she read them through she realized they explained nothing. She hesitated, then sealed and stamped the envelopes. They would have to do.

But just as the leaving had been almost painless, the arrival was almost frightening. The winter landscape was barren and already darkening. From the passenger seat of the transit van, Buryan church looked like the finger of doom pointing into a metal-grey sky. The driver, talkative at first, had long settled into a gloomy silence but now, as the road gave way to the track of Penhailes Farm, he commented, 'It's like the world's end, innit?'

The windows of the farmhouse were already lit but no one emerged to open the gate for them. Hope did it herself and could hear the sea crashing against the rocks below. The sound seemed too solid for water; it boomed imperiously, demanding the space that this tiny peninsula occupied. She shivered as she closed the gate after the van. She thought of Fay at the other end of the country in small, beleaguered Orkney; of Chatty, a true innocent in Paris. For a fleeting instant she pictured Jack pacing the empty rooms of Horsley House but she banished that thought as soon as it occurred. The wind tore at her hair and held her jeans against her legs. She fought her way back to the van. This was her choice; for the first time in her life she was on her own.

The walk down the tiny combe to the cottage was a nightmare and had to be negotiated half a dozen times. She might not have brought much but what she had was in unwieldy polythene bags – materials and sewing things, all the sweaters and cardigans she had been able to find, blankets and duvets and pillows, boxes of tinned food, milk powder, candles; Chatty's little radio and some batteries, spare torches, a string bag of vegetables because Jack had said he would throw them out otherwise, photographs; finally her mother's sewing machine.

She primed the three oil lamps, filled them from the can in the kitchen and lit them before total darkness engulfed the small valley. By their light she could see that the table was laid as it always was in readiness for her arrival; and for two people. Surely she had said in her note that she would be alone? There was kindling in the range, buckets of coal in the hearth. After they had lugged the machine into the little sitting room out of the way, she lit the fire and took the kettle into the scullery to fill it at the pump.

The driver said bleakly, 'We got to wait for that to burn up 'fore we can boil a kettle?'

She found herself smiling. 'No. I'll check that there is oil in the paraffin stove and we can have a cup of tea in about ten minutes.' She indicated the table. 'Help yourself. That ham will be home cured.'

'Any tomato sauce?'

Her smile widened. 'No.'

She made tea and watched the driver eat heartily while she stowed a few of the bags in the sitting room and unpacked some of her tinned food. She knew now that this was what she wanted. When she had stood on the staircase in Paris just over a week ago, her subconscious had envisaged exactly this. When she and her mother had talked about the passage of time she had longed for something in the past, perhaps something she had missed earlier in life; she had wanted – whimsically – to turn back the clock and do things differently. Well, perhaps this was how she might do that. She was back to a beginning of sorts. Now . . . here and now . . . she was going to find out what sort of person she really was. Whether she could live on her own. Entirely on her own.

She walked back to the van with the driver and watched him reverse carefully to the farm-yard gate. As she followed the light of her torch back to the cottage, she imagined, as she had imagined often in the past, the journey back into Buryan and then Penzance and Hayle and Truro and the bleak heights of Bodmin Moor. The sense of isolation deepened again. This was a different land; she'd always known that, but with Jack or the girls it had been deliciously different. Now, she was conscious of its dangers. If she fell at the top of the combe and was trapped between the cliff wall and the side of the house, she would probably die before anyone found her. She edged carefully along the muddy bank until the smoke from the fire told her exactly where she was, then she straightened and walked down the side of the combe and into the lamplit kitchen.

She told herself that isolation was synonymous with peace. She need not see Jack. She need not be constantly reminded of that scene in the Petersens' cottage at Sandhurst. She could sit down and begin to write again to Chatty. And then, tomorrow, she would write to Fay.

Nine

That night the winds came. They blew from the south-west so they should have been warm but there was ice in their breath which the radio told Hope was 'the wind-chill factor', made worse by their speed of around 90 m.p.h.

Hope was not asleep. Her feeling of isolation had been compounded by disorientation which effectively banished any sense of comfort. She lay on her back in the darkness, cold and uncomfortable, missing her electric blanket, angry with herself for not bringing a hot-water bottle, wondering whether she should go downstairs and search for a brick to heat in the dying fire. Somehow, now, her isolation seemed to mark her out; she was reminded of her mother telling her that during the blitz when Daddy was out with the ambulance crew, she had cowered beneath the stairs quite certain that the whole of the Luftwaffe were looking just for her. 'I think that is what typifies the true coward,' she had said objectively. 'It's a severe form of egotism.' When the wind first struck, tearing up the little valley and slamming into the house with the force of an express train, Hope knew exactly what her mother meant. At the top of the valley, exposed to all weathers, Penhailes Farm would be taking the brunt of the gale, yet Hope still felt the demon wind was looking for her alone.

She sat bolt upright in the double bed and while the gale shook the little house like a terrier shaking a rat, she fumbled for matches and lit the candle. For a moment, while the wind took breath, the flame burned tall and she could see the tiny room intact around her; then the flame cowered as the gale struck again; it guttered, making shadows jump crazily on walls and ceiling. She guarded it with cupped hands, but draughts were coming not only from the window but from under the roof itself. Even as she registered this, the corrugated iron lifted and with sickening force banged down above her head. She crouched, waiting for the plank ceiling to splinter, but other sounds took over – rattling windows and, downstairs, the heavy front door clacking against the lock as if someone were trying to get in. Then the wind gave a banshee shriek before lifting the roof again and hurling it down on to its supports.

She scrabbled out of bed and stumbled downstairs, terrified that the top of the house would fall in. The little scullery seemed solid; she stared at the black window, imagining the cliff face collapsing through it. Another furious gust girdled the house, and, trapped in the narrow space, pushed at the glass so that by the light of the candle she could actually see it bulging inwards. Yet it held.

The kitchen was taking the brunt of the wind, the door crashing madly against the bolt. She opened the lamp and lit it from the candle, put it on the floor and shoved the table hard against the door. The banging there ceased but only to make more space for the rattling windows and clanging roof. The cacophony was awful. She closed her eyes and put her hands over her ears for a moment before forcing herself to look around the ground floor for any damage. A steady drip in the sitting room announced a leak. She pulled some of the polythene bags over the furniture and sewing machine and found a bucket for the drips. Then she went back to resurrect the fire in the range. She felt better when that was burning, though the flames leaped and cowered more than the candle's. As the wind piled behind the house it created up and down draughts in the chimney which had the fire roaring one minute and dampened down to a glow the next. The trouble was, it was gobbling at her small fuel stocks; she had used a bucket of coal last evening and was already into the third. Two more to go and then the fire would have to go out. Somehow the thought was terrible. She riddled out ash, dampened it hissingly from the kettle and banked the fire at the back. Then she refilled the kettle and sat it squarely in the front, intending to make tea. There was never any time. Leaks sprang in the bedroom and, downstairs in the famous throne room, there was a sudden backwash from the cesspit and she was back and forth with towels and disinfectant, sobbing with effort and terror and disgust.

At 5.30 a.m. by her watch the wind seemed to abate slightly. At long last she made a pot of tea, not wanting it but knowing she must drink it, must sit down and ignore everything else. As she raised the cup to her mouth it shook uncontrollably, so that she had to hold it in both hands and drink the contents quickly. And as she replaced the cup in its saucer she heard the wind coming from the sea again, whipping the trees in the copse, screaming up the valley and meeting the resistance of the house against the cliff with the boom of a cannon. The iron roof replied with a pitiful clang, the fire sucked itself deeply into its own ash and then a hail of stones and grit was flung at the window, the flames leaped around the kettle and Hope pushed herself out of her chair to dampen the fire again.

By the time the late dawn revealed some of the devastation, she was bone tired. She had drawing-pinned the curtains to the window frames in a pathetic attempt to block flying glass if the wind broke through. It proved a mammoth task to get a knife beneath the pins and pull them out. But the glass had held and the banging roof was evidence that it was still there too. She peered through the filthy windows and saw that the valley was full of debris – branches and uprooted bushes; Widdershins had acted like a dam to all the pathetic flotsam of the night. Even as Hope stared, one of the alders from Marble Arch shot up the valley, slammed against the bedroom window and clawed itself to the ground. Broken windows were still a very real threat but she was too tired to replace the drawing pins. She dragged herself upstairs; the roof was clanging dismally now like the old-style fog warnings at sea. Buckets had overflowed and she took them downstairs and emptied them in the shallow sink and took them back again. She rolled up bedding and took it down to drape over chairs around the fire. Beneath it the mattress was dry. She found more polythene bags, emptied them of books and sewing materials and tucked them over and around the bed. Upstairs and down, the cottage looked as if it had been vandalized. She stared around dully then collapsed into a chair and as the wind steadied into a piercing whistle, she fell asleep.

A loud rapping on the window woke her and she started up with an exclamation.

'It's me!' Bella Penhailes's voice was loudly relieved to hear a sound from inside. 'Let me in, girl! This wind is lifting my skirt over my head!'

With a gasping laugh, Hope dragged the table away from the door and pulled back the bolts.

'Didn't think they'd hold.' She pushed a chair to the hearth. 'I'm so glad to see you – I never thought Widdershins would get through the night!'

'Damn Widdershins! What about you? You said you wouldn't be bringing Jack, but I thought the girls – someone – 'ud be with you. Why didn't you come to the farm?'

Hope shook her head. 'I couldn't leave. Anyway, I couldn't have stood against that wind.' She looked around the tiny room. Incredibly, everything was intact. After the awfulness of the night she felt, now, a terrific sense of belonging. She and Widdershins had survived together. She shook her head again, smiling wryly. 'I think I'm here for good now.'

Bella stopped fiddling with her clothes and stared for a moment, then said, 'Should'a' come down myself, but fact is, Gaffer's sick. Flu, I think. 'E 'ad pneumonia last winner so I don't let 'im out when weather's bad.'

Hope showed her concern, made more tea, fed the last of the coal on to the fire, asked Bella about more firing, milk, bread, butter, cheese.

' 'Ow long you staying?' Bella's eyes were sharp. 'You din't mean what you just said? You couldn't live 'ere. Not the year through. Jem were diff'rent. This was a palace after barns and hedgerows.'

Hope looked at the lean, dark face and said quietly, 'A palace for Jem. A haven for me.' She eased her aching back. 'Things have gone wrong, Bella. I'm on my own now. And this place is mine. It's in my name.' She smiled around at the draped bedding, the buckets, the ash-covered hearth. 'I had a feeling for it, you know. Immediately I saw it, it seemed to . . . belong to me. And me to it. I'll be all right – for goodness' sake don't worry about me.'

Bella did not give up without an argument but in the end she sighed sharply and stood up. 'Gotta get back. Gaffer will want breakfast, storm or no storm. Slates came off the dairy roof and I must get 'old of Perkins.' She too straightened with some difficulty. 'Meant to tell 'ee. We're on the telephone now. Thought it better when Gaffer were badly. So if you need to . . . get in touch . . . with anyone, you don't have to go into Buryan no more.' She felt the pillows experimentally. 'They're not too bad. Make up a bed down 'ere, why don't you? Sleep it off. When Perkins comes, I'll send 'im down to put some more rivets in that there roof. 'E can bring you some coal down too.' She glanced out of the window. 'Saw some logs, I wouldn't wonder.'

Hope remembered she had a saw. She had thrust it under the staircase last night. She could saw herself some wood. She waved goodbye to Bella and turned back into the kitchen. For the next two hours she put her house almost to rights. And then she slept.

It was still light when she roused to more banging. For a dreadful moment she thought the demon wind had come back but then there was a clumping sound over the kitchen and she realized someone was working on the roof. She glanced through to the scullery and, sure enough, a ladder was wedged between house and cliff face. The daylight was disappearing again and she hurried outside with a sudden resurgence of energy.

'Mr Perkins?' He was a typical Cornishman, stooped from years of working in the tin mines, small, whippy, strong. 'Thank you so much. I was asleep. Is there much damage?'

'Naw.' He paused to remove nails from between his teeth. 'Galvanized is either on or it's off. And yours is on!' He gave a mighty swipe with his hammer. 'And now it's on more than it were before!'

She laughed. 'Shall I make some tea?'

'Wouldn't mind,' he said. 'I'm going to put some o' that there mastic stuff inside. Kin I go through your trap?'

He shinned down the ladder, shouldered it and manoeuvred it expertly through the front door, the kitchen and up the narrow stairs. Hope lit the paraffin stove and boiled a kettle of water for tea, then found the hacksaw beneath the stairs and went outside to cut some wood. There was no sign of any coal so she snapped off twigs for kindling and sawed, tugged and broke up enough wood to have a fire during the evening. At some point Mr Perkins brought out two mugs of tea and took the hacksaw from her for a spell. She stood in the path of light that came from the open door, sipping her tea, watching her breath vaporize with the steam, feeling the exhilaration that came from physical exertion. And then the two of them dragged the firing to the side of the house where the old dilapidated part of the cottage hung grimly on to Jem's renovations.

'Used to be the sheep pen,' Mr Perkins panted. 'All this rubbish – could be useful. Wedge that old window acrorse 'ere, my maid. Keep some of the rain off the wood. Store your kindling inside.'

He left at six o'clock, promising he would come tomorrow with a load of logs. 'They'm in a state up at farm. Peter kin't be driving the tractor and Bella never learned. She's going to 'ave 'er 'ands full, what with animals and wind damage. I'll load up as much firing as I kin and drive down mid-mornin'. Now will 'ee be all right? I've rodded through the soil pipe and I reckon it'll be 'an'some now. You got bread and milk?'

'Everything I could possibly need. I know you

think I'm crazy, Mr Perkins, and I'm sorry I've made work for you, but this is my home now. I have to stay here.'

'I dun't think you're crazy, my girl. I think you'm very sensible. If you wuzn't sensible, you'd be up with Bella now a-crying and a-screaming. Good luck to you, I sez.'

'And good luck to you too, Mr Perkins.' Hope watched him walk crabwise against the rising wind and out of the light from the cottage. And then she began to lug some of her fuel supplies indoors.

That night, as the wind got up again, she made up her bed on the kitchen floor in front of the range and slept like the dead. The storm blew with only half the strength of the night before but there was plenty of rattling and banging. Nothing disturbed her until the fire went out and the cold seeped in, then she crawled out of the nest of duvets, shuffled into the throne room, fetched more blankets and pillows, pulled on another cardigan and curled up again. When she woke up it was dimly light and her watch showed seven thirty. She had slept since nine thirty the night before. She went into the scullery and lit the paraffin stove and made tea and while it brewed she lit the fire in the range. The joy of sitting propped by pillows, sipping tea in the fire glow, was almost animal. She was still frightened of the future, but the minute-by-minute battle of the night before had showed her clearly that there was no point in worrying about the future. To get through a day and a night was quite enough; in fact it was a triumph. She sipped her tea then leaned over and reached for the small transistor radio. The weatherman was forecasting gales in the south-west, speaking of the devastation of the early flowers. She made a sympathetic face over her mug. The Penhaileses went in for mixed farming and any crop failure was sure to affect them badly. And then she started to wonder whether she could make a garden on the sheltered side of her small combe. Just enough to support winter greens, and maybe some kidney beans and potatoes.

That day flew by and so did the next three. She stacked the logs which arrived by tractor and cleared the branches and leaves from around the house. The winds returned so that the sense of constantly battling with the elements stayed with her and pushed out all thoughts of Jack and the girls. On the third day, which she was surprised to discover was Sunday 24 January, she visited Peter Penhailes. He was swathed in a blanket and sitting next to the fire in their tiny parlour. His appearance shocked her out of her self-absorption.

He grinned up at her. 'Before you can say anything, my maid, I'm better than I was and not so well as I'm going to be!'

She smiled obediently and took the chair he offered opposite him. 'Bella is worried, Peter. You went to look at one of the cows. The cowshed isn't really the place for you at the moment.'

'She said Buttercup wasn't right. I 'ad to see for myself. Vet's coming tomorrow and 'e'll come inside and give me the verdick.' He grinned again. 'An' what about you? Down on the end of the headland in that weather. I've 'eard all about it from Perkins. Sawing up the trees, down in the cove yesty picking up driftwood.' He stopped grinning. 'You gunna be all right, my maid? On your own? 'Ow long for?'

She shook her head. 'I don't know, Peter. I'm not looking at the future, only tomorrow. I had to be by myself. My mother died on December 14th, you know. And the girls are both away so . . .'

'That friend 'o yourn. Aunty Andy, young Chatty did call her.'

'Gone away too.'

'She were a lovely apple with a rotten core. Set Jem back a bit, I kin tell you. We 'en't seen 'im since that 'appened.'

'What d'you mean?'

'Young Charity told us. She thought it were funny. But Jem is a deep one. Dun't expect he thought it were very funny. 'E guessed she'd tell us and 'e 'aven't showed 'is face since.'

'Oh . . .' She did not know what to say. Jem Trewint was deep, she knew that, but that he had been upset by Mandy seemed unlikely somehow.

There was a pause then he said heavily, 'I liked your ma. She were gentle and she were strong. And she will be missed. But he's a good man is Jack Langley. An' he thinks the world of you, my maid.'

She shook her head again. 'I don't know, Peter. Maybe he does, maybe he doesn't.' She looked up into the thin face and remembered that Peter had fished with Jack several times. They had shared whole days together. She said,

'I don't like him, Peter. In fact . . . I'm sorry . . . I can't bear to think of him.'

'Can you tell me what he's done?'

'No.'

'All right then. He's hurt you. Wounded you deep maybe. An' you've come to Widdershins to be healed.'

'Not really. I've come to Widdershins to learn how to live again. Properly. Myself. If I am wounded then I don't really expect to heal. I would like the wound to be cauterized though, then I can forget it.' She heard the bitterness in her voice and for a moment was ashamed.

He was silent for longer this time; it was almost dark in the little room. He said at last, 'That dun't sound much like a forgiving time. Dun't forgiveness come before forgetting?'

The door opened and Bella came in and flicked on the light. Hope blinked; she was un-used already to the harshness of electric light. She said, 'I don't think forgiveness comes into it, Peter.'

Bella said, 'Cup a tea, my 'an'some? And a slice of heavy cake. I got one for you to take back and half a dozen eggs and the flour you wanted and some yeast. Did you say you got salt and sugar?'

'And a lot of tinned food too, Bella. I certainly don't reckon on starving!'

They sat around the fire and Bella told a tale about Perkins's sister who had married into the gentry and then produced a baby who was strangely dark-skinned.

'She do swear it's a throwback to one of the Godolphins born the wrong side of the blanket and sired by their black page! But there's an Asian family run an Indian takeaway in the village and Fennie Perkins always loved her Balti curries!'

They all laughed and Bella said that Hope had done the gaffer a power of good and she must come as often as she could bear it because he'd take more notice of her than he would of his own wife. So, scolding, she ushered Hope into the kitchen and loaded her with provisions and said more soberly that the doctor wanted him to go into the new hospital at Truro for a proper rest. 'It's a toss-up whether he'll worry more being away from the farm or on it!' She tried to laugh.

Hope said, 'Look, you mustn't let me be a nuisance. If you need any help let me know but otherwise—'

'You ain't no nuisance, girl!' Bella looked for a moment as if she might hug Hope but then thought better of it. 'It's a real treat for me to have another woman handy-like. An' the gaffer – he d'like to see you. Always said you reminded 'im of some film star he'd seen on a race course.'

'*National Velvet*,' Hope said automatically, then, seeing Bella's bewilderment, added quickly, 'And I'll come up when I need milk, Bella. Or if I can't make a decent loaf of bread!'

They both laughed and Bella swung the gate shut after her and Hope shone her torch ahead of her feet and began the slow trudge down to Widdershins. For an instant the terror of that first day caught at her throat and then she forced herself to stop and look at the clouds racing over the moon and the sea shouldering itself inexorably into the cove on her left while the wind-flattened furze rose to the top of the headland on her right. She thought: this is my world now, the weather, the sky and the sea and the land; friends . . . and foes.

The winds fluctuated but did not go away and the local radio news told of spoiled cabbage fields, early potato haulms blackened and wind-burned, the first of the flower crops decimated. Another of the Cornish mines closed down; no cabbage cutters needed this year; more unemployed. Sometimes Hope felt guilty at her gradually won peace of mind. Her isolation still marked her out – at times she felt she was the only person in the land; but that made life special and important rather than fearful. She got up at first light and went to bed three hours after dark. When it rained she worked on getting the inside of the cottage tidy and organized; she tried to make bread – and tried again; she sewed new curtains because the drawing pins had ripped the ones that had in any case hung there for the past twenty years. When the rain stopped she went outside and collected wood and stacked it carefully at the end of the cottage where once had been the sheep pen. She found an old door leaning there and each night she put it against the outside of the kitchen window and wedged it in place with rocks. It protected the glass and made the room warmer. She hung a blanket at the door and with the odds and ends from the new curtains she began to appliqué moon and star shapes over it. There was a feeling of being under siege.

She stacked her tinned food on the scullery shelves, tea and coffee on the mantelpiece above the fire to keep dry. When she unrolled her bedding at night and snuggled into it, she would make mental lists of future needs. Books – lots of books; batteries for the radio and her torch and perhaps a larger torch; a bigger store of paraffin and a hot-water bottle. Two hot-water bottles . . . and some aspirin. She must not be ill. That would wreck everything.

Two weeks after she arrived, with the forecast of a sunny morning but rain spreading from the west in the afternoon, she visited Peter. He was no better and still refusing a hospital bed. She limited her time with him to half an hour because his breathing deteriorated when he talked, then she bought a decent loaf of bread from Bella and trudged home as the promised storm clouds started to blow in from the Scillies. She decided to use the last of the dry weather to saw and stack more wood in the sheep pen and was just hauling a broken branch to the sawhorse when two figures appeared on the neck of the headland. She was already so used to solitude that to see anyone was a surprise; two people could well be a threat. She thought wildly that she must get a dog. And then the smaller figure waved madly and she knew it was Fay.

They met at a run on the brow above the cottage and grabbed at each other, both weeping uncontrollably. Martin stood by them, patting them alternately, smiling, saying, 'Come on now. Cheer up.' Fay blubbered into her mother's neck, 'I didn't mean to do this. Cry and hug and things. I was so *angry* with you.

And now . . . now I'm just so p-plea . . . sed to see you.'

Hope blubbered back, 'I know my letter was hopeless. Like me. Hopeless. But I didn't want to interrupt your studies.'

They might have gone on like that for some time with Martin standing on one leg and then the other, but the inevitable rain began and Hope ushered them inside, laughing and embarrassed, scooped her bedding up and into the sitting room and put a match to the fire.

'My God, don't you keep the fire in?' Fay took the kettle into the scullery and pumped some water into it. 'Mummy, it's January! You'll get hypothermia!'

'I was out all morning. At the farm. And cutting wood this afternoon. I'm afraid I might run out of fuel. If the weather closes in.' She fed sticks on to the fire basket, took the kettle from Fay and wedged it on to the trivet. 'You get obsessional about the fire. You hoard it, protect it. It's more than just heat. It – it's a symbol of something or other!' She laughed. 'Anyway, I've laid the spare blankets as insulation in the roof space and done what I can about the draughts down here. It gets warm very quickly.' She wiped her eyes with the back of her hand and smiled. 'I really am very cosy here, Fay. You mustn't worry.'

'Well I do. I am.' Fay sat at the table with a thump and took Martin's hand. He held on to her and pulled out a chair for himself. Fay tightened her mouth against more tears and looked around. 'Last time I was here it was with Gran. The Female Four. Remember?'

'Of course.' Hope fetched mugs and the teapot. 'It's one of the reasons I came. I wanted to turn the clock back, I suppose.' She smiled at Martin. 'Sorry about all this, Martin. You drove Fay down here, did you?'

'We drove together,' he amended carefully.

'Yes. Good. Did you . . . was it . . . all right at home with your parents? New Year and everything?'

'Traditional. I think Fay enjoyed it as much as possible. In the circumstances.' He sounded just faintly . . . disapproving?

Fay said, 'We went back to Sheffield for the start of term. I rang home. You had taken Chatty to Paris. Sounded marvellous. But I guessed it had been . . . difficult. I mean, I know you and Dad would have preferred her to stay at school and go on to art college or something. So I guessed Henrik and Mandy were behind it.'

Hope looked up from pouring tea, surprised. 'Why?'

'Well, they've always been our . . . sort of . . . mentors, haven't they?'

'Oh, I see. In that way. Yes.'

'Then I rang again. Only a week later. And you'd gone and they'd gone and there was no phone down here and apparently no phone in South Africa and Dad sounded not a bit like Dad. And then I got your letter and then Chatty rang me and was going to give up the job and come over and I said not to do that because I could do it. So I was going to take a train to Gloucester and Martin said he'd borrow a car and drive me.'

Hope pushed mugs slowly across the table

and sat down in front of hers. Apart from the crackling of the fire there was no sound; they were waiting for an explanation.

She said, 'I'm so glad Chatty didn't throw everything up.'

'So was Dad.'

Hope sighed. 'How was Dad? Did you stay at Horsley?'

'Yes, of course. Dad is in a terrible state. He's on the phone nearly all the time. Henrik tied up the businesses so tightly that he seems to have left Dad with nothing.'

'Oh God.' But she sensed Fay's criticism. She realized that from everyone else's point of view her departure must seem like desertion.

'Yes. I loved him, Mum. I loved Henrik and I trusted him – I would have trusted him with my life.'

Hope nodded. 'I think you could have done that. He loved you too. He loved all of us. That's why they stayed so long, risked so much.'

'But what they're doing . . . it's theft! They're destroying us!' She leaned forward. 'They're realizing all the assets, Mum. It's all – somehow – in their names. They're just . . . taking it! All of it. And you're letting that happen!'

'I can't do anything, Fay.' Hope was genuinely surprised. 'I'm no businesswoman – you know that.'

'It's been one big scam! And you're leaving Dad to fend on his own . . .' Fay began to sob again and Martin put a protective arm around her.

Hope stared at the two of them, so obviously a

couple now. She said quietly, 'What did Dad tell you? About us.'

'Nothing that made sense. Just that you were so grieved about Gran and about Mandy—'

'So he *told* you about Mandy?'

'Well of course. That she wouldn't even say goodbye to Chatty in person! That she delivered a few home truths on the phone. That you couldn't take it!'

Hope closed her eyes for a moment and then opened them wide and said, 'And what did you think of that? What did you think about me coming down here?' She held up a hand as Fay began to speak. 'Martin. Tell me the truth.'

He waved his free hand helplessly. 'We thought . . . perhaps . . . some kind of nervous breakdown. Your mother, Fay, Chatty and then your best friends . . .' He stopped waving and reached across the table. 'Nothing to be ashamed of! You feel totally isolated. Grief will do strange things – and sometimes we turn against those we love the most . . .'

She could almost hear them discussing her. Fay's incredulity, Martin's efforts to find justification. She stood up abruptly and went to make up the fire. She watched the flames lick around the new log and turn blue.

'A frost tonight,' she said conversationally. 'That's what Bella says. When the fire's blue there's frozen dew.'

'Mummy, *please*! I'm not a baby. What's happening to you?'

Hope looked back at them and saw their disapproval. Quite suddenly there was no longer any point in trying to protect them. 'All right,

I'll tell you. Dad has been having . . . what is it called? . . . an affair . . . with Mandy. Henrik probably arranged it because he's impotent and it's his way of making sure Mandy has some sexual pleasure. And maybe he gets a kick out of it too. They are – were – after all – the complete voyeurs, weren't they?' She felt the usual bile in her mouth and went abruptly into the scullery. When she came back Fay and Martin were wearing identical expressions of shock. She said, 'I'm sorry. Perhaps I shouldn't have told you. Dad probably doesn't want you to know. But you have to accept that I am not coming back. And in any case I don't know why we have to pretend any more. Maybe it's a question of protecting you – that's why your father hasn't said anything – but living here . . . facing reality . . . makes all that seem puny. Almost unimportant. Except that – it can't be yet, can it? Otherwise I wouldn't be sick every time I remember seeing them.'

Fay swallowed visibly. 'You saw them?' she whispered.

'That doesn't matter. Please don't ask me about it – please don't talk about it. Perhaps I should have stayed on and tried to patch things up – I couldn't. He said it was over but there's nothing to stop him going to South Africa. Now. If I'm right out of the picture. And if he doesn't go . . . I can't go back. That's all there is to it.' She came back to the table, sat down and took a sip of tea. 'This is how I have reacted. You must just accept that. It's probably not a very courageous way to behave, but I am not a courageous person.'

There was a long, long silence. Hope wondered

if it would go on for always and they would get up and leave without saying another word. But at last Martin cleared his throat.

'You are courageous,' he said. 'We saw some of the damage done by the winds. And when we left the car at Penhailes Farm, Mrs Penhailes told us how you'd stuck it out that first night. That takes courage.'

She shrugged briskly. 'Of a sort. Of course. The other kind . . . living with a man I no longer like or respect . . . that's different.'

Fay said quietly, 'Poor Dad.'

Hope looked at her for a moment and Fay stared back. Her eyes were intensely blue and her blond hair made her look Nordic.

Hope said in the same quiet voice, 'Poor Henrik. Dad messed it up for himself. Henrik had to stand by and watch it happen. He loves you, Fay.'

Fay, with the cruelty of youth, shrugged her shoulders.

Martin cleared his throat. 'I feel I've got no right here—' he patted Fay's hand as she began to protest, '—and now is probably not the time to say it, but I'd like your mother to know, Fay.' He looked at Hope. 'We're living together, Mrs Langley. And one day we'll get married. Is that all right with you?'

Fay was suddenly pink, her chin thrust forward determinedly.

Hope laughed. 'More than all right,' she said. 'I was afraid that my mess might put you off!' She stood up. 'There's nothing stronger than tea in the house. But I bought a proper loaf from Bella this morning – I've been making my own bread but it's so hard! Let's have bread and cheese and another pot of tea. And I think I brought a tin of biscuits – we could open them.' She leaned over and put one hand on Fay's cheek, the other on Martin's. 'Listen. It's not the end of the world. Think about it. If Mandy and Henrik leave us without a bean . . . well, that's how we started. Maybe it's better that way. A clean break. A really fresh start!'

Fay was smiling with a trembling mouth, her eyes full of tears. Martin had his arm around her shoulders, holding her tightly. Suddenly he held out his free arm and Hope went into it without embarrassment.

Ten

It was all so odd, the way the whole topic of Jack
and Mandy and Henrik was swept under the
carpet. Hope had been doing just that ever since
it happened, but she had not expected Fay to be
able to do the same.

They left the next morning. Fay explained
that it would take about ten hours to reach
Sheffield. 'The car overheats now and then and
we have to stop and let it cool down.'

From that Hope gathered that they did not
intend to call at Horsley on the return journey.
They were respecting Hope's wishes not to talk
about it, and they did not want Jack to talk about
it either.

As the daylight waned that Sunday afternoon,
Hope had made a meal from packets and tins
and sorted out extra bedding from the sitting
room while Fay had given Martin a quick tour of
the little valley, the depleted copse, the swollen
rill and the view down into the cove. He had
been impressed, not only by the wild beauty of
the place but by its obvious vulnerability.

'Yes, but normally it's so sheltered.' Fay
was trying to reassure Martin, but also herself.

Widdershins was no longer the idyllic summer place she remembered. 'The Penhaileses put the cottage up long before the war for one of their workers and when Dad bought it, he had it repaired.' She gave Hope a quick sideways glance. 'Jem Trewint did it, didn't he, Mummy?'

Hope nodded briefly, not bothering to tell Fay that the repairs had been instigated and paid for by her sewing. She felt no relief from having told Fay the truth; in a way she regretted doing so. She should have left that to Jack.

When they had cleared away the supper things, they pushed back the furniture and made up beds as best they could. Then Hope packed the fire down with dampened ash and cinders and as the rain drummed relentlessly on the iron roof they rolled themselves into duvets and tried to settle down. She had wondered whether she should offer them the bedroom which was watertight now, but she'd left it to them and they had assumed they would sleep downstairs. She doubted whether any of them would be able to sleep at all, but within an hour their steady breathing told her that however worried they were, they had succumbed to the rigours of the journey. She smiled wryly to herself. She and Fay were very much alike; they pushed unpleasant things to the backs of their minds, ignored them, found something else to keep them busy. Wasn't that why she herself had come to Widdershins, where the day-to-day effort needed just to survive filled her thoughts completely?

In spite of the noise, both of the young people slept until dawn. Fay lay as she always had, arms upflung, head turned slightly, hair straying across her face. Martin curled himself neatly like a cat, but by the dim glow from the range Hope saw that at some time during the night his arm had emerged from his duvet and draped itself protectively across Fay.

She walked with them to the car and waved them off with mixed feelings. She could tell Fay was still totally bewildered and torn; anxious for her mother but desperate to get away from the whole problem. 'No, no breakfast, Mummy. We'll stop somewhere. Just a cup of tea – honestly!' Yet she had hated leaving her mother too. 'Please come with us. We'll help you to clear up and everything. You could live in Sheffield – get a job . . .'

Hope had laughed. 'I've *got* a job! I've never been so busy in my life!'

And then they were gone and she played her usual game of following them in her mind along the farm track to the lane which led eventually to Buryan and civilization. She wondered whether they would talk about her and whether Martin might say something like, we haven't heard your father's side . . . it's always six of one and half a dozen of the other . . . But Fay knew Mandy. Surely Fay would realize that Mandy had to be responsible for what had happened.

Hope let herself into the cottage and stood for a moment staring at the cold teapot and the three mugs. It was the first time she had not laid all the blame on Jack. For a split second the memory of Jack and Mandy slid into her mind and this time she stopped looking at Jack and saw Mandy . . . that tight smile of triumph on the upturned face, the gripping hands . . . Hope went quickly into the throne room and crouched like an animal.

And then she stood up and took a deep breath and planned her day.

In the middle of February it seemed as if spring had arrived. On St Valentine's day – a Sunday this year – Hope scrambled down the cliff path into the cove. The tide was out and the old *Mirabelle* lay on her side in the cave like an exhausted whale. The sea sparkled crazily and small wavelets filled the pools and washed around the standing rocks caressingly. Hope took off shoes and socks and rolled up her jeans to paddle. It was cold but absolutely delicious and she laughed aloud as her toes half sank in the sand. On a sudden impulse she ran up the beach and stripped off her outer clothing and – ridiculously modest in bra and pants – ran straight into the sea without giving herself time to think. She fell into it when she was knee-deep and floundered out into deeper water shouting with a kind of pagan joy. It was a ten-minute immersion at the most; she knew by that time that she was getting dangerously cold and she stumbled back up the beach and put on her jeans and sweater over her wet body, picked up her other things and ran as far as she could up the path before hanging on to a rock and fighting for breath. But she was warm. The slow, panting climb back to the top, the warm wash-down in the scullery, the clean clothes, the breakfast tea and toast, were all rewards and relished more than usual. With an enormous sense of well-being she hung out washing and then went on with the latest job which was clearing her vegetable patch. Already the bank between the cottage and the heathland was full of snowdrops. She lifted them carefully to transplant, then forked into the springy turf and started the endless task of removing the stones. She had taken advice from Peter about planting. Many local farmers were replanting damaged early cabbages and cauliflowers and Hope intended to walk into Buryan and catch a bus into Penzance to buy plants as well as carrot and parsnip seed. Peter had let her have some lettuce seed which she was raising in the sitting room and she had trays of cress which she regularly put into sandwiches. She promised herself that as soon as she felt able to sleep upstairs again she would drag the sewing machine into the kitchen and begin to make something she might sell. But the fascination of making Widdershins into a home filled her days. When she ran out of soap and tinned food it might be a different story.

She worked until she was hungry again. It was two o'clock and the sun was still strong but before she could make her usual lunch of tea and sandwiches, the sound of the tractor interrupted everything. Mr Perkins had said he might manage a trailer of coal, as much as six hundredweight. She ran down to the narrow space between the cliff and the house. She had wedged logs in here to make a bunker and covered it with more polythene. She rolled back the cover and went back to the front of the cottage. Sure enough, there was Mr Perkins but no trailer on the back of the tractor.

'Came to take you up the 'ouse!' he called. 'Peter ain't too good. Asking for you.'

She wasted no time in questions but closed and locked the door and tore up the rise to the tractor. Clinging to the back of Mr Perkins's metal seat she jolted with every molehill and rabbit hole. He had propped open the farm gate and drove straight up to the back door of the farmhouse.

' 'E's in bed. Go on up, my maid. I'll wait 'ere for amblance.'

She ran through the kitchen and up the back stairs. In the big front bedroom, Peter was propped high among pillows, an ancient cardigan around his shoulders. Bella was supporting him as he coughed helplessly over a bowl.

'Brought up blood,' she said briefly. 'At least 'e d'know 'e got to go in whether 'e likes it or not.'

Hope hovered helplessly, willing him to breathe again between each bout of coughing. When at last he lifted his head, his eyes closed with exhaustion, she could see sweat beading across his forehead.

Bella said, ''E wanted to see you. So now you're 'ere you can just 'old 'is shoulders a minute while I get a few things together.' Her voice was curt with anxiety; she moved to make room for Hope and did not take away her arm until Hope's was in place. Hope's only physical contact with either of the Penhaileses had been a brief handshake and for a moment she felt embarrassment for Peter rather than herself.

And then, as she realized the thinness of the shoulders and the heaviness of the head as it fell against her neck, a rush of tenderness filled her and she cradled him protectively, easing the pillows into his back with her elbow and making small murmuring sounds of reassurance.

He stayed very still within her arm while Bella rushed around the bedroom opening and shutting drawers and muttering to herself. And then as the sound of the arriving ambulance came from outside and she went down to see the paramedics, he stiffened slightly.

'It's all right, Peter,' Hope soothed. 'Nothing to worry about. Bella will come with you. They'll give you some oxygen and you'll feel better straight away.'

He whispered something and she bent her head to listen.

'Wanted to see you, girl. Look after Bella. Won't you?'

The thought of anyone looking after Bella would have been funny in other circumstances. Hope swallowed. 'I . . . I'll do my best.'

He took three shallow breaths then whispered, 'Thankee, Hope. You'm strong. An' she do need someone to lean on.'

The paramedics in their orange jackets came swiftly into the room. Hope was moved kindly but firmly aside and a mask was put over Peter's face. His eyes closed again, this time with relief. Hope thought he was smiling behind the mask. They swathed him in a blanket and strapped him into a chair; a drip appeared from somewhere. Hope followed the entourage downstairs and waited by the back door.

Bella had her top coat on; her hair was wild. She felt in a pocket and rammed on a knitted hat. 'Get the keys off Perkins, will 'ee? Lock up for me. Dun't know when I'll be back.'

'Listen. Will you let me drive in after you? I can bring you home later, when you have settled Peter.'

Bella's face almost crumpled then. She said, 'It would be that good to see you. Truro. You know 'ow to get there?'

'Yes.' Hope had never been to Truro, never driven Peter's ancient Wolseley.

As the ambulance drew away, bumping over the ruts in the lane like the *Mirabelle* taking the waves under her bow, she turned back to the barn where Mr Perkins had donned Bella's overall and was already milking the four cows. She glanced at her watch; it was gone four o'clock. She wondered how long he could stay but he anticipated any questions.

'I'll 'ang on 'ere till you gets back,' he volunteered. 'Don't worry about locking up. Keys are on a 'ook just inside the kitchen door – take the car keys off. Bella don't drive, so car en't bin out since Peter was took bad.'

It took a long time to start the car. The petrol gauge registered a full tank so she pulled out the choke and doubtless flooded the engine and then had to fidget impatiently for a timed five minutes before trying again. This time it fired and died on her. Belatedly, she found out how to lift the bonnet and checked the oil and as if grateful for this consideration the engine fired again and then settled into a steady chug. She said aloud, 'Peter would be proud of you. Now it's up to me, I suppose.' But it was surprisingly easy to reverse the big old car into the yard and then out into the lane. It continued to chug amiably while she went back and closed the gate, then it pitched and tossed down the lane with good-tempered rolls, quite used to such conditions. It was only when she was driving through Buryan that she noticed her hands on the steering wheel. They were covered in mud, her nails dirt-rimmed, from picking out the stones on her little vegetable patch. And Peter had entrusted Bella to her!

She drove carefully past the reservoirs and through Penzance and then she was on the A30 and following the signs to Truro and the big new hospital at Treliske. She slid into the biggest parking space she could find and spent valuable moments checking where the lights and wiper controls were for the return journey, then locking up Peter's precious car before making her way to the reception desk.

There was a terrible feeling of déjà vu as she waited for the girl at the desk to find out what was happening to Peter. This had all happened before, last November. Suddenly Hope realized that it was exactly two months since her mother's death and so much had happened in those two months – and was still happening. She shivered and wished herself back at Widdershins. She'd had nothing to eat since her after-swim toast and probably wasn't fit to be in charge of anything or anyone . . . Except that she had promised Peter she would look after Bella. Then the girl turned from the screen, smiled and said, 'He's in the special care unit, but Mrs Penhailes is on her way down to the waiting room.' She gave Hope directions. 'She might not want to go home immediately of course. They could have asked her to leave while they made him comfortable.'

Hope nodded: it was consoling to think of Peter being made comfortable.

Bella did not find it in the least consoling. 'I just 'ope they know what they're doing,' she said when she joined Hope five minutes later. 'All them tubes. An' 'e's 'ardly lying down! They got 'im propped up on an ironing board or some such contraption! Comfortable it ain't!'

Hope went so far as to take her hand; it said a lot for Bella's distress that she did not reject it. And so they waited while the staff did their best and then Bella went back and saw that in fact Peter was more comfortable than he had been for a long time and already drowsy.

'He's got his own special nurse. Introduced 'erself to me, she did. "I shall be looking after your husband through the night," she says. Nice smile. 'Er name is Angela. She comes from Malpas.' Bella made a grunting sound which Hope gathered was approving. 'Peter got an aunty lives that way. They might have a few acquaintances in common. When he gets to talking.'

Hope squeezed the acquiescent hand and asked what was going to happen next.

'Well, 'e's settled for the night. An' the doctor 'as looked at 'im. An' 'e'll come and 'ave a word in a minute.' She sounded suddenly fearful. 'You'll stay with me, won't you, girl?'

'I will indeed, Bella. And then we'll get back

and have something to eat and I can bring you to see him tomorrow.'

Bella said, 'What about the milking? Perkins was repairing the barn. Will 'e 'ave done it?'

'He'd started before I left.'

'That sister of 'is. Fennie. Perkins and 'is wife is looking after 'er cos 'er 'usband put 'er out. That baby *was* started at the Indian takeaway, it all came out later. Perkins will want to get back 'ome—'

'He said he would wait until we got back. Try not to worry.'

'I don't know what I'd do without you . . .'

Luckily the doctor came along then and saved Hope the chore of giving the reassurance she needed herself. But as he talked of tests and X-rays Hope knew just how Bella was feeling. Three short months ago she had listened to similar words from the consultant who had examined her mother at Gloucester Royal Hospital. With a sinking heart she recognized the phrases; Peter was younger than Milly had been, much younger. He stood a chance. They could operate. But before the tests had even happened, the three of them knew that he had cancer.

Hope spent that night at the farm and the next morning before it was light she went with Bella into the barn and had her first lesson in hand-milking cows. She had hardly slept on the lumpy horsehair mattress in the bedroom that had been used by Bella's mother. After the cosiness of her nest of duvets on the floor of the kitchen, it was cold and unwelcoming on the single iron bedstead. She watched, bleary-eyed, as Bella rested her forehead against Buttercup's flank and gently washed the udders and then began the rhythmical milking.

'She's used to me now. When I took over from Gaffer . . . back 'fore Christmas it were, she did kick the bucket over reg'lar. I tole 'er 'ow it was. Gaffer 'ad the flu and if she wanted 'im to do it again she had to put up with me for a spell.'

Hope listened to Bella's deliberately monotonous voice and could have leaned against the other flank and dropped off. She longed for Widdershins and her solitary way of life. There seemed little prospect of resuming it, however. That morning the doctor saw them again and put it to them that, as soon as Peter was strong enough, he would advise an operation. The X-ray showed a growth in the left lung. It might be possible to remove that lung altogether in order to stop any spread of the cancerous cells to the right side.

Bella did not break down. She went in to see Peter with a smile on her face and it was not until they were driving home that she said grimly, 'A farm isn't no place for a man with one lung. But 'e won't go anywhere else.'

Hope swallowed. 'Could you get someone in, Bella? A manager perhaps.'

'We got a few cows and a few sheep . . . early potatoes, kale . . . we don't need a manager, girl. We need a worker.'

'There are agencies, aren't there? For seasonal workers?'

'Aye.' Bella was silent for a long time then she said heavily, 'Nothing for it. I'll have to ring round. Not all the cabbages went with the storm. We need cabbage cutters for a start.'

But Bella had left it too late. So the next day, before they went to Treliske, the two of them took the sharp curved knives, donned gloves and went into the field partially protected by the Cornish stone hedges. Between them they filled six crates by midday and wedged them in the boot and on the back seat of the Wolseley.

'The wholesalers are down by the docks,' Bella told Hope. 'But gen'lly we can offer them trailers full. I dun't know what to tell you to do, girl. Could be you won't get rid of 'em.'

Hope said, 'Well, we'll have tried, Bella. That's all we can do. Give Peter my love and tell him everything is fine. That will do him more good than anything the doctors give him!'

Bella smiled her grim smile and walked slowly up to the main door, her back bent. Hope waved and drove off again, her own back aching sympathetically. She had already determined not to go to Penzance; there were shops in Truro after all. She had no idea how one sold fresh produce so she parked the car as near to the shops as she could get and went straight into the biggest supermarket she saw. She had heard that the staff in such places were specially trained and she hoped they would not be as dismissive as she thought the local Cornish shopkeepers would be. There was a large vegetable section just inside the automatic doors and she went up to the first assistant she saw there and asked who was in charge of buying vegetables. The young man obviously thought she had a complaint. 'I am the manager actually,' he said. 'How can I help you?'

She said, 'I have parked my car about five minutes away. Inside it I have six crates of cabbages which survived the storms last month. Would you be interested in buying them?'

He looked startled. 'We have wholesalers, madam. I don't think the company would approve of me bypassing the usual channels.'

'These were cut just this morning. And when the schools come out and the next customers come in, surely fresh cabbages would be a point of interest?' She wondered what she was talking about. But he nodded.

'I'm sure they would. And I'm sure they would sell. But you have to realize that our wholesalers would be put out – and that's mild – if we got our supplies elsewhere.'

'Would your wholesalers be interested then?' she asked. She heard her own voice with amazement. She could only do this for Bella and Peter.

'Possibly. But they are in London. The vegetables come up by road each morning.'

'What a waste of time when the stuff is grown on your own doorstep!'

'I'm sorry. That's how it is.' He looked genuinely regretful.

She tried one more time. 'Do you know if there's anyone local who would take our stuff?' She bit her lip. 'I've never been to Truro before.'

He was surprised again and she found herself explaining about Peter. 'I live nearby and we cut the cabbages and I thought I could get rid of them while his wife visits him but I can't really go all the way into Penzance . . .' She ground to a halt and smiled apologetically. 'Sorry. You can see I'm new to all this.'

He said, 'My uncle keeps a general grocery down by the river. Behind the cathedral. He might take a couple of crates. No more.'

She was delighted. 'That would be marvellous. Tell me his name and where to go—'

'Hang on, I'll phone him. He reckons firms like this one will put him out of business. This could be a gesture of – of – reconciliation!' He grinned, glad to be helping. She went with him into an office alongside the check-out desks and pretended not to listen as the young manager tried to persuade his uncle that this was the right thing to do.

'Don't you see, Matthew! This is something you can do and we can't! Put a couple of crates outside the shop – people will buy because fresh greens are so short just now – then they'll come in and get something else . . . Well, seems to me you got to look for gaps in the market these days . . . Yes, as a matter of fact that *is* what they taught us on the course. Makes sense to me. And if you weren't such a stubborn old . . . You will? Shall she drive down to you? Yes . . . a lady. Well . . . youngish.' He turned his head away. 'I think you could say that. A bit like Elizabeth Taylor.' There were a few more exchanges then he put the receiver down. 'Straight down Lemon Street, Mrs . . . ?'

'Langley,' Hope supplied. 'Hope Langley.'

'Follow the river and you'll see the shop on a corner. Matthew Hampton is his name – it's above the shop. He calls it Hampton Court. Bit of a joker. I'm John Hampton.'

Hope smiled. 'I can't thank you enough, Mr Hampton—'

'He can only manage two crates.'

'I know, but it's such a good start. I was beginning to think I'd have to take them back to the farm.'

They parted almost like old friends and Hope decided she liked Truro. She drove immediately to Hampton Court and was greeted by an enormous jovial character in a fisherman's smock who grinned at her approvingly, stacked the cabbages, paid her a fiver for each crate and gave her directions to another shop just outside the little city. They bought a crate but knew of no other possible outlets. She drove back into the middle of town, intending to get a cup of tea before returning for Bella. And there, getting out of a battered truck, was Jem Trewint.

She paused, terribly tempted to pretend she had not seen him. Her last sight of him had been with Mandy and somehow he brought the very essence of Mandy with him. But it was too late; his face lit with pleasure and he came up with outstretched hand, pumped hers and – of course – asked after her mother and the girls.

She told him briefly about Milly. 'Yes. It was awful. But of course she was over eighty and she did so well, right up to . . . anyway, both girls are away. Fay is at university reading English and Charity is in Paris hoping to become a fashion designer.' He waited and after a long pause she said, 'Our friends, the Petersens . . . Mandy was with us last summer . . . they have left too. A job in South Africa, I believe.'

'You believe? You're not in touch?'

'No.'

'I see. Sorry. I thought you were . . . well,

close.' He made a gesture, half turning. 'Would you like a cup of tea somewhere? Not if you're in a hurry of course.'

'I have to pick up Bella from Treliske hospital before dark. I was going to get a cup of tea anyway.' They fell into step naturally. 'I've not been to Truro before. I like it very much.'

'But what is wrong with Bella?'

She told him about Peter. Which meant explaining that she was living in Widdershins. He asked no questions about that but when they were seated at a plastic-topped table he said abruptly, 'You know I made a fool of myself with your friend? I think Chatty saw us. So I didn't turn up again. Sorry.'

Her eyes widened and then she looked down at the table. 'That's all right. You didn't have to tell me.'

'I didn't turn up at Penhailes either. That's why I didn't know about Peter.'

'I see. I hadn't thought about that.'

'They've been good to me. Both of them. I had a chance to repay them.'

She glanced up; his black eyes were miserable. She said, 'I'd forgotten how direct you are.'

'No point in being anything else, is there? I'm a simple man. I want to be close to the earth and the sea and the sky and when I get time try to put things into paint. When I saw you and Jack, back in '67, it was wonderful. To me, you were Adam and Eve. I enjoyed repairing the cottage. Felt I was helping the two of you to live an idyll. Then Mandy Petersen exploded into everything. I knew it was . . . wrong. Stupid. Spoiled it for me. I thought it might spoil it for you.' He shook his head and his straggled hair caught on the collar of his dungarees. 'So I kept away from the headland. I shouldn't have done that.'

Hope felt her face flush; not only with embarrassment but with sheer distaste.

She said in a stifled voice, 'I'd rather not talk about it.'

'All right. Sorry. I'd better be on my way. There's a market here on a Friday. I help out and sometimes I sell a picture.' He finished his tea. 'Give Bella my best. I might pop in and see Peter.'

She took a breath. 'You could help him now, actually. At the farm. He's going to have an operation to remove his lung. If you could spare the time . . .'

He was about to stand up but he relapsed into the chair. 'But Jack . . . surely you've left Jack at the farm?'

She stared at the cruet. 'Jack's not with me. Work . . . And so on. Bella and I have been quite . . . busy. We cut those cabbages this morning – I've sold three crates but there's more in the back of the car. There's an awful lot to do and I haven't been back to Widdershins since Sunday. The milk will be sour . . . I just wondered if you could come back with us now. Perhaps.' She shook her head and forced a smile as she looked up. 'It's too much to ask – I know that. You've got a room in Penzance, didn't you say? A studio? And you come here and sell paintings—'

He said, 'I'll go and see the chap. About the stall. And I'll met you back at the car park.'

He did not wait for a reply and she watched him manoeuvre around the small tables and stride off down the street and wondered if this was really a gift from above or whether it meant more complications. Was he still in love with Mandy? Was this a connection she just did not want? She thought longingly of her solitary life at Widdershins; somehow, although she had left her world, another world seemed to be coming at her.

She left the little café and crossed the square to the cathedral. The long nave stretched before her and the sudden peace after the hubbub of the little city was strangely moving. She sat for a while in a pew at the back and stared down to the chancel steps and the altar beyond. Was there a message for her here? Was this what she was trying to do – create an area of calm in the middle of life? Wouldn't it be wonderful – and easy – if her mother suddenly appeared and sat by her and told her what to do . . . and her father the other side. She waited, almost holding her breath. Then an elderly couple went down the aisle and he dropped his walking stick and couldn't bend to pick it up, so Hope leaned over and passed it up to him and the moment had gone. She stood up and went slowly into the wonderful February sunshine and the first thing she saw was a billboard outside a newsagent's opposite. It said 'American kidnapped in Lebanon'.

She turned and made for the car park. She wondered whether she would be able to get home to the cottage this evening and listen to the news on her transistor and go to sleep in her little nest by the fire. And then she felt guilty. 'For Pete's sake, Hope Langley!' she whispered furiously as she let herself into the Wolseley. 'Can't you stop thinking about yourself for ten minutes on end!'

So then she made herself think of Bella and Peter and as Jem Trewint appeared she blew her nose and dried her eyes, even more furious with herself.

Eleven

The good weather continued for the rest of
February. Between the three of them they
cut what greens were left and Jem stacked them
in his truck and took them to the market.
The money was not worth the labour, but the
psychological effect was worthwhile; windblown
and exhausted, they counted it on to the kitchen
table, then put it in an empty jam jar on the
mantelpiece as if it were a trophy.

'When the gaffer gets back, we'll have a treat,'
Bella promised.

'We could fetch an Indian – might get cheap
rates.' Jem grinned; he knew all about Fennie
Perkins.

He took over the bedroom with the horsehair mattress and Hope was able to go back to
Widdershins each night. She moved her bedding
back upstairs and promised herself that once
Peter came home she would resume her solitary
life. At present she drove Bella in and out of
Truro each day and helped with the evening
milking, but with Jem installed in the farmhouse
and Peter back home there would be very little
she could do to help.

Peter looked wonderful for the first few days after the operation. He was on an epidural drip and back in the general ward two days afterwards and though he went back a step when the drip was removed, by the last day of the month the doctor was talking of sending him home.

'Everything seems to happen on Sundays,' Hope said when they got back that afternoon. 'Fay and Martin came on a Sunday and Peter went into hospital two weeks ago. And now they say he can come home again.' She grinned. 'I almost forgot. That morning – two weeks ago – I went for a swim!'

Jem grinned back. 'Don't believe you.'

Bella plonked the teapot on the table. 'She's mad enough.'

'Nothing mad about it. Look at the sun now!'

'OK, let's do it again.' Jem poured tea and stood up to drink his. 'She's right, Bella. It's been like spring for a fortnight now and it won't last. Let's go and have a swim before the sun sets.'

Bella smiled grimly and said she had better things to do with her time but when the other two dragged her along the headland and down into the cove her only protest was that they hadn't brought towels. She stood by, at first appalled then chuckling as they raced into the sea fully clothed. And then, as they floundered about splashing and kicking in the waves, they saw her walk slowly into the cave and put a protective hand against the side of the *Mirabelle*.

Hope stood up, chest deep. 'Oh God. I'd forgotten for a moment. Let's go home.'

'He's not going to die.' Jem dashed the water

from his face and pushed back his long straggly hair. 'He's *not* going to die! He's strong. He'll survive this.'

They waded out and clambered soggily along the cliff path, Bella bringing up the rear, grumbling at them reassuringly. And then they separated; Hope to follow the rill up to the skimpy Marble Arch and Widdershins, Jem and Bella to take the cliff path back to the farm. 'Light the fire as soon as you get in,' Bella reminded her. 'Once we see the smoke we know you'm all right.'

So Hope did so and remembered that Peter had been grey-haired when she saw him first back in 1967. Though he seemed to have stayed the same he must surely be over seventy now. She was beginning to see what he had meant when he asked her to look after his wife; the way Bella had touched Peter's old boat had been more revealing than anything. Hope shivered as she stripped off her wet clothing. What would Bella do without her gaffer?

It was a leap year so it was the twenty-ninth of February when Peter came home. Jem and Hope had turned the little-used front parlour into a bedroom and lugged the big double bed downstairs. With a fire in the grate and most of the furniture moved into the dairy, it looked welcoming and there was a view of the yard so that Peter would see his beloved Buttercup when she came in for milking. Jem fetched him home and Hope left them to their own devices until the afternoon. She had had a long letter from Chatty that morning and something about it had encouraged her to pull her mother's sewing machine into the kitchen and rummage through one of the bags of material. She machine-quilted the leftovers from the curtains and made two cushion covers. And then in the middle of the afternoon she trudged up the headland to the farm to see how they were doing.

Although Peter had been out of his hospital bed and sitting in a chair for the past three days, Bella insisted he stayed in bed. 'At least for two-three days,' she said, her voice changing from bossy to pleading. 'Once you'm out o' bed, there's no keeping an eye on what you do!'

Peter smiled and agreed to her terms. 'For your sake, Bell,' he insisted. 'I could take my turn with the cows now if need be.'

'Well, need not be,' she said, smiling with relief. 'Jem does the milking in the morning and the girl and me takes it in turns with the after-noon milk. She's coming on a treat is the girl. D'you know, that blessed Buttercup din't kick the bucket over once when she started! She just sat there for a bit till Buttercup looks around at 'er to see what's 'appening, then she says, quiet-like – it's my turn now, my lovely, I knows you understands the position.' Bella tried not to smile but her mouth turned upwards. 'An' that blessed cow understood every word she did say. No trouble at all!'

Peter nodded. 'She's a good maid,' he agreed. 'An' the cow en't too bad neither!'

Hope protested. 'I just did what Bella told me to do! And it doesn't always work because I still can't make a decent loaf of bread!'

He laughed. He looked so happy to be home but so frail. Hope risked dropping a quick kiss on his head before going out to the barn.

She did indeed feel an affinity with the four cows and milking was a strangely peaceful time. When she had cleaned the udders and left the animals with their hay, she carried the pails of milk into the dairy for Bella to deal with and took off her overall and washed herself with a feeling of enormous satisfaction. Bella was right, it was good to see Peter warm and in bed as if somehow they could keep him safe.

Three days later it rained, the first rain for over a fortnight. Jem drove the tractor down the slippery incline to the cliff above the scullery and tipped down a load of coal. After the constant attention needed to feed the range with wood, it was a luxury to sit by the glowing coals and watch the rain pour down the windows. Jem told her to stay put until the rain gave over. There was no more work to be done in the fields and he and Bella between them could manage the milking. Mr Perkins had called to see Peter and brought Fennie and the new baby with him. Peter was trying to get Bella to take Fennie on to do some of the work.

Jem said, 'Apparently she's a dab hand in the dairy. In fact she can turn her hand to anything.' He grinned. 'She looks like an Indian squaw. Has the baby in a shawl on her back. She never leaves him for a minute.'

Hope wondered whether Peter could afford to pay both Jem and Fennie Perkins and as if he read her thoughts, Jem said, 'It would have to be a business arrangement. Not a friendly arrangement like you and me. I'm not sure whether Peter can afford it.'

Hope was silent for a while then said diffidently, 'Jem, I think – as you have no time for painting or anything else – you ought to make this a business arrangement. If you stay much longer.'

He looked surprised. 'I have free board and lodging. Use of the car and the tractor. Couldn't ask for much more than that, could I?'

She shook her head. 'Fennie will have that too. And for her baby.'

'Yes. But you know what I mean. She's not a friend. You . . . me . . . we've been around a long time.'

There was no logic to that argument but Hope knew that he was right. She said, 'I have to admit the car is useful. I must go into Penzance as soon as the rain gives over. I should have gone ages ago. I need to find an outlet for some of my stuff. And I certainly need to know how much is in my savings account. I brought some cash with me so I've been able to buy milk and bread and stuff from Bella and pay Mr Perkins for mending the roof, but there's not enough to pay for this coal.' She smiled blissfully. 'Look at it! Isn't it beautiful? The way it makes those caverns and things. It reminds me of when I was a little girl . . .' She laughed. 'I was making toast for tea and the fire was too hot on my face so I stuck the bread on the end of an umbrella and opened it up to protect myself from the heat and the next thing I knew the whole lot was on fire!'

He laughed too. 'What happened?'

'Panic. Mummy stuffed the whole thing in the fire and the smell of burning cloth went through the house!' She sobered. 'I'd forgotten that. It's one of the marvellous things about being down here. I discover things I'd forgotten.'

He nodded. 'Yes. Cornwall is packed full of memories. The ones you don't want . . . it will keep them for you.'

She glanced at him. He had been a hippie back in 1967. Now he was just a very shabby, middle-aged man.

She said, 'You've buried lots down here, Jem. Haven't you?'

'Oh yes. My conscience is somewhere on the Lizard peninsula.'

'Not all of it. Otherwise you wouldn't be helping Peter and Bella right now.'

'I had to grow a new one. Everyone told me I didn't have a conscience. Well, I did, but I think it must have died anyway. So . . . I buried it.'

She was angry. 'Who told you that?'

'My family. My wife's family.'

'Your wife? I didn't realize—'

'She's dead. And the baby.' He glanced at her and smiled slightly. 'Such a silly story really. We thought we could live down here on fresh air. And then she was pregnant. And she went into labour when I was . . . out of it. And died.'

'Oh my God! Oh Jem! Oh, how terrible!'

'Yes. It is, isn't it?' He sounded conversational and she did not know what to say. Had there been an inquest? Was he sent to prison?

He said, 'I'd better go. They might need me. I'll come with you to Penzance if you like.'

Without thinking she said, 'No thanks. I'd rather do it by myself.' She meant she would rather be alone when she went around the shops with her samples. But he flushed.

'I'm quite safe now. I don't do drugs any more.'

'No – of course not – I didn't—'

He shook his head. 'Don't worry. I told you – I buried it all. Where it happened.' He opened the door and the rain slanted in. He said, 'You've left your husband, haven't you? I recommend this part of the country for a burial ground.'

He closed the door after himself and she watched him walk down the little valley and then back on himself to where he had left the tractor. She shivered.

The first fine day she borrowed Peter's Wolseley and drove into Penzance armed with the cushion covers. She parked along the front and walked up Market Jew Street with some trepidation. If there were no takers for her sewing and not much money in her savings account, she wondered just how she would manage. She hesitated outside a gift shop and then funked going inside and continued up the hill to the bank situated just behind the statue of Sir Humphry Davy. Shouldering her bag, she produced her account book and asked for an up-to-date statement. The girl went away then returned with a slip of paper and pushed it across. The balance showed seventeen hundred pounds.

'There must be some mistake.' She glanced behind; no one was waiting. 'I'm sorry to be a nuisance but I know that I had under a thousand pounds in this acount.'

The girl looked surprised. 'I did check. Apparently a payment was made only last month.'

She knew exactly what had happened. Jack had half suggested supplementing this account when she left him. And somehow he had done so. Where had he got the money from? She had no idea and if she queried it and the whole thing was frozen, there would be no way of getting any money out. She smiled, rolled her eyes, and wrote a cheque for cash. The girl looked at her sharply and checked her signature with great care before asking how she would like the money.

'Tens, please.'

She felt like a thief as she left the bank and had to stop herself from running back down the street. She deliberately paused at the shoe shop opposite the bank and stared in at the spring collection of sandals and then turned left down the Causeway and went into the first suitable shop she came to. As usual it was not possible to speak to the owner, who was also the manager. 'She does buy local craft stuff. But just at the moment . . . I don't think so. We do things like this for Christmas – lovely presents they'd make. Possibly for the holiday trade too. Now . . . in between times . . . Can you come back in another month or two? Just after Easter would be ideal. And rag rugs . . . do you do rag rugs?'

Hope nodded. 'Large or small?' she asked.

'Both. Can't promise anything, mind. But last year everyone wanted rag rugs like they had in the old Cornish cottages.'

Hope felt justified now in going back to the car; she had done her bit and though she had never made a rag rug in her life she was sure she could do. Anything rather than smocks; the thought of getting in touch with Mrs Martin was almost as bad as getting in touch with Mandy or Henrik. She bought some groceries and a lot of tinned food and lugged it back to the car park with difficulty. She was still feeling like a criminal on two counts. She started up the engine and addressed the unknown owner of the Causeway Craft Shop. 'Well, I didn't actually lie to your assistant about the rugs' – and then as she drove past the railway station she thought of Jack and added in a grimmer tone, 'If you think you can buy anything from me, Jack, think again! I'm not going to touch that thousand!'

It took half an hour to drive back to the farm, but it was like a different world and she breathed a sigh of relief as she left Buryan and turned down the track. Bella met her in the farmyard and said, 'There was some post for you so I told him to leave it here. Save going down the head-land when it's so muddy.'

She handed over two envelopes. One was addressed in Fay's italic script; the other was from Jack. It was as if she could not get rid of him.

'Come on in and have a sit down, girl,' Bella said. 'You'm looking all-in.'

Hope stood helplessly for a moment, the car keys still in one hand, the two letters in the other. Then she said, 'I have to go, Bella. Here's the Complan and Peter's keys. Is he all right?'

'Nurse came and he got weighed. He's put on two pounds and he had to breathe into a machine and it was good.' Bella gave her grim smile. 'Reckon 'e's all right.'

'Give him my love. I'll be up Saturday. I can milk if you like and then we can play dominoes.'

'That'd be nice.' Bella walked with her to the farmyard gate then said, 'You will read it, my 'an'some? You wun't just throw it away?'

Hope looked at the sharp black eyes on a level with her own. She wondered just how much Bella guessed.

'As a matter of fact, I need to read this.' She turned and stared out to sea. 'He has paid some money into my account, Bella. It puts me in a false position. I left him. I don't want his money.'

'Mebbe . . . he still feels responsible for you.'

'I don't think so.'

Bella sighed deeply. 'Poor lost soul,' she said and turned back to the farmhouse.

Jack had handwritten his letter. He had been declared bankrupt and the computer had been one of the many assets sold to pay his debtors. He had not managed to save the house; everything that was jointly owned had gone. But a very small amount of cash had been paid into her account.

The windpower project was financed largely by Henrik and he took everything with him when he went to Cape Town. It is obvious that Henrik was in dire straits himself and had been planning to leave as soon as he had sold what he could. It is useless to try to tell you how sorry I am. I wanted – I always wanted – to give you so much. And now there is nothing. I am thankful that you left when you did. I don't think I could stand seeing you and knowing what I have done. The good things to come from our marriage are the girls. Think of them, Hope, and try to obliterate the rest. You should be able to make something from Widdershins if you sell in the summer. I know you will find work; you are talented. I will not ask forgiveness. Perhaps just forgetfulness.

With best wishes, Jack.

She looked up from the letter. The daylight was fading. The clocks would go forward very soon now and then the summer would start and she would be planting her beans and digging some early potatoes. She went outside and walked down the combe to the alder grove. The rill bubbled carelessly over the floor of pebbles towards the cliff and the sea. She said aloud and incredulously, 'With best wishes . . . with best *wishes!*'

Chatty wanted to come for Easter. Hope wrote and invited Fiona too but when she met the train at Penzance, Chatty got off alone. She was delighted to see her mother.

'I thought I'd have to get a taxi and money is in short supply! Whose car?'

'Peter's. You haven't been reading my letters properly. I told you all about driving Bella into Truro. She can't drive so Jem and I use the car more or less when we want to.'

'Jem and you?' Chatty slid out of her backpack and put it on the back seat. 'Does that mean anything?'

'Of course not! Don't talk like that, Chatty, for goodness' sake. I don't think I can bear it.'

'Reminds you of Andy-Mandy,' Chatty said lightly. 'Yes, I know I'm barging in where angels fear and all that stuff. But I can't spend this precious weekend pussy-footing around. Fay will be phoning and giving me the third degree. I need to know exactly how you are, what you are eating, how you are coping in the cottage without much money or transport, whether there's anything with Jem . . . well, there are two questions settled. You've got transport and there's nothing between you and Jem.'

Hope sighed and drove along the huge arc of Penzance front then turned right to get on to the A30 for Buryan. She said, 'I think I'd temporarily forgotten your full-frontal attacks. You're not called Chatty for nothing, that's for sure!'

'You're beginning to sound like Bella! Oh, look at the Mount! Oh my God, I'd forgotten how beautiful it is! How long are you staying down here? I must bring Fiona some time. She's never been to Cornwall . . . How is Peter? Oh of *course*, you wouldn't give poor Jem a second look, would you? Like Dad, he's blotted his copy-book with Mandy for evermore!'

'Chatty!' Hope was seriously angry. 'Don't talk to me like that, please. You sound absolutely . . . *crass*! You have no idea at all of what has happened.'

'I have actually. Fay has put me in the picture.'

'Yes. I realize she will have done that. But . . . events are one thing. What happens after the events is quite another.'

'Causes and effects?'

'Yes. All right, causes and effects. And—' She took a hand from the steering wheel as Chatty opened her mouth, '—I do not want to talk about it. Certainly not with you!'

'OK.' Chatty still sounded light. Was it some carefully prepared ploy? She placed her mother's hand back on the steering wheel. 'Concentrate on driving and let me look around. Remember, the last time I was in this part of the country, Gran was still alive and Mandy was still my aunt. She was on my side. I need to look around a bit differently now. Can you understand that?'

'Oh God.' Hope breathed deeply. 'Of course. I forget that you are still adjusting. I've had almost three months to get used to things.'

'And I've had the toughest but the best three months of my life so don't think I've been all pale and starving in my garret. By the way, it's a wonderful garret – thanks ever so much for getting it for us.' Chatty twisted and turned, taking everything in, but still talking lightly, conversationally. 'It's been absolutely marvellous, Mum. I can't thank you and Dad enough. Dad managed to rescue some money for me – and I've still got Gran's lump sum, bless her cotton socks. And you got Fi and me that gorgeous flat – and I'm beginning to understand what people say to me and even manage a reply now and then!' She laughed, tipping back her head and showing her long, creamy neck. Fay was supposed to be the beautiful one but Hope realized suddenly that Chatty had an attraction Fay lacked; a kind of vibrancy.

'Oh God, there's Buryan church. Does it look like the forbidding finger of God or what!' She turned to her mother excitedly. 'Listen, if it's still decent weather tomorrow, let's have a swim in the cove!'

'Fine. I've had two so far. Both at low tide. Nothing rough. We had a wonderful spell at the end of February.'

'Oh Mum – well done!' She looked surprised and pleased, then went on irrepressibly, 'Oh Mum, you should have seen the trees in the Tuileries! Oh it's so beautiful. Here too.' For a long moment she said nothing else and then, suddenly, she blurted, 'Mum, think about this. Both you and Dad were . . . bereft. Stripped of everything. But you are swimming in Cornwall and he is in a flat in Gloucester, sick and alone.'

'Enough, Chatty! I mean it – don't say any more!'

'He told me you wouldn't talk about it. He was right.' She glanced at her mother's tight face. 'Sorry. Really. Sorry, sorry, sorry. I love you and I want us to have three wonderful days together.' She looked at the small, bleak terraces of miners' cottages opposite the church. 'Just remember that I miss Gran too. But I also miss Dad and I even miss Mandy! There. No more.'

She spent the twenty minutes between Buryan and Penhailes Farm chatting madly about her life in Paris. But those last words had acted like an electric shock on Hope. And yet it was so obvious. She expected both the girls to miss their father as much as they must miss her and Milly. But Mandy . . . did Chatty really mean that she was missing Mandy?

'There's the sea! Oh Mum! There's our very own sea! I'll get out and open the gates. Should I knock and say hello to Bella and Peter now?'

Hope shook her head. 'Peter sleeps in the afternoons. We'll wait until tomorrow morning. I'll put the car away and we'll just walk through.'

She drove into the shed which until a few years ago had housed the farm's pony and trap, and waited while Chatty collected her backpack. She wanted to ask Chatty how she could possibly miss Mandy. But she did not. That night as she listened to the unusual sounds of someone else in her small domain, she came to the conclusion that Chatty had meant she was only too glad Mandy was missing from their lives.

On Easter Sunday morning they swam in the iron-cold sea and then, tingling yet relaxed, they borrowed Peter's car and went to church at St Buryan. Bella was cooking a chicken with roast potatoes and fresh cauliflower. Hope and Chatty took on the dishing up and they ate at a small table in Peter's room and then, while Peter rested, the three women joined Jem cutting and crating cauliflowers for next week's market. Bella and Hope started at one end of the field, Jem and Chatty at the other. At one time the silent Bella straightened her back, grinned at Hope and said, 'Dun't that girl o' yourn ever stop talking?' And Hope smiled back as Chatty's clear voice floated across the field while Jem's monosyllabic replies acted as punctuation.

'The funny thing is,' she replied, 'the girl she works with – and lives with – is exactly the same. I cannot think how they manage.'

'Set one of they kitchen timers for ten minutes

each, I wouldn't be surprised,' Bella returned.

But that night when Hope and Chatty were sitting by the fire drinking tea and nibbling at a biscuit from one of the new tins, Chatty said unexpectedly, 'Jem was really smitten with Mandy. I reckon she broke his heart as well as Dad's.'

Hope almost gasped. And then she realized Chatty was being provocative.

'You are *terrible*, Chatty. We were listening to you, Bella and me. You didn't give Jem time to say a word!' She shook her head, then added, 'And you know I won't talk about Dad.'

'All right. No Dad. But you're quite wrong about Jem. He said several words.'

'He grunted. Just to keep you satisfied.'

'It was the way he grunted. And the places where he grunted. And his body language.' She sorted through the biscuits and found the last chocolate one. 'It's no good you looking like that, Mum! Jem still has feelings for Andy-Mandy!'

Hope looked into the caverns of coal in the range and remembered her last conversation with Jem. She said sombrely, 'You don't know anything about Jem, my love. Be careful what you say to him.'

'About his wife dying?'

Chatty looked satisfied with her mother's reaction. She waited until the exclamations were over then said, 'No, of course he didn't tell me. But . . . you remember that all-night party thing Mandy and I went to? In St Ives? It was dead boring actually, but I heard someone mention the name Trewint so I listened hard.'

She made a face. 'So did Andy. And she thought she could offer consolation.' She shrugged. 'And apparently she did. Only it was on a short-term basis!'

'Oh Chatty. You sound so . . . cynical. I know it's all awful, but honestly, the real people are like the Penhaileses. They live from day to day by the weather and the sea. They're . . . *decent*!'

Chatty looked at her for a moment then forced a schoolgirl giggle. 'If I sound cynical, let me tell you, you sound very, very old hat!'

Hope smiled too but said, 'Well, old hat or not, that's what I'm aiming for.'

Chatty stopped giggling. 'You and Dad were always decent. Like Gran and Grandad.'

'We started off that way, yes. Then we moved away. I'm trying to move back.'

'Without forgiving Dad and Mandy?'

'Without thinking of them. And before you say I'm not facing up to anything, let me agree with you!' Hope leaned forward to push a coal into place. The cavern flickered with light and grew into a miniature cathedral. 'I've gone further than that. I've simply turned my back on them.'

Chatty was silent, staring into the fire like her mother. When at last she spoke it was to deliver one of her usual bombshells.

'Andy won't care, of course. But Dad . . . I'm in Paris having a whale of a time, Fay's all wrapped up with being in love with Martin and the Orkneys and the bloody Icelandic sagas, you're down here . . . As far as he can see, we've all turned our backs on him.' She looked up. 'I suppose if you and Jem had a fling together it would help.'

Hope made a sound very like a squawk, then aimed a pantomime punch in Chatty's direction.

Chatty protested, laughing. 'I mean it, Mum! You've got to face things in order to forgive them. And you've got to forgive Dad and Andy, otherwise – knowing you – you're not going to be able to get a grip on that decent life you're talking about!' She sobered and leaned forward. 'I'm surprised you took Communion this morning. You are not in a state of grace!'

Hope sat back, really shocked. 'Chatty, that's going too far.'

'No, it's not. Talk it over with Gran when you get to bed – I take it you can face Gran?'

'Oh, Chatty . . . I thought you didn't believe in an afterlife?'

Chatty ignored that and swept on, 'And Jem's the same. Don't you see? He can't forgive himself – more than that, he can't forgive life for playing such a horrible trick on him. So it could help you both. Have you considered it?'

Hope felt suddenly irritated. 'No, I haven't. And if you have any more agony aunt solutions, kindly keep them to yourself. And wait until you're a bit older too. It's all very well discussing me as a – a case – with Fiona Tabb in the cosmopolitan atmosphere of a Paris flat, but I'm not a case, I'm your mother. And don't you forget it!'

Chatty drew her lips into a rosebud and pretended remorse. 'Sorry, Mum. But I've always been the one that caused you headaches. Surely you haven't forgotten that?'

'Not at all.' Hope could not maintain disapproval for long but she had had enough for one night. She gathered herself together and stood up and then suddenly leaned over and kissed Chatty's curly mop of hair. 'You're all right, Charity Langley. We were comfortably off and now we're not, and you haven't griped about that once. You're not a bad human being. On the whole.'

Chatty actually flushed with pleasure. Then said, 'I was going to mention that you haven't griped about it either. But that side of things . . . making money – it didn't bother you, did it? It mattered to Dad, not to you.'

Hope said, 'It wasn't at the top of my priority list, no. But then, Chatty, you mustn't forget I've never had to do without anything much.' She brightened. 'Don't you see, that's why this – living here at Widdershins – is so exciting and worthwhile.'

Chatty watched while she damped down the fire for the night, then said, 'Yes. Yes, actually, Mum, I can see that.' She too stood up and made for the sitting room where Hope had put the airbed. Then she said, thoughtfully, 'Poor old Dad. He doesn't stand a chance, does he? Not against this place.'

Twelve

That summer Hope realized that she was learning how to be content. The effervescent joy she had known as a girl, the deep happiness she had felt with Jack and the girls, the fun she had had with Mandy, even the nostalgia she had shared with her mother . . . they were gone. This new happiness was something she found in the hard physical labour of collecting and stacking fuel, looking after her garden on the slope of the combe, walking along the headland to see Peter and help with the chores on the farm, sawing the old doors which she'd found in the wood store to make shutters against next winter's gales. The shop in Penzance's Causeway could sell as many rag rugs as she could make, but they took a long time to do and sold for much less than the smocks had done. But the rugs and the cushions made enough money for her to replenish her tinned food and buy two precious hot-water bottles. Bella refused to take any money for supplying her with bread and milk and butter. Jem told her she could apply for unemployment benefit but that might well mean 'they' would find her a job. She kept away from all bureaucracy; she had always paid the old-style rates on a standing order and presumably that would still go ahead. She wondered about water rates. The water in the sink and the toilet flush came from a well sunk at the back of the cliff.

The only thing that marred that summer was watching Peter's slow decline. He said he was in no pain at all; he walked slowly around the farm and to the small knoll above it where he could see, far below, the cove where the *Mirabelle* leaned against the wall of the cave. Sometimes, when he was strong enough, he would play dominoes in the evenings with Jem or with Hope. Once, when they were all together, Bella behind his chair rubbing his back with some special emollient from the hospital, he said, 'I feel like a king.'

'One of they Romans waited on by slaves, I wouldn't wonder,' Bella said tartly, leaning forward to slide her thumbs between his shirt and spine.

'Aye.' Peter chuckled appreciatively. 'But they never seemed to realize how lucky they were! And anyway, reckon I can beat them. Don't think there are many who 'ave 'ad such a good life as me.'

For once, Bella did not sharply remind him that there was more to come. Tacitly she was beginning to accept that Peter's time was running out. Instead, she paused for a moment and looked across the bedroom and through the window to the farmyard. 'We 'aven't done bad, 'ave we, Gaffer? Getting you back from Dunkirk was the worst thing. It's been easy since then.'

Hope, listening as she gazed at the dominoes, longed to ask about that time and why they hadn't had children. But Peter leaned forward and placed his domino with a chuckle.

'I know you cain't go, my 'an'some. So there's another game done with.' He turned his head slightly to address Bella. 'You're right as usual, Bell. We ain't done so bad. The two of us.' He sighed. 'I better get to bed while I can. Goodnight to the two of you.' He grinned at Jem who was boxing the dominoes. 'Your turn tomorrow, my lad. Neither two of you 'ave beaten me yet!'

She made small rituals out of her breaks: breakfast after an early morning swim was taken with the door open and always consisted of bread and honey washed down with at least two mugs of tea. She worked outside whenever possible, looking after the burgeoning garden, weeding, taking the ferns back another few inches to make room for beets and carrots and turnips. Her three wigwams of runner beans were heavy with blossom and promised much for the late summer. She picked wild fruit too and bottled it carefully as she had seen her mother do before the days of freezers. Bella unearthed a small hand churn from her cellar and she learned how to turn the paddles slowly and rhythmically until the yellow bubbles appeared at the edges of the milk. When the butter hardened she delighted in patting it into shape and imprinting it with the acorn on the other side of the wooden pats. Her contentment was earned; never before had she worked so that she fell into bed exhausted each night and slept deeply until the iron roof began to expand and creak above her when the sun shone on it.

After Easter she received another two letters from Jack. He was living in a bed-sitting room in Gloucester and there was a communal phone in the hall; he printed the number carefully in case she needed to get in touch with him. Bella said he telephoned at the beginning of June to ask how she was. Chatty must have given him the Penhaileses' number and for a moment Hope was annoyed with her, and then realized how ridiculous that was. She felt not the slightest inclination to write or telephone him. Some days she did not get time to think of him until she settled for bed. She really had turned her back on him.

In August the girls came together, just the two of them.

Although already she liked Martin and was prepared to like Fiona Tabb, it was wonderful to have them to herself. They seemed to enter into the spirit of Widdershins immediately, rolling out of bed each morning either to swim in the cove or wash in the rill according to the tide and then joining her in whatever she had to do. Fay showed a great talent with the rugs, ripping rags and laying them in coloured bundles ready to thread and knot each evening. Chatty tried to take over the churning but, impatient as ever, had to give up before the butter started to form.

'Why don't you just take off the cream?' she asked. 'You could probably sell it – or we could use it.'

'We already make enough for the three of us.

And how on earth could I sell cream?' Hope took over the paddles. 'Look, try singing to it.' She began to hum and beat with her foot but it was no good: Chatty really wanted to sketch a winter coat she'd thought about two nights ago. And when it rained she used the machine and made some children's dungarees from the material in the bit-bag. When they made one of their excursions into Penzance she took the dungarees and sold them with the latest rag rug and cushions. She was delighted when the assistant asked for more. 'I could get into this way of living,' she crowed on the way home.

The girls stayed ten days, then Chatty's holiday was over and Fay wanted to spend time with Martin. Hope knew she was going to feel bereft. There had been no futile discussions; no questions; they had not tried to remind her of the past or talk to her about the future. Fay suggested she took half of 'Gran's money' as a standby and that was the nearest they came to talking about what had happened. Hope said briefly, 'Any standby would be for you. That's how Gran would want it.'

She drove them into Penzance for the train and watched it pull out with her heart sinking rapidly, and for a few days after that there was a dragging sensation in her abdomen, not helped by the weather which decided to turn wet and windy. On the Sunday she braved the surf and had a dip before breakfast then picked the beans from her three wigwams and spent the morning cutting them into jars and salting them down. The scullery was packed with tins and jars of food and she took a housewifely satisfaction in adding the dozen jars of beans to her store. She labelled them and added them to her list and was looking around smugly when she heard Jem call from the front of the house.

'Come on in – for goodness' sake, it's raining again, don't just stand there!' She opened the door and ushered him inside. 'I wondered about walking up to the farm after tea. Seeing if I could help with the milk.'

'Thought you might.' Jem did not sit down. 'Bella said best not wait though. There was a phone call for you. From Chatty.' He saw her face and said quickly, 'Everything is all right. But she wants to talk to you and she's hanging about in the design room at work because the phone at the apartment is on the blink.'

'It's Sunday.'

'That's what Bella said. And those places are a bit spooky when they're empty.'

'It must be serious, Jem. Are you sure she didn't give a hint?'

'Bella took the call. She said it was nothing to worry about. That's all I know.'

Hope dragged a cardigan over her shirt, picked up a bag of beans she had cut for the Penhaileses and followed Jem outside. It was mid-afternoon, hazy, with a mist blowing from Mounts Bay that was damp on her face.

'It's going to rain hard,' she said knowledge-ably.

Jem smiled. 'You're getting the feel of things, aren't you?'

She said, 'If Chatty needs me, I'll have to go. And I can't imagine being anywhere else. Not now.'

He nodded. 'That's the trouble with Cornwall.'

She greeted Bella and asked after Peter who was taking his afternoon nap. Bella gave a curt nod. 'Din't eat 'is dinner. 'E'll 'ave to 'ave that Complan muck for 'is supper whether 'e likes it or not!' She was ironing fiercely and expertly and glanced up long enough to say, 'That number – for your girl. It's on a bit of paper by the telephone.'

Hope was able to dial direct and was amazed when Chatty's voice immediately came on the line.

'Of course I'm all right. It's only four days since I was with you!'

'What's that got to do with anything?'

'Nothing. It's Dad. Fay didn't want to upset you but she got off the train at Gloucester to go and see him. She phoned me straight away and we weren't going to say anything but then we thought we ought to. She stayed with him till today but now she's on the train back to Sheffield, so I'm doing it.'

'Oh Chat! Obviously I'm not going to get upset when either of you go and see Dad. How could I?'

'Mum, listen. He's not well. Depressed. He went into hospital for some treatment. And the doc – well, psychiatrist, I suppose – got him to talk about Mandy. We don't know if that's why he did it. Something must have been the last straw. Anyway . . . he took an overdose last Tuesday. If Fay hadn't decided . . . She found him on the bed. There was a note. It sounds horrible, Mum. Poor old Fay . . .'

Hope stared at the natural granite wall. She said in a stifled voice, 'Are you saying he is dead?'

'No – no, sorry. Of course not. We would have had to tell you immediately. No, he's all right and he's back in hospital and he begged – absolutely begged – Fay to join Martin and not to tell you. So she is joining Martin and she told me.'

'So it was a cry for help?'

'Mum. He didn't know Fay was calling in. And if she hadn't . . . It was absolutely meant to be. Probably something to do with Gran. They were close, weren't they?'

'I don't know.' Hope drew a deep, shuddering breath. 'Why are you telling me now? This happened on Tuesday and I suppose they pumped him out and he's all right. Why are you telling me now?'

'Mum, for God's sake! We're talking about Dad! They pumped him out. Yes. But he's not all right. And when they discharge him – which they will do because beds are so short – what's going to happen then?'

'I don't know. Neither do you. He'll be under some kind of supervision, I suppose. Anyway they won't send him out until he's . . . all right.'

'Aren't you going home?'

'You mean to Gloucester? That's not home, Chatty.'

'You're not, are you?' The voice suddenly became conversational. 'Sorry. Didn't mean to sound like that. Why should you? It's OK. I shouldn't have phoned – you're quite right. Now look, I don't want you to worry. I'll ring Fay and if she can't make it, I'll go. But she'll make it. Martin will drive her down – they're the obvious choice—'

'The obvious choice is surely Mandy?' Hope pushed her knuckles against the granite. 'Has anyone phoned Mandy?'

'Mum, will you kindly stop talking like that!' Chatty's voice changed again; she coughed and said hoarsely, 'I don't think I can bear it.'

There was a short silence. Hope thought she heard the far-off sound of a Parisian taxi honking its horn. It was incredible to think that Chatty was in that enormous room, full of tables and machines and fabrics and smelling of oranges . . . she was here on this headland in Cornwall; Fay was in Sheffield. And Jack . . . Jack was in a hospital ward.

She said, 'I'm on my way, Chat. Sorry. I'll be there in five hours. Sorry.'

Chatty gulped, 'Oh Mum. Are you sure? I mean . . . you have to really, don't you? But not tonight. You don't have to go till tomorrow. Jem will drive you into Penzance.'

'If I don't go now I might change my mind. There's a train at five-something-or-other. I'll go straight to Dad's bedsit and you can ring me there. Make it as late as possible. I don't know when the train gets in but I'll have to have a taxi. Midnight. Is that all right?'

'Yes. Of course. Take care. Oh Mum—'

'Stop worrying. You did the right thing. Thanks, Chatty. You're a wonderful daughter.'

Chatty, suddenly relieved and irrepressible, said, 'I know.'

Hope told Bella briefly what had happened.

'You must 'ave the car, my maid. It's what Peter would want. No, I wun't 'ear any more about trains. You will need a car when you get there – Gloucester's a bit bigger than Penzance, I reckon. Dun't argue no more. Get back to Widdershins and pack yourself up and come back as soon as you can. Jem's in the barn – tell 'im what's going on and 'e can get the car out for you.'

Bella was galvanized into activity, folding her ironing blanket and putting the clothes horse by the window where it would get any sun that might break through.

'I'll pack you up some food for the journey.' She almost pushed Hope towards the door. 'No more arguin', I said. Just get a move on. You'll want to be over Bodmin before dark, that's for certain sure!'

Hope went into the barn. It smelled sweetly. Jem was milking early, his head in Buttercup's flank, his movements automatic. He listened while she told him what Chatty had said and then what Bella had said.

'Bella just . . . just rose to the occasion.' She tried to laugh. 'She really is incredible.'

'Yes. I suppose that's how she reacted when she took the *Mirabelle* to Dunkirk back in 1940.' She barely registered this second reference to Dunkirk. He added, 'Your hand is bleeding, Hope. Put some plaster on it when you get to the cottage. How long will you be?'

'I don't know. An hour. No more.'

'Go then. This mist might get worse this evening and you want to be over Bodmin before then.'

273

She shook her head. 'It's going to rain,' she said.

And rain it did. The wipers could barely cope with it. It started just past St Germans and by the time she reached Jamaica Inn visibility was down to a few yards. It took three hours to reach Okehampton and another three to Gloucester. She left the motorway with a sigh of relief and drove through Quedgeley and down the Bristol Road and over the Cross and then turned right into Eastgate Street and left into Clarence Street, and right again into Russell Square which was the address on Jack's last two letters. There was a lot of demolition work going on in the run-down old square and number five looked as though it might be the next victim. It was a tall old house, the side ripped off to reveal a grate hanging in mid-air, strips of wallpaper festooning the trees and briers which had grown protectively around it. In the rain and with the street lights swaying precariously, it looked unwelcoming to say the least. For the first time since January Hope felt a pang of sympathy for Jack. This was a grim place to be. But she was thankful to have arrived and rammed on Peter's old sou'wester before scrambling into the rain. This could be awkward; it was gone eleven o'clock. She wondered what on earth she would do if no one answered the door.

It did take two knocks and a long time but eventually a light appeared in the transom and there were sounds of bolts being drawn. A middle-aged woman stood in the open doorway looking so much like a cartoon of a landlady that Hope smiled involuntarily. Her first words took Hope by surprise.

'We'd given up on you! Thought you must have postponed your trip till tomorrow! Come on in. Mrs Langley, isn't it? Your daughter said you'd be wearing an oilskin hat.'

Hope shouldered her bag and squashed herself past the woman into a narrow passage with a flight of stairs at the end of it. There was a smell of onions which was not unpleasant. She said, 'My daughter phoned you?'

'Yes.'

'I could have done that. I didn't give it a thought.'

'You were worried.' The woman finished re-bolting and turned. She was wearing a kimono printed with sunflowers; her hair was in rollers. 'I understand that. I divorced my hubbie ten years ago. Still have him round for his Christmas dinner.' She held out a ham-like hand. 'I'm May Jennings. I've made up his bed for you and switched on the electric blanket. I know it's not cold but this rain . . . Mr Langley's got a little electric ring up there, so you can make yourself a drink if you like. There's powdered milk but you can borrow some proper.'

'No, I'm happy with the dried. It really is kind of you.' Hope was stunned. Six hours of driving in bad conditions made this sudden respite over-whelming.

'All right then. We'll have a chat in the morning. Your daughter said she would be ringing about twelve. Just to check you'd got here all right. So I'll leave you to answer the phone.' She plodded ahead of Hope up the stairs. 'It's the top of the house, I'm afraid. Not a room I generally let but my friend Miss Marchant said your husband would be quiet and respectable and for your sake I should make an exception. Down on his luck, she said.'

'Miss Marchant?' Hope queried incredulously.

'The secretarial school you went to many years ago?' She gasped a little laugh. 'I know. Funny how things work round full circle, innit? What's that saying about nothing being new under the sun?'

Hope shook her head. It was all too much.

Jack's room was small, with a sloping ceiling, but pristine. 'Your other daughter tidied it all up after the ambulance came.' Mrs Jennings sounded crunchingly tactful. 'And I've stripped the bed of course and put in another mattress and pillows. You don't need to feel funny about it.'

But strangely enough Hope did feel 'funny' about the room. She unpacked her things and made herself a drink while she waited for Chatty's phone call, and the events of the day seemed to settle about her in the tiny twelve-by-twelve attic room like . . . she sought for a word to describe how she was feeling . . . like the ash from the range. Deadening. And dead. She had reacted to Chatty's news reluctantly and in doing so had tried to stir some life into old embers; to feel some real personal concern for Jack, with whom she had been in love all those years ago. And what came from the embers was . . . this ash.

After Chatty had phoned and she lay in bed, she tried deliberately to imagine how Jack must have felt lying here with his life in pieces about him. Had there been any embers for him to stir into life? And if he had really finished with Mandy, why had her name provoked the suicide attempt?

She shivered in spite of the electric blanket. With all her soul she longed for Widdershins and the sound of the sea. She turned her thoughts away from Jack with some difficulty and tried to imagine Bella launching the *Mirabelle* almost fifty years ago and setting out for France and her Peter. And eventually tears came and she turned her head into the new pillow and wept. She had been sick before, she had felt ill before. But these were the first tears she had shed since she had seen Mandy and Jack together in the Sandhurst house.

The hospital had been opened in Edwardian times as a lunatic asylum. Gloucestrians still referred to it as the loony bin and as far as they were concerned once a patient was there, for however short a time, the label stuck. There was a lot of room in the visitors' car park but no apparent security measures. The days of the padded cell and wailing had gone with the advent of the hypodermic. A male nurse took Hope into a sitting room furnished with chintz armchairs and coffee tables full of magazines.

'Jack isn't dressed yet. I'll tell him he's got a visitor.'

She was suddenly panic-stricken. There were other people around; she did not know what to do with herself. She had not planned what to say or do. Why on earth was she here anyway? She said, 'He might not want to see me. It might not be good for him to see me.' She had expected a talk with a doctor first, a chance to back out of the whole thing.

'Oh, he'll be delighted,' the nurse said casually and disappeared.

Hope looked round nervously. There were half a dozen people in the sitting room. Two of them were playing draughts. One sat reading a newspaper. The others were talking to someone in a white coat. There seemed to be an argument and she drifted sideways to the window which opened on to a lawn edged with flower beds. It was closed against another storm, but she still felt safer there. She had not reckoned on being frightened. Depression was, after all, just another word for madness. Was Jack mad?

The woman in the white coat said suddenly and loudly, 'Well, the chiropodist is waiting and someone's got to be first, someone's got to be last and someone else has got to be in the middle! And if none of you can agree, I'm going to say – Billy, you're first. Jim next. Andy last. Now skedaddle, for goodness' sake. I've got better things to do than listen to the three of you acting up. It doesn't hurt! OK?' They shuffled in front of her just like schoolboys, then one of them, presumably Billy, stumbled out of the room and the other two settled with newspapers.

The woman came over to Hope. 'You're Mrs Langley and you've come to see Jack?' She held out a hand. 'I'm Dr Davis. Everyone calls me Glenys. Shall we sit down? He'll be a while. He's scared of seeing you.'

'You told him I was coming?'

'One of the girls rang. They're on the phone all the time.' She hesitated then said, 'You were a close family, Mrs Langley.'

It was not a question but Hope flushed and nodded, then added, 'Well, at least I thought we were.'

'Yes. And now your daughters – both of them in different ways – say you have detached yourself.'

Hope sensed criticism. She said defensively, 'I couldn't live a lie. So I went away. Yes, in that sense, I have detached myself. But not from the girls. They had left home anyway.'

'Quite.' The doctor smiled. 'Though I think you will agree that when children leave home for the first time, they need – more than ever – to know there is a secure family behind them.'

'I think they know that. They have both been to stay with me.'

The doctor smiled. 'The older one, Fay. She said you'd all had a wonderful time.'

'Yes.' Hope wondered why she felt guilty.

'You've spent a lot of happy times in this little Cornish cottage,' she said.'

'Yes.'

'You and your mother and the two girls.'

'My husband would join us when he could, of course.'

'And last year, when your older daughter went to Iceland, your friend came down in her place?'

Hope swallowed. 'That's right.'

'Interesting how it always worked out that there were four women . . . your daughter said

279

you called yourselves the Female Four. It must have been fun.'

'Yes.'

'But your husband rarely came. Perhaps he felt he was intruding on this all-female group?'

'No. Not at all. He was busy and he wasn't very keen on . . . the simple life.'

'Yet he bought the cottage for you?'

'Yes. He knew I loved it.'

'I see.' The doctor smiled again. 'Well, I'll leave you to it now. I think Jack will be discharged quite soon and it would be most helpful if you could be with him when he talks to the occupational therapist. There will be rehabilitation procedures and you probably know his strengths and weaknesses better than anyone else.'

She said quickly, 'I can't be responsible for him. You must understand that.'

The doctor smiled. 'I simply meant that you know whether he can boil a kettle, make an omelette. That sort of thing. It's in case he qualifies for any domestic help.'

Hope relaxed. So no one was assuming she was coming back to look after Jack.

The doctor – Glenys – stood up slowly. 'Of course, there are other strengths and weaknesses. You would know about those too. You might be able to help him there, you might not. He tells me you are not actually divorced.'

'Not yet.' Hope clenched her hands. 'I think I must be straight with you. There is no question of a reconciliation.'

'No. We realize that. And so does Jack. There is absolutely no pressure on you at all.' Glenys smiled. 'He has mentioned a brother. Giles. In Australia. Apparently Jack toyed in the past with the idea of emigrating there himself. He has . . . indicated . . . that in the future he might like to join him.'

Hope felt enormous relief. 'That might be best of course. A new start.'

'Quite.'

The doctor glanced behind her as Jack appeared in the doorway. Her smile widened and she got up and went to him.

'Hello, Jack. How are you this morning?'

In spite of her easy, familiar style, Jack stared at her blankly. Eventually he said, 'All right.'

'Your wife has come, just as Fay promised she would. Come and sit down and have a nice talk together and I'll organize some coffee.'

She led Jack forward as if he were an invalid and in fact Hope could see how frail he was. He wore a T-shirt and an old pair of flannels she remembered from years ago; his feet were in slippers, no socks. But it was his face that shocked her. His thick, floppy hair was almost white and his cheeks had fallen in so that he looked lantern-jawed. His eyes stared at her for a long moment and then flicked away. She stood up, formally.

'Hello, Jack.'

His eyes flicked to her again and he said, 'Hello.'

Glenys eased him into a chair and left them. He stayed exactly as she put him, bony knees almost under his chin, arms hanging.

Hope forced a smile. 'Jack. You don't seem to recognize me.'

'Sorry.' His eyes focused for a moment. 'Sorry. Sorry.'

'It's all right.' She found herself leaning towards him. 'It's all right, Jack. You were desperate and you thought it was the only thing left. But it's not. Truly it is not.' She held his eyes and saw a faint glimmer of recognition in their depths. She leaned further and took his flaccid hand. 'It's me, Jack. Hope.'

He looked at her and a faint frown appeared. Then he shook his head. 'No hope,' he murmured and at last he moved, leaning back in the chair so that his hand fell from hers; turning to look out of the window.

She sat there not knowing what to do. Part of her was angry and wanted to shake him and say he couldn't get out of things like this, he had to come back and face up to what was happening. The other half was horrified.

One of the other men – presumably Billy – shuffled back into the room and another one stood and made to go out and then paused and looked down at Jack. 'He's drugged up to the eyeballs,' he commented. 'Keep going at him. Only thing to do.'

The anger disappeared; the horror remained. She nodded up at the man and took a deep breath. 'Jack. It's Hope. Your wife. We have two daughters, Faith and Charity, and we call them Fay and Chatty. Fay is blond and beautiful and somehow serene. Like my mother. Milly. You remember Milly. And Chatty is dark like me and never stops talking.'

The words came out jerkily with long pauses in between. The whole thing was surreal and unnatural, like a scene in an old-fashioned film about shell-shock in the First World War. Her horror was compounded by something else. Embarrassment. How could she possibly feel embarrassed at a time like this? Yet she did and found herself glancing around furtively in case the draughts players or newspaper readers were listening.

There was no response from Jack; she followed his gaze and looked at the garden outside the window. A shaft of sunlight was highlighting some sunflowers and she said spontaneously, 'Oh look at those! Aren't they beautiful? There were some self-seeded ones at the end of the combe and I'm collecting the seeds. The birds love them.'

She looked at him and to her surprise he smiled. She said eagerly, 'You heard that, didn't you?' She turned to the view of the garden again. 'You don't want to talk about people, do you? People hurt and do damage. That's how I felt when I went to Widdershins. I wanted to immerse myself completely in – in growing things and looking at the sea and the flowers. And . . . oh dear, you know what I mean!'

And he did. She was convinced he knew what she meant though she hardly knew herself. His face did not change and his eyes stayed fixed, but now they were looking instead of staring.

She said, 'The daisy shapes are the best, don't you think? I love the racemes but the daisies look as if they're turning their faces up to the sun. And is that phlox? Such an old-fashioned flower. Hollyhocks too.'

'Hope,' he said suddenly. 'Hope.'

She was so certain that he was referring to the abstract that she said quietly, 'There is always hope. Always.'

When Glenys Davis came back, she found them sitting side by side, silent but apparently at ease.

'How's it going?' she asked in her breezy and deliberately unprofessional voice.

Hope smiled. 'I wondered whether we could have a walk around the garden? Perhaps this afternoon? Jack is tired now.'

'That would be excellent.' She bent to Jack and said, 'Fish and chips for lunch, Jack. Everybody's favourite.'

Hope took that as dismissal. She stood up, said her goodbyes and went out to the car park. She was crying again. It was ridiculous. Yet, perhaps not so ridiculous after all. If Jack's brain was damaged from the suicide attempt then he really had gone. And they had been so in love. A long time ago.

Thirteen

That afternoon Hope returned to the hospital but Jack was sleeping and when he woke his eyes were dull again and he made no response when she suggested a walk in the garden. She sat by his bed trying desperately to interest him in something outside his head. The room was small but adequate for his needs. She sorted through his locker and found a Gideon Bible and a tooth mug.

'Jack, we must make a list – a shopping list.' She smiled brightly. 'You could do with a bottle of lime juice. Your favourite. Do you remember?' He frowned slightly; she was getting used to that small, rather puzzled frown. 'I've brought some grapes.' She tried to lengthen her smile into a grin. 'That's what you bring people in hospitals!' He continued to frown, though not at her. She broke off a grape and took his hand. 'Come on, Jack. Eat a grape.' Obediently he raised his hand and mumbled the grape between his lips.

Hope was appalled. She had assumed that they would take up this afternoon where they had left off this morning. Instead it seemed he had taken one step forward and two back.

At four o'clock a tea trolley came round and she saw with even more horror that Jack was given a feeding cup.

'No cake?' She included the nurse in her rallying question. 'He's usually a great one for a slice of cake!' She hated her own voice; the condescension, the indulgence, as if Jack were five instead of almost fifty.

The nurse shook her head. 'They're all too sleepy in the afternoons,' she replied in exactly the same tone. 'They come to in time for supper, never fear!'

Hope made up her mind suddenly. 'In that case, I'll go and do this shopping and come back about six thirty and we'll have our walk in the garden then.'

Very matter-of-factly she stood up, leaned over and dropped a kiss on the top of his grey head. The effect was startling. Jack recoiled as if she had struck him; the feeding cup slopped sideways on to the bed and tea gurgled over the sheet. The nurse leaped forward to snatch up the cup and mop at the spreading stain.

'You are a naughty boy!' she said, only just managing to retain the indulgent tone.

Hope found herself saying, 'Sorry. That was my fault. Sorry, Jack. I made you jump. No damage done.'

'The sheet will have to be changed,' the nurse said tightly.

'I meant, no damage done to the patient,' Hope replied just as tightly. She picked up the cup and went to the trolley to refill it. 'There you are, Jack. It's not a bit hot, I'm afraid. Drink it as soon as you can.'

'It's not meant to be hot. Some of them would scald themselves.'

'Yes. I see.' Jack would be at the mercy of this woman when she was gone, so she smiled. 'Makes sense.'

The nurse wheeled the trolley to the door and banged through it. 'We do our best,' was her parting shot.

'Oh dear, Jack.' Hope held the feeding cup, determined he should drink the tea while it was still warm. 'I've put my foot right in it there, haven't I?'

Just for an instant she thought he was going to smile at her above the spout. But then his gaze became unfocused again and he drank like a child, gulping loudly.

She bought biscuits, and cheese in a carton with a plastic knife, apples, lime juice, some special tissues and a copy of *Treasure Island* which he had once told her was his favourite book of all time. And then she sat in the nave of the cathedral for an hour. She made no attempt to pray because she no longer knew what to pray for, but she tried to open her mind in case her mother might be able to send a thought into her head. Nothing happened. Unbidden, other thoughts used up the space she had left: the last time she had been in a cathedral was in Truro, and there had been a man who had dropped his walking stick. Nothing else had happened then either. Although before that, Jem had arrived back into their lives and made life at Penhailes possible for Peter. She wondered if he had been 'sent', and then smiled because a more unlikely messenger from the gods was difficult to imagine. She looked around her, wondering if someone else might appear today, but the nave stretched echoingly up to the choir and beyond that to the Lady chapel with its threadbare banners. She sat back and stared unwinkingly at the east window until her whole head was filled with the jewel colours of the stained glass. Colours. Vibrant, life-enhancing colours. She got up and walked down the tiny court into Westgate Street and bought a cravat, rainbow coloured and gaudy and probably in execrable taste. And then she found a phone box and rang through to Bella.

'Oh my 'an'some, I'm that glad to hear you!' Bella did not sound her usual dour self at all. 'Those girls of yours, they haven't given us no peace at all since you bin gone! An' that poor Mrs Jennings must be fed up with them. You 'aven't been back to the room all day – whatever are you up to?'

Hope told Bella exactly what was happening. 'Don't pass this on to the girls, Bella. I'm not sure how bad he was when Fay was with him, but he's pretty bad now. I suppose it's the tranquillizers. The doctor was talking about discharging him when I spoke to her this morning, but as far as I can see there's no hope of him being able to look after himself for a long time yet. I certainly don't want Chatty considering coming home – nor Fay.'

'What about you coming home here, my girl?' Bella sounded anxious. 'I can't see as 'ow you'll be able to leave 'im in a room on 'is own.'

'I'm going to put my cards on the table when I

talk to his doctor again. He'll have to stay in the hospital. We couldn't look after him, Bella. None of us. It – it's awful.' Unexpectedly, she sobbed. 'Just awful.'

'Now, now. Come on. That don't sound like you, my maid!'

'I know. I keep on crying. It's getting on my nerves!' She snuffled a laugh and after a moment Bella joined her. Then, offering what comfort she could, the older woman said that Jem had been down to Widdershins and picked the beans and watered the salad bed and everything looked very well.

'Don't rush to get back, my girl. That Fennie Perkins came this morning with a load of groceries. Cleaned my windows, she did. And scrubbed out the dairy.' There was a little pause then she added, 'Peter took the baby on 'is lap.'

Hope too paused, sensing something important. When Bella added no more, she said hesitantly, 'If you're sure. I think I might have to stay longer than I planned. Perhaps as long as a week.' The thought made her want to cry again. She wanted quite desperately to hear the sea and watch the sky for signs of the weather.

'All right then. And both your girls are going to phone you again tonight. So try to get back to that there lodging house in decent time.'

'Yes. Give my love to Peter.' The phone went dead in her hand and the money clinked into the box. For a moment she felt as if a lifeline had been cut. Then she shouldered her bag again and went out to walk to the car park.

Already it seemed as if she had been driving to the hospital for ages and she had to remind herself that yesterday she had still been at Widdershins. This time Jack was in the sitting room waiting for her; he stood as she came into the room and turned towards the open window like an automaton. She followed him into the formal garden and managed by a little skip to walk by his side. It was as if he had been drilled into some kind of performance. He walked perhaps three steps and then stood and looked at the nearest bush. Deliberately she said nothing; after about five seconds of complete silence he took another three steps and stopped again. Rigid with the sheer unnaturalness of it all, Hope did not wait for him but continued walking until she came to a seat bowered in a lavender hedge. She settled herself on it. The perfume was all-enveloping. She closed her eyes and breathed deeply.

The rain had stopped and it was a quiet, still-damp evening. Somewhere a peal of bells sounded raggedly and on the roof a dove gave a throaty coo. She opened her eyes and saw that Jack was standing uneasily in front of her.

'Sit down, Jack.' She patted the bench. 'Sit down and smell the lavender.'

He sat down obediently and for a long time they were absolutely silent, as if enjoying the scent and the gentle sounds together. Hope had no way of knowing how Jack felt, but she knew she was gradually tensing up like a spring. She had dumped her bag unceremoniously on one of the chairs in the sitting room so she could not offer him a biscuit or a sweet, and for the life of her she could not come up with any mundane remark about the weather or the garden.

And then, just as she felt she must get up and leave, he spoke.

'When are you going?' he said.

His words were so normal, so tactless that, without thought, she laughed and came back, 'Thanks a lot, Jack! I've only just arrived!'

She turned her head to look at him and he blinked hard and shook his head. 'I mean when are you going back to the cottage?'

She stared at him, amazed. It was as if he had been away and suddenly a door opened and he was there again. 'Not yet. Dr Davis thinks I can help to settle you back at home.'

'No.'

'It's just to check with the Social Services.' She thought he did not want her to see his weakness. It was just like Jack. He had to be in charge; the protector and provider. This was the old Jack. From being a zombie he was suddenly logical. She smiled. 'Nothing very drastic, Jack.'

'Not Dr Davis,' he said.

'That's who suggested—'

'No.'

She felt her nerves tightening again. 'Yes, Jack. It was Dr Davis who spoke to me when I arrived this morning.'

'No . . . *Glenys*,' he said. 'Glenys. Not Dr Davis.'

She was tempted to nod and indulge him in this and then could not.

'They are one and the same person, Jack,' she said levelly.

'No,' he repeated.

She burst out, 'This is a nightmare! You're there and then you're not there!'

Incredibly, he said woodenly, 'Yes.'

'Oh Jack! Oh, I'm sorry! Can't you wake up?'

'No.'

'Listen.' She leaned forward, desperate to help him. 'Bells. Can you hear them?' There was another silence and she thought she had lost him again, then he nodded once. 'Good. It's bell-ringing practice. At a church somewhere. Wouldn't you say?' Another pause and just as she was giving up, he nodded again. 'Right. That's not a nightmare, Jack. That's real. And the doves? Can you hear them? And the lavender – surely you don't think the lavender is a nightmare?'

There were no more responses but she went on steadily, reminding him of his perceptions, leading him to see and hear and smell and touch. Gradually her own tension dissolved and when she ran out of words she was able to sit, silently relaxed, accepting his presence, assuming he was accepting hers, so that it was a shock when he said suddenly, 'I must go.'

She stood up immediately. 'Of course. I've brought some things. You know, we made a list this afternoon. I'll bring them into your room and put them in your locker.'

He said immediately, 'No!'

She felt her face flush. 'Oh. No, of course not. If you don't want . . .'

'No,' he repeated. He started back down the path to the windows of the sitting room and she fell in behind him. He would have continued to walk across the room and through the doorway but she stopped him and offered him the bag she had brought. He took it and held it at arm's length.

'Biscuits and things. Put it all in your locker, Jack.'

He looked at the bag and then at her and at last said, 'Thanks.'

She said, 'One more thing.' She delved into her handbag and brought out the cravat and before he could move she put it around his neck and tucked it into his shirt. 'Rather Noël Coward, don't you think?'

He tucked his chin in so that he could see the cravat; he looked almost affronted.

She said quickly, 'It was the colour. I loved the rainbow effect. Reminded me of the east window in the cathedral. I went to sit there and . . .'

Her voice trailed away aimlessly as he looked up again and right into her eyes. Her own eyes widened; he was seeing her. At long last, he was seeing her.

He said quietly, 'Go back to the cottage, Ho. Don't wait for me any more. Go back.' And he turned and went through the door. Hope watched him walk down a long corridor and turn left, out of sight. Ten minutes previously she might well have decided to extend his stay here and leave him to it. Now she knew she could not do that.

Over the following week, Hope tried to establish a routine. She visited the hospital three times a day but stayed no more than an hour each time. In the mornings she would pass on messages from the girls, Bella and Peter. Then she would read the headlines in that day's paper. In the afternoons she would read a chapter of *Treasure Island*, sitting by his bed, insisting he had at least two biscuits with his mug of tea. In the evenings they sat in the garden and she took him through what he could hear and see, spread some of his crackers with cheese and shared a little picnic with him.

On bank holiday Monday she arrived with a bone-china cup and saucer in the afternoon and as soon as the nurse had wheeled the trolley away she transferred the tea from the feeder to the new cup.

'Sit in my chair, Jack. Those cups with spouts are only for when you're in bed. That's right. Tastes better, doesn't it?'

The usual long pause before the single nod. He sat there like a duchess, holding the saucer with one hand, the cup with the other. 'You can crook your little finger if you like,' she teased. But she had no response and when he had finished the tea she read again, breathing the words 'black spot' dramatically. She flicked her gaze to his face and thought there was a trace of a smile. But that evening he was not in the sitting room waiting for her and when she found the male nurse to enquire about him she was told he did not want to see her.

She stood there in a complete quandary. She was still his wife and presumably could ask to go to his room again. But . . . she was not really his wife any more and if he didn't want to see her . . . did it mean he could cope alone now? Was this a kind of beneficent farewell on his part?

The nurse smiled. 'He's quite OK, you know.

We haven't got him locked up or anything. This happens sometimes with attempted suicides. They simply don't want to see their families. It's a kind of embarrassment.'

It reduced the awful enormity of everything to a trite prognosis, terribly tempting to accept. But Hope knew there was more to it than embarrassment.

Dr Davis – or Glenys – was away for the weekend so she made an appointment to see her on Wednesday. Tuesday was awful. Jack refused to see her at all. She felt at a completely loose end all day, kicking her heels in the city until midday then going back to the hospital only to be told Jack was still refusing any visitors, and then on the spur of the moment driving out to Sandhurst in the afternoon. It was very warm but windy – itchy weather, Mandy used to call it. Mandy had had some frank and telling phrases. 'I feel as if my bra is full of fleas!' she had said one muggy day before a thunderstorm. And when Hope was pregnant she had called for her to go shopping and said, 'Go and throw up and then put on a clean smock and your kangaroo pants and a new face!' She had always been able to make something funny from something not a bit funny. Hope wondered, just for a moment, how she would cope with the awfulness of Jack's illness. What was funny about the strangely dual personality who was trying to shut himself away from everyone and everything?

Hope drove very slowly past the terrace of houses. The gardens looked tired at the end of the summer; the river was low and a line of glistening mud edged each bank. She pulled into the pub car park and went inside to ask if she could have a pot of tea and some sandwiches. She must make some plans. She would sit outside and decide what she was going to say to Glenys Davis tomorrow. Could she possibly be absolutely frank and ask whether she could go back to Cornwall by the end of the week? It was so obvious that there was no chance at all of Jack returning to the room in Russell Square. Mrs Jennings was kind enough but the facilities were fairly basic and he really would go crazy in the room at the top of the house.

She took tea and cheese sandwiches into the little garden and sat at one of the wooden tables and tried to think what might be best for Jack. Was there a convalescent home for cases like his? And if so, how much would the National Health pay, or was that the Social Services' province? And was she really thinking entirely of Jack's welfare or was she just desperate to get back to Cornwall?

At the end of an hour she was no further forward with her thoughts and plans. She went back to the car and drove on down the road, intending to turn in the driveway of the Petersens' old house. It was uncomfortably hot now and a pungent smell from the river drifted through the open windows of Peter's car. She hoped it would rain tonight and wash some of the city dust from the immaculate paintwork. When she got back she would clean it, polish the chrome and glass, make it shine again. She wished there was something she could get for Peter and Bella. If she went into the tiny shop in St John's Lane tomorrow perhaps there would be a decent second-hand telescope. Jem could set it up for Peter in the bedroom on a tripod or something. Bella would enjoy that too.

She swung the car into the gateway of the drive and put it into reverse to back into the road again. And then paused, embarrassed. Someone was pegging clothes on the line at the back of the cottage. How stupid of her: obviously the house would have been sold or let or something. She backed hurriedly around the hedge and was about to drive off when something caught her eye. The dress that hung limply from its pegs in the heat of the afternoon was familiar. It was cut on the cross; silk, coral-coloured. Mandy's favourite colour. Mandy's favourite dress. 'My vamp-'em-quick frock,' she had called it.

Hope edged the car forward a yard. Whoever was doing the pegging out was invisible now. The line suddenly ascended as it was propped high and then a woman swung around the corner of the house, pulled open the door and went inside. It was Mandy.

The male nurse greeted her as she got out of the car.

'Mrs Langley. I'm sorry. I've been talking to Jack, but he insists that he cannot see anyone. You have an appointment with Glenys tomorrow morning, I see. Perhaps she will override his decision. You understand, I cannot do so.'

'Of course not. I wouldn't dream . . . I mean, if he doesn't want to see me then obviously I respect that.' Hope tried to smile reassuringly. 'Perhaps I'll see you tomorrow then.'

'I won't be on duty until Thursday this week. I'll see you then, I expect.'

'Yes. Give Jack my best wishes. Just say . . . oh . . . I hope he will come for a walk in the garden with me tomorrow.' She was about to get back into the car and then she stopped. 'I wonder . . . do you know if Jack has had a visitor this afternoon – besides me, I mean?'

He turned. 'No. No one else. I did wonder whether any of his old colleagues might pop in. Strange. People are still scared of mental illness.'

Hope drove away slowly, scanning each car she passed on the way down to the ring road. If this whole situation had verged on a nightmare before it had suddenly become a full-blown version of a very bad dream indeed. She had got the impression that Henrik and Mandy had left the country for ever; possibly because they owed money. One of the reasons for their prosperity had been that Henrik neatly avoided paying any British taxes. Yet they had neither sold nor let the house and now they were back. Or at any rate Mandy was back.

Hope had thought of little else since she left Sandhurst that afternoon. Like a terrier worrying its prey she had gnawed and torn at the problem of Mandy's sudden reappearance with a kind of terror. They – she – had come back for something. What was it? It had occurred to Hope quite late in the afternoon that if Mandy were alone she could only have come back for Jack. In which case, had Jack asked her to come back? No. Surely not. And yet . . . and yet . . .

It was only a temporary relief to know that

Mandy had not called at the hospital. She would hardly go later today, it was already seven thirty. And tomorrow . . . she might go tomorrow afternoon. Not in the morning. Visiting times always used to be in the afternoons and that was what she would remember. So there was still the appointment with Dr Davis in the morning. She could warn her about Mandy. Explain that it was when he talked about Mandy before that he had decided to end his life.

Mrs Jennings met her just inside the front door.

'I thought it was you. Your old teacher's here. Miss Marchant. We've had a nice cup of tea and a walk in the park. But the park isn't what it used to be and this nasty wind blew us all which-ways so we came back because Dorothea thought it would be nice to see you again.'

It was the last thing Hope wanted to do but she admitted to herself that perhaps it was for the best. Alone in that attic room she might have read or gone to bed early; no way could she have stopped chewing on this new problem. Whereas now, she smiled and shook hands and accepted a small sweet sherry and sat in one of the overstuffed chairs grouped around the net-curtained window and listened while Miss Marchant exclaimed over all the years that had intervened since their last meeting.

'It was just after your first baby was born,' she recalled. 'Faith. Such a lovely old-fashioned name. And you called the next baby Charity? Faith, Hope and Charity. And the greatest of these is charity. Does that ring true, my dear?'

Hope smiled. 'Charity is the biblical term for

love, isn't it? I wouldn't be surprised. Though it is Faith who is in love at the moment.' She spread her hands. 'Mrs Jennings will have told you about my marriage breakdown. Both girls are dealing with it very well. I am very proud of them.'

Miss Marchant did not comment on this; Hope got the impression that she did not approve of marriage break-ups. She did not appear to have changed in the last twenty years. Her skin might well be wrinkled but beneath the careful powder it was not obvious and her long, patrician nose still gave her a general air of disapproval. Yet she was friendly with Mrs Jennings who, after all, was divorced.

Mrs Jennings hovered with the sherry bottle. 'And how was your poor husband today, Mrs Langley?'

Hope shook her head to the sherry and continued to shake it slowly. 'I'm afraid he would not see me at all. It was very disappointing. He seems to shut himself away for long periods. Even when we're walking in the garden, there are times when he is simply . . . not there.'

'Is that just with you? What is he like with the staff?' Miss Marchant accepted more sherry and leaned forward. 'Surely he must be more . . . forthcoming . . . with them? They would not be considering discharging him otherwise.'

'I've got an appointment with his doctor tomorrow morning. I need to find out a lot of things. It's very difficult to know what to do. I wondered about convalescent homes. I would rather not stay here too long. Relying on neighbours to look after things back in Cornwall—'

Miss Marchant said suddenly and firmly, 'In sickness and in health.'

Hope looked at Mrs Jennings who lifted her shoulders helplessly.

Miss Marchant said, 'I can hear you both saying those words, my dear Hope. In sickness and in health. A very solemn promise.'

Hope put her glass down carefully and placed her hands on her lap. She was wearing a cotton skirt with big patch pockets on the front. After a while she put her hands into the pockets.

'I don't love him any more, Miss Marchant.'

'That has got nothing to do with it.' Miss Marchant was beginning to sound like an angry prophet. She repeated, 'In sickness and in health. Nothing about falling out of love.'

'But . . . wouldn't it be hypocritical? I actually dislike him!'

'You dislike what he has done. I don't think you dislike the man who is in the hospital, Hope. Otherwise how can you visit him and try to help him as you are doing?' She held up her hand as Hope began to speak. 'But I still maintain that in the circumstances your feelings for your husband don't enter into this.'

'Oh . . . I don't know.' Hope felt wretched.

Mrs Jennings said, 'It's only like me with Alf. He left me and he's gone downhill ever since. But I can't see him on his own on Christmas Day. Poor old devil.' She sipped delicately at her glass. 'You don't have to like him, my lamb. Staying near at hand for a bit and keeping an eye on him . . . it's no more than you'd do for one of your sick cows!'

Hope laughed. And then she couldn't stop.

Mrs Jennings joined her and, after a startled pause, so did Miss Marchant. But when Hope left them and went upstairs, the new problem was still there. Had Mandy come home to look after Jack . . . or to claim him . . . or to torment him? It was ridiculous to want to protect him from another woman. But she did.

She could not sleep and knowing that she would probably drop off at dawn, she set Jack's small alarm clock. She did not want to risk Mandy turning up at the hospital before she could see Dr Glenys.

She woke to its insistent note in the middle of a dream. It had something to do with Mandy but she could not remember quite what. There was a little ache somewhere in her chest, and she tried to sleep again, just for a few minutes, so that she could study Mandy's smile.

Instead she dragged herself out of bed and went to the next floor and the bathroom. It occurred to her to wonder whether she herself might be running away from Mandy, because, like Jack, there was a part of her that wanted to see that mocking smile, the golden hair, the sheer craziness of Mandy Petersen.

She splashed cold water on her face and shivered in spite of the humidity.

Fourteen

'Please call me Glenys. It helps to bridge the patient–doctor gulf.'

Hope was sitting in another room furnished with a desk and a computer but both chairs were on one side of the desk. She forced a smile.

'The trouble is, I think at least one of your patients thinks of you as a dual person. Dr Davis and Glenys.'

'Really? That is most interesting. I take it you refer to Jack?'

'Who else?'

Hope realized she was sparring and that meant she was on the defensive. Glenys realized it too and did not immediately respond. Instead she moved the computer keyboard closer to the modem and put an elbow on the free space.

'Has anything happened?' she asked.

'Not a lot. We walk in the garden. I talk. Sometimes he replies appropriately and sometimes he nods or shakes his head and sometimes he does neither.'

'And you think we are going to shove him out into the cold, cruel world to fend for himself when he is so obviously unable to do so?'

'Something like that.' Hope leaned forward. 'Doctor. Glenys. Is my husband suffering from brain damage?'

'He could be. He is certainly suffering from despair.'

'Obviously. Terminal despair.'

'He was. Perhaps he is still. Although I don't think so.'

'I don't agree. If he is sent home now I think he will again try to end his life. And probably succeed this time.'

Another silence. Hope felt herself being studied. The doctor said, 'What had you in mind? A lengthy stay here? That's not a good idea.'

'No. I can see that.' Hope realized her words could be construed as insulting but for some reason she was angry. 'Are there places like convalescent homes? Rehabilitation centres? Some halfway-house arrangement?'

'Yes. Waiting lists a mile long. There are private ones. Expensive.'

'No good.'

Glenys sighed and stood up. 'I can see how difficult this is for you. Naturally you are concerned for Jack. You were married and must have been happy at one time. Now all you want to do is to forget the marriage and go back to your new life. And he is around your neck like an albatross.'

Hope was shocked at this description. Was that how she saw Jack? She said, 'I certainly cannot leave him until I feel he is . . . safe.' She would not have used that word before she had seen Mandy back in Sandhurst. Mandy was a danger. She went on quickly, 'The thing is, although he has responded at various times during the past week, I am left with the impression that he doesn't welcome my presence. In fact I make him worse. He wouldn't see me at all yesterday and I shall be surprised if he sees me today.'

'He has said he does not wish to.'

'You see? So if I cannot help him, is there anyone who could?'

'You mean, one of your daughters? No, I don't think so. In fact I would hope not. The fact that he is desperately trying to reject you is an excellent sign of recovery.' She smiled at Hope's expression. 'Don't you see? He is thinking of someone else. He doesn't want to ruin any more lives.'

'Oh God.' Hope got up violently and walked to the window. The rain had still not come and someone was watering the roses 'I can't cope with this.'

Behind her she heard the doctor sigh. 'I know what you want me to say. You want me to come up with the address of a small hostel where he will be monitored and cared for and yet have his freedom.' There were sounds of things being moved around on the desk. 'I can find him somewhere. Yes. But you know how many holes there are in the system. I cannot give you any guarantees. However it seems to you, he has made progress since your arrival. But I cannot ask you to stay. Obviously.'

Hope said flatly, 'No, I cannot stay. And anyway what good would I be if he won't let me anywhere near him?'

'Oh, I think you are capable of breaking that barrier, don't you?'

Hope sensed a sarcastic undertone that infuriated her. She turned. 'You think I am manipulative, don't you? It was Jack who smashed our marriage. And I mean, *smashed*.' Glenys said nothing but smiled slightly and Hope exploded. 'He slept with my best friend! Probably for ages!'

Glenys said quietly, 'And you cannot forgive him.'

'Forgiveness does not enter into it! I simply don't want anything more to do with him!'

'And here you are, pitchforked into making decisions for him. He probably made all the decisions, did he? And now everything is down to you.'

'And I don't *want* that!' Hope controlled her breathing with difficulty. 'Listen. There is another way.' She came back to the desk and sat down. 'I think you know who I mean when I say . . . Mandy.'

Glenys was surprised at last. 'What on earth are you suggesting? Posting your husband off to the other woman? With blessings? Surely they would have left the country together if there were still anything between them?'

'No. Mandy knew which side her bread was buttered on! She had – has – a very indulgent husband.'

'Then it is unlikely she would agree to taking on a sick man.'

Hope paused and took another breath. 'She is back. In this country. Here. I saw her yesterday.'

Glenys took her elbow off the desk and sat

straight. 'What did she say? Is she going to visit Jack?'

'I didn't speak to her. But I can't think of another reason for her to return. They owe a lot of money to people. The Inland Revenue too.'

The phone on the desk rang suddenly and they both jumped. Glenys picked it up and listened and then said, 'I'll be out soon.' She turned to Hope. 'Mrs Langley. Your husband was having therapy before the suicide attempt. We think that when he spoke of Mandy Petersen his distress became unbearable. I would not like him to see her.'

'You can stop her, surely?'

'This isn't a prison. I can try to stonewall her but if she is as determined as your husband says—'

'She is determined.'

'It will be difficult.'

Hope sat back. 'Then there is only one thing for it.' She sighed, suddenly – and for the first time in the last week – relaxed. 'I'll go home. Today. Now. And I'll take Jack with me.'

Once she had said it she knew that it had been the only solution all along. Widdershins had saved her sanity; it would save Jack's. She was sure of it, so sure she smiled widely at the doctor. 'There won't be any problem about discharging him, will there?'

'He is a voluntary patient. But whether he will agree to leave with you . . . indeed, whether it is a good idea, I am not sure.'

'Doctor – Glenys – you have just spent nearly an hour trying to convince me to stay with him!

And now, when I am suggesting staying with him all the time, you are having doubts!'

'Mrs Langley, he is being cared for medically. He is on a programme of certain tranquillizing drugs—'

'I know. I've seen him under the influence. A zombie.'

'You asked about brain damage. We cannot rule that out. There was a gap between his heart failure and the arrival at hospital. The paramedics resuscitated him, of course, but it could be—'

'But you don't really think he has permanent brain damage.'

'I think he is deeply traumatized. Which in some ways can be worse. From the carer's point of view.' She fiddled with a pencil on the desk. 'Your daughter told me that the conditions in Cornwall are quite primitive—'

'That is why it is the best possible environment for him. There is so much to do, just to survive.' She saw Glenys's expression and swept on regardless. 'It's a healing place too. The sea and the sunsets and the headland itself—'

'Your daughter also told me that her father never really liked it down there.'

Hope was brought up short. That was true. That was the real reason for Jack never sharing their holidays.

She said, 'That was the old Jack. He was always striving for something . . . beyond his ken, I suppose. Material things. Success.'

'He wanted that for you.'

'I didn't want it.' Her eyes opened wide.

'But . . . Mandy did. Was that why he turned to Mandy?'

Glenys fiddled with the pencil again. 'Mandy represented a lot of things. We know that. What we don't know is how important she came to be. For Jack.'

Hope was silent, still staring at Glenys. Glenys picked up the pencil and put it in a holder and said, 'If you are successful in rehabilitating your husband . . . it could well be that he goes back to this woman. You need to know that a complete recovery for Jack must mean that you leave him free to make his own choices.'

Hope swallowed. 'I see that. But – at the moment – we are surely agreed that Mandy is a danger to him?'

'Yes. But I must emphasize that ultimately – when he can free himself of the terrible guilt – he might want to be with her.'

'I know. I accept that.' Hope realized she was tense again and tried to relax. 'I am not possessive about Jack. I am certainly not jealous of Mandy. In a way . . . it would be very easy for me to let her take over. But if she has some hold over him – and she obviously has – then I would rather try to protect him for a while.'

She put her hands to her head and tried to think through what she wanted to do. Glenys sat very still, waiting. At last Hope said, 'Listen. Let me have a supply of whatever he is taking and a detailed list of instructions. I haven't registered with a doctor myself yet, so I can do that for both of us and ask whoever it is to get in touch with you. And there are very good neighbours near at hand. The cottage is not as cut off as it sounds.' She smiled. 'We have a proper flush toilet!'

Glenys laughed and then sobered. 'All right. It is a most unusual convalescence but it could work. I want you to promise me that if it gets too much for you, you will ask for professional help.'

'Of course.'

'Then . . . you will have to bear with me for a while. There's a lot of paperwork and I must talk to Jack and convince him this is the right thing to do.' She stood up. 'How will you feel if he absolutely refuses to go with you?'

Hope had already thought of that. 'He will say no. To you. But please go ahead with the paperwork. I'll go back to his bedsit and pack everything into the car.' She too stood up and looked at the doctor. 'He will come with me.'

She felt almost hunted as she drove back to Russell Square and told Mrs Jennings what was happening.

The plump face lengthened with concern. 'I don't let that room normally – as I told you. It will be there if he needs it. Or if you need it, come to that.' She was definitely flustered out of her usual monumental calm. 'I knew you was taking Dorothea's words to heart. I could have killed her really. All right, I keep an eye on my old man but that's no reason for you feeling guilty. Your husband is in good hands. It's not as if you were deserting him – well, sounds to me as if he did that to you in a way.'

Hope was touched. 'It wasn't only what Miss Marchant said. It's just that he can be so quiet and peaceful in the cottage in Cornwall. Really think what he wants to do, where he wants to live. In a way, it'll be like being born again for him.' Hope started up the stairs two at a time. She still felt a sense of urgency. It was ridiculous but she half expected Mandy to knock at the door any minute.

'That's a nice idea,' Mrs Jennings panted, following as fast as she could.

Hope said over her shoulder, 'I'll take my own stuff down to the car. And perhaps you can tell me what is yours and what is Jack's.'

'Well, like I said, unless it's something he particularly needs, you can leave it . . .' but she trailed up anyway and got in Hope's way while she picked up various things and put them down again. 'No books, see. Nor papers. Oh, there's this one – *Treasure Island*, a kiddie's book by the sound of it.'

'I'm reading that to him. What about the alarm clock?'

'That belongs here. There's a pair of his shoes in the cupboard, and socks. Just the one pair. I suppose your daughter took the others into hospital for him.'

Hope picked up the socks. They were carefully darned. She clutched them to her for a moment before putting them in her bag. 'They're twenty years old actually. Just a silly keepsake. My first attempt at darning.'

They parted almost affectionately. 'Sisters under the skin,' Mrs Jennings said as she handed one of the bags to Hope. Hope grinned suddenly. It was a remark Fay would appreciate, having met her father's landlady. She must remember it.

It was one o'clock when she arrived at the

hospital and the trolley was being pushed down the corridor loaded with the remains of lunch. She knew she ought to report at reception or go straight to Glenys's office, but she followed the trolley and turned left for Jack's room, rapped on the door and went in.

He was lying on the bed but propped up, not in his usual somnolent post-prandial state. As he turned and saw her he straightened and swung his legs to the ground. She glanced at his locker and saw two tablets there.

'You haven't taken them,' she said conversationally.

His throat moved as he swallowed but he said nothing. She smiled, went to the locker and swept them into her hand. 'Good. Perhaps that's how we can go on. Are you ready to leave? I've brought the car right up to the entrance.'

He looked at her and then away. 'No,' he said.

She said, 'It's the only way, Jack. Widdershins is a haven. A sanctuary. I have proved it. Don't be frightened of it.'

'No,' he said.

She smiled. 'No? You certainly are frightened. And if you're not frightened of Widdershins, what is it? Are you frightened of me?'

There was a longer pause and when he said no at last, she told herself that at least he had given it thought.

She said, 'You are frightened I will try to drag you back? I represent everything that went wrong?'

He said violently, 'No!' And then looking at her again, 'Me!'

She shook her head. 'That's part of your illness. That will go. And this Tarzan talk will go too, I hope. It's wearing, to say the least.' She went to his locker and began to shovel everything out into a plastic bag. 'I thought they would have done this already. I want to leave as soon as possible, Jack. We'll take it steadily. Stop at Okehampton for a cup of tea. Penzance for some shopping.'

She heard him breathing; almost panting.

'I cannot come with you,' he said.

She turned and smiled. 'Congratulations. A whole sentence.' She straightened. 'Jack. I didn't want to say this. You have to come with me. I am your only hope . . .' She tried to stretch her smile into a grin. 'Did you hear that – I am your only Hope!' She saw the complete incomprehension in his eyes and said with great deliberation, 'Mandy is back. I've seen her. She must know you are here. So you cannot stay.' She paused and watched his face change. Yes, it was Mandy. He was terrified of her. Or of himself? His own vulnerability?

She said gently, 'Come on, Jack. We are nothing to each other any more. Just two people who need care. Widdershins will give us that.' She watched him swallowing again, desperately, but he said nothing. She could almost feel his mind seeking a solution and finding none. She knelt by the bed and fitted sandals onto his feet. Somehow the familiar shape of his toes, the crooked nail where Chatty had dropped a brick on it, the long upstanding vein over his left instep, the rough skin on his heels . . . all made her feel a strange, impersonal pity for him.

She buckled the straps and looked up at him. 'It's all right. Honestly. I know I can do this absolutely objectively. No emotional strings, I promise.' She smiled again. 'Listen. I need someone to saw and chop wood. It's an endless job. Once the fire has to be kept in it eats up fuel. I've made some makeshift shutters too. They need hingeing on to the windows. And if you could clear more of the furze and dig out the roots, I could put in some winter cabbages.' She waited, crouching before him. He said nothing and kept swallowing. She said, 'Jack, did Fay tell you about Peter?' He looked at her. 'He's got lung cancer. They've done what they can but he loses weight all the time. You could sit with him. Perhaps play dominoes. He likes playing dominoes. You could make such a difference to Peter.'

Very slowly, painfully slowly, he eased himself off the bed and stood up. She gave him the plastic bag containing his belongings and put his anorak over her arm. She walked ahead of him down the corridor purposely looking straight ahead, assuming he would follow her. When she reached the room where Dr Davis had seen her earlier, she tapped and went in. Glenys looked up from the computer. Hope walked to the desk and knew that Jack was behind her because Glenys's face lightened.

'Oh . . . Jack. I am glad. This could be really . . . exciting. Yes.' She smiled. 'Yes, exciting! Have you got everything? Toilet bag – shaver – clothes?' She turned to Hope. 'Sorry we didn't pack. He was so against it earlier. But in any case, I got everything together as you asked.'

She stood up and reached for a large envelope labelled with Jack's name. 'A supply of tranquillizers. Nothing else. But I have included a list of the drugs he has had and you can take it all to your doctor if necessary. Is there a contact telephone number?'

Hope took the proffered pen and wrote down the Penhaileses' number. She glanced out of the window. Beyond the garden the drive swept to the car park. There had been a dozen cars there when she arrived and there were a dozen now.

She said, 'I think we should be on our way. Thank you for your help.' She shook hands. 'Have there been any phone calls?'

'No.' Glenys came around the desk and went with them into the corridor and shook hands with Jack. 'I wish you all the best, Jack.'

Hope went ahead and unlocked the boot to thrust in Jack's few possessions. Then she opened the passenger door for him and went round to the driver's side. He was still in the entrance; Glenys was talking; he shook his head; she said something else and he nodded. Hope contained her impatience somehow. She told herself she was being ridiculous; no way would Mandy come here without phoning first. And if she did – if she arrived at this moment – what could she do? But Jack was frightened and Hope had a feeling that he was frightened of his own reactions. Would he go with Mandy if she asked him? Hope bit her lip. Mandy could give him so much; the luxury of the Sandhurst cottage for a few days and then – maybe – the sunshine of Cape Town.

He clambered awkwardly into the car and she

leaned across him to pull over the seat belt and clip him in. He didn't smell like Jack; he smelled of the hospital.

She said, 'Jack. Have I bullied you into this? Would it be better for you to wait for Mandy?'

He did not reply. She had not expected him to. She looked at him and saw the fear again. She said, 'Listen. If you really hate it at Widder-shins, I will bring you back. Any time.'

His grey eyes were bewildered as well as frightened. She felt the pang of pity again. She patted his hand and turned the ignition key and they drove slowly to the gates and then very quickly on to the A38 and the motorway. No strange car followed them. Hope felt faintly ridiculous. What on earth had she thought would happen?

The rain started at Bristol. Like the journey up-country last week, it made driving very diffi-cult and slowed them considerably. She parked behind the shops at Okehampton and found an umbrella on the back seat.

'Come on, Jack. I must have a break. We'll find a snack bar or something and have a cup of tea.'

He did not want to leave the safety of the car; she was not surprised; after the hospital it was his one point of reference. She opened the umbrella and risked dashing down the road in search of the sort of café which would put tea into polystyrene cups. It was nerve-racking and her relief when she got back to the car and saw Jack still sitting there was enormous. She gave him his cup and then had to take it back to remove the lid and put in the sugar. And then he held it in both hands and brought his head down to it. She blinked and opened her own cup. For the first time she wondered whether – physically – she could cope.

After a while they drove on past the castle and out again on to the A30. She had always divided the journey into sections with interim goals; first Bristol, then Exeter, then Okehampton and then Jamaica Inn. This afternoon the leg from Okehampton to Jamaica Inn seemed endless. She leaned forward in the driver's seat, her nose almost touching the windscreen in an effort to see through the rain. Jack did not speak a word and she thought he had gone to sleep until the long hill up to the inn when a car came off Bodmin Moor apparently determined to ram them. Then she heard Jack gasp just as she braked. The other car missed them easily and she made no comment at all, but she registered that Jack knew what was happening.

She did not stop in Penzance; it was six o'clock and most of the shops would be closed. 'We'll be coming in soon,' she told Jack. 'I want to have a look round the second-hand shops. I thought I'd get Peter a telescope. If we get any more summer he'll be able to use it up on the knoll. Above the cove.'

Jack said nothing. She thought with dread of the muddy walk down the headland from Penhailes Farm; she saw Widdershins through his eyes. The ragged patches of garden, the piles of wood. It probably looked like a gypsy encampment.

She said, 'I should have put your shoes on, Jack. Those sandals will be hopeless.' She realized wryly how unsuitably dressed they both were. 'We're going to be absolutely soaked by the time we get indoors!'

The journey finished almost too quickly. One minute the finger of Buryan church was pointing menacingly through the rain, the next they had turned into the open gate of the farm and were bumping across the yard towards the coach house. And Jem must have been looking out for them because he was there with the doors wide open, waving them in, grinning like a Cheshire cat.

'Have you had this weather all the way down?' He opened the passenger door wide for Jack to alight. 'Bella and Peter were worried. Dr Davis rang just before one o'clock and it's almost seven now.'

Hope got out wearily. 'It did seem a long drive both ways,' she admitted. 'But it's good to be home.' She looked across at Jem who was standing helplessly by Jack's door. She put her head back into the car. 'Come on, Jack. Out you get. We're here now.' Nothing happened and she spoke to Jem. 'Leave him for a minute, Jem. We've got a couple of bags we need to take with us. Everything else can stay here till the rain gives over.'

He said, 'I'll walk down with you. Let's go and say hello to the others.'

Hope heard Jack whimper and said loudly, 'We're tired, Jem. Could you go in now and make our apologies? We'll see Bella and Peter tomorrow.'

He hesitated. He too had heard the whimper. Then he said, 'Yes. Of course.' He came around the bonnet and joined her. 'Just leave the doors – leave everything. I'll see to it later.' He stared at her through the darkness of the garage. 'Can you manage?'

'Yes.'

'I've taken stuff down. Bread and milk and some butter and cheese. Plenty of lettuce ready to pull. The tomatoes are looking good too.'

'Great!' She spoke with false heartiness. She could see that Jack was sitting very still, his chin touching his chest. 'We could do with something to eat.' She nodded meaningfully at Jem and he drifted out of the garage. Then she went around to the passenger side. 'He's gone, Jack. You need not see anyone. Come on. Can you carry this? And I'll have the coats and try to keep them dry under these plastic bags. The umbrella's hopeless, it'll be inside out before we get across the yard.'

It was indeed a bleak evening and when she had coaxed him out of the car she had to start all over again to get him to the other gate and through on to the headland. Once there, with the full force of the rain beating on them, he seemed slightly more purposeful and put his head into the wind. She led the way, squelching through the mud, giving up on trying to keep to the dry edges of the path. They got to the little escarpment below which the cottage nestled. She sniffed. 'Oh, Jack! Smell that smell! Sea and earth and . . . best of all . . . Jem has lit the range! I can smell the smoke! That's what I call a welcome home!' She almost ran along the top of the cliff and down into the valley and then back up to the door. By the light of the fire she could see the table laid just as it had been back in 1967. She had not bothered with a tablecloth since her arrival in January and the starched white linen sparkled like frost. She could have wept. It was going to be hard work looking after Jack. But at least she was home.

The next few days were indescribably difficult. She told herself the fault lay with her because certainly Jack was no trouble. She gave him the bedroom to himself and took to sleeping next to the range just as she had done last winter. She did this mainly because she was worried he might wander off in the night or set fire to the house, but also because she needed to get him right out of the way. His presence should have been unobtrusive; he hardly spoke, he did what she told him to do, he came with her when she went to the farm and stood like a statue while Bella exclaimed on his thinness and how they would soon put some fat on his bones. He let Peter pump his hand; he even sat and watched while Hope and Peter played a game of dominoes. But his presence was in fact very obtrusive. She could not forget him for a moment; he was her responsibility as a child would have been. That first night she could not sleep though she was bone tired. The thought of him upstairs was a violation of her privacy and solitude. As day succeeded day and nothing changed, she wondered how long she could bear it.

His first Sunday at Widdershins began as

usual. She took him a cup of tea at six thirty and went down to the rill to splash the icy water over herself. The sun was already warm on her face as she walked back up the combe. It was going to be a golden Michaelmas day. And she had to spend it regimenting Jack into some kind of routine. She sighed.

When she got back he was standing by the table, dressed after a fashion but unable to make any decision about what to do next. She usually told him to sit down while she got the breakfast, but this morning she did not say a word. She cut bread and butter and spread her own gooseberry jam on it, made more tea and sat down herself. After some hesitation he sat opposite her.

She said casually, 'Pour the tea, will you, Jack?' He did so; his hand shook and some of the tea went on to the cloth but she made no comment and merely watched as he dabbed at it with his handkerchief. He appeared not to see the plate of bread and butter and jam, but he drank the tea and then sat very still looking out of the window. She switched on the little radio. There had been flooding in Bangladesh; a new report about Mandela's illness; a humorous account of how England and Wales were coping with the all-day opening of public houses. She commented, 'I bet not many Cornish pubs will open all day.'

To her astonishment, Jack said with quiet conviction, 'Eventually they will.'

She stared at him, hardly believing her ears. He did not look round, his grey eyes were not seeing the little valley with its cultivated banks.

But he must be listening to the radio and he had responded to her remark!

She took a careful breath. 'They don't think much of Sunday working though. So let's take the day off. I'll cut some sandwiches and we'll go down to the cove and sunbathe. We can't miss out on a day like this.'

She expected him to come out with one of his monosyllabic refusals but he said nothing and she fetched cheese and cut more bread and packed it in a tea towel with tomatoes and lettuce. It was infuriating when he continued to sit blankly at the table while she cleared away and heated water for washing up. He had always been so helpful and had chivvied the girls into helping too.

They followed the rill down to the cliff path and clambered down to the strip of sand left by the tide. She immediately spread a towel and lay down and, after one of those agonizingly indecisive moments, he squatted on his heels and looked at the sea.

She tried to ignore him. She told herself that this gentle sunshine was good for him, that she need not be anxious for him, that the journey back to health was a long one and that she must be patient. But they had been here for the best part of a week now and he had eaten only when she told him to and then like a bird; she was frightened to let him use either the saw or the axe and after two or three hours with a spade she saw that he was white with exhaustion. She found it unbearable to have him standing in the middle of the garden watching her hoeing, so she set him to stacking wood and that was just awful because he took a log at a time and stood by the woodpile, obviously quite incapable of working out where to put it. She was extending their visits to Penhailes Farm because she did not know what else to do with him. And that meant that she wasn't doing the work herself. It was a diminishing spiral and she had no idea how she could put it into reverse.

She closed her eyes, unwilling to see him squatting there helplessly, so she had no idea when things began to change. She might even have slept for a few minutes. When she opened her eyes next he was still there, but with a difference. He really was there; inhabiting his body again and registering . . . something.

She stayed very still. It occurred to her belatedly that the sea was a way out for him. Was that what he was registering – an escape? She tried to swivel her gaze without moving her head; where was the tide now? Was it coming in, about to swamp them, or was it retreating?

And then he stood up and moved away and immediately she was getting up too. But he was not walking towards the sea. He had spotted the *Mirabelle* leaning against the cave wall. She sat back down on the sand and watched him, objectively curious. He reached the boat and began what seemed to be a careful inspection. He ran his hands along the keel, then picked up a stone and scraped experimentally at the paintwork. It came off. He got on to his hands and knees and crawled under the stern and she could hear him knocking the other side. When he emerged he was festooned with bright green weed and he stood and pulled it off. His actions looked so normal she wanted to weep. He meandered back to her after that; she saw that he was exhausted again.

'You must eat, Jack. All that inspection . . . come on. Cheese, tomatoes. You need your strength.'

He ate obediently as he did everything. But when he had finished he said, 'Peter will have pitch. I'll give the keel a coat of pitch.'

'Not today. Today is Sunday. Tomorrow. If you eat your supper.' She grinned as she spoke. It was like a gift from heaven when his mouth turned up too.

Fifteen

They walked up to the farm that evening and stood on the knoll with Peter, watching a magnificent sunset. Hope deliberately said nothing about the *Mirabelle* and neither did Jack. She was disappointed but not surprised. Each time he seemed to be breaking through the fog, his retreat was swift and total. Peter asked if they had had a good day and after waiting for Jack to reply, Hope supplied a response. 'Actually, it's been a wonderful day. We had a picnic in the cove.'

'Did you swim?' Peter asked.

'No.' It had occurred to her but the risk was obvious with Jack in his present state.

'I'll let you have some of my sea soap. D'you remember, I gave you some before? When you came down first? Best to choose a nice deep pool when the tide goes out and use it like a bath.'

Hope smiled. 'Are you telling us we're getting smelly, Peter?'

Peter grinned back. 'I'm telling you how you can save yourselves a lot of trouble!' He glanced at Jack. 'I think you could do with a shave, my lad. Let's go back now and you can have a lend of my stuff.' He was sitting on a rock and stood up with some difficulty. 'Give me your arm, m'boy.' He hung on to Jack who stood like a statue. 'No need for you to come down yet, my maid. Have a bit o' peace and quiet by yourself for five minutes.' He grinned at her doubtful expression. 'Don't worry, I en't going to let him have my cut-throat razor!'

She smiled back shakily. Sometimes she thought Peter understood everything. She perched on his rock and looked out to where the Longships light was just beginning to show. Any time to herself was precious and, determined to make the most of it, she consciously emptied her mind as she had done in the cathedral not long before. Again, nothing happened except that gradually a kind of peace seemed to bathe her. She closed her eyes and smiled, letting the last light from the sun glow against her lids. How could she think nothing was happening when she was getting this injection of tranquillity? After a while she opened her eyes again and saw that the sea was darkening and the streaks of sun-red sky were gone. And so was the moment. As if on cue, Bella's voice came from below, calling her. She leaped up, immediately anxious about Jack.

Bella appeared, panting, holding her side.

'Someone on the phone. Wouldn't give a name. Told 'em you'd ring back. Thought you might want to do it while the gaffer is 'elping Jack with his shave.'

It was strange; Hope knew who had telephoned. She had felt Mandy's presence behind her ever since she had seen her in the Sandhurst garden.

She nodded slowly. 'Yes. Thanks, Bella. It was a woman's voice, was it?'

'Yes. But it weren't neither of the girls 'aving one of their jokes. And if it had been that doctor, she would've said.'

They fell into step together. Jem was bringing the cows into the barn for milking. The kitchen light shone across the yard. 'That's where the gaffer and Jack are,' Bella said. 'Too much for Gaffer to get upstairs nowadays.' She opened the door and stood aside. 'I'll be in the bedroom. I'm going to put that little electric fire on. Bit chilly tonight.'

'All right. I won't be long.' Hope walked down the hall to where the telephone sat by the coat stand. Her breath was catching in her throat and she swallowed. Bella picked up a piece of paper and gave it to her and she saw that it was the number of the Sandhurst house.

Bella, as perceptive as Peter, said urgently, 'He's getting better. I can see 'ee's getting better, my girl. Don't let nothin' spoil that!'

Hope dialled the number slowly and surely. She had no idea what she was going to say. When Mandy's voice came across the line it was as if the past nine months melted away. How very, very much she would like to be able to say, 'I'm making rag rugs now. D'you think you could sell them as relaxation mats for the lady-in-waiting?' There had always been a sense of space with Mandy; freedom; limitless horizons. One of her favourite replies to a question had been 'Why not?'

She must have paused a bit too long because Mandy's voice changed; it became less certain. She said slowly, 'Is that you, Hope? Can't you speak to me?'

Hope spoke just as slowly. 'Why couldn't you leave us alone? How did you find out?'

'I went to see Chatty.'

'She hasn't told me about that.'

'I promised her I would not get in touch with you. I suppose she didn't want to worry you. She's so . . . lovely, Hope.'

'I know. And you have broken your promise to her.'

Just for a moment, the old Mandy surfaced. 'I crossed my fingers anyway!' Then she sobered. 'Yes. I did break my promise. I had no intention of keeping it. I haven't changed, you see.'

'No. That is why you must stay away from us.'

Mandy said, 'I am not *ruthless*, Hope!'

'Oh, I think you are.'

'Don't confuse a lack of ruth with realism!' Mandy tried to laugh and then stopped and added seriously, 'You are not realistic, Hope. You cannot make Jack well by isolating him in that place. He never liked it down there. What makes you think he will feel differently now?'

'He needs a sanctuary.'

'He can't stay in a sanctuary for ever.'

'Of course not. When he needs it no longer, then he can make up his own mind about what to do with his life. At present, he cannot do that.'

There was a pause. Bella came out of the bedroom with a blanket over one arm and sidled past Hope and into the kitchen.

Mandy said, 'Listen, Hope. I think I am in love with Jack—'

'You *think*? You think you are in love with him! You left him – do you remember that? You left him penniless and alone. And you *think* you love him?'

'I've come back. I've left Henrik and I've come back. For Jack.'

Hope was gasping for air. Behind her in the kitchen, Bella laughed and then, quite out of the blue, someone else laughed too. She stopped breathing and listened hard. The laughter stopped but it had been Jack's laughter.

She forced herself to breathe evenly and said, 'Did you say you weren't ruthless?'

'He loves me too, Hope. At some point you have got to face that.'

'Let's get back to realism, shall we? Jack knows exactly what you're like – he knew before I did. The sexual favours . . . he knows he was just one in a queue.'

Mandy said quietly, 'You bitch. I didn't know you had it in you, Hope.'

'I've learned a lot in nine months, Mandy. It's called survival. And I have survived. And I intend Jack to survive too.'

'On your terms. What options are open to him, Hope?'

'The whole world will be open to him at some point.'

'Does that include me? Be honest, Hope. Could you bear it if he chose to come to me?'

'Yes. If it is a free choice.'

'You're not keeping him for yourself? So that you can punish him for the rest of his life?'

Hope gasped again and then leaned her head against the granite wall.

Mandy's voice came quietly in her ear. 'If I had been a few hours earlier at the hospital, he would be here with me now. You know that, don't you? That's why you ran away.'

Hope tried to straighten and could not.

Mandy's voice was insidious in her ear. 'You know we had something you never had. You saw. That afternoon. Here in the bedroom. You saw and you know. Admit it, Hope.'

Hope felt bile in her mouth just as she had all those months ago. The hall stand was to her left and she held on to one of the pegs, frightened she might faint.

And then the kitchen door opened and Bella said loudly, 'The new man, my maid. Clean-shaved and ten years younger, I'll be bound!' She saw Hope was still on the phone and clapped a hand to her mouth. But not before Jack had appeared in the doorway, spruce and . . . incredibly . . . smiling gently at her. Bella said, 'Sorry – sorry. Come on, my 'an'some. Give 'er a few minutes more!' And the door closed on them.

Hope turned back and said strongly, 'Jack had the choice, Mandy. In the hospital, he had the choice of coming with me or waiting for you. He knew exactly what he was doing. He chose to come here. Perhaps that answers your questions. All of them. And I will make you a promise which I will keep. Next spring I will ring this number again and you can talk to him. But you must give him that much time.'

Mandy said, 'I'm making no promises. You

wouldn't believe them anyway, would you? But if Jack needs time to think things over, then so do you. And think about this, Hope. I loved both of you. I loved all of you. Fay and Chatty. You and Jack. To sleep with Jack was just one step nearer to being one of you. But as time went on, I fell in love with Jack. Separately. I still love Henrik but I was in love with Jack. I tried not to be, but every time we were together, it became more obvious. We didn't talk much. But I am sure he feels the same as I do. He loves you. But he is in love with me.'

Hope stared at the granite.

Mandy said, 'Are you there? Did you get that? I want you to think about it, Hope. Really think about it.'

Hope whispered, 'How long . . . how long had you and Jack . . . been together?'

Another pause, then Mandy said, 'You didn't know. You thought it was just that once.' She sounded almost regretful. She said angrily, 'Haven't you talked about it?'

'I couldn't. It made me physically ill.'

'You . . . *fool*! You don't know anything, do you? You are what you always said you were – hopeless!' Across the line there came what sounded like a sob. Then her voice hardened. 'Since Chatty went to school. You must have realized. God, you and Jack were hardly an item after that!'

Hope stood very still, no longer seeing the granite wall. The familiar nausea was engulfing her.

Mandy said, 'Anyway, Hope, you weren't so in-nocent with my husband if I remember correctly!'

The wall seemed to be bowing inwards. Hope whispered, 'What do you mean? Henrik never ever . . .'

'Oh come off it! He kissed you – under the mistletoe first of all. Don't tell me that was the only time! He bought you diamond earrings. Was always patting you, doing things for you! You knew he was impotent. You knew that was his way of making love to you! Don't deny it, Ho. He could talk you into anything!'

Hope felt her knees begin to give way. She said nothing.

Mandy said urgently, 'Listen, Ho. I love you. I still love you. I didn't want you to know – there was no need. Because of Jack, I loved you more. Don't you get that? Can't you try – just for once – to forget all those rules you were somehow indoctrinated with? See how it could possibly be for someone else? Someone like me who has nothing – no family, no husband, no children? For Jack too – he was on his own till he met you, wasn't he? Why isn't it possible for us to bond together without all this silly pain and affront and fear and—'

Hope replaced the receiver and turned towards the stairs and the bathroom.

Bella found her there an hour later, sitting on a stool, exhausted after vomiting again and again. She turned, startled, as Bella entered unceremoniously.

'That bolt hasn't got no catch,' Bella explained briefly. She opened the cabinet and took out cotton wool swabs. 'Good job we got plenty of medical stuff. Nurse keeps us well supplied.' She rinsed a swab and leaned over

Hope and with unexpected gentleness she began to wash her face. 'Expect you ett something you shouldn't of. Blackberries?'

Hope closed her eyes momentarily. 'Probably,' she said.

Bella finished her job, dabbed Hope's face with a dry swab and then took her arm. 'Come and lie on the bed for just a minute. I'll make you a hot cup of tea. Jack is all right. He's with the gaffer and they're playing dominoes.' She waited and when Hope did not comment she said, 'I said they're playing dominoes. First time your Jack has done that.'

Hope said without any interest, 'Yes.'

She let Bella lead her into the bedroom where Peter had been taken so ill. There was a single bed there now and Bella sat her on it and picked up her feet and placed them under the eiderdown. Then she went away and Hope stayed very still, staring at the dark ceiling, trying desperately not to think. When Bella brought the tea she elbowed herself up against the brass bedhead and took it. She discovered she wanted it – needed it – and she gulped at the hot, sweet brew and hardly noticed the roof of her mouth burning a protest.

'Take it steady, my maid.' Bella went to the window. 'There's Jem bringing Buttercup in. She's always last, is Buttercup.' She drew the curtain across and went on conversationally, 'I reckon we might have a match there.' She snorted a gruff laugh. 'I don't mean for Buttercup neither! I mean for Jem. He's taking a great interest in that Fenella Perkins. Well, I should call her Fenella Phillips except old Sid Phillips

333

has chucked her out to fend for herself and the baby.'

Hope let the steam from the mug float up her nose and into her head. Her face felt sore.

Bella came to the bed and tried again. 'I reckon that lets you off the hook, don't it, girl?' She grinned meaningfully. Hope looked at her through the steam. 'You know. What your Chatty said when she was down back last Easter. Trying to fix something up for you and Jem?'

Hope blinked. 'She told you that? I thought it was a bit of a joke.'

'Course it was. But you can 'ave a joke back now, can't you?'

'Can I?' Hope continued to look uncomprehendingly over the tea.

Bella sighed. 'Never mind, girl. But if you try 'ard enough, you can see everything as a bit of a joke.' She sobered. 'Though not when I see the gaffer 'olding Fennie's baby. Oh dearie me. That tears my chest to pieces.' She stood up and went to switch on the light. It was a sixty-watt bulb shaded by a deeply fringed, crocheted cover. Not a light by which to read in bed.

She opened the door. 'When you've drunk your tea, come on down into the gaffer's room. I'll cut a few sandwiches. An' just remember, there's only one thing what's final and that's death.' She grinned again. 'While there's life there's hope! Perhaps that's why you got your name, my maid.'

Hope stared at the door, still clutching her mug of tea. Bella had not been able to have children – was that why it tore her chest to pieces to watch Peter with a baby? Hope let her thoughts wander around the sheer pathos of the elderly childless couple; she even allowed tears to well into her dry eyes. Bella's tragedy and redemption had something epic about it; nothing sordid, nothing brutal. There was loyalty and fidelity and strength . . . Suddenly she was crying properly. Chatty had started school twelve years ago; longer than that. Jack and Mandy had been 'together' all that time. It was unthinkable. She remembered times with Jack – *her* times with Jack – when he must have come straight from Mandy.

And then she thought of Henrik.

She felt her stomach begin to cramp again and shut her mind quickly while she gulped the rest of the tea. She thought wildly that if Jem wasn't setting his cap at Fennie she would sleep with him – tonight, now. And then shut her mind on that too.

And then she swung her legs off the bed and went downstairs.

The next few days were the most difficult of her life. If Jack had been under her feet as before, she could not have stood it. But somehow, via suggestions and questions from Peter and mono-syllabic replies from Jack, the two men had worked out a system for recaulking the *Mirabelle* and with Jem's help they got down into the cove at each high tide and waited until it had ebbed far enough to begin work. Jem would take over from Peter after a couple of hours but he did not try to take over Jack's job. They were both there to make absolutely certain Jack had no intention of walking into the sea. After a few days, it became obvious that that would not happen. As the tide came back in so Jack would take the sea-water soap and wash himself in a pool and whether anyone was with him or not, he would shoulder the bag of tools and climb the cliff path again.

Hope did not go down into the cove when he was there. No one seemed to find that strange. Another pattern was emerging; before, Jack had not let her out of his sight unless he was in bed. Now, he hardly noticed her; it was as if all his energies were going into tarring the *Mirabelle* and rediscovering himself. She would see him standing by the rill looking down as before, but now seeing his feet; as if he had never seen them before. Sometimes in the middle of their breakfast he would lift a hand and stare at it almost wonderingly. It was the same with objects. He particularly liked the preserving jars in the scullery. One day she walked home after milking the cows for Jem and found him with a jar of the bramble jelly she had made the day before, holding it against the light.

He put it on the table. 'Ruby,' he said.

She thought how ironic it was that a week ago this would have delighted her. Now she said shortly, 'Bella gave me some apples so I picked the blackberries.'

He frowned at her, recognizing the lack of interest in her voice. Then he seemed to gather his whole body together and blurted, 'What did Mandy say?'

She stared. In any other context this would have been an amazing breakthrough. She swallowed convulsively. 'Nothing.'

There was another of his interminable pauses. Then he said in the same strangulated rush, 'Everything is different.'

'Yes.' She went to the window and looked down the combe. The garden looked well cared for now. The bits of wood had been stacked and the whole area was neat. She said, 'She told me what I already knew. And yet . . . I suppose I couldn't face it.' She lifted her eyes and watched a gull riding the wind. 'I knew you and Mandy had been . . . together . . . before that time. When I saw you.' Like Jack, she could hardly speak. 'I suppose I hadn't realized it was such a long-standing . . . thing.'

He said nothing but she could hear him breathing very fast. And then realized he might be weeping.

She said, 'We'll just have to live from day to day. I was wrong – nothing is different. Not really.' She could not bear to look round at him.

After a while he said hoarsely, 'I'll go.'

'No. You can't go. Not now. You're not well enough. Wait a few weeks. At least till after Christmas.' She waited; he said nothing more. She took hold of the window frame and held on to it. 'Are you in love with her, Jack?'

'No!'

And suddenly she couldn't take any more and cried out passionately, 'Then why? When Chatty started school – that's when she said it started! Did you think then that she was – she was – better than me?'

She felt him coming towards her and gave another enormous cry. 'Don't! Don't touch me! I shall be sick!'

He stopped in his tracks and then edged around the table and opened the door and went out. She did not ask him where he was going; she did not care. It was dark when he came back home and she had already made up her bed and been to the rill to wash. He put his handkerchief on the table. It was stained wine-red but it was full of blackberries. He waited for some sign of approval and when there was none he gathered up the handkerchief again and took it into the scullery. She heard him reach down the colander and then begin pumping water into the sink. She called, 'Leave them. I'll see to them in the morning. Go to bed now.'

There was a moment of silence, then he walked slowly upstairs. It was only as she listened to his shuffling steps that she realized he had been walking upstairs normally for a week now.

She roused when he left the house very early to begin work on the boat then drifted into a shallow, troubled sleep for the space of a dream. She dreamed that he was alone in the cove and that a little wind whipped sneakily around from Land's End and chilled him. The wind brought a storm and the sea began to crash into the shore. She could see his shoulders shaking with cold and his grey hair darken with the spray coming off the rocks. Suddenly the sea was everywhere, around his legs and over the boat. A wave lifted him to the ceiling of the cave and he looked right at her as she lay in her nest of quilts, warm and safe. He was not asking to be rescued; he simply looked. And then looked away. When the wave receded he was no longer there. She was free.

She turned over and slept deeply until the sun beamed through the curtains and woke her. Then, for the first time since she had spoken to Mandy, she made him honey sandwiches and a thermos of tea and took them down to the cove. She halted halfway down the cliff path and looked out to sea. It was a perfect day: the last day of September. The tide had ebbed to the rock where she had first changed into her costume back in 1967. There was no wind; no waves. She swallowed. There was also no Jack. She went on slowly, her eyes on the boat. It gleamed blackly, its hull exposed to the sunshine. Jack must be on his back on the other side. But she knew he was not. She knew that her dream had been a wish and that her wish was fulfilled. She was free.

And then she saw him. He was in the pool behind the rock. Suds floated out from his body; he was washing. She closed her eyes, not knowing whether the rush of emotion was relief or disappointment. She put the sandwiches and thermos on the sand by the boat and went back up the path. She did not know whether he saw her or not. She thought with a kind of desperation: what are we going to do when winter comes and we are shut in the cottage together . . . ?

October brought rain and letters from Fay and Chatty. She read them, smiling slightly because they wrote as they spoke; Fay with a quality of reserve, Chatty almost illegibly as she tried to make word pictures of the autumn collection and Fiona's boyfriend who was an art student.

She knew she should read them aloud for Jack to share, but somehow she could not. She left them both on the table for two days then folded them and put them on the mantelpiece. She did not know whether he read them or not.

And then three days later came a letter for Jack. The envelope was typewritten but it was obviously from Mandy. A little while ago Hope might well have opened it or even kept it from him. She simply handed it to him without comment and went upstairs to change his bedding. The rain drummed on the iron roof and outside the window on the bank that protected Widdershins from the sea, a seagull huddled, head sunk into neck, delicate grey plumage funnelling raindrops off the body. She stood with her arms full of sheets and pillowcases, looking out at the dreary scene and wishing that Jack might find the words to tell her he wanted to go back to Sandhurst and Mandy. It would be hard to find again the wonderful peace she had had when she first came to Widdershins but she could do it eventually if she were alone. With Jack, it was now impossible.

She shook her shoulders and went downstairs again. Jack stood, typically bent, holding the edge of the table. The letter was in front of him but as she went in he pushed it towards her. She halted, still clutching the bedlinen to her chest like a buffer. 'No thank you,' she said curtly and retreated into the scullery. She was busy pushing the sheets into the old-fashioned dolly-tub when he came in behind her and held the letter out.

She said fiercely, 'I don't want to see it. It's

your letter. It's for you. Not for me. And if you don't take it away, I shall be sick.' She glanced round at him and said desperately. 'Go *away*! D'you hear me, Jack? Just go away and take the filthy thing with you!'

He flinched and turned hurriedly into the kitchen and she jammed the sheets right down and shook soap powder on top of them and took the kettle of water off the paraffin stove to pour over them and hardly knew what she was doing. The cottage was so small and he and the letter were still only three or four paces away. She pumped more water into the kettle and put it on the stove and hung over the shallow yellow-stone sink, longing to keen and wail her horror aloud. But two minutes later, when she heard him go outside into the rain and could have wailed with impunity, she no longer wanted to do so. She found herself running after him to tell him to put on his anorak. He was gone; she went around the corner to the ruined part of the cottage where they had stored all the fuel and where she had strung a line for drying under cover and he was not there. Through the rain she could see the grove of alders and no one was sheltering under them. She was stiff with anxiety and clenched her hands into fists by her side. 'Damn you, Jack Langley! Damn you!' she said into the rain and went inside to slam the door violently. The letter lay on the table as she went into the scullery; she could see that in fact it was meant for both of them. 'My dear Hope and Jack . . .' it began.

She did the washing, rinsed it and hung it out; came back indoors and remade Jack's bed; laid kindling in the range; cut bread and peeled potatoes. It was Thursday; they had omelettes on Thursdays so there was nothing else to do. She had intended to borrow Peter's Wolseley and go into Penzance with the last of the rag rugs but it was too late now. Somehow that was also Jack's fault. She went into the little sitting room and sat at the sewing machine, making some denim dungarees from the pattern Chatty had left. At three o'clock Jack had still not returned. She was hungry and cold and still stiff with tension. She gave up the machining and put a match to the fire and was sitting as close to it as possible when Jem arrived.

He stood by the door dripping like a dog. 'We saw the smoke. Thought something was wrong,' he said.

'I was cold,' she said briefly.

'Sorry.' He shook off his oilskin and sat opposite her. 'What's up? Where's Jack?'

'I don't know. Nothing's up.'

He looked at her sharply. 'You must know where he is. It's coming down like stair rods. He'll be soaked.'

'That's up to him. He's free to get wet or stay dry. I'm not his keeper.'

'You've had a row,' Jem said flatly.

'Can you imagine having a row with Jack?'

'Well, quite. It would have been a great stride forward.' He tried a small laugh but she did not join him. He said, 'Come on. What's happened?'

She shrugged. 'He had a letter from a friend. Your friend too, actually. Mandy. He wanted me to read it. I told him I would be sick if I did. He

342

kept on pushing it in front of me. So I told him to go away. And he went.'

'What time was this?'

'After the post had been. Nine-ish. Ten-ish.'

'It's nearly four o'clock, Hope.'

'Yes.'

'Is this the letter?'

'Yes.'

He picked it up and read aloud. ' "My Dear Hope and Jack. I don't know what to say. I love you both. You already know that. Please read this. I will write again. I want you to know you are always in my thoughts. Mandy." ' He put it back down. 'Not too bad, really. She doesn't go on much. Women usually do go on quite a lot.'

She said woodenly, 'Yes.'

'It was one of the things I liked about her. She always had a quip for everything. But then she shut up and got on with it.' Hope put a hand to her mouth. He smiled and said, 'You can't take it, can you, Ho? The fact of the matter is that for Mandy, sex was casual. Really casual. No more than a passionate kiss under the mistletoe.'

She remembered the mistletoe years ago. The kiss that Mandy had given to Jack and that had gone on and on. Mandy had bought that kiss; paid for it with good money. She tightened her hand over her mouth and made a small sound.

Jem said levelly, 'We should go and look for Jack.' She shook her head violently. He stood up with the same kind of violence, came over to her, pulled away her hand, put one of his under her chin, the other at the back of her head and tilted it towards his own head. He kissed her angrily at first and then with a kind of unwilling tenderness. She responded in exactly the same way; pulling against him, trying to stand up, beating at his shoulders and chest. And then, she subsided. She felt her mouth soften against his. The terrible tension of the day began to dissolve. She made another sound, still despairing but in quite a different context.

When at last he lifted his head, she found she had closed her eyes. She opened them; he was looking at her intently and she felt herself flushing hotly like a schoolgirl. He said quietly, 'Are you ashamed of yourself?'

'No! Yes!' She tried to smile. 'Why should I be?'

'Exactly.' He pulled her up. 'Get your mac on. Let's go and find Jack.'

It was such an anti-climax. She stared at him, her mouth still trembling.

He said in the same very gentle voice, 'I'm Jem. Who was seduced by Mandy and who is seriously considering making an honest woman of Fennie Perkins and I have never made any commitment to anyone or anything since I killed my wife and baby. I fell in love with you when you were twenty-one and looked exactly like Elizabeth Taylor. You still look like her and I still love you. But I would let you down and you couldn't take that. Fennie will be able to take it. Even so, it's a big and dangerous gamble she will be taking on.' He kissed her again. 'D'you see what I'm getting at?'

'I don't care. I—'

His voice was less gentle. 'No. No, Hope. I'm not going to be a pawn in your private revenge.' He turned and started shrugging into his oilskins. 'Come on. It will be dark soon.'

She said, 'I'm not coming. Why should I chase after Jack? He's a grown man and if he wants to stay out all night—'

He caught hold of her roughly. 'Listen, Hope. You were prepared to go to bed with me just now. It wouldn't have meant much, but you know all about me and you were prepared to do it. Jack did the same with Mandy. And now he's ill and needs you. You are coming with me to look for him!'

'You have no right—'

'I told you I love you. That's true. I'm not doing this for Jack's sake, I'm doing it for yours. If he's wandered off across the moor and you don't look for him, you won't like yourself, Ho. OK?'

She swallowed against a return of the sickness. And then nodded.

Sixteen

There was no wind but the rain beat against
the ground with enormous force, smothering
their calls, bending them over with its sheer
weight. They went beyond the rill to the very tip
of the headland and by the time they got there
the darkness was impenetrable and it was too
dangerous to clamber around the rocks. Hope
tugged at Jem's sleeve and shouted in his ear, 'I
think he might have tried to walk into Buryan –
got a bus to Penzance and then a train.'

Jem switched on his torch and peered at her
from beneath his sou'wester. 'You sound fairly
sure.'

She shrugged; it was a habit she had lost since
coming to Widdershins, now it had returned.
'Mandy's house at Sandhurst has to be a better
deal than this.' She tried to smile. 'Don't you
see, Jem? This is what is hurting my pride.
I knew when he left the house that somehow
or other – without money or decent clothes –
he would find his way back to her.' Her smile
inverted itself. 'Sorry. That's why I fell into your
arms. It wasn't really revenge – at least I don't
think so. It was a need for comfort.'

Jem said, 'Oh God! Fennie and now you!'

'How do you mean?'

'Nothing. Come on, let's get back. I'll stay with you if you like.'

She did not know whether she wanted that any more. They tramped back to the far side of the rill and she paused there to hold her side and fight for breath. Below, far below, the tide was creeping in heavily. There was not much wind so the waves were reduced to a menacing swell. In an hour they would lift the *Mirabelle* up to the roof of the cave. She hoped that Jack had made sure the two anchors were down. If the boat floated free she would certainly be wrecked by morning, smashed against the rocks or swamped.

She said, 'Have you been down to the boat today?'

'No. Too wet.'

'The tide has been out though. I wonder . . .'

'He wasn't there when I came down from the farm. There was still enough daylight to see him. He definitely wasn't there.'

'He wasn't working. Not in this weather. But he might have been in the boat.'

They ran to the cliff path and slithered down it. Already six inches of water covered the cove with each swell. They shoshed through it and reached the exposed hull of the *Mirabelle*. The ladder was in place. Jem leaped for the bottom rung and pulled himself up then reached down for the torch. Hope stood inside the cave out of the incessant, numbing rain. The anchors were both winched against the hull. The boat would go with the first swell that floated it.

Jem called down, 'He's here! In the wheel-house! Seems to be asleep! I'll have to go aboard.'

She shouted back to tell him about the anchors. 'Winch them down as soon as you can! We've got to secure Peter's boat!'

There was a lot of crashing about and shouting above her. The water was building up around her legs. She leaped for the ladder and scrabbled frantically to get a purchase on the side of the boat so that her head was level with the deck. Inside the wheelhouse she could see by the waving torch that Jack was slumped into a corner. Jem was trying to haul him up by his arms. The door opened with a crash and she could hear him yelling, 'Get up, you ungrateful swine! She's been looking for you – get up and get yourself over the side!'

She called out, 'Jack! Quickly! The water is rising and Peter's boat will be damaged!' She swung back down herself; the water came over her gumboots and filled them heavily. Jack half fell beside her and leaned against the hull. She snapped, 'Now is not the time to withdraw into your private world! Come and help me secure the anchors!' She sloshed to the stern of the *Mirabelle* just as Jem let go the anchor chains and they rattled into the sea. But it was Jack who roused himself and packed rocks around the anchor heads and asked Jem for chain slack so that the old boat could rise with the sea. Already the hull was righting itself on the swell and then falling back against the fender tyres with the receding water.

Jem landed by them with a splash and

manhandled them both across the cove. 'Keep going, for Christ's sake! We're going to be cut off at any moment – move! Hope, go in front. I'll manage Jack. Take off your boots – leave them.'

She reached the cliff path and leaned back to pull Jack beside her. His hand was like ice. He reached with his other hand and grabbed Jem and then they stood for a moment just above the water line, breathing heavily.

At last Jem said, 'I think I've had enough of you two for a while. Jack, I don't want to hear why you were trying to drown yourself and scuttle Peter's boat. Hope, I don't want to know how you feel about Jack. You can both stew in your own juice.' He switched on his torch, shouldered past both of them and strode up the path. At the top he waited until they drew level and delivered a parting shot. 'I'll tell you something. You make me feel very much better about the muddle I made of my life. At least I didn't wallow in self-pity.'

They watched the torch disappear towards the farm before turning for the cottage. Suddenly Hope was so weary she wondered how she could negotiate the steep path down into the valley, but somehow she did it. She was angry, she was ashamed, but most of all she was exhausted. The realization that, if she and Jem had made love an hour ago, Jack would be dead and the *Mirabelle* wrecked was too enormous to consider. She would think about it in the morning; she would think about everything in the morning.

In complete silence they crowded into the kitchen and she lit two lamps and carried one of them into the scullery. The fire in the range had gone out but when she brought in kindling and coals, Jack was resurrecting it from the drying wood in the hearth. She watched him; it was the first time he had done it and she remembered how important the fire had been to her when she first arrived. He looked terrible; white, almost blue. His hands, sunburned and rough from gardening, were obviously stiff with cold and when he broke some wood across his knee he winced suddenly. The water in the big kettle was still hot and she poured some of it into a bowl, pushed him into the chair, took off his sandals and lifted his feet into the warm water. He made sounds of protest which she ignored but when he tried to remove his feet she said angrily, 'Listen. If you're going to kill yourself, don't let it be my fault! D'you understand? I am not going to have anything to do with it!' She straightened and pushed the kettle well into the fire to boil it for tea and when she had made it she wrapped his hands around the mug and then filled a hot-water bottle. Later, after they had eaten the omelettes and some creamed potatoes, he began to look a little better. There was a certain grim satisfaction in that. She thought: nurse and patient. That's what I had forgotten. Nurse and patient.

It was incredible that after that night they could go on as before. The next morning Hope still did not think about it; she dared not. The whole stupid and terrifying day was simply unthinkable. There had not been much to choose between Jack's behaviour and her own. Her anger died and left her with shame. Eventually, in the middle of the day, she spoke abruptly, half to herself and half to Jack.

'There's nothing we can do about it – we have to forget it and go on.'

He stared at her and she repeated her words with a kind of impatience. He did not give his usual acquiescent nod; he was still looking white and he moved stiffly. She thought with a sinking heart that this time he had gone back more than just two steps.

But, incredibly, go on they did just as before with Jack gradually regaining those two steps, alternating between deep silence and sudden responses, as if nothing had happened. Hope let herself imagine that some pattern or reason would develop that would make everything a little more logical, a little more acceptable. Then she would be able to come to some decision and everything would suddenly be clear.

Meanwhile, they had to eat and drink and wash themselves, cut the cabbages and the last of the beans, experiment with other vegetables, take their turn with milking the cows, playing dominoes with Peter, pretending this was a normal life.

It would have been so much easier to believe in the pretence if it hadn't been for the letters. They arrived at regular intervals and were always addressed to Jack but inside started with 'Dearest Jack and Hope'. During the first three weeks of October no fewer than eight of them were left at the farm. The same message was repeated in each. 'Still thinking of you and loving you both.' They were like water drops wearing away a stone. Hope could feel her nerves tightening in spite of all her good intentions to remain utterly detached. She had no idea how Jack felt about them. He simply read the single sheet and left it on the table.

Towards the end of the month Hope borrowed Peter's car and went into Penzance with the last of the season's rugs and the dungarees. The manager of the Causeway shop told her regretfully that there would be no call for holiday goods until next spring. She wrote herself a cheque and did some shopping and drove back to Widdershins with a feeling of desperation. There were still eight hundred pounds in her account but she could no longer afford to ignore Jack's contribution. And when that had gone, there was no way they could go on living on the headland.

That night she sat down and wrote to Mrs Martin care of Expectancies in Gloucester and then she began to sketch a smock. She took her sketches with her when she went to the farm the next day. Jem was still avoiding her but Fennie was in the dairy scrubbing the stone shelves with a will.

'Would you wear something like this, Fennie?' Hope opened the sketchbook and held it out. 'I thought of quite a coarse material. Something that will hold its shape. Denim. Heavy linen.'

Fennie put her small head on one side. She was years younger than Jem but not unlike him with her long hair and dark eyes.

''S all right. But all that heavy stuff round your arms . . . too much of it, I reckon. Why don't you make it sleeveless? And a real deep scoop neck. Then you could wear it on its own in the summer and with a sweater underneath in the winter.' She grinned. 'You seen the latest maternity stuff? Those overall trousers? Like clowns' outfits they are. Some of the girls at clinic wear them – they're that proud of being pregnant they don't want to hide it no more!'

'I know what you mean.' Hope nodded thoughtfully. 'Why should they hide it, after all? Thanks, Fennie. I'll work on both those ideas.'

'Din't know you were a dress designer. Thought it was your daughter.'

'Yes, she is. I'm not. But I have to make some money! This is how I used to do it.'

There were no letters from Mandy for a whole week. Instead came long screeds from the girls, a photograph of Fiona Tabb modelling what looked like a petticoat. The weather suddenly improved and Jack told Peter he would like to finish off the work on the *Mirabelle*.

'Dun't think I can get down there any more, m'boy,' Peter said regretfully. 'And Jem's off into Truro most days to the market.'

'I don't need anyone.' It was the first time Jack had made a bid for any kind of independence. 'It won't take long. Nice weather.'

They all looked at Hope. She almost shrugged.

'I'll help you down with the tools and things tomorrow,' she offered.

It was Jack who shrugged.

The weather was glorious but there was a definite chill in the air. The tide was in during the early morning so Hope worked in the garden. Fennie appeared at ten with a letter addressed to

Hope. She tore it open immediately. It was from Mrs Martin, who said she could take as many smocks as Hope could make.

'Good omen, Fennie.' Hope was overjoyed and deeply thankful. She did not need much money but they could not grow all their food and she would have to get Jack some warm clothes for the winter.

They went inside. Jack was fiddling with some wallpaper on the kitchen table. He had been doing something entailing her tape measure and cutting-out scissors for the last two days. He had found the wallpaper in the roof space when he clambered up to check on Mr Perkins's repairs and had not volunteered any explanations so Hope had not asked questions either.

'I've taken your advice, Jack,' she said, pushing the kettle into the coals. 'Written to Mrs Martin. She can still sell the smocks apparently. So we'll keep our heads above water!'

He glanced up and flushed slightly. There was the usual silence and Fennie spoke kindly as if to a child, 'And what are you up to, m'an'some? Making something, are you?'

He looked across at Hope and just for a split second they shared something; a wish to laugh. And then it was gone.

He said, 'A kite.'

'Oh. That's nice,' Fennie sat down; she had obviously shot her bolt.

Hope fetched mugs and made some coffee. 'Jack has been interested in windpower for a long time,' she said, sounding exactly like a schoolmistress but still stunned by that moment of shared amusement.

'Oh. Is that so?'

'Yes.' She smiled. 'I think I'll pack our lunch, Jack. It's nice enough for a picnic and it will give you more time on the boat.' She passed Fennie a mug. 'Leave your work on the table, then you can go on with it when we get back. It will be dark quite early.'

He took his coffee and cupped it in both hands as he always did now. He said gratefully, 'Thank you.' There was another brief moment of understanding between them and she knew he was thanking her, not only for the coffee but for giving him some kind of status.

It was a halcyon day in the cove. Sheltered by the headland, Hope sunbathed for a precious hour after lunch and then, seeing that Jack was thoroughly absorbed with a repair to the wheel-house, she partially undressed and went into the sea. She swam beyond the headland and lay on her back looking up at the sheer cliff that protected Widdershins from the worst of the weather, and feeling strangely optimistic. And then she rolled over and there was Jack on the shoreline waiting for her. Her albatross.

She swam slowly into the shallow water, stood up and waded ashore. She felt faintly ridiculous with straight sleek hair and sodden under-clothes.

'Have you finished?' she asked curtly.

'Yes.' He was loaded with tools and paint-brushes. He said uncertainly, 'Towel?'

'Haven't brought one. I won't stop to dress. I'll run on ahead. Is that all right?'

He nodded and she went to the rock where she had left her clothes and then hurried to the

355

path, shivering once she was out of the direct sunlight. She knew she should have taken off her wet things and put on the dry clothes but in so many ways Jack was a stranger now and she could not bear to dress in front of him. And he must have felt the same because long after she was dried and dressed she saw him in the garden walking down to the alders by the rill and staring at his feet. He was still carrying his tools and when she opened the door and called to him that the kettle was on, she saw he was also carrying a pair of gumboots. He held them out to her.

'They're mine! I took them off . . . that night . . .' She was astonished. 'Where did you find them?'

'On the beach. Washed up into the cave.'

They gazed at each other with a kind of startled recognition. Then he turned the boots upside down just inside the door, straightened and mumbled something.

'What did you say?'

'Sorry. I'm sorry.'

She felt the muscles of her throat tighten convulsively.

'I'm sorry too, Jack. Really sorry.'

On 5 November Jem appeared with another letter from Mandy. Hope had forgotten how marvellous it was not to see that familiar postmark. Jack had gone up on to the high ground to test his kite so she took the letter between thumb and forefinger and put it on the table.

'You've been almost human lately,' Jem said. 'I hoped no more of these would come.'

She shrugged. 'I don't take any notice of them anyway,' she said.

'Oh yes you do. You are always unbearable when they come.' He grinned but she did not grin back and he went on quickly, 'Listen. There's going to be a bonfire in Buryan village tonight. How about taking Peter to see it?'

'You? Me? Bella?'

'All of us. Jack and Fennie and Nathan too.'

'I thought you didn't want anything to do with us.'

'I didn't that night. But you're doing a good job. You and Jack. You both seem more . . . settled. Perhaps it cleared the air.' He looked at her. 'I didn't like being used, Hope.'

'Sorry. I didn't mean to . . . use you.' She glanced at the letter on the table. 'Pity that's come. They do upset him.'

'Not you?'

'All right. They upset me too.' She took a quick breath. 'Anyway . . . tonight. If Peter really wants to go . . . is he up to it?'

'He can stay in the car. Bella and Fennie would like it.'

'The baby too?'

'Call him Nathan, for God's sake! That's his name!'

She looked surprised. 'Sorry. Did you say I was unbearable?'

'Nathan will be my son if Fennie agrees to it. He's the light of Peter's life. And you never call him by his name.'

She was aghast. 'Oh Jem. I didn't realize, honestly. I like Fennie a lot – and the . . . and Nathan. And it's lovely you're going to be part of them. She's so sweet and kind. Is that why you've come to deliver the letter? To tell us about you and Fennie?'

'I wanted to see you. Heal the breach. And ask you to come to Buryan tonight.'

'I don't think Jack will want to cram into the car with all of us. And I can't leave him here.'

'Don't be silly. If you drive Peter and the girls, Jack and I will walk. He'll agree to that.'

'It's four miles, Jem!'

'It will do us good.'

'Well, if Jack agrees . . . Yes, it would be a good thing to do.'

Jack agreed as he agreed to anything she suggested. They left Widdershins as it got dark and walked up to the farm and Jack and Jem left immediately on foot while Bella and Hope got Peter into the car and well wrapped in rugs. He was as excited as a schoolboy and when they passed the two men striding along the side of the lane, he leaned over and sounded the horn, laughing at their instant response.

'You're worse than young Nathan 'ere!' Bella scolded. She leaned towards the back of Hope's head. 'Screamed the place down, 'e did, because Fennie wanted 'im to have something out of a tin!'

'They said at the clinic he's got to be weaned,' Fennie protested.

'Never mind what *they* say,' Bella came back. 'It's what '*e* says what counts!'

Peter laughed again and for some reason they all joined in. Hope thought suddenly: this is being almost happy. Just thoughtlessly happy.

They were early and managed to park outside

the church so they had a perfect view of the guy sitting on top of the edifice of dried bracken and old beds and chairs. When the fireworks were lit Hope forgot to watch because it was a joy to see Peter's reaction; the thin planes of his face were lit suddenly and he looked like the young man he must have been once. She could see why Bella might have fallen in love with him.

And then Jem and Jack arrived and went to buy hot dogs and amazingly Peter, whose appetite was becoming more and more uncertain, ate his with relish. Fennie went off with Jem and Jack sat on the back seat holding Nathan, smiling gently. At one point Bella asked him if he was all right and Hope heard him say very clearly, 'More than all right.' Then, as if he were hearing his own words and wondering at them, 'More than all right.'

She turned and looked at him in the sudden glare of a rocket but this time he did not meet her eyes and she was foolishly disappointed. And then of course she remembered Mandy's letter, unopened, waiting for him on the table back at the cottage.

She drove back quite soon because Peter's spurt of energy did not last. He sat in his chair holding Nathan while Fennie fed him strained spinach from a teaspoon and he pushed it out with his tongue until his bib was bright green and then at last she fed him herself and he was content. Hope followed Bella into the kitchen to tell her about Mrs Martin and the smocks.

'Fennie said as how pleased you were.' Bella grinned her congratulations. 'So you can buy a few Christmas presents? Have your girls along?'

'Oh yes, I hadn't thought of that. How lovely.' She sighed. 'It's been such a nice evening, Bella. Thank you.'

'Dun't thank me, my girl. It's you what makes it. Peter thinks of you as a daughter – always has done from the minute he met you.'

'Oh Bella . . .' Hope could have wept. 'You're so . . . unjealous!' She laughed. 'Is there such a word? I think you're very generous. You don't mind, do you? That Peter looks on me as a daughter and is always nursing Nathan – you don't mind?'

Bella looked surprised. 'Course I don't mind. Oh, I did at one time, I suppose. When I knew 'e couldn't have children, I was angry – full of anger. See, 'e didn't tell me until we'd been married a bit. An' I s'ppose I felt cheated. An' I went a bit wild.' She gave her toothy grin. 'Can't imagine me going wild, can you, girl? But I did. Then . . . well, I realized it was 'im that mattered. I went and fetched 'im from France, you know. In the old *Mirabelle*. 'E was that surprised.' She laughed. 'We bin all right since.'

Hope said, 'I thought . . . I thought . . .'

'You thought it was me couldn't 'ave children? Good. I dearly hope everyone thinks that. Makes it better for 'im, dun't it?' She looked up. 'That's why I never nurse the baby. An' I don't show anyone how fond I am of you, either, my maid. It might upset Peter.' She stood up and went to the door. 'Thought as much. 'Ere come the weary travellers!'

Jem and Jack came in looking the worse for

wear and smelling strongly of cider. Hope got up immediately.

'I think we'll go home before Jack falls asleep.'

She was so bewildered by what Bella had told her that she forgot to say goodnight to Peter. She almost hustled Jack across the farmyard and on to the cliff path and when he stopped her with a hand on her arm and pointed to the clear, frosty night sky, she just nodded and went on ahead. By the time he came through the door she had rejuvenated the fire and lit the lamps.

He stood looking around, bewildered but probably also fuddled with the unaccustomed drink.

At last he said, 'What's wrong?'

She was making coffee and looked at him, surprised. 'Wrong? Nothing. Not really.' She sighed sharply and went on, 'I thought I could run away from . . . everything. But life has a way of – of – knocking on the door. However far you run.' She put the kettle back on the trivet. 'Bella was telling me tonight that Peter could not have children and he didn't tell her until after they were married. Yet she still went over to Dunkirk to rescue him. Can you imagine that?'

He nodded, then said, 'Yes.'

She sighed. 'Yes. I suppose I can too. Bella is . . . big, isn't she? She hasn't forgotten anything and she doesn't seem to need to forgive anything. She just accepts it.'

But he nodded and then picked up the letter which for a blessed moment she had forgotten. It was still unopened and, as she had done, he held it by a corner between finger and thumb.

She nodded too. 'Mandy. I told her not to

come and see you until the spring. She's kept that promise anyway.'

He moved to the range and very deliberately lit one corner of the envelope and when it was burning threw it on the back of the fire. And then he came back to the table and picked up his coffee mug.

She watched the envelope turn black and curl up and then fly up the chimney like a child's letter to Santa Claus.

She said, 'There could have been something important in it this time.'

He cradled his cup. 'Yes,' he said, as he always did. But he was smiling.

Seventeen

It was amazing – perhaps ridiculous – the difference it made not to see any more letters from Mandy. They kept arriving and Jack kept burning them. It was a symbolic act which reassured Hope that her high-handedness in bringing Jack down here was justified. Beyond that she dared not go. She accepted now that both of them needed time to rehabilitate. She had imagined her own recuperation had been accomplished in the time she had spent at Widdershins alone. But though it had given her the strength to deal with moving Jack down here, she realized, after the events of the past month, that she was as vulnerable as he was. Mandy's shadow had darkened her life. It was still there, but every time Jack burned one of her letters, it seemed to lift a little.

She was able to live from day to day again; to consider the future in terms of food and fuel. The basic conditions at Widdershins helped her; she thought they helped Jack too. It was an enormous step forward that, as the days short-ened, they were able to share the tiny cottage without discomfort. In the evenings they would clear away their meal and then Jack would take over the kitchen table. He was still thoroughly absorbed with planning and making paper prototypes of kites; sometimes she would see him trying out a model down on the headland. At the beginning of December, he asked if he could look at her store of materials. He chose a few remnants of nylon net and when the weather kept them from the garden, he sat with needle and thread, sewing industriously. Hope, emerging from the small sitting room where she too was sewing, smiled at the scene of domesticity. He had wedged the fragile frame of his kite between his knees so that it looked rather like an old-fashioned tapestry frame. He looked up and caught her smile and smiled back. It was another of their wordless exchanges. She went into the scullery to make some tea, telling herself that these moments of communication had happened three or four times at the most; she still felt a lift in her spirits.

They took it in turns to visit the farm so that they were never in each other's way. Jack helped Jem with the planting and even went with him to the Truro market with some of the produce. Hope still did the afternoon milking stint and spent an hour with Peter. More often than not she read to him; occasionally he found the energy to talk. The doctor looked in before Christmas and suggested that another operation might be possible. Peter told Bella that he had decided against it. Hope was there; she stood by the bed knowing he had chosen his moment to make it more bearable for Bella.

'I'm all right as I am. It's been a good life but I

don't want to hang on to it much longer.' He grinned. 'You know those sort who allus want to order another drink just when the landlord calls time? Don't want to be like them.'

Bella said sturdily, 'I dun't hear no one calling time.'

'You 'aven't got the time to listen, my maid!' Peter laughed. 'You and that babby . . . a natural, you are.'

Bella looked stricken and he added quickly, 'Don't keep trying to hide it from me, Bell.' He grinned. 'D'you remember Nanny Trenwith?'

Bella nodded. 'Aye. She lived Bodmin way. People travelled miles for one of 'er cures.'

'They said she were a white witch. Children loved 'er. So people trusted 'er.'

'She 'ad a man when she were a young woman. Killed in the Boer War, 'e was. She never 'ad anyone else.'

He nodded. 'She was like you in that. If you 'adn't a-come to France almost fifty years ago, my maid, you woulda been like Nanny Trenwith. You wouldna looked at another man—' She tried to interrupt but he held up his hand. 'And the children woulda flocked to you. But you've always pushed them away, 'aven't you? For my sake – don't think I don't know that!' He chuckled. 'No need any more, Bell. You stick to little Nathan. You be Nanny Penhailes for little Nathan.'

Bella looked as if she might retreat into her armour as usual and then quite suddenly she said, 'I never wanted anyone else. You was enough for me, Peter Penhailes. I 'ope you know that.'

His smile widened. He patted Hope's hand but he spoke to Bella.

'Maybe I didn't always know it, my maid. But when you came for me . . . when I saw the old *Mirabelle* coming right into that beach at Dunkirk . . . never mind the Stukas and the Messerschmitts . . . I knew then.'

Bella nodded. 'So did I.' She grinned. 'It weren't made in 'eaven, our match. But we worked on it, eh, Gaffer?'

'We did.' They spoke to each other above Hope's head, but it was as if they were talking to her. Peter said gently, 'We've always been kind to each other. That's important. Being kind to each other.'

Bella said, 'Putting up with each other – that's what I'd call it!'

He looked up at her and she shook her head at him. 'You always were sentimental, Gaffer. You 'aven't changed.' She turned. 'I'll make you a hot drink and if you want to do me a kindness, you'll drink it!'

She left and Peter lay back on his pillows for a moment and then rallied.

'Look after her, my maid. She is only the strong one for my sake. When I'm not here—'

'She will have Jem. And Fennie and the baby.'

'They won't want to stay. He's an artist, not a farm worker. There's the flat in Penzance. Fennie will want a school for the baby and a bit of life for herself. And if Jem tries to make her happy that's where they will go.'

They were quiet while Hope thought about that. It was true. She would stay here on the headland; with or without Jack it was home now.

Bella too would stay. But if Jem and Fennie made themselves into a family it would be because they shared a strain of rootlessness. And probably not much else except that urge to make a life together; to be kind to each other.

She looked down at Peter. He was so frail, eyes closed, scarcely breathing, yet still concerned for her.

She said in a low voice, 'I know what you're trying to tell me, Peter. Working at a relationship – growing it almost. Jem and Fennie . . . you and Bella. But Jack and I are different. We had the world. Our match *was* made in heaven. And he . . . threw it away.'

Peter opened his eyes and looked at her directly. 'I don't know anything. Not really. I'm not the wise man you think I am, my maid. I don't think Jack intended to throw anything away. Perhaps that makes him a fool. I don't know. Maybe he thought you didn't care any more? I just don't know. But I can see you're learning to live together now. Properly. You're . . . almost friends. I can see that – whatever you say.'

'I don't think we're friends, Peter. Jack is ill. And I am looking after him. We have to live together . . . for a while. Until he is well enough to decide on his own course.'

There was a long silence; Hope thought he might have gone to sleep and she began to loosen her fingers from his. Then he said, 'What if he decides to go to his brother's place in Australia?'

She smiled and squeezed his hand. 'Then . . . so be it.'

'And if he decides to throw in his lot with . . . this woman? Mandy?'

'The same. Peter, I am just a nurse and he is a patient.'

'You would let him go?'

'I would have no option.'

Peter drew in a breath then released it. 'This is the important question. Answer me truthfully, my girl. If he wants to stay with you – what then?'

She stared at him wide-eyed and could not answer.

He said, 'Right. You do not know. Not yet. But keep asking yourself that question. Because if the answer is yes, then the other two questions are going to have different answers.'

She swallowed. 'Peter . . . I don't know what you mean.'

He half closed his eyes in sheer weariness. 'I mean that if you reach a time when you would agree to him staying with you, then . . . if he chooses to do anything else, you must launch your own *Mirabelle* and go to his rescue. It won't be his decision, it will be yours.'

Bella came in then and Hope stood up to leave. Bella said, 'Jack's here, my girl. He was worried about you.' Hope looked at Peter and saw he was smiling again.

The girls arrived on the 23rd. Jem met them at Truro and brought them to Widdershins in his truck. It was dark, the night full of stars. Jack and Hope met them in the farmyard and helped them to gather their many bags from among the cabbage and cauliflower stalks. There were some that had to be left for Bella and Peter; a strange shape for Nathan which jingled as it was taken out; French perfume for Fennie and a hatbox for Jem.

'It's a gorgeous embroidered cap,' Chatty confided as soon as they were out of earshot. 'If he wears it in the market the whole world will come to his stall!'

Fay took Jack's arm. 'How are you, Dad?' She breathed deeply. 'I just know this air is making you better! When I think of your room at Gloucester and that hospital . . . it's nearly three months since then.' Jack said nothing and she turned to Hope. 'How is he, Mum? I can feel muscles that he didn't have before!'

'Yes. I daresay.' Hope sensed Jack's discomfort and said to Chatty, 'I wondered if that rail crash in London might have delayed the trains. How was the journey?'

'Fine.' Chatty turned to look at Fay through the darkness. 'In other words, lay off Jack, OK?'

Even Jack laughed at that. Chatty went on, 'I've decided to call you Ho and Jack. You've been Mummy and Dad for far too long. And by the way I am now known as Chat. OK? You can call me Cat or Kit, but not Chatty any more. I'm designing a terrific logo for when I am famous. Just a smile in the air. Like the Cheshire cat – you know?'

Fay said resignedly, 'She is unbearable. She's been like this ever since we met at Birmingham. I'll have to go on calling her Chatty. She's more talkative than ever.'

So the girls covered Jack's silences and –

strangely – made Hope more conscious of them. She was always pleased and surprised when he spoke but she was so used to his monosyllabic replies, his body language, that she hardly registered the long silences between them any more. It was all so different from any other Christmas she had ever known. Last year had passed in a haze of bewildered grief for her mother; Mandy and Henrik had taken over all the arrangements and made some kind of celebration for everyone else. She could barely remember it; immediately after it, the suspicion had grown that Jack had misused her mother's money and then had come the frightful visit to Sandhurst. Previous Christmases were almost spoiled by that awfulness. She remembered how busy they had always been: shopping, cooking, games for the girls. There was none of that this year. She had brought in armfuls of holly and ivy and tucked it around the picture rails. There were cards from Bella and Fennie and, unexpectedly, from the manager of the shop in Penzance. If Mandy had sent anything it had been burned by Jack. Hope had sent off a big parcel of clothes to Mrs Martin in Gloucester, but there was no response as yet though she had hoped for at least a card.

Chatty, looking at the meagre display with great care, said, 'Nothing else, Mum? I thought you might have had a card from Mandy actually.'

Hope glanced through the window; Jack and Fay had gone for a walk and there was no sign of them yet.

'I know she came to see you. Was it all right?

I wanted to say something when I wrote but . . . I didn't know what to say!'

Chatty looked stricken. 'She got in touch with you? She promised me faithfully—'

Hope gave a painful smile. 'She had her fingers crossed.'

'Oh my God. Oh Mum, I'm so sorry. What happened? She didn't just turn up here, did she? How did Dad take it?'

'She telephoned the farm. We spoke. It was rather . . . acrimonious.'

Chatty said again, 'Mum, I am so sorry. But so long as she didn't actually turn up. Not yet. Dad's not up to seeing her yet.'

'She wrote to him. Until just before Christmas we were getting letters from her two or three times a week.'

'Mum!' Chatty was stricken again.

'They were addressed to him, but the messages were for both of us. The same thing over and over again. She loves us both.'

Chatty stared. 'I can see it didn't do you much good. What about Dad?'

'It was like a presence . . . for me at any rate.' Hope bit her lip. 'I suppose Dad could see the effect it was having. He started to burn them without opening them.'

'Good old Dad! Surely that helped?'

'Of course.' Hope was ironing, taking the old-fashioned flat irons from the front of the fire basket in turn and clapping them on to the damp jeans which were spreadeagled on the kitchen table. The steam hid her face. She said, 'I don't want to talk about it though, Chat. Do you mind?'

'No. Yes. In a way I do. Because that probably means it's all pretty unbearable. And I was hoping things were very much better.'

'They are getting back to some kind of norm. Whatever that might be. But for a time they were very much worse.' She changed irons. 'Was it the same for you when she turned up in Paris?'

Chatty sat down holding the Christmas cards. She stared into the heart of the fire. 'I don't know.' She sighed. 'It was strange, Mum. She was hanging about outside the design room when Fi and I left one night. That was a shock – not a pleasant shock either. But she acted – well, like she always did. Hugged me and then hugged Fi as if she'd been waiting for her to appear in her life. You know, delighted. And then she took us to dinner and said she'd left Henrik.' She glanced almost furtively at her mother. 'D'you know what she said? She said she was tired of living with a man who was no more than a pimp! Anyway, then she said all she wanted to know was how you were. And Dad. I told her that he was really ill. And . . . honestly, Mum . . . she was devastated. Really devastated.'

'Yes. I gathered that.' Hope folded the jeans and put them over the new clothes horse which Jack had made. She took another pair from the basket and laid them on the table. 'Were you upset, Chat? I'm so sorry you had to be involved.'

'That was it. The thing. I mean . . . I felt strange. But . . . it was like turning the clock back. Having Andy-Mandy back again.' Chatty said miserably, 'Mum, I was really glad to see her. I'm sorry. I feel awful saying that to you.

But – she was so special to me. D'you remember my first day at school?'

Hope remembered and wondered whether it had been then that Mandy decided to seduce Jack.

Chatty said quickly, 'You're not going to be sick, are you?'

Hope straightened, only then realizing she was crouching over the table.

'No. No, I don't think I am.'

'Listen. Don't let's talk about Mandy. It's Christmas.' She leaped up and took the iron from the trivet. 'I'm going to finish the ironing. You make us a cup of coffee and let me tell you about the spring collection.' She banged the iron on to the jeans and said through the steam, 'Have I been calling you Mum? What a very retrogressive step!' She laughed. 'Sorry, Ho. Oh Ho, I'm so sorry.'

Hope reached for the coffee jar and smiled. 'Don't be,' she said.

They were sharing a late Christmas dinner with the Penhaileses; Hope had made an adapted pudding from the summer fruits she had bottled and was supplying the vegetables. Bella had personally wrung the necks of two chickens.

'It's a real do-it-yourself Christmas,' Fay said grimly. 'I'm so glad I am a vegetarian.'

'Only when it suits you,' Chatty taunted. 'Don't forget we had a meal in Birmingham. You had a burger if I remember correctly.'

'A vegetarian burger,' Fay said piously.

They exchanged presents as soon as they got up. Hope had made both girls patchwork skirts

as her mother had so often done for her. Jack
had a 'winter warm' made from one of the many
blankets she had brought from Horsley. The
girls had got both of them woollen hats, gloves,
scarves and socks. 'They're boring but we've got
to keep you warm,' Fay announced. Then there
was perfume for Hope and aftershave for Jack.
'To offset the lack of sanitation around here!'
Chatty said.

They all went to Buryan church in the morning, driving Peter's car, leaving Bella and Peter
to listen to a service on the radio. It was a
surprise to find Jem, Fennie and Nathan already
in one of the back pews. 'We walked,' Fennie
confided. 'Thought it would be nice. And give
Peter and Bella a bit o' time on their own.' She
smiled matter-of-factly. 'You know, being as
it will be their last Christmas together.' Hope
looked, shocked, at Jem, who tightened his
mouth wryly, and then at Jack. His gaze met
hers and held, and then, to her horror, his
eyes filled slowly with tears. No one else saw.
Fay had taken Nathan on to her lap and Chatty
was asking Fennie what he had thought of his
present. She shuffled into the seat next to Jack
and took his hand.

The carols were all familiar, the sermon
very short. Afterwards they squashed into the
Wolseley and drove back to the farm and then
the Langleys walked back to Widdershins, intending to have a snack and spend the afternoon
walking the coast path. But unexpectedly Jack
stood up from the table as soon as he had
finished his sandwich and disappeared upstairs.

Chatty yelled out, 'Don't be long, Jack! We've

only got a couple of hours before we have to go to the farm.'

There was no reply. Some noises came from overhead; bumping and scraping.

Fay said, 'Oh Mum. He's still so . . . unpredictable. He hardly speaks. Never explains anything. How are you coping?'

Hope said truthfully, 'Very well. I don't know what this is all about.'

They were soon to know. Jack came gingerly down the stairs carrying two large box kites. Hope laughed aloud, recognizing the tapestry frame and nylon curtaining immediately. He gave one to Chatty, the other to Fay. They almost filled the room and the girls backed against the wall with them.

Hope said, 'Your father has been working on these for the past month!' I didn't know they were for Christmas – they are presents, are they, Jack?'

He nodded.

Chatty said, 'They're great, Jack! Absolutely great! Come on, Fay. Move! I want to get through the door and try mine up on the moor!'

So they abandoned the walk and spent the next two hours running crazily along the top of the cliff until the kites floated high above them like enormous white moths, needing only a gentle tug now and then to keep them in formation.

Fay was ecstatic. 'Dad! They're beautiful. So ethereal. Oh, Martin will love this – will I be able to take it to bits so that I can get it home?'

Jack nodded and then glanced at Hope. They had both registered that Fay was calling her Sheffield flat 'home'.

Chatty said, 'Come on, Ho! Take mine. I want to get a photograph of it. No way I can fly this in Paris. It will have to lodge with you.'

Laughing, they spent the rest of that grey Christmas afternoon flying the two kites high above the smoking chimney of Widdershins. And then, when they had reeled them in and were climbing down the cliff again, the low grey cloud parted as if on cue, and a misty sun made a red path towards them across the sea. They came to an involuntary halt above the valley. For once Chatty found nothing to say; they watched as the cloud slowly gathered the sun into itself again and then they exchanged a smile and went on down the path to the cottage. 'A quick cup of tea, then we'll go to the farm,' Hope said. 'Bella asked us to get there before it was dark. And I'd like to help Jem with the milking.'

Fay and Chatty groaned and mentioned their feet and legs. Hope busied herself with the kettle and teapot and thought that she and Jack must be physically fitter now than their own children. She smiled at them as they crowded round Jack, asking him to show them the prototype for the kites and to tell them how he had designed the fragile frames to catch the small wind that was blowing that day. She had no doubts about their psychological health. They had somehow coped with the marriage break-up and the loss of their grandparents and honorary aunt and uncle and now they were doing their utmost to help. They were not a bit put off by his strange silences, in fact gentle Fay supplied answers for him.

'Martin has explained a lot about aerodynamics

to me,' she said, her blond hair falling all over Jack's sketches. 'If you lift here, then you have to drop there. Yes?' Jack nodded. Fay said, 'Dad, you always had a feeling for this sort of thing, didn't you? It wasn't just the income it brought in. It was the – the – sort of – *meaning* – of the air we breathe and the way it moves. And why!'

Chatty rolled her eyes at her mother and Hope grinned back and said, 'Where's the enigmatic grin got to, Kitty?' She shook her head. 'Cheshire cat indeed!' she said. Then added for good measure, 'Jack and Hope forsooth!'

Bella was waiting for them by the kitchen door. She was wearing Peter's old tweed coat and a cap and looked like a scarecrow.

'They're here!' she yelled behind her and Jem and Fennie crowded out, similarly wrapped up. 'Peter can't manage it.' Bella herded them towards the gate. 'An' we got to hurry 'cos we need a bit o' daylight.'

Chatty said, 'What's going on? I thought we were going to be doing presents and cooking dinner—'

'Not so much talking, young Charity!' Bella huffed and puffed ahead of them up the knoll and down the other side. 'We've left the gaffer in charge of Nathan and we don't want to be long!'

Jem was laughing. Fennie said, as excited as a schoolgirl, 'That's what we're doing! We're doing presents!'

'Shut up, young Fennie!' Bella ordered. They had reached the top of the cliff path and she beckoned them on. Obediently they all shut up and followed her lead. They reached the cove and began to tramp across it towards the cave. 'We 'ad to be certain of the tide,' Bella explained. 'It's mostly for Jack, o' course, but it's our present for all of you 'cos you'll all use it.'

For a heart-stopping moment, Hope thought Bella and Peter were giving them the old *Mirabelle*, but then Bella struggled up the soft sand right into the cave and past the newly tarred hull and there, pulled up past the wrack that marked high tide, was a dinghy, just under eight foot from stem to stern and about four foot in beam. It was a stout boat, all timber, with heavy oars shipped across its seats and rowlocks like medieval ankle irons.

Bella said, 'We din't know what to get. Started thinking about it weeks ago. And then Jem saw this advertised. He's done it up.'

Grinning, Jem said, 'Test driven it too, Jack. What d'you think?'

Jack was staring with the others, speechless as usual but to the point of being stunned. Hope felt her throat closing on tears.

Fay said solemnly, 'It's the best present anyone could give anyone! It reminds me of the story in the sagas about—'

Chatty said, 'It's wonderful. It's like giving us . . . a new life!'

Fennie said, 'They thought – Bella and Peter – that you could go fishing, Jack! You used to go with Peter in the *Mirabelle* and you liked it, didn't you?' She spoke indulgently as she always did to Jack. 'Peter said you liked bringing home the food for Hope. That's why you like the gardening now. Peter said—'

'Shut up, Fennie,' Bella ordered again. 'I

378

reckon they're pleased. Now come on, you two. I got to get back to my pots. An' you got to get back to your babby, my girl. Leave 'em to 'ave a good look.'

But Fennie could not be subdued. 'There's something else too! Only we 'ad to show you this while it was still daylight!'

This time it was Jem who said, 'Shut up, Fennie.' He paused as he passed Jack. 'With all the muscle power you got at your disposal, why don't you lug it as far up the cave as it will go? And moor it to a rock as well. Just in case we get some gales.'

The three of them tramped off, well satisfied with the reaction they had got. And still Jack stood as if turned to stone, staring at the dinghy. The girls crowded around it, rocking it to feel its weight, lifting an oar at a time, clambering into it and trying each of the seats.

Hope took Jack's arm gently. 'It's like being ten years old again, Jack. Like getting the present you always wanted and didn't even know you wanted.' She knew he was as close to tears as she was. 'The *Mirabelle* is beyond us . . . in any case it will always be Peter and Bella's boat. But this . . .'

He blinked and turned to look at her. He said, 'They trust me. To go out. To fish. They trust me.'

It was more than he had said all day. She nodded slowly, seeing another facet to the gift.

Chatty yelled, 'Mum, you'll never be able to use these oars – you'll have to leave it to Dad,' and Hope noted that she was Mum again and Jack was Dad.

He said very quietly, 'Will you trust me too, Ho?'

She nodded again and then as Chatty reiterated, 'Poor old Dad – you'll have to do all the rowing!' she smiled. 'Sounds as if I've not much choice,' she said.

With some difficulty they manhandled the boat further up the cave and tied the mooring lines to rocks. Chatty badgered them to promise they could all go 'for a sail' the next day.

'Boxing Day,' she said solemnly, 'is a corruption of boating day. Didn't you know that? Everyone who has a boat is duty-bound to take it out on Boxing Day!'

Fay hugged Jack. 'Oh, isn't it just lovely?' She abandoned the sagas for a moment to say, 'It's just like the boat in my book – d'you remember, Granny gave me that lovely book with pictures? The *Owl and the Pussy Cat* boat!'

And it was rather like a boat from a picture book, so the girls decided it must be called the pea-green boat. And by the time they had clambered back up to the knoll and down to the farm again it was already known as *Sweet Pea*.

Peter had got up and was sitting by the kitchen fire and the big table was already laid. They thanked him; they thanked Bella, Jem and Fennie again – although she kept telling them it was nothing to do with her – and at last settled down to give the more prosaic presents that they had bought. Nathan had already had his: it was a hardwood frame from which were suspended bells and rattles of all shapes and sizes. He demonstrated it with a will. Jem looked very much the artist in his beaded African hat and

Bella and Fennie were delighted with their scarves and perfume. Peter accepted his parcel from Jack and unwrapped it slowly. It was Jack's copy of *Treasure Island*. Hope had not known about it. She offered to read it to him later that evening. Jack said quietly, 'Let me read it for you, Peter.'

Just for a moment there was a surprised hiatus in the babble around the fire. And then before anyone could cover it, Bella brought in a basket. 'This is for all of you but mainly for Hope.'

She plonked the basket in front of the fire. Inside was a puppy, not long weaned by the look of it, black and white with a feathery tail and limpid brown eyes. Hope looked at it and it looked back at her.

'Oh . . . oh!' she said. Chatty and Fay made similar noises. The puppy struggled out of the basket and went to each of them in turn and back to Hope again.

'She knows,' Peter said. 'She knows she's got to look after you. I bin telling her ever since she arrived that she's got an important job to do.'

'You'll 'ave to 'ave 'er seen to,' Bella said more prosaically. 'She's crossbreed as you see but she's mostly collie and they're good guard dogs. She'll let you know if anyone comes.'

Hope said wonderingly, 'We've never had a dog. How . . . lovely.'

She smoothed the silky coat and watched as the little animal, wriggling with delight, moved to Jack. Fay was cooing, 'Look at those eyes . . . oh, you darling girl!' And Chatty was leaning over to tickle behind her ears. 'What shall we call her? Two names in one afternoon! *Sweet Pea* and . . .'

Jack said something so quietly no one heard except Peter and he nodded. 'Why not? It's a proper name. A proper woman's name.' He patted his knee. 'Come here, my girl. Little Milly. Little Millicent. Come to Peter.'

And Milly wriggled her way ecstatically across the hearthrug for yet more attention.

It was not late when they walked back to Widdershins. Hope held Milly beneath her chin, glad of the warmth of the small body although with the cloud it was a mild night. Jack carried the basket and the girls managed dog food between them. Somewhere out on the moors a fox barked and Milly's small body tensed and then quickly relaxed again. Before going inside they put her down and tried to tell her that this was her new home. She snuffled around the doorstep and then set out for the sound of the rill and used the trees of Marble Arch to good effect.

'What a clever girl,' Chatty extolled, delighted. 'Hope, look! She's made a proper little puddle! Isn't that the cleverest thing you ever saw?'

They let her find her own way back to the door and then in her excitement she tried to trip everyone up as they moved carefully around lighting lamps and feeding the fire. Hope put her basket to one side of the range and lifted her into it and the girls went on repeating the last exercise while Hope and Jack made coffee and laid the table with mince pies and cake.

'I couldn't eat another thing!' Fay expostulated, but then did a fine job on the mince pies. Chatty lay full length in front of the fire feeding tiny pieces of dog biscuit to Milly by hand. Jack and Hope sat either side of the table, Jack with his hands wrapped around his coffee mug as usual, Hope smiling dreamily at the girls.

Fay took a deep breath and said, 'Would anybody mind if Martin and I got married next year?' She looked from her mother to her father. 'We thought we'd wait until after I've graduated. Martin is doing his doctorate but that's all right because he's being seconded by his firm. We could afford to start buying a flat just behind the university. I might . . . just might . . . get a job in the library. Ancient Scandinavian history section. I was talking to the chief librarian just before we came down for Christmas and he seemed to think—'

Hope interrupted. 'Never mind all that. Brilliant – but outshone by your first request! You've obviously thought it all out – cut it and dried it completely!'

Fay flushed. 'It didn't seem a good time to be talking about marriage.'

Chatty rolled over onto her back and looked up. 'Idiot! They're thrilled. Can't you tell? When Hope starts talking like Mandy it means she's thrilled.'

She realized what she had said and clapped a hand to her mouth, then released it sufficiently to blurt, 'Mum – sorry. Sorry, really.'

Hope said in her most sensible voice, 'Don't be silly, Chat. Or Cat. Or whatever. But yes. We are thrilled.' She glanced at Jack. 'Aren't we, Jack?'

His eyes were wary but he nodded.

Hope smiled. 'Let's hear some more of those plans, Fay. Have you fixed a date? Seen the vicar? Bought the flowers and dress?'

'Oh Mum . . .'

'Well. Sounds as though you and Martin have gone into it fairly deeply.'

'We knew. Straight away we knew. Don't you remember?'

Hope thought back. 'Yes. I remember. You were effulgent.'

'We get on so well too. We can be in the same room working. Never get on each other's nerves. In fact Martin says he can work much better when I'm there. And I'm the same.' Chatty made vomiting noises and Fay said, 'Shut up, Chatty. I had to put up with you rabbiting on about Mark Jinty when you were at school!'

Surprisingly, Chatty did shut up, a fact that Hope promised herself she would think about later. Meanwhile they discussed Martin, his parents, the Orkneys, Sheffield and the housing situation and, reluctantly, money and finances.

'We don't expect you to have to pay for this wedding, Mummy. Daddy, please don't look like that! We don't *want* a big wedding. Martin never goes inside a church unless it's to examine their heating system. We're going to a register office and then we'll have lunch or tea somewhere – just you and Martin's parents, not even his sister – and then off to Norway. Don't forget Chatty and I are pretty rich. We've got Gran's money. I've hardly touched mine.'

'I'm saving mine for when I start my own business,' Chatty said.

Hope said, 'You'll be twenty-one by then of course. And I was twenty-one. So . . . oh Fay . . . I think it's good. I suppose we knew that you would marry Martin one day anyway. Oh, I'm pleased.' She glanced at Jack. 'We're both pleased. Aren't we, Jack?'

And he nodded and then said, 'Yes.'

The next day they launched *Sweet Pea* and rowed sedately around the cove in a dead calm sea with Milly in the stern barking at each stroke. When the girls begged to be allowed an oar each, Jack changed places with them and put out a mackerel line baited with a spinner. That night they had soused mackerel with one of Bella's loaves spread liberally with home-made butter. The next day they went out again and Chatty stood in the boat and slid out of her tracksuit to reveal a swimming costume. Amid loud protests she dived into the icy water and swam ashore. Jem and Fennie came down to see what all the noise was about and found them all floundering in the shallows as they pulled *Sweet Pea* ashore helped by a leaping, barking Milly.

'She's already taking to the water, I see,' Jem commented as Chatty ran past him carrying the dog, both of them shivering.

Fennie said, 'You must be mad. Look at all of you. Wet up to the waist.'

'Tell Bella not to cook tonight.' Hope rested, hand on side, while Jem took her place. 'I'll bring some mackerel. We've got far too many for us.'

'All right.' Fennie grinned, looking at Jack. 'He's that pleased with his present. Poor dear. It's nice to see 'im looking happy, innit?'

Hope looked across the cove to where Jack was bent double pushing the heavy boat into the cave. Beneath his new blanket-coat, his arms and shoulders were obviously powerful; his jeans rolled to his knees made his legs look stronger and thicker than usual. She remembered seeing him in the hospital four months ago and being shocked at his emaciation.

She said slowly, 'Yes. I think that's what it is, Fennie. But if it's not, at least he is focused. On something outside himself. I'll never be able to thank you enough for giving him this boat.'

Fennie laughed. 'Don't be daft. Peter rang up this bloke and told 'im straight. He said 'e'd never asked no favours in the past and 'e wouldn't be around much longer to ask 'em in the future, so 'e expected a good answer! Jem went to pay for it and collect it. We 'ad it for a song.'

Hope was afraid to laugh in case she cried. Instead she said, 'I think this has been the best Christmas I can remember. Isn't that amazing?'

'No. Not really.' Fennie scuffed her toe in the sand. 'It's the same for me, innit? I was dumped by old Sid Phillips, I'm skivvying for Bella in return for bed and board for me and Nathe. Nathe's dad dun't want to know. But Jem says one day we'll get married and we'll run a little stall in Truro market and Bella and Peter love Nathe like 'e was theirs. An' you an' the family are here for company . . . I can't remember a better Christmas neither.' She paused for breath and then added, 'It's 'cos o' Peter p'r'aps.'

Hope found Fennie's frankness more easily acceptable now. She nodded. Across the sand Jem came running chased by Fay. Jack followed carrying the fish. Somewhere above them Milly barked. She and Fennie began the steep climb to the cliff top. She thought, I must remember this moment, keep it in my head and bring it to the front of my mind every Christmas from now on.

But on the Wednesday Fay was going back to Sheffield and it was harder to part with her this time than before. They had two more days with Chatty and then she too left. They stood on the platform at Penzance, waving until the train disappeared around the curve of Mounts Bay. It was another very still morning and they walked from Penzance station up Market Jew Street into the Causeway. Jack had brought Chatty's kite with him and while he took it into a small toyshop halfway along the cobbled street, Hope at last bought a telescope for Peter. And then she went into the bank for a statement and had to deduct the cost of the telescope from what was there. She bit her lip. Still no word from Mrs Martin.

She met Jack at a little teashop and they ate an early lunch there. He was pleased with his negotiations.

'I set it up for them to see and showed them my sketches. They liked it. They'll have four for the Easter holiday. Maybe more later.'

'That's great, Jack.' She meant that it was great he was able to tell her exactly what had happened; that apparently he had also explained his kite to the shop owner. He nodded. 'Yes,' he said. And she realized what he meant and belatedly added her congratulations.

She showed him the telescope. It was expensive, with its own tripod, but she had felt she had to do it.

'We're down to five hundred, Jack.' She took out the statement and spread it on the table. 'But that's all right. It will get us through till Easter. And then I'll go to the Social Security office and see what's what.'

He said nothing. She knew he was frightened of bureaucracy in case it meant an end to their isolation. She brightened deliberately. 'Anyway, if your kites do well, Jack, we'll be fine!'

She knew from bitter experience that the kind of sales made in Penzance would not cover their basic living costs. But he too brightened and they walked back down the steep street to the car park and she drove home through Newlyn and Mousehole as if they hadn't a care in the world.

Eighteen

There were no January gales to contend with in the New Year. Several days were bright and sunny and Jack gradually took to going out in *Sweet Pea* for short fishing trips. Hope was nervous at first and hung around the top of the cliff path to watch him, but he managed so well that eventually she took it for granted. As Jem said matter-of-factly, 'If he'd wanted to top himself after that night in the *Mirabelle*, he could have done it a dozen times. He learned something that night – you both did.'

Meanwhile she discovered how to salt fish and the cottage gained another smell, not so pleasant as before. On the 21st of the month, another letter postmarked from Gloucester arrived and she was about to hand it to Jack when she saw that it was addressed to her. She ripped open the envelope and a cheque for £320 slid on to the table. She gave a little cheer. She and Jack were breakfasting late and she pushed it over the table for him to see.

'I'd given up,' she admitted. 'Obviously Mrs Martin waited until she had sold all of them.'

She heaved an exaggerated sigh of relief. 'That will tide us over for a bit. I suggest we keep the five hundred as a sort of insurance and live on what we put in from now on.'

Jack nodded; he did not look enthusiastic.

'Sorry, Jack. I know you hate talking about money – thank God we don't need to do much budgeting here.'

He said nothing but picked up the envelope and looked inside. There was no covering letter, nothing except the cheque. He looked carefully at the envelope.

She watched him apprehensively and when he put it down she said, 'You don't suppose . . . How much did Mandy give us that first Christmas?'

She did not think he would answer but at last he said, 'Nine hundred and sixty pounds.'

'For twelve smocks. That's about eighty pounds for each smock. And I sent four smocks to Mrs Martin.' She stared at him. 'Four eighties are three hundred and twenty pounds.' He said nothing. 'There's no reason to suppose . . . I mean, if she sold the others for a hundred – or ninety-nine – or whatever the mark-up was – then presumably she would also sell these for that price.'

Still Jack was silent but he did not put the envelope back on the table.

She looked at the cheque. The handwriting was not Mandy's. She said, 'In real terms, eighty pounds is not the same price as it was twenty years ago. So it's just coincidence. Surely?'

He spoke at last and said miserably, 'I don't know.'

'Jack. I cannot burn a cheque for three hundred and twenty pounds.'

He shook his head vigorously.

She said, 'That's settled then.' She folded the cheque and put it on the mantelpiece and lifted the teapot from the hob. 'Another cup of tea?'

He shook his head then added, 'No thanks.' He crumpled the envelope and threw it on the fire. 'I'd like to swim. Will you come with me?'

She was astonished. 'You haven't swum since we arrived!' She glanced through the window; it was not sunny and she quailed at the thought of immersing herself in the icy Atlantic. But it was the first time he had asked her to do anything with him.

'All right. I'll come.' She grinned. 'Milly will enjoy it anyway!'

If the girls had been with them it would have been an adventure; silly but fun. Jack took it very seriously, going upstairs to change and arming himself with towels and the sea soap. He set off down the valley and then the cliff path as if he could not wait to get into the water. He left her the cave for changing and went behind a rock. Long before she had taken off her outer clothes he was wading into the sea. Milly followed him closely but hesitated as the waves washed her chin. Hope ran down to join them, gasping and screaming as the iron-cold water lapped over her abdomen. Milly yapped frantically in sympathy and then as a small wave lifted her off her feet she saved her breath and paddled towards Hope. She had galloped in and out of the water before but never gone out of her depth. Hope rolled on to her back and paddled alongside her. The whiskery black face was a picture of sheer determination. Hope laughed aloud and called to Jack to come and look but he was swimming strongly out to sea, apparently immune to the intense cold. At some point when she was getting anxious, he turned and shouldered his way through the water to where they were playing in the shallows and began lathering himself and Milly with the soap. He too laughed and leaped up and down to keep warm. Milly escaped and swam in to the shore and ran along the sands, then turned and hurtled back into the shallows, barking crazily.

'What? What is it?' Hope looked round and saw what Milly could see. It was a seal, looking like another Milly, its head well out of the water, staring at them with obvious curiosity.

'Oh Jack! Look!'

He too turned and they both looked into the drowned eyes of the creature and then back to each other. Quite spontaneously, Jack reached out for her hand and swung her towards him and they looked again and with Milly still barking, they waited until the seal decided they were not a threat and disappeared beneath the water.

They let go of each other almost self-consciously and walked back up to the beach to dry and dress as best they could. Then they panted back up the cliff path and stood as usual at the top, looking out to sea, getting their breath again. And it was then that Jack said quietly, 'Better now. Not so . . . dirty.'

She looked at him, shocked, and then quite suddenly she understood.

'That cheque. It was that cheque. Wasn't it?'

He shook himself, looking like Milly. 'We were bought and paid for. Before.'

'Oh Jack. You think it came from Mandy.'

He shook his head though she knew he was not convinced.

She said, 'Listen. If you think it came from Mandy, I will burn it. Is that what you want?'

'No!' He had never sounded so definite and she was strangely disappointed. 'I meant . . . it made me remember. Things.'

'All right.' She leaned down and towelled Milly, wondering what it was she wanted him to say and do. The cheque had brought back memories which made him feel unclean; so unclean he had needed to swim and wash in the sea. But he did not want to burn the cheque.

She straightened. 'Come on. Milly's shivering. Let's get back to the cottage and get warm.' She smiled at him. 'That was marvellous, Jack. Especially seeing the seal.'

He nodded as usual and then frowned as Milly started to bark. They both waited and Jem came around the rill and held up his hand to them.

'I thought you must be down in the cove.' He patted Milly. 'You've got a visitor. I came on ahead to warn you. Bella was trying to hang on to him but I think he must have escaped her now.' He grinned. 'It's OK, he seems a decent chap but he didn't give a name. I reckon he's from your hospital, Jack. Said he only needed five minutes of your time.'

Hope raised her brows and glanced at Jack, wondering how he would take it. 'That's decent of him,' she said. 'Looking in on you. If he's on holiday down here, it's quite a lot of time to give up.' Jack said nothing; it was obvious to her that he did not like the idea of anyone at the hospital keeping an eye on him. 'Shall I go on alone and make your excuses?' she suggested. 'You can go back with Jem and have half an hour's visit with Peter.'

But he shook his head and took the lead, determined to get the interview over with as soon as possible. Hope and Jem followed with Milly running from one to the other and then deciding to get thoroughly wet again in the rill. Hope laughed and gathered her up into the soggy towel and carried her up the valley to the front door. And then stopped. Jack was standing by the table holding on to the back of his chair. Getting out of the chair next to the range was the familiar figure of Henrik.

It was as if a hand clutched her heart; definitely a physical sensation. She remembered so many times shared with Henrik . . . Comforting times, now poisoned because they had not been the friendly, innocent times she had thought. She gasped, just as she had gasped when she went into the sea. Then she turned to Jem.

'It's all right. It's an old friend.' Jem frowned because it was so obvious the atmosphere in the tiny kitchen was anything but friendly. Hope unwrapped Milly and put her down. She said in a low voice, 'It's Henrik Petersen. You had better leave us.'

Jem was also still for a moment; then he said, 'Will you be all right?' And when she nodded he turned away. She went inside and closed the door behind her. It was very quiet: the fire settled itself; Milly whined, sensing something unnatural in her small, secure world; Jack hung on to the chair.

Hope forced herself to speak naturally. 'Henrik. I'm not going to say we're pleased to see you. But you're here and obviously you have come for a reason. So sit down. Jack, you sit down too. I'm going to make some coffee.' Henrik subsided and, after a small hesitation, so did Jack. Hope swallowed; she was terrified she might be seized with the terrible sickness. She looked across at Jack; he was staring at Henrik as if he had never seen him before and she wondered what poison Mandy had dripped into his ears. She moved into his line of vision and smiled at him and, unexpectedly, he nodded back. Suddenly she thought that whatever was going to happen, whatever catastrophe Henrik had brought with him, nothing mattered except that Jack was well again. She knew it; quite suddenly, she knew he was well – more than well, better than he had ever been. Milly seemed to catch her mood and crept quietly into her basket next to the range. Hope settled the kettle into the coals and reached for mugs.

'We have been swimming, Henrik. The three of us.'

He said conversationally in his precise voice, 'It must have been cold.'

'It was. Very cold. But invigorating.' She spooned coffee into the mugs and walked around him to the scullery for milk. His hair had almost gone from the top of his head. She remembered again their closeness: how he had picked her up from the flower bed when she was in labour and carried her to his car; how often he had made coffee for her, washed up, met the girls from school.

He addressed Jack. 'Mandy has told me you were ill. I wanted to phone. Write. Tell you how sorry I was. How sorry I am. But she said I must not. She said I must keep away.'

Jack made a sound. Hope moved between them again as if to protect Jack. She said, 'That was good advice. Yet you are here.'

Henrik was silent. Hope made the coffee and passed him his mug. She sat next to Jack. 'Well?'

He said haltingly, 'I am not sure how much you know. How much Mandy told you. Will you tell me this . . . have you seen her since she returned to this country?'

Hope put a hand on Jack's arm. 'No,' she said.

'She wanted to come back to put things right. We became . . . bankrupt. As you know. We should have left Britain years ago. We did not. Because of you.'

He paused and Hope said, 'Sorry, Henrik. You can't blame us for losing your money. We lost ours too. And my mother's. Jack almost lost his life.'

'I do not blame.' Henrik looked down into his mug and the steam clouded his face. Hope wondered whether he was weeping. He said at last, 'I transferred a lot of money to Mandy. We had to be careful. I put it into the shop. Expectancies. You remember.'

Hope did not look at Jack. She said, 'We thought the shops had gone. With everything else.'

'The two went. The Gloucester shop . . . I had come to an agreement with Mrs Martin that she would run it for us. It was Mandy's special project. And it was your special project. We thought you might agree to . . . taking it over. You and Jack. It would have supported you. Been some small recompense for the loss.'

Hope glanced at the mantelpiece. The cheque was still there, tucked behind one of the candlesticks.

'We knew nothing of this,' she said. 'We thought you had lost everything just as we had. Mrs Martin told us she had the lease of the shop.'

Henrik lowered his head further. 'I told her to give out that information. I have other names, Hope. They are a kind of . . . insurance.'

'So you still own the shop. And you still own the house at Sandhurst.'

'Mandy owns the shop. And . . . it would seem . . . she has sold the house at Sandhurst.' He looked up suddenly and she saw his eyes were full of tears. 'I cannot find Mandy. The telephone at Sandhurst was not answered. And then it was answered by someone else who said they had bought the house. I telephoned Mrs Martin and she says that Mandy moved into the flat above the shop but she is not in at the moment. She has not been in at the moment for one week. So I fly to Gatwick and hire a car and go to these places. She is not there. I cannot find her. The only other place I can look is here. She has told me about the cottage and how to get to it. So I drove to Penzance last night and found a hotel. And this morning I have come.'

Hope said, 'She is not here.' She glanced through the window. The cheque had arrived this morning. Was it possible that Mandy would arrive soon after it? Was it her way of letting them know she was coming? For a moment she lost control of herself and said shakily, 'Has she gone into the haunting business now?' Jack covered her hand with his. She glanced at Henrik. 'She has phoned and written. I made her promise not to turn up here. Because of Jack. But she is constantly . . . hovering. Her presence is always . . . there!'

Jack said, 'It's all right, Ho. It's all right.'

Henrik sat up straight. 'You know. Oh God. You know she has come to take Jack back. She has told you.'

Hope said passionately, 'I did not *kidnap* Jack, Henrik! He was ill! He took an overdose and he was really ill! He was ill and thin and . . . dreadful!' She heard herself sob. 'He was in no state to make up his mind. All I did was to give him space. Give him time. Surely that wasn't unreasonable?'

'She said she would not tell you. She said she was coming home to help you. She promised she would not say it was because she was taking Jack away.' He looked past Hope at Jack. 'Was it because of Mandy? Did you want to end things because of her?'

Jack gripped Hope's arm. 'No,' he said clearly.

Hope swallowed on sudden nausea. Jack took a deep breath for the sheer effort of speaking. And then spoke. 'It sounds . . . absurd. But it was because I was nothing. I was just in the way of everyone. A bit of rubbish that needed clearing . . .' Again she heard herself sob.

Henrik said, 'She thought it was because of her. She telephoned to tell me what had happened. She thought it was because she had left you.'

Jack spoke in a strangled voice, 'No.'

Henrik said slowly, 'She wanted it that way. She wanted to be . . . that important. I am sorry, Hope. I am causing distress. I do not know how to be tactful any more.' He sighed. 'Do you hate her very much?'

Hope tried to think straight. She said at last, 'I want to hate her. I want to hate both of you. But when I heard her voice on the phone . . . when I saw you sitting here . . . it is very difficult.'

Henrik clutched his coffee mug. 'It is. You see, we have – Mandy and I – a very difficult relationship. We are not lovers. But we are more than friends. It is complicated. Mandy needs . . . other people. I have gone along with this. I have kept a distance. Until we met you. The two of you represented – for us – what we did not have and wanted very much. Quite simply, we loved you. Can you understand that? Does it embarrass you, Jack?'

Jack did not reply; Hope could feel his misery almost tangibly.

Henrik went on slowly, feeling his way. 'At first, it was all right. We wanted to help you and we plotted to do it. Together. You with your designing and sewing, Hope. Jack with the course . . . the computer course. You recall.'

'Yes,' Jack said suddenly.

'And then, it was different. Somehow. I think I

399

might have fallen in love with you, Hope. It was Fay. I wished – so much – that Fay had been mine.' Jack made a sound and Henrik held up his hand. 'Nothing happened, Jack. It was . . . quite simply, a fantasy. Also for Mandy and Chatty. But it became very, very difficult for us to leave. And then, it became very, very difficult for us not to leave. We knew what we were doing. Leaving you without money or home. And we did it.' He closed his eyes. 'It was criminal. Literally. And we did it.'

The nausea was threatening to overwhelm Hope. But Jack's hand was on hers and she could not push it away and stand up. She said on an indrawn breath, 'Why? For God's sake, *why?*'

Henrik said, 'Self-preservation. Emotional and economic.'

She breathed a shallow laugh. 'That is so you, Henrik. Emotional and economic. Your emotions, your economics.'

'My dear . . . my dear, dear Ho. Can't you see that if we had stayed we would have done more damage still? We were in love with you – don't you understand that? We saw our . . . desertion . . . as liberating you! And I might have gone to prison if we'd stayed. And I couldn't have guaranteed Jack's freedom.'

'A truly altruistic desertion then?'

He actually flushed. 'You have every right to be angry.'

'I am not angry because you left. I am angry because you have come back and are trying to explain everything away.'

'I did not know what else to do, Ho. I must

find Mandy. She is – at the moment – what you would call a loose cannon.' He saw her expression change and added quickly, 'She is very vulnerable, Ho.' He gestured towards Jack. 'You are concerned for Jack for the same reason I am concerned for Mandy. Has she said anything in the letters you have had? Any clue to her state of mind?'

Hope swallowed again. 'She said the same thing over and over again. That she loved us. We have burned them . . . lately.'

'So she could have sent quite recent messages that you know nothing about? She could have told you where she was going?'

Hope closed her eyes on the nausea and tried to think about the seal. Jack said, 'She is not here and we don't know where she is. Go away. Please go away. Hope is going to be ill.'

Henrik levered himself out of his chair with difficulty, then he felt in his jacket pocket and found a card. 'This is my hotel in Penzance. I will stay for three days more. Will you telephone if there is news? Please?'

Jack nodded and then pulled Hope to her feet so that Henrik could open the door. They did not wait to see him walk down the cleft and then back up on to the cliff. Jack closed the door and put his back to it; Hope stood in the scullery doorway staring at him. At last he said, 'Are you all right?'

She nodded. It was as if they had reversed roles; she could not think of a thing to say. He went to the chair so recently vacated by Henrik and plumped up the cushions.

'Sit down, Ho.' He took her arm and led her

around the corner as if she were an invalid. 'I'll get us some lunch. Sit. Close your eyes.'

She did exactly as he said; she was cold and the warmth of the fire seeped into her legs and worked its way through her body. It was only when she stopped trembling that she realized she had been shaking for a long time. She listened to Jack moving about; filling the kettle again and cutting bread. When he said, 'There is tea by your right hand and I have put cheese on toast in the side oven to keep warm,' she felt hot tears well behind her closed eyes. She wanted to thank him, to tell him that she was tired in a way she never was after working in the garden; that it had nothing to do with their swim. It was a tiredness that came from fear. And she did not know what she was frightened of. But if she spoke what would she say?

She felt the tears slide down her cheeks and Jack must have seen them because she heard him move to the linen cupboard and then a handkerchief was gently put in her limp hands. She put it to her face and held it there, ashamed of this breakdown. It smelled of the green soap she used and the fresh air and the flat irons. And that made her weep more. There was very little that was disposable at Widdershins; handkerchiefs, towels and dishcloths were all washed and boiled assiduously. People. Were people disposable? Henrik and Mandy were the most disposable people she had ever met. Her parents had gone. Peter would go quite soon now. How long would Bella be there without him? When would Jem and Fennie take Nathan back to 'civilization'? Would Jack go too?

She made a moaning sound and pressed the handkerchief hard against her face as if to blot out all her thoughts. The next instant Jack's arm was behind her neck and she was being tucked into his shoulder. The moaning rose to a sharp keening sound and he tightened his hold; she released the handkerchief and held hard on to his shirt. She felt, quite literally, that she was drowning. And he knew exactly how she felt because he was lifting her higher in the chair as if clearing the water and his voice was not soothing; it was loud, trying to get through to her.

'It's all right! I've got you. It's all right . . .' He kept saying it, louder and louder. It was so long since she had heard Jack speak loudly; she gasped and sucked in air and clung to him. He was her only chance of survival. She knew it, clearly and desolately. He could save her if she would let him. Could she let him?

Jem came back before it was dark. He tried to sound casual.

'You two all right?' He stood in the open doorway for a moment, then came in and closed the door behind him. The sun had gone and the air was bitterly cold. 'I saw him go ages ago but then Bella and I had to turn Peter and it was time to do the milking . . . What's up, Hope?'

Jack was clearing the table. She had sipped her tea and eaten two mouthfuls of the cheese on toast; now she was huddled into the chair staring at the red caverns of the fire.

Jack indicated the other chair. 'Sit down. Hope isn't feeling too good.'

Jem stared in surprise; it was immediately obvious that Jack was different.

'Oh God. Was it awful?'

Jack glanced at Hope and when she made no movement he said, 'It's a mess. Mandy has disappeared and he had come looking for her. Obviously Hope thinks she's out there somewhere.'

Jem sat down slowly. 'Christ. You're not scared of her, are you, Ho? She's not going to come at you with a knife or anything?'

There was no reply. Jack hung up the last mug and sat down. 'She could do that actually. But it's not really that. She represents all that has gone wrong.' He glanced at Hope and met her eyes and nodded. 'Henrik too.' He sighed. 'It's an invasion. And we can't repel it.' He smiled wryly. 'No drawbridges any more.'

Jem said, 'The headland is its own drawbridge. And anyway you need them inside yourself. I thought you were well equipped that way, Jack.'

Jack shook his head. 'No. Hope has been my drawbridge.'

'Not any more, eh?' Jem leaned across and put a hand on Hope's knee. 'Say something, Ho. You're always so clear-headed. Tell him everything is going to be OK.'

She transferred her drowned gaze to his hand and then his face. She whispered, 'Peter.'

Jem sat back. 'God. This is not good, Hope. Are you trying to copy Jack or something stupid?'

She whispered again, 'Peter.'

'He is no worse. No better either. The nurse

phoned – she was held up somewhere. So we turned him in the bed. Bella rubbed his back and settled him down for the night.'

She went on looking at him while tears filled her eyes again. He was embarrassed and said, 'Hope. Don't. He's comfortable and he's with his Bella. There's nothing else anyone can do.'

Hope nodded and blinked her eyes and then turned back to the fire. She said very clearly, 'Disposable.'

Jem did not stay; he had coped well with Jack's illness, he could not cope with Hope's. 'I'll send Fennie down, shall I?' he asked Jack.

'No.' Jack was amazingly decisive. 'Tomorrow . . . we'll see.'

And when he had gone, Jack went to the range and reached down the cheque which had arrived that morning. He held it out to Hope; she stared at it and put a hand across her mouth. Jack tore it across again and again and then scattered the postage-stamp pieces on to the range. They flared and were gone.

He said, 'There's soup in the scullery. Shall I heat it? Then we could have some of the pickled mackerel.' He smiled. 'Just for a change.'

He waited and after a few seconds she smiled too.

Nineteen

For two days Hope was ill. She knew she was ill because her bones ached and her skin itched. Sadness, sometimes fear, lay upon her like a blanket too. When she felt able to get out of the chair by the fire she wandered to the window and peered through it apprehensively. On the third day Fennie came down with hot pasties wrapped in greaseproof paper, a bunch of grapes and a hand of bananas.

'Jem told us you wanted to be left alone,' she said. 'But Bella said if one of us din't come and see you, she'd come herself.' Fennie drew her mouth down. 'She 'ardly leaves Peter's side, so you can see she's mighty worried.'

'Tell her I'm better but I don't want to come up to the house yet in case I bring germs with me.' Hope forced herself to speak normally. One of the wonderful things she had learned from Jack's illness was that dialogue was not necessary. She had frequently spoken to Jack and supplied his responses. He was doing the same for her now. The last two days had been blessedly and wonderfully undemanding.

'You sound all right.' Fennie was almost put

out. 'Jem was reckoning you were as bad as Jack was!' She looked from one to the other. 'Jack's talking again – and sensible too. And you're just the same as per usual!'

Jack laughed so that Hope did not need to. She said, 'We went for a swim. I might have picked up a chill then.'

'That's what it was!' Fennie lengthened her face still more. 'Never 'eard of anyone so daft as you lot. Swimming in midwinter. Wonder the dog is still alive.'

Hope ignored that. 'Look at this fruit! Oh Fennie, thank you.'

'Jem got it from Truro market. Nothing to do with me.'

'What about the pasties?'

'Well, yes. I did make them. Bella 'asn't got the time any more.'

Jack glanced at Hope. 'Is Peter very bad?'

'Not much longer, I wouldn't think. Nurses are coming each day. I wonder they don't give 'im something. We wouldn't treat an animal like it, would we?'

Hope said, 'I'll walk back up with you, Fennie. There might be something I can do.'

'Well, I wasn't going to say anything 'cos we're managing all right and Jem said to leave you in peace. But your eldest girl did ring. Last evening. She said not to worry you but when you're next at the farm can you phone her.'

'You weren't going to tell us?'

Jack said swiftly, 'I'll go.'

'We'll both go. Whether we can help or not, we want to see Peter.' Hope put the pasties in the side oven and took her coat from under the stairs. He would have stopped her but she seemed charged with new energy. 'I'm all right, Jack. Really. I need to . . . break the pattern . . . forget the nightmare. You know.'

He nodded. 'I know.'

They walked behind Fennie who was obviously still nonplussed by their good health. 'Jem said as how you were at death's door! Honestly, men make such a fuss about illness.'

Milly followed, delighted to be out and about again. Jack held his blanket-coat around him and did not offer a hand to Hope. She shivered in the clear air, realizing that she had not felt it on her skin for three days. She thought of the sea and shivered more; how had she got into it . . . why had she got into it? Had it indeed been the kind of cleansing Jack had needed? She tried to recall the wonder of seeing the seal's head emerging from the swell but Henrik's grey and thinning hair came between then and now. Henrik who had loved her and Fay, but had loved Mandy so much more. Hope shivered again; she knew nothing about love; not really. It was deep and dark and frightening.

Fennie was saying something about food and she forced herself to listen and reply. 'Yes, of course we've eaten properly. Jack cooked a cauliflower. So we have had fresh vegetables.'

'Bella wanted Jem to get oranges. She swears by oranges. But they weren't worth buying, so he reckoned.'

'We've done well. I take it you are doing the cooking at the farm, Fennie?'

'Yes. Peter and Bella mind Nathe for me.' Fennie looked round and said soberly, 'It's awful really. Not a proper life at all. But Jem tells me it wun't be for long. Tidn't right, is it? Waiting for someone to die.'

Hope said nothing but Jack's voice came strongly from behind. 'It's good for Jem, Fennie. Remember that. He needs to see . . . the process.'

'Because of 'is wife, d'you mean?' Fennie shook her head. 'I don't get it. Oh, I know what you're saying. That were unnatural and he felt responsible. And this is natural and nothing to do with 'im. But death is death. There's no getting away from that.' She reached the farm gate and leaned on it, breathing heavily. 'Jem's been waiting about too long. What 'e needs is to get on with everything. Have a baby and look after it. Take life in his own hands . . . live it.'

Jack smiled. 'He needs you, Fennie. Black and white. Simple and direct. Jem will be all right.'

She grinned too. 'Course 'e will. Take no notice of me. I'm just so . . . sad. Really sad. I'm not used to 'anging about not able to do any-thing much.' Her grin widened. 'When I got bored before, I went down the takeaway and ended up with Nathan!' She sobered. 'There's nothing I can do about Peter. An' he's a lovely man.'

They went indoors where Jem was stacking logs next to the range. He looked up warily.

'How are you?' he asked both of them.

Hope nodded. 'I'm all right now. Think I must have got a chill from the swim.'

'Funny chill,' Jem commented.

Jack said frankly, 'You know what it was, Jem. It was seeing Henrik. Cured me and knocked Hope for six. But she does seem all right today.'

'Cured you? Just like that?'

'I was well on the way. But there were still . . . bogeymen.' He laughed at Fennie's expression. 'Henrik was one of them. But when it came to it, Henrik was . . . after all . . . just Henrik. He dumped all of us up to our necks in mire. But he didn't reckon on Widdershins. And all that goes with Widdershins.' He leaned down and picked up Milly. 'It's just like you said, Fennie. We've had to get on with life.'

Hope knew the words were directed at her. They had formed her philosophy all along. She had been so certain that she was doing the right thing by bringing Jack here. And he did seem . . . better. Better than his old self. Did it mean that she had to let him go now? Not next month or the month after, but now? Why should that seem like an end instead of a beginning?

She said, 'I'll ring Fay before I see Peter. Is that all right, Jem?'

'Sure. But she did say there was no urgency, so don't worry.'

She went into the hall and picked up the receiver. Jack was behind her. 'She could be at a lecture. Anything,' he reminded her as she began to dial.

She nodded and then started to count the rings. When the fifteenth rang out there was a click and a voice said, 'This is Fay and Martin's flat. May I help you?'

At first Hope tried to believe it was an answering machine. She avoided Jack's questioning gaze and waited for the bleeps. Nothing happened until the voice said again, 'Is anybody there?' She turned and faced the hall stand. Peter's cap dangled at eye level. The voice said suddenly, 'It's Ho. It is Ho. Isn't it?' She squeezed her eyes tightly shut. Mandy said, 'It's me, Mandy. Talk to me, Ho. Please. I'm staying with Fay and Martin. I had nowhere to go and I was going to break my promise and turn up at Widdershins and then I thought of Fay and I rang Chatty for her number and couldn't get her so I just turned up. She's moved – well, you know that – so I had to go to the university and make some enquiries – it was like being a detective!' A laugh tinkled over the wires. 'It's a bit awkward because Martin is all Scottish and disapproving. But they're out all day anyway, and I usually go out in the evening, so it's not too bad.' She paused. Hope could not speak; she laid her cheek against Peter's cap and fought the usual nausea. 'Darling? Are you there? Why don't you say something? I want to know whether I can come down now. It's almost February and that's almost spring. Surely Jack is well enough now to make up his own mind? We could take it slowly, Ho. Perhaps I could stay at the farm and visit each day? I don't want to rock the boat, darling. But you're not interested, are you? And I do love him. That's why I've stuck it here all this blessed winter. I'll take him to Cape Town with me. Henrik won't mind. We'll look after him together.'

Jack said, 'Give up, Ho. She's not there. We can try again later.'

Mandy said excitedly, 'Is that Jack? Is he with you? Jack?' Hope tucked the receiver under her chin. Mandy said loudly, 'You've found your voice, Jack? They said at the hospital that you could barely string two words together! But you said something then, Jack. Say it again.'

Hope took a deep breath and said, 'Henrik is here. In Penzance.'

There was a stunned silence from the other end. She risked a quick glance at Jack; he looked tense with . . . with what? Excitement?

Mandy's voice dropped a register. She said, 'How does he look?' When Hope said nothing she went on, 'Old. He looks old, doesn't he? We're both getting old, Ho.' She paused then said, 'Is he . . . angry?'

Hope tried to recall whether Henrik had been angry. At last she said, 'I don't know. He wasn't very . . . sorry. Neither of you seem to be sorry. For anything.'

Mandy said, 'We are sorry, Ho. But . . . surely Henrik explained? We had no option. We did what we could. I tried to get Chatty settled in Paris – that succeeded excellently, Ho. You cannot deny that. And Henrik safeguarded the Gloucester shop so that you and Jack—'

'You did not tell us about that. In fact it seems you have been running the shop. Not that we – not that I – would want anything to do with your shop.' She paused. 'Chatty – Chatty deserved the introduction you arranged. But since then she has made her own way. Don't forget that.' She paused again and when Mandy did not speak she added almost reluctantly, 'I was grateful for the way you spoke to Chatty . . . that day . . . on the phone. It hurt her at the time but it also toughened her.'

'I meant what I said. She needed toughening.

She needed to know what she was doing, not let life push her here and there.'

'Like I have?'

'Did I say that? Well, yes. Exactly.'

Hope said, 'Maybe that was true. I don't know. But I do know that you wouldn't last five minutes down here. And I have.'

Mandy said, obviously nonplussed, 'Quite an assertion. Especially coming from you.' She forced a sudden laugh. 'But you still can't face me, can you? And you certainly won't allow Jack to do so.'

Jack obviously heard those last words because he held out his hand for the receiver. Hope said, 'You promised us some kind of recuperation time. Till the spring.'

'And I've kept that promise. But now I can hear Jack talking. So he is cured. And Henrik has come over to find me so time is – is—' she sobbed a little laugh, '—of the essence!' She hardened her voice. 'Listen, Ho. I shall have to go back with Henrik. He knows how I feel and he will be happy for me to bring Jack with me. That means a new life for Jack – a good life – money, sunshine. And me. Can't you see – just for once – past the end of your nose?' She sighed sharply, impatiently. 'Tell me one thing. Has Jack slept with you since he arrived?' Hope did not reply and Mandy laughed tightly. 'You see?'

Jack took the receiver from her hand and said very quietly, 'Mandy. This is Jack. You're right, I am cured. Hope and I will catch the train and be with you tomorrow. Goodbye.' He replaced the receiver.

Hope whispered, 'I can't. You must go. She's right, you are cured.'

'We go together.'

'No. The time for deciding has come and I shall only inhibit . . . you.'

'The time for deciding has come for you as well as me.' He smiled suddenly. 'I'm as rattled as you are. But it's something we've got to do.' He turned towards the old dining room which was Peter's bedroom. 'Come on. Let's go and tell Bella and Peter what is happening.'

She followed him helplessly. She knew only one thing for certain and that was that she did not want to leave Widdershins. She could not face the outside world.

Peter was propped high on pillows, the neatly turned-down sheet stopped at his waist and he wore a shawl over his pyjama'd shoulders.

'Helps with his breathing,' Bella explained shortly, cutting across his welcome. 'Don't try to talk, Gaffer.' She pulled up two chairs. 'Sit down a few minutes, the pair of you. We want to talk to you.'

They sat side by side, trying to summon smiles for the sick man. Hope glanced at Bella; the gaunt, lined face was as grim as ever but every movement was slower.

Jack said, 'I'm better, Peter. Did Jem tell you?'

Peter grinned irrepressibly. 'You been better for some weeks, lad. Only you couldn't believe it.'

Jack nodded. Bella said, 'I thought I told you not to talk?' She looked at Jack.

'We've said ever so often. You seemed to get

414

better on bonfire night. When we went to Buryan. D'you remember?'

'I remember.'

Hope tried to smile. It was true that they had built some kind of life together over the past weeks but that could disappear immediately they saw Mandy again.

Bella said, 'Anyway. We thought you should know. We've changed our wills. We were going to leave the farm to you. But then we decided not to. We're leaving it to Jem. We talked about it a lot.' She took Peter's hand and he nodded. 'That cottage is where you should be. If we lumber you with the farm it wouldn't be fair. But we're leaving you some land. The fields up to the farm gate will be yours. They're not bad fields, rocks everywhere but in between . . . you could grow daffodils and early potatoes for the market. Cauliflowers and stick beans later in the year.'

Both Jack and Hope stared incredulously. It was Jack who stammered, 'We don't want . . . anything. What are you saying . . . thinking?'

Bella glanced at Peter, who nodded. She said firmly, 'We 'aven't got relatives. They've all died. And you . . . specially Hope . . . our family. It seemed quite straightforward and we decided on it some years back. But then . . . it's a responsibility. It – it—'

'Subtext,' Peter breathed.

'That's what the slisster man said. He meant that underneath it all was a sort of request – an – expectation – from us – to you to stay together and work the farm. An' you might not want to do that. An' yet you might not feel you can sell it.' She looked grimmer still. 'Jem and Fennie won't feel like that. If they keep it on it will be because they want to.' Suddenly she looked pleading. 'You understand. Don't you?'

Hope said, 'Oh Bella. Peter. I don't think I can bear any of this. Like Jack just said – we don't want anything except you.'

'You're 'appy in that cottage. And you wun't be able to keep it going unless you 'ave more land. But not too much because if Jack goes, you want to be able to work it on your own. Bit of seasonal help p'r'aps. You've proved you can do it. And with a bit more land and your sewing jobs, you can support yourself. Jem will give you a hand, you know that. We've talked about it a lot, the gaffer and me. That's what we want. Now you know. No more talking because it's settled.'

She forced a grin. 'You can stop looking like a pair of cod on a line. And tell us what that daughter of yours wanted.'

There was a little silence then Jack said, ' "If Jack goes". That's what you said, Bella. And you and Peter have talked about it a lot.'

Bella said, 'She brought you down to make you better. Not to 'ang on to you. That's all we know.'

Jack said heavily, 'You know far more than that.'

Bella said briskly, 'P'r'aps. P'r'aps we just think we know. What we do know is that she 'as made you better. An' somehow or other, she's made herself ill. Oh, I know, she's supposed to be suddenly better today. But I don't believe that. Do you?'

Jack said, 'No.'

'Well then. What are we going to do about it?'

Jack bit his lip, suddenly unsure again. 'We're going to Sheffield. To see Fay.'

Peter tried to sit up straight. 'What 'as 'appened? Is she all right?'

'As far as we know. But Mandy Petersen is with her.' Jack looked directly at Peter. 'The Petersens make Hope ill. They seem – always – to be on the edge of her life. I thought the best thing would be to face them.'

'Didn't 'elp much when she faced the chap the other day, did it?' Bella asked dryly.

Jack took a deep breath. 'No. Sorry. I was so sure it was the right thing to do.' He took Hope's hand and held it between both of his. 'Don't worry, Ho. I'll go. Dammit, what am I thinking of? Mandy Petersen is my problem, not yours. I'll go up tomorrow.'

Hope did not know what to say. She stared at Jack helplessly. Was this how it was all to end? Jack going back to Mandy so – so – obediently? She looked across the bed at Peter and was surprised to see him smiling right at her.

'Time to launch the *Mirabelle*,' he murmured.

She thought she knew what he meant. Now was the time to do what Bella had done all those years ago; now was the time to rescue Jack.

She said, 'I'm coming. And we won't go by train. We'll phone Henrik at that hotel in Penzance. He can drive all of us up there in that car he hired.'

For a moment she thought Jack would argue, but then he smiled wryly and said, 'Very practical, Ho. Two birds with one stone.'

She was still looking at Peter as if she expected

something more from him. Did he really see this as being a rescue mission? All she was doing was acquiescing to something . . . that was more like it. Agreeing to a return of the old status quo?

Peter closed his eyes and, momentarily, she followed suit. Somewhere along the way, probably since Henrik's arrival, she had lost her tenuous control of the situation. She no longer knew what she wanted. Whether it was the best for Jack or the best for herself. Or simply to face the two people who were proving to be her own personal nightmare.

Bella said quietly, 'If you go before I see you again, take care of each other.'

Coming from Bella it was like an ancient blessing. They both smiled at her but she was looking as grim as ever.

It was Jack who rang Henrik's hotel and arranged for him to pick them up the next morning. Henrik was all for starting immediately but Jack vetoed that. 'Hope has not been well. Tomorrow will be quite soon enough.'

Hope had already gone into the barn where Jem was herding the cows into their stalls. She needed to share some of their ruminatory quality and as she washed Buttercup's udders and then drew the stool closer and began the age-old rhythm of milking, she felt her neck and shoulder muscles gradually and tremblingly relax. She butted her head into the cow's flank. 'I'll be back,' she whispered. Then she realized what she had said; she was already leaving Jack out. Just for a moment came a return of the panic and fear. She let it wash through her. And then she said aloud, 'I can do this.' And she felt one of Bella's grim smiles curve her mouth. Because the irony was that she had no idea what it was she had to do.

Henrik arrived at ten o'clock the next morning. Hope and Jack had eaten their pasties the evening before and had toyed with tea and toast at breakfast but there had been no point in lighting the range that morning so they were oddly disorientated. Keeping the fire going had become a way of life for both of them.

Henrik knocked tentatively and then called, 'It is me. May I come in?'

Jack opened the door. 'You came in last week,' he reminded him only half humorously. 'Sit down at the table for a few minutes. We are almost ready.'

Hope managed a tight smile of greeting and then went into the scullery to line up the lamps for their return. Jack came behind her with a box of kindling. 'All right?' he asked quietly.

Hope said, 'I think this is how Peter must have felt when he knew he was going to have an operation.'

Jack made a face. 'It's not unlike, is it? And if it can cure any of us, then so be it.'

Hope hated the fatalism of that. She said, 'It did not cure Peter.'

'No.' Jack sounded sombre for a moment, then patted the back of her hand. 'Whatever happens, Ho, please don't forget what a good job you have done here. Making a home and a living. Putting me back on my feet.'

'I've done nothing.' She wanted desperately to cry. 'Absolutely nothing. You've cured yourself.'

He shook his head, frowning at her. 'We won't

argue that one.' He pumped some water into the sink and began to lather his hands. 'Ho . . . you – you know everything now. It was unbearable to me at first – that Mandy had told you . . . everything. That was why I tried to drown myself and the *Mirabelle* that night. But you stuck it out. Put up with me. And . . . I have felt . . . we have become almost friends.' She glanced at him quickly. Someone else had said something like that before. More than friends. She could not remember who.

He said, 'You won't forget that, will you?'

She put matches on the window sill and stared out at the cliff face two yards away. 'No,' she said. 'I won't forget.'

It sounded very much like a farewell.

They clambered to the top of the cliff and the car. They had a holdall each and Jack carried Milly under his spare arm. He was wearing his blanket-coat over one of Peter's old canvas fishing smocks and the puppy snuggled her nose beneath the collar. Hope had bought walking boots from a second-hand shop in Penzance and he wore those with the hat, gloves and scarf the girls had given him.

'You look as if you expect to be on an Arctic expedition,' commented Henrik.

'It will be much colder up there,' he replied.

Hope knew she would feel awful anyway when she met Mandy but she had made no effort to compete. She wore her jeans and a roll-necked jumper as usual and tucked her Christmas scarf inside her duffel coat. Her hair had grown down into her neck through the winter and was threaded with grey; she had scooped it into a rubber band like Fennie did. She tried to see Jack and herself as Mandy would see them; Jack still gaunt but so obviously strong and fit; herself without make-up, the etched lines from nose to mouth no longer due to laughter. Her normally healthy colour had sallowed over the past few days and she knew her skin looked almost jaundiced. She glanced at her hands and saw that her nails were broken and worn down. She never looked at her hands. She made a whimpering sound and Henrik said, 'Sit in the front, Ho. Jack won't mind.'

But it was the last thing Hope wanted. The memories of Henrik helping with Fay and getting her lunch for her as she worked were now completely repellent.

'Jack will sit with you and I can lie down on the back seat.'

'You are still unwell?'

'Yes.'

She did not enlarge on this and neither did Jack. She could tell that Henrik was surprised at the change in both of them but he made no other attempt to organize them. Jack helped her into the car and pulled a folded rug over her knees. 'You'll be all right?' he asked in a low voice. She reverted to a quick nod. 'I'll take Milly up to the house and open the gates for you.'

Hope watched him stride ahead of the car. Henrik switched on and they bumped along after him and through the farm gate.

'Jack is looking well. Better than he has looked for years,' he commented. She said nothing and he went on, 'Why are you here, Ho? Do I gather you are not going to try to . . . change . . . whatever happens?' Again she did not answer. Jack opened the gate from the other side and they went slowly through it. Henrik said, 'Ho, I understand. There is a need to see Mandy again. A need to see Mandy and Jack together, perhaps?' He looked at her in the mirror and sighed at her expressionless face. 'I will just say to you . . . if he comes back with us . . . with Mandy and me . . . I will look after him. You need not think that the last four or five months of nursing have been thrown away.'

She met his gaze with a complete lack of interest. And then the gate was closed behind them and Jack jogged up to the car and got in.

'Jem said to tell you, Peter rallied this morning. He had some porridge and drank some tea.'

At last she spoke. 'Good.' And then she smiled.

The drive was indescribably tedious. Now that they were on their way she wanted them to be there, to be face to face with Mandy, to see Jack face to face with Mandy. By the time they climbed to the heights of Bodmin Moor she felt she had been in the car much too long. It was an enormous relief when Henrik said, 'We'll stop at Okehampton for lunch, shall we?' She did not want lunch but she wanted to put more space between herself and Henrik. They went to the White Hart and had vegetable soup and braised beef and Henrik had a fruit tart afterwards. She pushed her food around her plate as Chatty had done as a small girl and then asked for a glass of water because she could not swallow.

Jack said, 'Try to eat your meat, Ho. You will feel better for it.'

But it was no good. 'I should have had fish,' she said unhappily. 'My stomach is used to fish.'

He said, 'Don't worry. It will soon be over.'

She was still hearing those words when they got to Birmingham and she eventually fell into a fitful sleep. The misty-grey day had dissolved into early darkness by then and the orange lights lining the ring road flicked over her closed eyes with a nightmarish strobe effect. Beneath the car rug she shivered uncontrollably. She heard Jack say, 'All right, Ho?' But she could not move her mouth to reply to him.

Henrik said, 'She's asleep. I can see in the mirror. She has been asleep since we passed Worcester.'

She wanted to deny it. Jack grunted. Henrik said, 'Is she really ill, Jack?'

She did not hear Jack's reply but he must have said something because Henrik said very clearly, 'Do not worry. I will take her back to Cornwall myself.' And she whimpered and then was deeply asleep.

Fay woke her, saying, 'Is she all right? She looks shattered.'

Henrik's clipped voice replied. 'Have you a spare bed, Fay? She needs sleep – proper sleep.'

'Henrik.' Fay's tone was not welcoming and she gave him no more greeting than that. 'Yes.

She is sleeping with me. Martin is with a friend. Mandy has gone to a hotel. Dad, can you get that side . . . Mummy? Darling – we're either side of you. Just swing your legs round . . . that's it.' The fair hair brushed Hope's face and she sneezed. 'Are you all right? You sound very wheezy.'

Hope forced herself out of the blessed state of semi-consciousness and said, 'I'm all right. Your hair tickled my nose.' She managed a laugh. 'How marvellous to see you, Fay. Let me just reach for my bag. But Martin – I can't be held responsible for throwing him out of his own home!'

Jack forestalled her with the bags and dropped a kiss on Fay's nose as he did so. 'It does sound rather drastic,' he agreed. 'Where are you sending me?'

'You're in the flat too. I thought it would be nice to have a quiet evening. Just the three of us.' She glanced at Henrik. 'You will want to see Mandy privately, I expect. She is at the Centurion.' She paused. 'Please don't bring her round until tomorrow. Or stay put and meet at the hotel. Easier perhaps.'

Henrik stood by the car looking abandoned. The Victorian terrace was lit by a dozen windows, the street by replicas of the old gas lamps; it looked welcoming and homely in the drizzle that had now set in.

Fay said firmly, 'Goodnight, Henrik.'

They climbed the stone steps to the front door and went up an elegant flight of stairs to a balcony landing. Fay did not let go of her mother's arm until she fitted a key into the door.

She turned and gave her a grin. 'Martin put a couple of plants and a deckchair out here the other day and told Mandy she could use it as a sitting area!'

Hope looked around. The enormous effort of waking up and behaving normally was paying dividends. She actually felt better. She smiled. 'How sensible. Martin is definitely our kind of son-in-law!' They both laughed.

Inside, the flat consisted of an enormous room overlooking total blackness which Fay said was a walled garden, and a row of doors on one side which led to a kitchen and a bathroom and two bedrooms.

'It's easy to keep going.' Fay flung open doors, obviously proud of her first home. 'And because this room is so big, it doesn't matter that the rest of the place is tiny! No windows in the kitchen or the bathroom and the extractor things hardly ever work, but if it's boiling hot in the summer we shall cut sandwiches and sit in the garden. What do you think?'

Hope felt better by the minute. 'It's lovely. And look at those cushions – and the miniatures! I'd forgotten Granny gave you those. You've made a proper home here, Fay.'

Jack dumped the bags inside the door and closed it thankfully. 'Just to be out of that car!' he said. 'But yes. This is very nice. How is Martin?'

'Fed up,' Fay said frankly. 'He didn't think much of Mandy arriving here without so much as a phone call! Apparently she went to the college office and made quite a fuss about being my long-lost aunt – you know, typically Mandy.

He didn't think it was funny.' She looked at her father apologetically. 'He's biased. We went to see Mum that first January, just after the awful storms. He doesn't really understand how Henrik and Mandy sort of grew into our lives.'

Jack sighed. 'I don't think any of us understand, Fay. That's why we're here.'

Fay made a face then said quickly, 'Look. Sit down by the fire. It's an original gas fire – isn't it lovely the way it pops? I've got a sort of vegetable casserole in the oven and I'll bring it in on trays and you can tell me about *Sweet Pea* and Milly and Jem and Fennie and Nathan and Peter and Bella . . .' She was moving into the kitchen, laughing as she went.

Jack said quietly, 'In other words, she doesn't want to talk about us and the Petersens. Who can blame her?'

'I don't want to, either.' Hope leaned towards the fire. 'She's offering us a breather, don't you think? And it's so cosy here. It reminds me of those pictures of Sherlock Holmes's rooms in Baker Street.'

'The journey was awful. Were you really asleep?'

'After Birmingham. Yes.'

'Henrik told me about Cape Town and how marvellous it was. They've got a house with a swimming pool.'

'And an eight-foot-high security fence?'

He laughed and shook his head. 'It wasn't mentioned.' He eased himself into the cushions. 'I have to say something, Ho. In case there's not another chance.' He smiled in the direction of the kitchen. 'She's wonderful, isn't she? And

426

so is Chatty. We must have done something right.'

She swallowed. 'Yes.'

'And you. Ho, you have been a good friend to me. I know you hated me. Perhaps you still do. But you launched your own special *Mirabelle* and came for me. And since then . . . no one could have had a better friend.'

She stared at him. 'Launched my *Mirabelle*?' Her voice sounded thick and stupid. 'That's what Peter said.'

'That's how I see it too, Ho. And I wanted to say . . . thank you.'

'Oh. You mean . . . when I came to the Gloucester hospital.' She shook her head. That seemed such a simple rescue compared with the complication of this one.

The kitchen door opened and Fay came into the living room wheeling a trolley. 'Martin made it,' she said proudly. 'It's a bit wonky this side and I have to watch it doesn't get caught in the rug. But three tiers, no less! So here's a tray each and some cutlery. Serving spoons.' She removed the lid from a casserole with a flourish. 'And here are braised onions, carrots, swede, parsnip – I've thrown in some beans too. And the stock is my own!'

Jack said, 'Fay! It smells wonderful. And what's this – garlic bread? We haven't had any garlic bread for ages! We're hungry.' He looked across the hearth. 'Aren't we, Ho?'

She was. She would have to think about everything else tomorrow. Tonight Fay had made them supper and was going to look after them. She said, 'This is heaven, darling.'

'And . . .' Fay looked at them both with big eyes. 'There is enough hot water for you both to have a bath. Each. And when I say hot I mean hot!'

They laughed. Rather loudly and rather too long.

Twenty

Hope slept with Fay that night. It was odd and inhibiting to know that she was sleeping where Martin usually was. It was 1989 and the whole of society had changed in the 'sixties; Hope was a child of the 'sixties, but it made no difference. She lay on her back, stiff and unyielding, until she knew that Fay was asleep. Only then did she curl over and away from the spread of golden hair on the next pillow. For some stupid reason – as much for her own reaction as anything else – she then wept.

The next morning, she woke at six o'clock to the wholly unfamiliar sound of a milk float whining along the street. The room was dimly lit from outside and she could see that Fay had apparently not moved an inch during the night and still did not, even when Hope slid sideways out of the bed. She pulled her big fisherman's sweater over her nightdress and crept to the door. The living room smelled of last night's casserole and she thought that they really did need an extractor fan that worked. She went into the kitchen and switched on the light. She filled the kettle and plugged it in and found matches so that she could light the gas fire. It was bitterly cold, a different kind of cold from the iciness of the headland; harder, totally unyielding. She hovered over the fire, rubbing her arms through the oiled wool. When the kettle clicked itself off she found tea and a teapot and assembled breakfast things on Martin's 'wonky' trolley. Then she poured three cups of tea and took one in to Jack.

She did not immediately realize he was not in the single room. After the light of the living room, she couldn't see anything for a while and whispered, 'Jack? Here's a cup of tea. Shall I put it on the floor?' When there was no reply she felt blindly along the bed and then back to the door to switch on the light. And then she just stared at the empty bed for a long time, clutching the teacup in front of her while her mind jumped crazily around possibilities.

She must have made some noise because Fay's voice came blearily from next door. 'Is everything all right? Mum?'

Hope forced herself to turn round and go back to the other bedroom.

'I've made tea. Dad must have gone for a walk. Can you manage two cups?'

Fay saw nothing odd in that. 'Oh yes. Easily.' She got out of bed, pushing her hair back. 'Let's go by the fire. It gets cold in here in the mornings.'

Hope said, 'High ceilings, I expect.'

'Yes.' Fay dragged on a dressing gown. 'Oh, you are a darling. Breakfast and everything. Shall we do toast by the fire like you do at Widdershins? I just love sitting by the range doing toast. Not quite as good by the gas but almost. Haven't used the toaster here since Christmas! Martin thinks I'm mad.' She smiled. 'But he bought me a toasting fork all the same!'

It was exactly the kind of thing Jack would have done all those years ago in Sandhurst. Hope smiled and watched as Fay squatted on the hearth rug and fitted a piece of sliced bread to the end of the long toasting fork. And suddenly it was as if lots of small things came together and made a pattern. Henrik's visit nearly a week ago, Jack's insistence that they should meet Mandy face to face. And now his sudden disappearance, natural though it might be.

She said quietly, 'I don't want Dad to leave me.'

Fay's head came round quickly, her blue eyes alert. 'Oh . . . Mum!'

'I know. I never thought I would say that. Especially after . . . well, I never thought I'd say it.'

Fay moved the toasting fork. 'He won't,' she said. 'If you ask him to stay, you know very well he will.'

'Ah. There's the rub.' Hope tried to smile. 'I can't ask him to do that. There was a sort of unspoken agreement. I would take him to Widdershins, make sure he had peace and quiet. Until he was well enough to decide what he wanted to do.' She sighed. 'I shouldn't have come here, Fay. My presence is definitely not required.' She frowned. 'I can't think why I came.'

Fay turned the bread and said decisively, 'Because you wanted to. You might not be able to ask Dad to stay in so many words, but you certainly weren't going to let him just . . . disappear.'

Hope forced herself to sip her tea. She felt as if she was on the edge of a cliff. 'It was seeing that empty bed. I think I knew then. Oh Fay, what a mess. I've been such a fool.'

Fay did not deny it. 'Mum, we're all fools at one time or another. Luckily most of us don't have someone like Mandy anywhere nearby.' She put the toast on a plate. 'Butter that and eat it. You look as if you've seen a ghost. You'll be all right, Mum. Everything will be all right.' She reached for another slice of bread. 'Actually, I'm glad to have you to myself for a moment. I want to say how wonderful it is to have Dad back. Properly back. How did you do it?'

'Widdershins did it, not me. Though when I went to pieces he seemed to pick up where I left off.'

Fay could not get over it. 'Three weeks ago he was still practically monosyllabic. Now he's completely normal!'

Hope smiled. 'Neither of us is that, Fay. But I know what you mean. Actually, for a long time now Dad has been getting better. It's not such an overnight recovery.'

'No . . . OK.' Fay nibbled her lip. 'Probably Mandy has been going downhill just as gradually. I have to tell you . . . Mandy isn't quite . . . as she was. Which is probably just as well because the Mandy we knew would have simply come to Widdershins and wrecked everything.'

'Yes. I thought she would. What's happened?'

'I'm not quite sure. She is sort of . . . rudderless. Her drive has gone. She's sold the house at Sandhurst and is trying to sell the shop, so she's got money. In any case Henrik probably has funds tucked away somewhere over here. But she is acting as if she is penniless. She said she couldn't afford to stay at the Centurion. When she arrived here she practically begged us to take her in. Martin didn't want to. But after the first shock, I began to feel almost sorry for her.'

Hope sighed. 'She does that. Makes you feel you are the only person who can make her happy.'

'This is taking things one step further. You always knew that Mandy could cope. D'you remember when she came and took over at school on Chatty's first day? She simply swept everything before her.' Fay added another piece of toast to the plate. 'That's gone. She thought she was setting herself free when she left Henrik. But she can't manage without a man.' She sat up on the chair and buttered the toast. 'Surely she cannot think it will be Dad? On the strength of one silly indiscretion – all right, more than an indiscretion – a great big mistake?'

Hope opened her mouth to say that the big mistake had lasted twelve years. Then she closed it. It had taken her a long time to accept that Jack had been unfaithful for so long and it would be cruel to inflict such a confidence on Fay. But now she saw how simple it must seem to Fay; more than an indiscretion, certainly, but only one mistake.

She said, 'Dad and I don't exactly . . . talk. Since he began to speak again, we haven't had a chance. So I just don't know how he feels. OK, he looked after me at the weekend but of course I have looked after him so I daresay he felt . . . well, he had to really.' She too sighed. 'I meant to remain absolutely objective. You know, the perfect nurse.'

Fay managed a grin. 'Bit difficult when you've lived with the patient for so long,' she commented. 'Listen. Eat that piece of toast I so lovingly prepared and I'll get ready for work.'

'Work? You haven't dropped your course?'

'No.' Fay smiled reassuringly. 'I'm doing every Wednesday at the library. Cataloguing and so on. They pay me and it's good experience.'

Hope felt bereft. 'I thought you would be here.'

'I had yesterday off. To get Mandy and Martin settled and then to clean up.' Fay took her mother's hand. 'I mustn't be around when you have your meeting. You know that very well. This is something the four of you have to thrash out between yourselves.'

Hope gripped the slim fingers. 'You seem so confident. So . . . unworried.'

'That's because I know how it's going to work out.'

'No. You don't. You think you know us. But we don't even know ourselves.' She released Fay and looked around the room. 'What if Dad doesn't come back?'

Fay said starkly, 'Then that is his solution. He has run away again.' She straightened her back. 'But he won't do that. Not a second time.' She looked down at her mother. 'Darling, you are not . . . positive. When Martin and I visited

434

you a year ago – and at Christmas – you seemed to know what you were doing. What has happened?'

Hope said miserably, 'Henrik came. And . . . I suppose . . . it brought it all back again. The – the mistake. I simply felt that if your father left with Henrik, I couldn't bear it.'

'You would bear it. It would be hard again. Going back to Widdershins and starting all over again. But you would bear it.' Fay crouched in front of her mother. 'Listen. D'you remember how you used to joke – against yourself – about being hopeless? Hope-less?'

'Of course. And that is exactly how I feel.'

'You meant that you felt useless. Didn't you? We all feel pretty useless at times. But not hopeless.' She cupped her mother's face. 'Dad thought he was Hope-less. And he tried to finish everything.'

Hope clasped her hands tightly. 'But . . . he's not *here*!'

And as if on cue, there was a tap at the door. Fay scooped her dressing gown around her as she stood up and opened it; and there was Jack looking sheepish.

'I didn't have a key. Someone from the ground floor let me in. Not very happily.'

Fay stood aside. 'That's because of Mandy,' she said. 'She always forgot her key and got them to answer the door. They're fed up with it.'

Hope was so glad to see him she could have wept. 'Did you – did you have a nice walk?' she asked.

'Yes. It was very dark – no stars – but I think I

got a feeling of the place. The sky seems to be light over there. The railway station?'

Fay was making for the bathroom. 'Smelting works,' she said briefly. 'You know, Sheffield steel and all that.' She grinned. 'Help yourself to toast and tea, Dad. There are some eggs in the kitchen if you need any protein.'

Jack smiled at Hope as he sat down. 'This is nice. Not what we're used to, but nice. How did you sleep? How are you feeling?'

'Better.'

'You look better.' He munched on some toast. 'This won't take long, Hope. And then we'll be free.'

There was a long pause while she waited for him to say more and when he did not she asked tentatively, 'What do you mean? Free?' She tried to sip her tea. 'Free of the Petersens?'

'More than that. Free . . . free of the past, I suppose. Free of guilt and anger and bitterness.'

It still was not enough but she dared ask no more. Fay was so right, she was totally negative.

After Fay had gone, they went down to the hall and, at Jack's insistence, Hope dialled the number of the hotel. 'You are the one who makes telephone calls,' he urged her.

Henrik's voice eventually came across the wires.

'Mandy is still in bed.' He sounded unutterably weary. 'We have talked a great deal and she is tired. But please come round when you are ready. Perhaps we can have lunch together.'

'Lunch?' It sounded civilized and Mandy was rarely civilized.

'Why not? We have to pretend all this is normal, surely?'

'All right. Yes.' She replaced the receiver carefully and looked at Jack. 'Lunch. At the Centurion.'

'Fine,' he replied heartily. 'We'll go and look at St Peter and St Paul's and the Sheaf and the Don.'

She was startled. 'You sound like a tour guide!'

'I've done a lot of walking this morning.' He grinned. 'Now I'd like to see just where I walked!'

They tramped around the city for over two hours, almost forgetting the reason for their visit and enjoying discovering Fay's new home. The university itself was early Edwardian but the Cutlers' Hall was ancient, as were many of the public buildings.

When they stopped at a riverside café for a much-needed coffee, Hope said, 'We never did this sort of thing, did we? When I took Chatty to Paris there were so many tourists looking around. I thought then that perhaps we'd missed something important.'

'Discovering things together?' Jack looked wretched. 'I seemed to do a lot of travelling. It was always with Henrik. We went to one set of offices or another. Never got to know places. But I thought I'd done them anyway. Sorry, Ho.'

She shook her head. 'I didn't miss travelling. I don't think I wanted to go anywhere until you gave me Widdershins. And then that is where I wanted to go.'

'I never felt Cornwall like you did. I was always very conscious of sparing time to be with you all.

I could see you and Milly and the girls almost growing into the rocks but I didn't understand why.' He made a sound of disgust. 'What a fool I was.'

She said sadly, 'We were both fools. We let other people tell us what to do and when to do it.'

He did not ask about the other people. They were silent for a long time, then he glanced at his watch. 'We'd better go to the hotel.' He did not move. 'Ho . . . I rang Bella from a public phone box. Early this morning. Peter is not well.'

'Oh . . .' She had been pulling on her gloves; she stopped and put her hands on the table.

'When we were driving up yesterday I asked Henrik if he would take you back whenever you wanted to go. Could you bear it tonight?'

She said quickly, 'Not with Henrik . . .' Then she looked at him. 'Not alone.' It was obvious he was not including himself in these plans.

He said, 'No. Not with Henrik on your own. Stupid of me. On the train then – OK? I know you would like to spend time with Fay. But Easter is really early this year so you'll see her soon. What do you say?' She nodded once and he smiled. 'Actually I told Bella you would be home this evening. She was . . . really glad.'

'Yes.' She did not know what else to say. She was going home alone. And he seemed to think she would be pleased.

'Quite. Hard to imagine Bella being glad. But she was.' His smile deepened. 'She is a marvellous woman, isn't she?'

'Yes.'

He went to the counter and paid the bill and she wandered outside to wait for him. She could not quite believe in what was happening. Everything began to take on a dreamlike quality. The weather which had continued grey and drizzly seemed to be brightening and she was actually sorry because somehow the dreariness had matched and hidden her mood of complete desolation.

In the old days they would have taken a taxi to the outlying hotel. Now they walked there without a thought, Jack still slightly leaning, Hope deliberately upright, neither of them touching the other. When they reached the canopied entrance it did not occur to them they were out of place until Henrik rushed down the steps to greet them. 'Friends,' he explained to the narrow-eyed porter. 'Great walkers.'

Hope looked down at her jeans and then at Jack's blanket-coat and started to laugh. Then found it difficult to stop. Henrik took her arm and she pulled away sharply so that she would have stumbled back down the steps if Jack had not held her.

Henrik said, 'Sorry, Ho. Sorry. Take it easily. Please.'

Jack said, 'She is fine. We are both fine. Lead the way.'

Henrik hesitated then walked across the plush foyer and through mirrored doors into an enormous restaurant. It was almost full but Hope's eyes went immediately to the table in the window where Mandy's ash-blond head seemed to shine like a beacon. She glanced sideways at Jack and saw him staring too and pulled away from him just as she had from Henrik. He glanced at her, startled. She said, 'I'm all right. I can walk on my own.' And she went ahead of the two men, her damp curls sprouting from her head defiantly because now she knew what was happening she also knew she must learn again to stand alone, and she must learn it quickly so that no one knew anything of her weakness.

Mandy half rose. Hope tried to see what Fay had seen; someone who was without direction. It was not immediately apparent to her. Mandy's face was as smooth as enamel, her lips glossy, her teeth still even and very white as she smiled.

'Oh. Hope,' she said. Then she looked past Hope and said, 'Jack. Thank God you came. I did not know whether you would.'

He pulled out a chair for Hope and made no attempt to take Mandy's outstretched hand. 'Why wouldn't I?' His voice was hard.

She laughed and sat down again. Henrik sat next to her. 'I wasn't sure whether Hope would let you.' She spoke teasingly but Hope flushed.

Jack settled himself. 'Hope did not want to come with me. I insisted.'

Mandy spread her hands. 'Why? She is so happy down at Widdershins. You are happy, aren't you, Ho?'

'Yes.' Hope could not manage more. She swallowed experimentally. She was not feeling sick but she did not want to eat. However, Henrik had other ideas. 'Listen. We will order. And then we will say what we have to say.'

But Jack shook his head decisively. 'The other way round please, Henrik. We are very wary now. Let us have everything in the open, then

440

– perhaps – we can eat together.' He looked around. 'I have been trying to work out how I would apologize to all of you for what has happened. This morning – while it was still dark – I went for a walk.' A tiny, wry smile lifted his face for an instant. 'No inspiration came. I did untold damage to all four of us. I regretted it so bitterly I was . . . ill. As you know.'

He looked down at his hands and Mandy said quickly, 'There is no blame, Jack. We fell in love. How could we help it?'

He actually smiled at her. 'That is not true, Mandy. Not for me. Perhaps you could not help it but I could. I was in love with Hope. Yet I told myself this would not hurt her. It was separate. I told myself the sort of things men do tell themselves to justify infidelity.' For a second the old, lost look spread across his face. 'I cannot understand what I did or why I did it. So it is very difficult for me to forgive it.'

Mandy said, 'There is nothing to forgive. You are forgetting how wonderful it was—'

Hope leaned forward and said clearly, 'I forgive you. And I hope you forgive me for letting our marriage become sterile and meaningless.'

He turned to her eagerly. 'Do you mean that, Ho?'

'Yes. I can see now that I somehow lost interest—'

'No. Do you mean that you can forgive me?'

She turned in her chair to look at him. 'Yes.'

Mandy said in a high, joking voice, 'Hello! We're still here. This is Henrik and I am Mandy. We have been having an affair for the past twelve years, Jack. Had you forgotten?'

Ho flinched and looked back at the table. Jack said, 'I wish I could. But do not pretend it was more than it was, Mandy. Please. Nobody's relationship is perfect, but you and Henrik have always been necessary to one another. Anything outside that was . . . outside.' He turned again to Hope. 'You see, I thought it could be like that for us. That's how . . . influenced . . . I was by Henrik and Mandy. If they could do it and stay together, so could we. I'm sorry, Ho. It was stupid and wrong and – and – naive. The time at Widdershins has shown me just how completely unrealistic I was. That was why . . . last October. You remember. The *Mirabelle*.'

'I remember.' But she could not look up.

Mandy said loudly, 'Never mind the boat and the cottage and the pastoral bit. We know you feel a sense of duty to Ho, but you have to come back with us, Jack. Henrik and me. We can look after you properly. Decent food and decent weather. A decent *life*!'

Jack said, 'Don't be silly, Mandy. I have come here to beg your pardon and to say goodbye. No more.'

Henrik said in a low voice, 'Leave it, Mandy. Please. We have already gone into what has happened—'

Mandy rounded on him angrily. 'If you're going to start all that again . . . I have done – *those things* – as you called them, for you! You needed various people to be softened up! To listen to your plans! To advance money! To invest in your projects! So I slept with them! And that was why I slept with Jack at first! Because of his father-in-law's money!'

'I did not ask you to do that, Mandy.' Henrik spoke quietly and levelly.

'But you never objected, did you? So naturally I thought—'

'I had no right to object. I could not give you the sexual love you so obviously needed.' He sighed. 'I am sorry, Hope. Jack. You do not wish to listen to this.'

Mandy lifted her voice. 'Listen to *me*, dammit! I told Chatty ages ago that you were like a pimp to me! And pimps expect certain things from their girls!' She stopped, shocked by her own words. Then she said quietly, 'You lusted after Hope and the girls. Family. When you fetched and carried for them . . . that was your way of sleeping with them!' She looked at Jack, white-faced, pleading. 'Take no notice of all this, darling. You have got to come back with us – that is all there is to it.'

Jack glanced at Hope, then said firmly, 'I have sent plans off to a charity which sponsors projects in Africa. Plans of windmills that will pump water from deep below the surface and into the desert. I want to do something. I want to go over there and set up a scheme for them. I think I can do it now.' He looked at Hope. 'I was going to tell you about it. And then you were so ill and I wasn't sure . . .' She was looking at him as if she had not seen him before. He said urgently, 'Ho? Are you all right?'

Mandy said flatly, 'You can't go. Henrik will find work for you. Paid work. Charity work . . . it's not for you, Jack. You've always wanted money—'

He turned to her fiercely. 'I wanted money for

Hope. I always wanted to give Hope . . . the world.'

Hope said slowly, 'You have. You've done that. You have given me the world.'

He smiled right at her. It was the smile he had given her when he had carried her into Widdershins for the first time.

He nodded. 'I know. It has taken me all the autumn and the winter to see that Widdershins is your world.'

She had meant much more than that, but she said nothing because she was smiling back at him.

Mandy started to speak but Henrik overrode her. 'That's it, my dear. You tried to teach Jack how to live for the moment, and instead you fell in love with him.' He sighed. 'It wouldn't have worked, Mandy. You couldn't have been faithful to him. Let it go. Let it all go.'

For a moment Mandy was silent and then suddenly, shockingly, she began to wail. Like a child deprived of a toy, she lifted her head and keened her grief to the world. The other people in the restaurant were transfixed; there was no ignoring Mandy's grief. A waiter came hurrying.

'Is something wrong, sir?' he asked Henrik.

'Yes. Rather a lot.' Henrik looked weary. 'You will have to excuse us. We will not be lunching after all.' He looked at Hope. 'It's rather a lot to ask but will you and Jack help me to get Mandy upstairs?'

The three of them stood up and tried to encircle Mandy's chair. Suddenly she became a virago. 'Get off me!' She struck at Jack with claw-like hands. 'Judas! Judas Iscariot! You promised – you said we would live together for ever!' She grabbed Hope's sweater. 'Come with us, Ho! He's no good to you – come with us and it will be like the old days at Sandhurst! We'll laugh and be silly and go shopping – come with us, Ho! It's you really. It was always you. Fay has turned against me – she said I was sad and pathetic! That's what she said, Ho! Sad! You know how they say that word these days! Sad . . .' She collapsed, folding like a concertina into her chair, hands over her eyes.

Henrik said, 'Come on then, my dear. Let's have sandwiches sent up to your room, shall we? And then you can have a little sleep.'

She continued to weep profusely but she allowed herself to be hoisted out of the chair and guided across the restaurant. People were now busily ignoring them, talking intimately, exclusively. Mandy knew what was happening and her tears quietened to a whimper. 'Don't go, Hope. Please don't go.'

'I'm here, Mandy. I'm not going.'

In the lift they supported her as best they could. She said no more, hiccoughing helplessly on her sobs, but once inside her room she seemed to recover a little and sat on the bed, dabbing her face with a handful of tissues from the box on the dressing table. 'Is my mascara all over the place?' she asked Henrik.

'It does not matter, my dear.' He took the tissue and wiped her cheeks with great tenderness. 'You are ill. It is better this way. I will look after you as Hope looked after Jack. Do you not see how good that will be?'

'I am not really ill, am I, Henrik?' She stared at him with blurred focus.

'Oh yes, you are, Mandy.' He smiled. 'That is what you will be now. Ill. And there will be no more talk of pimps. Nothing like that.' His voice was soothing. 'You will look on me as your doctor perhaps. You will listen when I tell you what to do. Doctor's orders, yes?' He smiled down at her. Her mouth worked uncontrollably and then she too managed a travesty of a smile.

'Oh, Henrik,' she murmured. 'Thank you.'

Hope felt herself become rigid with distaste. Jack said quickly, 'Henrik. Is everything going to be all right?'

Henrik kept his eyes on Mandy. 'Yes. It is, isn't it, my dear?' Mandy smiled again and Henrik said, 'I will telephone to the farm in a day or so. Let you know how we are. Will that suffice?'

'Yes. I suppose so.' Jack glanced at Mandy uneasily. 'If she is having a breakdown, perhaps we should call a doctor?'

Mandy shifted her gaze to Jack. 'No! I am like you, Jack. I don't want a doctor. You had Hope and I have Henrik.'

Henrik moved to the door and opened it. He looked at Hope. 'It worked for you, Ho. It might work for me.'

She went quickly into the corridor and almost ran down to the lift. Jack caught her up as she pressed the button.

He said, 'Ho! It wasn't like that. Henrik is acting like some kind of Svengali figure! You were never like that!'

She said, 'I took you away from the hospital – practically kidnapped you—'

'Because you knew that if you didn't, I would probably be weak enough to let Mandy take me over! And that would have been wrong because you gave me freedom and she wanted to give me some awful form of slavery!'

The lift arrived and there were two people inside. Hope immediately turned and made for the stairs, closely followed by Jack.

He said breathlessly to the back of her head, 'Listen. I know how you felt in there. As if the whole thing was going on and on for ever and you couldn't stop it! But we stopped it ages ago. And I wanted – so much – for today to be the final break. I wanted you to see how silly and hopeless they both were. What Fay said – sad and pathetic – I wanted you to see that!'

She stopped on a half-landing and looked at him. 'Hopeless?'

'Yes. I meant hopeless. But in fact they are only hopeless when they are Hope-less.' He laughed. 'Come on, Ho, laugh! Right now! It's so farcical and stupid. We are us! I love you. More than ever. I admire you. More than ever. And I want you to know that so that when I come back to Widdershins in six months or eight months or a year or whatever, you can give me an answer.'

'An answer? What is the question?' She was still utterly bewildered but at least the horror in that hotel bedroom was receding. She did not feel sick.

'The question is . . . or rather will be . . .' His voice slowed right down. 'Do you love me too?'

She stared at him, clutching the banister as if she was afraid of falling down the stairs.

'I don't want you to go. I know that much.'

He smiled. 'That is why I am not going to ask the question yet. We'll go back to Cornwall on the train. Together. To be with Peter. But then . . . Ho, let me see what I can do with my poor redundant windmills! I read an article in one of the old newspapers at the farm. It was written about a man who had invented a pump which could be sunk to enormous depths. But the power needed to drive it was simply beyond the means of the Third World. So last time we were in Penzance I managed to get his number and I spoke to him from a phone box. He wants to see me. I've got together my old plans for power windmills and I think it can be done.'

She gazed at him. 'Jack. You're better. Really better. Stronger than you've ever been.'

'Yes. And it's your doing.' He gripped her hands. 'Ho, this is my way of launching the *Mirabelle*. Does that sound crazy? I wanted you to see that I was entirely unaffected by the Petersens. And if I am free of them, then that will make it easier for you to be free of them.'

She sobbed a little laugh. 'I thought I was the rescuer.'

'You were. Now it's my turn.' He shook her hands gently. 'You have already stood alone. Let me do the same, Ho. I'll be back. Nothing will keep me away. But I'll have done something. By myself. And what I have done will be for you.' He gave a shaky, upside-down smile. 'I can't think of any other way of doing it, Ho. Making a fresh start – a really fresh start.'

For what seemed a long time, she stood there on the stairs, holding his hands, looking at him. Then she sighed and said, 'I'm glad we're going back together tonight. On the train.'

'And on our own.'

'Yes. On our own. It's a long journey. It will be good to have a friend.'

Twenty-one

Fay was bewildered and anxious but also delighted.

'Of course you must go back immediately. If Bella has asked you . . . Oh dear, more sadness. It's so hard to imagine the headland without Peter there guarding it.' She looked expectantly from one to the other. 'But . . . you're still together. Does that mean . . . anything?'

Jack glanced at Hope who nodded. He said carefully, 'I want to give us some time. Your mother was happy on her own at Widdershins. She – she proved herself in a way I've wanted to – right from the start – and never quite made it.' He shook his head. 'Wrong goals or something. So I'm going to try to do something too.' He turned his mouth down diffidently. 'It might come to nothing. But my windmills were good, Fay. They really were. They provided power for – for anything! They could work pumps instead of dynamos.'

Fay nodded. 'I know that, Dad. You have a feeling for air movement. Like a bird using the currents. Look at our kites.'

His mouth turned up. 'Thanks.'

She too grinned. 'You're welcome. So you're going back into business? But not with Henrik?'

He shook his head violently to both questions. 'Couldn't if I wanted to. I've got to sell my ideas now. And I wondered . . . about the AfrAid people.'

Fay's eyes shone. 'Oh Dad.' She looked at Hope. 'Wouldn't that be marvellous, Mummy?'

'Dad's contacted someone.' Hope was fired by Fay's enthusiasm. 'It would be marvellous.' She was realizing as she spoke just how marvellous it would be. And caution reared its head. 'But it's all a bit nebulous. Don't be disappointed if nothing comes of it.' She had turned to Jack but Fay replied with some passion.

'If that door closes, Dad must go round trying others. He's got to keep on and on. The Red Cross and Oxfam and – and . . .'

Jack said dryly, 'I gather you approve.'

Fay hugged him. 'Oh, I do! For both of you. It's such a good thing to do anyway, but—' she leaned back and looked from one to the other, '—won't it help to – to – sort of put Henrik and Mandy into perspective? You know, as regards the – the – bitterness.' She rubbed her hands together. 'The general awfulness, the – the . . .'

'We know what you mean, darling.' Hope picked up her bag and fastened the top. 'Though I think a great deal of that went this morning.' She sighed. 'We have thought of ourselves as victims, and Mandy and Henrik as predators. But in their way they were as much victims. Of us.' She looked soberly at Fay. 'I left the Centurion feeling very sorry for Mandy. You were right, Fay. She has changed.'

'She's got Henrik,' Fay said rallyingly. 'He'll look after her.'

'He will. He certainly will.'

'Remember how he looked after me. And Chatty. That's his . . . thing.'

It made the scene in the hotel room a little more acceptable. Hope sighed again. It seemed that a great deal had happened during their twenty-hour visit to Sheffield and she hardly knew what to make of it all. Was she really going to 'forgive' Jack? Or was it simply that the sense of betrayal was lessening with time? And how much was due to Mandy's breakdown? Deliberately she let her mind go back to the cottage bedroom in Sandhurst. A different Mandy certainly . . . and a different Jack? She closed her eyes momentarily but she did not feel sick.

Jack said, 'There's a train at five-fifteen. We should leave now if we want to catch it.'

Fay darted around, finding biscuits and cheese and thrusting them into her mother's bag willy-nilly. 'You'll get a drink on the train. I'll ring for a taxi. Would you like me to phone Bella and tell her you're on your way? It'll be midnight before you get there. Oh, I do hope it won't be raining.'

Hope said, 'We haven't really talked, Fay. Are you going to try to see Henrik before they go back?'

Fay paused and thought. 'I'll leave it to Martin. He's so level-headed about all of this. But . . . yes, I would like to. And I hope they will call on Chatty too.' She paused again. 'Would you mind?'

Jack and Hope spoke together. 'No!' Then

Jack said, surprised, 'We've come such a long way. Do you feel that, Ho?'

'I don't know what I feel.' She followed Fay on to the landing and watched her run down to the telephone. 'I'm happy about Fay and Martin. I know that much. But the rest . . . it sounds fine, Jack. But I'm not sure. The mess is still there and there might never be a way of mopping it up.'

He put a hand on the banister and took a deep breath, then said slowly, 'That's why I must go. It doesn't matter where, but I must let you be alone. So that when I come back you will be sure.'

'And you will come back?'

'Yes. I'll come back.'

Peter died as he had lived, with great tranquillity. He was semi-conscious for two days, not seeming to recognize anyone though clinging to Bella when he roused and unable to relax again unless she was cradling him. On Sunday morning the nurse asked Jem and Jack to turn him so that she could rub his back, and as they lifted him gently, so he reared into a sitting position, gave a great gasp and collapsed into Bella's waiting arms. Bella held him to her and said very calmly, 'Has he gone?'

The nurse leaned forward and put her fingers to his neck. 'There is still a pulse. Talk to him, Mrs Penhailes. He will hear you.'

Bella bent her head until her mouth was close to Peter's ear; she began to speak, slowly and clearly. 'I'm only a step behind you, my 'an'some. Just a step. So we won't lose sight of each other.' She paused and smoothed the wispy grey hair. Then she took a breath. 'Thank you, Peter Penhailes. Thank you for giving me happiness in your company. For taking your happiness from me in exchange. For all the seconds and minutes and hours and years we have shared. For piling all the little things up . . . up and up, Gaffer, till they made a fortress.' She glanced at the nurse again and then put her mouth against Peter's ear and whispered something. And then she put both arms around him and held him tightly to her. And Jack took Hope's hand and followed Jem into the hall.

They stood very still, the three of them, listening to Fennie playing with Nathan outside in the sunshine. 'I'll catch you!' she called. 'I'm right behind you – I'll catch you!' The toddler shrieked and gurgled his joy and Hope reached for Jem's hand so that the three of them were linked. Jem cleared his throat and said deliberately, 'It's all we can ever hope for, isn't it? To be just one step behind.'

Hope forced herself not to cry. She said, 'It's enough. That is enough. One step.' She glanced at Jack and then Jem. 'It's enough. Isn't it?'

Jack did not reply but Jem said, 'It has to be. We have to make it enough.'

Hope stayed with Bella until after the funeral. There were flurries of frantic activity sandwiched between long periods when they looked for things to do. Jem and Fennie between them took over the outside work, and Jack joined them when he had done the chores at Widdershins. They were a tight group, set apart from the rest of the world by the terrible sense of loss, but forced into normality by Fennie and Nathan. Fennie had the truly innocent eye of someone brought up close to nature and her constant, natural references to Peter made him seem indeed only a step away. 'Your uncle Peter won't like you playing up like that,' she would say to Nathan when he pushed his food away. 'Come on, remember what he says, one spoonful for you and one for him.' Bella would smile her grim smile and take the spoon from Fennie. Nathan always ate for her.

The funeral in St Buryan church was simple and very traditional. They sang 'Eternal Father', the maritime hymn for sailors, and then at Bella's request, 'We plough the fields and scatter'. She said to the rector, 'Sea and land. He harvested both.'

The service was well attended. Small black-edged notices in shop windows reminded everyone when it would be. Jem must have posted a few in Truro as well as Penzance because Hope recognized John and Matthew Hampton from Truro. Matthew had regularly bought vegetables from Penhailes ever since that first time she had sold him two crates of cabbages. And as they shuffled into their pew, Fennie whispered, 'Dear Lord. My 'usband is here! Can you believe it!'

Jem and Jack walked either side of Bella. Later, when they picked Nathan up from Billy Perkins and Bella settled him on her hip, she said with her usual grudging good humour, 'For someone who din't have no children, I've done proud today, I reckon.' And Jack said, 'I reckon you've always done proud, Bella.'

There were sandwiches, pasties and some of Bella's Cornish heavy cake back at Penhailes. The watery February sunshine picked out every raindrop hanging from every leaf and created the kind of clear, pearly light beloved of artists. Jem finished the milking and wandered off to the knoll above the cove to look out at the glittering sea. Fennie's husband said that if she behaved herself he would take her back – but not the baby. She smiled peaceably. 'That's good of you. But actually I have got a better offer.' And she followed Jem.

After everyone had made their farewells and told Bella she would manage all right, never fear, there was a moment when they simply did not know what to do next. Hope and Fennie between them had cleared the crockery and washed up as they went along and everywhere was unnaturally tidy. Peter's bed had been put back upstairs and the dining room was as it had always been. Bella stood in front of the kitchen range, her busy hands hanging limply at her side; Jack returned from upstairs where he had been replacing all the bedroom chairs brought down for the occasion. Hope closed the front door and came through the hall, hesitating by the phone for an instant and then continuing into the kitchen.

They stared at each other. Jack said the first thing that came into his head. 'D'you remember that time you cut my hair, Bella? Peter made me shave at the sink and you grabbed the scissors and snipped away . . .'

Bella said, 'I remember so much.' She squeezed her eyes into slits and said in a stifled voice, 'And yet, so little.' She opened her eyes and held out restraining hands. 'It's all right. Just an instant of being frit.' She shook her head. 'It's the emptiness. Everything will be all right but so empty.'

Hope said, 'I'll stay. We'll work out a routine. No time for emptiness.'

'No. Don't do that, my maid. Go back with your man and sort out what you're going to do. Talk together. Be together.' She looked at Jack. 'You told me at some time that you were going to do some voluntary work, my 'an'some. You'll need to think it all over very careful-like. You've done your bit 'ere. You look to yourselves now.'

Jack held out his arm. 'Walk up to the knoll, Bella. Come on. Jem and Fennie and Nathan have gone up there. Let's stand and look down on the *Mirabelle* like we did before.'

She hesitated then nodded brusquely and took his arm. 'Then we can come back and have tea together and you two can get into Widdershins before it's dark.'

Hope smiled and followed them outside. Milly appeared from nowhere and ran ahead of them excitedly. Bella laughed, 'Silly dog,' she commented. 'She 'asn't done this since Gaffer died.'

Hope glanced at Jack who nodded. 'It's true. She curls up at home when I'm indoors. When I go out, she walks after me and just sits.'

'She knows,' Bella said certainly. 'She spent a lot of time on his bed. It's only natural she would know.'

They went slowly up the rise; Jem, alerted by Milly, came down to meet them. 'Fennie's gone down to the beach with Nathan. I waited for you.'

'How did you know we were coming?' Jack asked.

Jem looked surprised. 'You had to see the *Mirabelle*. The *Mirabelle* is the whole point, surely?'

Hope said quietly, 'The rescue ship.'

And Bella started to laugh. 'If you coulda seen me all those years ago! I was that angry – with myself and with Gaffer, but specially with them blasted Jerries – I told the *Mirabelle* where to go and she went!'

They started down the cliff path, laughing without knowing why. The tide was out and Milly chased after it, barking like a tiny canine Canute. Nathan was sitting, Buddha-like, patting the sand around him experimentally while his mother dug a castle. The others drifted slowly towards the cave and the beached fishing lugger. Beyond it, above the tide mark, lay *Sweet Pea*, well anchored to a nearby rock. The two boats symbolized so much. Jack put his hand on the keel of the *Mirabelle*, just as he had last autumn when he had first seen her. Bella stood nearby, smiling. Jem went to check on the rowing boat while Hope stood apart watching the three of them, not thinking, simply taking in impressions, registering smells, the touch of the damp air on her face, the over-bright sea almost hurting her eyes. She remembered something Peter had said. 'Just *be*, my maid. Don't try to think . . . don't worry . . . just know that you are you. In this place. Now.'

Bella was moving closer to Jack, saying something to him, quietly, earnestly. He stared into her dark eyes; she seemed to be holding his gaze very deliberately. Then he nodded. Immediately she turned and came back to Hope.

'I'm glad we came down here. Used to do it almost daily. It's a good place to be.' She linked her hand into the crook of Hope's arm. 'But enough's enough. Let's be getting back now. It'll be dark shortly and I don't want you and Jack falling down that cliff on your way home!'

As February gave way to March, the winds started up. Jack strengthened the downstairs shutters and made another set for the bedroom. Milly sat by the door each evening, growling as the gales rattled the latch. Once Hope had closed the gaily appliqué'd curtain, she would go back to her basket by the range and wait for the evening meal. The sense of being beleaguered was strong and comforting; the iron roof stayed firm and the shutters and curtains between them kept out all draughts; the oil lamps burned steadily and even a candle guttered only occasionally.

Hope said, 'Is it heartless to be content like this? How do you suppose Bella is feeling up at Penhailes, so alone?'

'Like you felt when I first came here. I was no companion, was I? A companion who was not a companion. At least Jem and Fennie will talk to Bella. And Nathan won't let her sink into despair for a moment. I couldn't speak. Sometimes I barely understood what you said to me. I remember you talking, though. I remember the comfort of your voice.'

She remembered too. She said in a low voice, 'I'm sorry, Jack. So sorry.'

He opened his grey eyes at her. 'Sorry? What on earth for? You nursed me – fed me—'

She said, 'I resented you, Jack. And then . . . later . . . I think I hated you.'

He was silent for a long time, then said slowly, 'Perhaps that made . . . what you did . . . even better.' He looked up from his plate. 'Anyway, I think I prefer the hate to the resentment.' He cleared his throat. 'Don't look like that. It is good you can tell me – we can be honest . . .' He straightened his back. 'Can you tell me how you feel about me now?'

She frowned. 'I've tried to sort it out. It's difficult. There's a sense of comfort . . . warmth . . . familiarity. But fear too.'

He was shocked. 'You're frightened of me?'

'Not of you. Of what might happen.' She shook her head helplessly. 'Jack, I dare not let myself think too much. I am happy with you. Here and now, I cannot think of anyone I would rather be with. But I can't go that one step more. The step that Bella was talking about . . .' She paused and then said in a rush, 'If it happened again . . . I couldn't take it.'

The pain on his face made her want to retract her words. She said quickly, 'I think I have accepted my part too . . . forgiven . . . both of us. Honestly. And I would like to forget. But I cannot.'

'I wouldn't want you to forget. I don't want to forget. But . . . listen, Hope. I won't go away. We'll stay here. Together. And then – like Bella said – bit by bit we will build up the trust again.

Make our own fortress. Oh God, Ho. I am so sorry. I will show you – day by day, I will show you—'

She shook her head again, this time very definitely.

'No. That is not the way, Jack. I cannot learn to trust life by keeping you here for ever! My God, that would change everything – Widdershins might even become a prison! And I would be a kidnapper!' She tried to laugh. 'You can't do that to me, Jack!'

'But you will always . . . remember. And so will I.'

She shrugged; not one of her old hopeless shrugs, but with acceptance.

'We've got to live with that. There's no easy way round it, is there? Sometimes it might get us down. But other times . . .' She smiled. 'Listen. Let's clear the table and you can finish your plans. And tomorrow you must go up to the farm and make those telephone calls.'

A gust of wind shook the little house and Milly growled in her throat.

Jack said, 'Oh Lord. Listen to it. I can't leave you here – on your own.'

'You can. You know I can manage perfectly well, especially now we have Milly.' She smiled. 'I want to be able to miss you, Jack. I want to really, really miss you! It's part of the – the process. Can you understand that?'

He nodded but smiled wryly. 'You see, Ho, I have no doubt at all about missing you. I am not so sure about whether you will miss me.'

'Yet you know it's the right thing to do?'

'I have to give you the same space you gave me,' he said simply.

She stood up and began to pile plates and mugs together.

He sighed sharply. 'Sit down a minute more. Let's be practical now. We must do some budgeting. Bella says that Peter has left us some money. To keep us going until we develop the extra land.'

'Is that what she was saying to you down at the beach after the funeral?'

'Among other things. Jem has some good ideas too. Vegetables for the summer then an early bulb planting for the spring flowers. It's the harvesting that is so tricky. We'll have to use Bella's agency. It's all got to be done so quickly and usually against the weather.' He indicated the windows. 'Listen to that wind and imagine what it would do to a field of daffodils.'

'We'd have finished picking by now,' she said. 'The really early ones are ready in February.'

He lifted the big kettle off the stove and carried it into the scullery for the washing up. 'It's a lot of very hard work.'

She rolled up her sleeves. 'Good. That's how we'll build our fortress – the one Bella talked about to Peter.' She pumped water into a bowl and stood aside while he topped it up from the kettle. 'And when you come back, I've got an idea for converting your kites into kits. We might be able to mail-order them or something.'

He laughed. 'Oh Ho . . . you make everything so full of it.'

'Full of what?'

'Hope,' he said simply.

*   *   *

Jack eventually left the headland at the end of
April. Before then he spent several separate
days in Plymouth, meeting with people from
AfrAid, discussing the logistics of transporting
components to Ethiopia and using local labour
to assemble them. His first contact had been a
man called Brian Dewey, and he visited Widdershins and met Hope.

'I feel that this sort of project involves the
whole family,' he explained to her, pumping her
hand, smiling from ear to ear. 'We don't exactly
leave our wives and homes. In one sense we take
them with us. They are there all the time, a
constant support. It's needed, I do assure you.'

Hope smiled back, liking his enthusiasm
instantly. When she heard that he and Jack
would be travelling together, she was delighted.
She listened to them making their plans as she
got a meal and did indeed begin to feel part of
the whole scheme. Brian said to her, 'This is one
of those happy coincidences that can't be wholly
coincidental. With this power source and my
pump, we can do something that counts. Really
counts. If Jack hadn't seen my article – if he'd
still been involved in his business – if, if, if—' his
grin widened further still into laughter, '—you
can't tell me it's all down to chance!'

Another two weeks passed after that visit. Every
day, in between the outside work, Jack would
make phone calls to finalize all the details of the
trip. On 8 April the weather was as balmy as
summer and in the suddenly longer evenings the
two of them pushed *Sweet Pea* into the water, lifted
Milly over the thwarts and rowed out towards the

end of the headland. Hope sat in the stern and watched Jack pulling on the heavy oars.

'You couldn't have done this eight months ago,' she commented. 'Widdershins has made you strong again in every way.'

He pulled away from the cluster of rocks where she and Jem had searched for him that long-ago November night.

'So much good has come out of Widdershins,' he said soberly. 'It's supposed to be . . . how did Bella put it? Okkard. Back to front. But it's looked after us. Turned us the right way around.' He shipped the oars and the bow lifted high on the first serious roller. Milly barked and Hope laughed. He said, 'It's provided a physical fitness programme for both of us, Ho. I couldn't have taken on this AfrAid project before Widdershins. And I couldn't have left you to cope on your own.' He grabbed the oars again and pulled the boat around to face the shore. 'Will you be all right?' he asked, suddenly anxious as he so often was.

'Barring the unexpected, of course. And what about you?'

'Likewise.'

They exchanged smiles. It was like a silent promise. She knew then that they would be man and wife again. One day. And they could both wait for that day.

The separation was punctuated by phone calls and letters. Jack sent her a kind of diary of what was happening to him. Every two or three weeks this would arrive from Massawa by airmail. Sometimes there were photographs:

Jack and Brian standing in the midst of scrub-land surrounded by Africans, dwarfed by tall drilling machinery. For a long time there was no sign of Jack's windmill. And then in August came a snap of a tall pillar surmounted by a trio of sails. Below it was a group of grinning people, tiny against the column of the windmill. Jack had scribbled on the back: 'Prototype number one. We are waiting for the kind of gales we had on the headland in March!' As always he asked how she was, whether she was content – strange that he never wrote 'happy' – and urged her to telephone to Massawa immediately if she wanted him to return. She replied with news of Penhailes, Widdershins, the people who lived there. And then her thoughts and feelings. She found it so easy to write to Jack though it was something they had rarely done in the past. She spoke of her kinship with Buttercup, the fact that she often talked to her mother, certain now that she was heard. When August became drowsy, the sea a sheet of glass, Jem took her out in *Sweet Pea* and taught her how to row with one oar like a gondolier. She put out a spinner and caught some mackerel and she tried to describe the overpowering smell in the kitchen when she smoked them. He wrote back by return outlining an idea he had for a smoke house down by Marble Arch. That letter pleased her more than any; it proved his thoughts were often with Widdershins. She liked that. The idea of the headland as a prison and herself as a warder still worried her at times.

Fay and Martin came to stay and brought a tent which they erected next to the several wigwams of beans. 'You can hardly tell the difference,' Fay said. 'We're going right back to nature!' They wanted to take her with them to the autumn show in Paris. Chatty and Fiona were still making tea and sweeping up, but they were also sewing hems´ and necklines and were going to be dressers for the models at the autumn dress shows. Jean Lascelles had asked them to submit designs for next spring and the big man himself, Jules Ferrier, had asked how the new girls were doing. 'The thing is, Ho,' Chatty said loudly so that Bella could share the call, 'we haven't got shoved out on our collective ears! That's enough for most people. To be asked to submit stuff . . . wow!'

Bella, mumbling disapproval at the use of Hope's name, called down the receiver, 'It's a question of respect, my girl!'

'Sorry, Bella!' Chatty's blithe voice floated into the hall. She could have been at Buryan, she was so clear. 'Anyway, you will come, Mother dear, won't you? Fay and Martin will do all the arranging and you can sleep in the flat – no expense spared!'

Hope hesitated and Bella leaned forward again. 'Course she'll be there! I'm going to see to my oven now so I'll say goodbye!'

'Au 'voir, ma belle!' Chatty carolled, then, suddenly serious, 'Ho. Must tell you. Mandy is coming. Please don't let it put you off. I couldn't forbid it or anything, could I? She got me the place, after all.'

So Hope went. And this time, with Fay and Martin too, she 'discovered' Paris. The autumn colours, the sense of energy and enthusiasm tempered by cool chic, won her over completely. She did not see Mandy until they took their seats below the catwalk, but then she was unmissable. She had let her hair go white – or perhaps Henrik had insisted on it – and had piled it up on top of her head so that she looked like a dowager duchess. She waved excitedly when she saw Hope and struggled along the line of chairs to say to her, 'Darling, you look marvellous. An earth mother or something.' She gave Fay a special, almost secret smile, and swept on, 'Fay darling, you could have been up there—' a nod in the direction of the catwalk, '—and your mother could have been the couturier. If only you'd taken my advice!' She raised her voice slightly so that no one could miss it. 'Cat has asked me round after. Champers in the cutting room – sounds like the title of a play, doesn't it?' The same rich, infectious laugh rang out. She leaned towards Hope. 'See you then, darling. Everything forgiven and forgotten? Yes?'

Hope felt a flood of amazement tinged with amusement. Mandy was so many things; certainly she was a consummate actress, certainly she was indefatigable.

Hope smiled gently and said the first thing that came into her head. 'Oh Mandy . . . you really are hopeless!'

Just for a moment the mask dropped. Mandy's smile became a grimace, the sky-blue eyes narrowed as if in pain. Then she recovered and laughed again.

'No arguing with that, Hope!'

The show was almost as amazing as Mandy. Hope had always been interested in clothes but had tailored her imagination to practicality and economy. Here, there were no such limits. The fabrics ranged from gauze to Harris tweed and seemed to take on lives of their own as they moved with the models and swung on each turn. In spite of her own circumscribed wardrobe, Hope was enthralled by the whole thing. She whispered to Fay, 'It's the shapes – how can they make a human body appear triangular?' And then with the next breath, 'No, it's the materials – look at that drape as she holds her arm up . . . a dying fall if ever there was one!'

Fay was unmoved until the final promenade when a line of girls appeared apparently wearing armour. Skin-tight lurex pants and tops that skimmed the body and turned into helmets; bangles by the ton, anklets, neckbands . . . a glittering, jangling display.

'That's my idea!' she whispered, not knowing whether to be outraged. 'I told Chat about the Nordic helmets and breastplates! She's stolen my idea!'

'Not entirely,' Hope murmured. 'Those neckbands are like African women wear. And the helmets are pure Batman.'

They congregated in the jumble of jewellery, feathers, pins and paper that was the cutting room. Mandy was already talking animatedly to Chatty. Henrik had appeared and was standing protectively close. As soon as he saw Hope he put his arm around Mandy and spoke over her head.

'How do you do, Hope. And Fay. And Martin if I remember correctly?' He offered brief handshakes. 'I think my wife has had enough. It is

468

very loud. We have flown here specially for this evening. It is good for Chatty, yes?'

Hope nodded. 'Of course.' She paused and it was Fay who said, 'You and Mandy – you are married? Chatty said something . . .'

'Yes. My first wife was killed. Sadly. Also my brother. Ski-ing. There was an avalanche.' He looked at Hope. 'He has a son and daughter, still young. We have suggested that his children come to stay with us. And it seemed right to be married.'

Hope nodded. 'You were made for each other.' Henrik flinched. She said quickly, 'I meant that, Henrik. And I am sure your nephew and niece will realize it.' She searched desperately for something positive to say. 'Congratulations,' she concluded lamely.

'Thank you, Hope.' He smiled at last. 'I understand I can say the same to you. Chatty tells us that you and Jack are now farmers.'

Just for an instant she wanted to tell him about Jack's AfrAid project. She wanted to tell Henrik how proud she was of him; how all the work he had done with Henrik had paid off in a way none of them could have imagined. But she did not. Africa was an enormous continent, but it held Mandy as well as Jack.

She said, 'We are very happy, yes.' And as the words dropped into the hubbub around them, she recognized their complete truth.

Henrik was smiling, relieved. 'So you have put the past behind you?' he asked.

She looked around him at Chatty fielding Mandy's excited exclamations, at Fay and Martin watching her anxiously. She laughed. 'Of course not! I wouldn't have missed my past for anything. My mother used to say the past was all rolled up like a carpet and you could get on it at any time. So it will never go away. All I know is that we can be happy again. No questions, no probings. Jack and I can be – will be – happy.'

Chatty looked round, saw her sister's expression and quite suddenly said, 'Mum. Mandy and Henrik are going. Come and meet Fi again. And Madame Solange who is my boss and is terrifying. See where I work. And I've got the most marvellous portfolio. What did you think of the lurex stuff? My suggestion.'

Fay said, 'Your suggestion, my foot. I was telling you about the Nordic women only last Christmas!'

The two girls went ahead; Martin put a hand beneath her elbow. Hope said, 'Mandy . . . Henrik. Goodbye. The very best of luck.' Martin was drawing her away; Mandy was looking lost. 'The children,' Hope said over her shoulder. 'You will so enjoy the children.'

Mandy smiled and patted Henrik's arm. 'He has always given me exactly what I have wanted,' she said, nodding. And then the crowds seemed to swallow them up and they were gone.

Martin said, 'Are you all right?'

'I am. I am all right, Martin. Thank you.'

He glanced over the milling heads. 'They're good at disappearing, aren't they?'

Hope laughed. 'So are we,' she said. 'It's only us who can see us.'

He stared at her. 'And I thought Fay was crazy,' was all he said.

*　　*　　*

Jack came home in November.

She was expecting him to arrive on the 27th which was a Monday, but on Sunday afternoon, when she was digging the dead bean vines back into the earth, Milly started barking and trying to run up the bank and she knew it was him.

She tore down the combe followed by a crazy Milly, scrambled up the bank on to the cliff and saw him running down the knoll towards her. He had no luggage and was wearing just a shirt and trousers. She stood still, watching him. At this distance his grey hair looked brown again and flopped over his forehead as it always had done.

She said aloud, 'Oh Mummy – Mummy, you were quite right. It's just a carpet after all. And we're on it. Together.' And then she ran to meet him.

He had left everything, including his jacket and blanket-coat, at the farm so that he could run down the headland to see her. And this time, because she had moved the table closer to the fire, he could carry her right over the threshold and put her gently into her chair. He knelt by her. He knew already how she felt; it was in every line of her body.

He said, 'Hope. Dear Hope. It seems such a long time. But nothing stopped, you know. I loved you more and more each day.' He rubbed his cheeks against her knees. 'I have always loved you. And you loved me too. And you weren't afraid to admit it. When you cut the holes out of those socks . . . I knew then.'

She said, 'I'm not afraid to admit it now, Jack.'

'Oh . . . darling Ho. Do you mean it? Because

I meant it when I said my love for you went on growing. It really did. Seriously. The last six months have had this amazing undercurrent of loving you. I never had to ask why I was there as Brian did – as so many of the workers did. I always knew.'

'So did I.' She stroked his hair – which looked white again – away from his eyes. 'You were right about the separation. It's like being on a hill – on the knoll overlooking the cove. Everything is in perspective. The underlying terror of the rocks at the end of the headland, the rough sea, the calm sea . . .'

'So . . . it's going to be all right?'

'Oh yes. I think so. Don't you?'

'I don't know. But for me . . . there is no alternative.'

They sat for a long time, holding each other, looking into the fire. Occasionally they exchanged tiny snippets of news.

Jack said, 'It worked, Ho. The wind blew, the dynamo charged, the pump went into action. And has been in action since. I'm working on solar power now.'

She breathed a laugh over the top of his head. 'Oh Jack. If only we'd known – years ago – that you were an inventor . . .'

Milly sat before them, ears cocked, knowing her time would come.

Hope murmured, 'Small beer, but I sold a dozen rag rugs and – wait for it – a maternity smock!'

'When Chatty gets going you can design for her.'

'What a pleasant thought. The Cat and her

Mother.' They both giggled. 'Mandy was at the autumn show.'

'You said. It was all right, I gathered.'

'I didn't tell her you were at the other end of Africa. Air travel is too easy these days.'

'Henrik wouldn't let her.'

'No. Probably not.'

'Are Fay and Martin married yet?'

'If they are they have forgotten to mention it.'

'Are they coming for Christmas?'

'Yes. Chatty and Fiona Tabb too.'

'Oh lord.'

'Yes.'

A long and contented silence, then Jack said suddenly, 'What's up with Bella?'

The silence became startled. 'I see her every day. I haven't noticed anything.'

'She's thin. Her eyes are sinking into her skull.'

Hope frowned and stroked his hair again. 'She has always been thin. Is it more than grief?'

'I don't know. She did say she was just one step behind.'

'Yes. But . . .'

'Shall we have a cup of tea?'

'Certainly. Or shall we go upstairs first? The bed is made up for two.'

He caught her hand and lifted his head to stare at her. 'Are you sure? There is no hurry.'

She kissed him. And he got to his feet and lifted her again and carried her upstairs as he had done that first time.

Bella lived through Christmas and was well enough to enjoy seeing everyone who came to Penhailes Farm. She fell for Fiona Tabb though she described her as a cheeky madam. Fiona fell for her too and sat at the kitchen table with her, sketching crazily on the back of old wallpaper rolls she found in the loft.

'It depends on the shape you want . . . see? A diamond? OK, then we'll have a choker neckline, sort of batwing sleeves and then a gorgeous taper right down to the ankles.'

'An' 'ow d'you think anyone 'ud walk in that skirt, then?'

'That's where the material comes in. Black jersey, I think, don't you? And what we'll do, Bella my beautiful, is . . .' a few deft lines of charcoal, '. . . we'll drape the back, so. Then there will be what amounts to a giant slit to give plenty of room.'

'Cheeky madam. I'm nobody's beautiful. Never 'ave been.'

'Oh you're beautiful all right. Only not everyone can see it.' Fiona looked up. 'D'you think I'm beautiful?'

'Not a bit. You remind me of a pug dog as a matter of fact.'

'Thanks, Bell. You remind me of a gypsy woman who cursed my mother once. But your Peter thought you were beautiful. And there's a student at the art school by the name of Jean-Pierre who thinks I'm the absolute bee's knees.' She narrowed her eyes. 'Pug dog, eh? That was below the belt.'

'You weren't too polite either.'

'Forget the gypsy. I just realized. You're a dead ringer for the Mona Lisa.'

Bella snorted. 'I allus thought she looked like a gypsy anyhow!'

They both rocked with laughter.

On the eve of the new year of 1990 Martin took them to see the lights at Mousehole. It was a magical evening. They sat in the verandah of the Lobster Pot and had a cream tea and while they were still 'emptying the pot', as Fay put it, the lights began to come on. The spouting whale, the little church, the boats, the cat, the robins, the lanterns; each one hailed with enthusiasm by the girls. As they drove back to the headland, Chatty said, 'This was special. I wish Bella had been well enough to come with us. It was so . . . special.'

When they reached the farm, Jem was waiting for them.

'She just went to sleep in her chair by the fire. And she didn't wake up,' he said simply.

They could hear Fennie crying in the dairy.

'She's put Nathan to bed and we're keeping out the way till the undertakers have been. Doctor came at half-past five and left a certificate.'

It was Chatty who broke the awful silence. She said, 'Half-past five. So she must have died just as the lights were coming on.' Her voice choked. 'She was with us. And we didn't know it.'

They trailed slowly into the kitchen where Bella still sat comfortably in front of the fire as she so often had done. Hope was full of thankfulness that she had known none of the illness Peter had suffered. She squatted by the chair and put her hand on Bella's and said – as Bella had done almost a year ago, 'Thank you, my friend. Thank you.'

And for a second, she could have sworn she

saw that grim old smile with which Bella had fooled so many people.

Jack told them all what Bella had said that day by the *Mirabelle*.

'She didn't want the boat sold and it's not going to be seaworthy for much longer. She went into it all – Trinity House coastguards, even the Royal Naval place at Culdrose. So long as we inform them so that they can clear the area, we have permission to do it.'

Hope said nothing. It was so like Bella. She could hardly bear it.

Fay said hesitantly, 'How will they do it, Dad? I mean – actually do it?'

'They tow it out with the lifeboat. It is soaked in petrol. They fire a flare right into it.'

Fiona Tabb had hardly spoken since New Year's Eve. Now she said desperately, 'Bella – Bella won't be in it, will she?'

'No. She wanted to be buried with Peter. This is something quite separate.'

'Oh,' Fiona leaned back in her chair. 'Oh, I am glad.'

Jem grinned. 'She had a sense of the drama, did Bella Penhailes. That's half the reason she took the old tub over to France that time. There was an old film with Greta Garbo where she was standing in the bows of a boat looking out to sea. Bella fancied the part for herself, I reckon.'

Jack grinned too. 'Well, we'll fix it for her, won't we?'

The girls all nodded and, after a second's hesitation, so did Hope.

*   *   *

But for her, the real farewell was in the scuttling of the *Mirabelle*. She would go to the little churchyard and look after the grave for years to come probably, but she said her goodbyes to Peter and Bella as the flare landed on the petrol-soaked deck of the carefully preserved lugger and the flames shot immediately into the pale blue sky of a perfect January afternoon. They stood on the gently rocking deck of the lifeboat and watched, hypnotized by the spectacle. The *Mirabelle* had been primed expertly and she did not sink until the flames had almost consumed her hull. And then, with a hiss, she was gone.

Still they were silent. The coxswain said quietly, 'Shall I go back to 'Curno now?'

Jem looked at Jack and then nodded. 'It's over,' he said.

Hope turned away and faced the shore. The girls were looking at her and she smiled at them.

'Well. Now we know why Bella wanted Jack to arrange all this. It's an end to the past, isn't it? Nothing to do with Bella wanting to be a film star!'

Fiona said, 'I'm glad I saw it though. It was a real Viking's funeral.'

Fay said, 'I should have said that! You're so right, Fi! A proper ending. Final. Forces you on to the future!' The wind blew her hair horizontally from her head; she had a sudden look of Greta Garbo.

Chatty grabbed Jem's arm. 'You said ages ago you'd tell us the story of how Bella went to France in the *Mirabelle* to rescue Peter. We've got to go back tomorrow. Will you tell us to-night?'

'All right. But that's it in a nutshell really. Except that she must have had the strength of ten men to launch the old tub and get it across to France on her own.'

The girls clustered around him. Martin and Fennie handed Nathan back and forth between them to keep him amused. Jack and Hope turned and stared at the place where two blackened spars still marked the spot where the *Mirabelle* had gone up in flames.

Hope said, 'Bella was so wise, Jack. So very wise. This is her way of making sure that we're all right. She's given us the *Mirabelle*.'

'More than that perhaps.' Jack put his arm around her shoulders. The wind was freshening and she shivered against him. 'Maybe she saw it as the *Mirabelle*'s last rescue.'

Hope held on to him until they were almost at the little jetty. Then she took a deep breath.

'I'm thankful we got that land cleared, Jack. I noticed this morning, the green is just coming through the earth.'

'If they all take, it'll be a sea of yellow,' he agreed.

'I love daffodils. Beautiful, intricate, complicated blossoms.'

He smiled at her. 'Like Bella Penhailes then,' he said.

And she laughed. 'Just like Bella Penhailes.'

THE END

THE KEYS TO THE GARDEN
by Susan Sallis

Widowed Martha Moreton was a devoted mother to her only child, Lucy, and when Lucy married Len on a golden July day, Martha tried hard to make the best of things. Len was a good man who would make Lucy happy. They wouldn't be living far away. And the arrival of grandchildren was something she anticipated eagerly.

Unexpectedly, Len's job took the newly married couple overseas, where their first child was born. But sorrow, not joy, came with Dominic's birth. On their return, Lucy's best friend, Jennifer, as flighty as Lucy was conventional, was anxious to provide her own kind of consolation . . .

Martha, who was experiencing unlooked-for and at first unwelcome changes in her own life, clung fast to the maternal bond that meant so much to herself and Lucy. Everything she had come to depend on was overturned, however, before Martha was able to find her own kind of happiness in a very different existence.

One of Susan Sallis's most poignant and involving novels, *The Keys to the Garden* explores the mother-daughter relationship with a rare insight.

0 552 14671 4

A SELECTED LIST OF FINE NOVELS AVAILABLE FROM CORGI BOOKS

14060 0	MERSEY BLUES	Lyn Andrews	£5.99
14579 3	SCORE!	Jilly Cooper	£6.99
14449 5	SWEET ROSIE	Iris Gower	£5.99
14538 6	A TIME TO DANCE	Kathryn Haig	£5.99
14410 X	MISS HONORIA WEST	Ruth Hamilton	£5.99
14686 2	CITY OF GEMS	Caroline Harvey	£5.99
14692 7	THE PARADISE GARDEN	Joan Hessayon	£5.99
14603 X	THE SHADOW CHILD	Judith Lennox	£5.99
14693 5	THE LITTLE SHIP	Margaret Mayhew	£5.99
14659 5	WHAT BECAME OF US	Imogen Parker	£5.99
14752 4	WITHOUT CHARITY	Michelle Paver	£5.99
10375 6	CSARDAS	Diane Pearson	£5.99
14715 X	MIDSUMMER MEETING	Elvi Rhodes	£5.99
12375 7	A SCATTERING OF DAISIES	Susan Sallis	£5.99
12579 2	THE DAFFODILS OF NEWENT	Sasan Sallis	£5.99
12880 5	BLUEBELL WINDOWS	Susan Sallis	£5.99
13136 9	ROSEMARY FOR REMEMBRANCE	Susan Sallis	£5.99
13756 1	AN ORDINARY WOMAN	Susan Sallis	£5.99
13934 3	DAUGHTERS OF THE MOON	Susan Sallis	£5.99
13346 9	SUMMER VISITORS	Susan Sallis	£5.99
13545 3	BY SUN AND CANDLELIGHT	Susan Sallis	£5.99
14162 3	SWEETER THAN WINE	Susan Sallis	£4.99
14318 9	WATER UNDER THE BRIDGE	Susan Sallis	£5.99
14466 5	TOUCHED BY ANGELS	Susan Sallis	£5.99
14549 1	CHOICES	Susan Sallis	£5.99
14636 6	COME RAIN OR SHINE	Susan Sallis	£5.99
14671 4	THE KEYS TO THE GARDEN	Susan Sallis	£5.99
14744 3	TOMORROW IS ANOTHER DAY	Mary Jane Staples	£5.99
14508 4	GRANNY DAN	Danielle Steel	£5.99
14740 0	EMILY	Valerie Wood	£5.99